CHRISTIAN
SHORT STORIES

CHRISTIAN SHORT STORIES

An Anthology

Edited by Mark Booth

Firethorn Press

© 1984 Waterstone and Company Limited,
edited by Mark Booth

Firethorn Press is an imprint of Waterstone and Company Limited.

First published 1984 in
The United States by
The Crossroad Publishing Company
370 Lexington Avenue
New York
NY 10017

First published in
Great Britain by
Waterstone and Company Limited.
193 Kensington High Street
London W8

Design and production in association with
Book Production Consultants, 47 Norfolk Street, Cambridge.
Typeset by Cambridge Photosetting Services, 19–21 Sturton Street, Cambridge.
Printed and bound by Richard Clay PLC, Bungay, Suffolk.

Library of Congress Catalog Card Number: 84-070839
ISBN(US): 0 8245 0673 1
ISBN(US): 0 8245 0674 X (pbk) ·

ISBN(UK): 0 947752 005
ISBN(UK): 0 947752 013 (pbk)

Acknowledgements

The editor and publisher wish to thank the following for their permission to reproduce copyright material:

John Cheever: 'The Low Boy' (first published in 'Some People, Places and Things That Will not Appear in My Next Novel', 1961). Reprinted by permission of Jonathan Cape Ltd in the UK and Commonwealth and Alfred A Knopf, Inc. in the USA. © The estate of John Cheever 1961, 1984.

G K Chesterton: 'The Blue Cross' (first published in 'The Innocence of Father Brown', 1911). Reprinted by permission of Miss D E Collins in the UK and Commonwealth and by Dodd, Mead & Company, Inc. in the USA. © renewed 1938 by Frances B Chesterton.

Graham Greene: 'The Second Death' (first published in 'Nineteen Stories', 1947). Reprinted by permission of William Heinemann, Ltd, and The Bodley Head, Ltd, in the UK and Commonwealth and Viking Penguin, Inc. in the USA. © 1947, renewed 1975 by Graham Greene.

Flannery O'Connor: 'The Artificial Nigger' (first published in 'The Kenyon Review', 1955). Reprinted by permission of Harold Matson Company, Inc. in the UK and Commonwealth and by Harcourt Brace Jovanovich, Inc. in the USA. © 1953 Flannery O'Connor. © renewed 1981.

Cover illustration: 'Coming From Evening Church' by Samuel Palmer reproduced by kind permission of the Trustees of the Tate Gallery, London.

Contents

Introduction

At a time when more and more human words are being printed, and a less and less significant proportion of them promote the Word of God, why should Christians look to short stories? How are short stories fitted to that toughest but most delicate of tasks, recommending the Christian view of life?

On the broadest historical perspective religion and stories seem indissolubly linked. Religious belief began as a response to stories, and at least until Renaissance times stories were primarily a way of teaching religion and morals.

The legend of Galahad and the Holy Grail is just such a story. Otherwise in strictly chronological order, the book begins with a nineteenth century retelling of the legend which has always been a model for Christian stories in the English speaking world. Embracing many aspects of Christian experience, it explores themes which will be found in later short fiction: spiritual quest, God's miraculous intervention, vocation, divine justice, trust in God and reward in Heaven.

The opening episodes of the story are pervaded by a majestic sense of the sadness of a world fallen from Grace, and therefore in decay. As the story unfolds the world is prompted by Grace, in the form of the Grail, to discern the meaning of the quest, and so to learn to hope for a better future. In this achievement of a sense of God's purpose for the world working itself out in a historical setting, *Galahad and the Holy Grail* looks forward to the crucial contribution of the short story to Christian literature.

The parable and the sermon number with the essay, the fable, the folk tale and the novella as prototypes of what we understand today as a short story. Parables were used by Jesus to interest, to educate and to inspire. They made complexities easily accessible and memorable. Theologizing and moralizing in the abstract can express only closed ideas, but a story, especially if invested with allegorical or symbolic overtones, can suggest unlimited areas of thought and feeling in a way that is peculiarly enriching.

Someone who is simply told that he ought to give alms to the poor is less likely to be moved to do so than someone who reads Oliver Goldsmith's heart-warming *A Curious Inconsistency of the Man in Black*. One of the earliest short stories in the sense that we understand the phrase now, it retains something of the form of a parable. The Man in Black is taught by his father, a clergyman, to love his neighbour as himself. Like his father he is repeatedly exploited by so called friends 'til he is brought to ruin. Life seems to have taught him that he had better 'look after number one', and he pretends that it has, boasting of his own selfishness and meanness. In fact his pretence is a transparent one. He believes everyone is taken in, but it is obvious that he can refuse no request for help. He gives a beggar a piece of silver when he wrongly believes his friend is looking the other way. So while worldly wisdom advises him to reject the teachings of the Sermon on the Mount, Grace works within him so that 'his heart is dilated with the most unbounded love', and 'his cheeks glow with compassion'. It takes a great writer of fiction like Oliver Goldsmith to create a character who is wholly lovable, so that our hearts go out to him and we want to follow his example.

Similarly, someone who is told in abstract terms that God will punish him if he does not respond to the promptings of Grace is less likely to be influenced than someone who reads Graham Greene's chilling account of the descent into Hell in *The Second Death*. Greene takes up the story of Lazarus, as it might have been, after Jesus raises him from the dead. When he first dies Lazarus feels that there is someone all around him who knows his past sins. He feels that he is going to be punished and that he can't escape. When he is raised from the dead, he believes he might be being given a second chance, and for two years he stops womanizing. But as the memory of his second chance fades, and scepticism about its meaning takes over, he reverts to his old ways. It is only when he dies for the second time, and feels God's judgement coming upon him again, that the true horror of his predicament overwhelms him: 'When one's dead' he realizes 'there's no unconsciousness any more for ever'.

Some stories might be described as suppressed parables. William Makepeace Thackeray's *Dennis Haggarty's Wife*, for example, retells the parable of the Good Samaritan with great panache. Jemima Gam, a girl very proud of her Protestant ancestry, rudely and cruelly rejects a proposal of marriage from Dennis Haggarty on the grounds that he is the son of an Irish 'Black Papist'. Like the Samaritan in a society of

Jews, he is not of the socially acceptable creed. When, years later, he chances across her, she is living in poverty, scarred and blinded by illness, and all her former, more eligible suitors have passed her by. Haggarty marries her, and 'is quite as faithful to her as he was when captivated by the poor tawdry charms of the silly Miss' he met all those years ago. The despised and rejected foreigner shows who the neighbour is whom Jesus commanded us to love.

Anton Chekov's sad and funny vignette *The Requiem* is a retelling of the parable of the Pharisee and the Publican. An arrogant, small-town intellectual, when asking a priest to say Mass for his dead daughter, describes her as 'the Adulteress Marya'. The priest rounds on him furiously, and berates him for his uncharitable attitude. He seems suitably cured, and he remembers his daughter's grief at her lost innocence. However such is his invisible complacency that, while the Mass is actually being said, he again calls her an adulteress. The soul of the sinful but repentant girl ascends to Heaven; the soul of her father, we must assume, remains in the balance.

Because the short story is intuitive rather than drily theoretical, and open-ended rather than definitive, it can be made resonant with ambiguities. The short story is not necessarily, or even ordinarily, reducible to a simple statement of doctrine; it is better suited to opening up areas of Christian experience to debate. *A Curious Inconsistency of the Man in Black*, for example, raises questions about how far love of neighbours should be qualified by love of self. *Dennis Haggarty's Wife* is a worrying depiction of people apparently beyond salvation. Jemima Gam and her mother are described as being among those wicked souls who are 'selfish, stingy, ignorant, passionate, brutal, bad sons, mothers, fathers, never known to do kind actions', and who 'are too dull to understand humility'. Can it be possible, as certain theologians have in the past asserted, that God creates some souls so innately wicked that they are inevitably damned?

Further, a story's ambiguities may also awaken what the Irish short story writer Frank O'Connor has described as 'the moral imagination', causing the reader to wonder, to look for answers in a much more active and involved way than would be probable if he were merely presented with an intellectual dilemma. William Canton's charming story *The Song of the Minster* describes the visionary experience of a sub-prior who begrudges money spent on finery for the Abbey, because he believes that it would be better spent on the poor. One night he is praying alone in the Minster, 'taking a cruel joy in the freezing cold', when suddenly the whole building begins to throb and drone with a mystical music, and the carved angels, the figures in the stained glass windows and the effigies on the tombs sing the 'Te Deum'. His experience teaches him the beauty of Holiness: 'he saw with unsealed eyes how churlishly he had grudged God the glory of man's genius and the service of His dumb creatures, the metal of the hills, and the stone of the quarry, and the timber of the forest; for now he knew that at all seasons, and whether men heard the music or not, the ear of God was filled by day and by night with an everlasting song from each stone of the vast Minster: We magnify Thee, and we worship Thy name; ever world without end'. He becomes one with the great monks who in their love of God were 'blithe of heart, and filled with a rare sweetness and tranquillity of soul, and . . . looked on the goodly earth with deep joy, and . . . had a tender care for the wild creatures of wood and water'. Ambiguity in this story raises questions about the relations between the command to love God and the command to love our neighbour; when they conflict, how are we to choose? As with *A Curious Inconsistency of the Man in Black*, the stated message of the story is creatively at odds with feelings the story is likely to inspire in the reader.

Because of the short story's tendency to ambiguity, and because its brevity encourages an implicit rather than an explicit mode of writing, the medium is a good one for inviting reflection on forces that are ultimately inexplicable, ultimately mysterious. Charles Dickens's *A Child's Dream of a Star* deals with the love between a brother and a sister and with their hope of being reunited in Heaven. This strange piece, which flits between the real and the visionary, and is written in a style which mixes the language of a fairy story with that of the Bible, rises to the level of intensity of a liturgy. The short story has none of the cumbersome qualities of the novel, and so is well equipped to capture these elusive aspects of insight and feeling.

Thomas Hardy's *Old Mrs Chundle* suggests, perhaps more subtly, that life's mysteries admit of a Christian interpretation. Hardy's pessimism was illumined by a wish to believe in the consolations of Christianity, as he expressed in the famous poem *The Oxen*.

Christmas Eve, and twelve of the clock
'Now they are all on their knees,'
An elder said as we sat in a flock
By the embers in hearthside ease.

We pictured the meek mild creatures where
They dwelt in their strawy pen,
Nor did it occur to one of us there
To doubt they were kneeling then.

So fair a fancy few would weave
In these years! Yet, I feel,
If someone said on Christmas Eve,
'Come; see the oxen kneel

'In the lonely barton by yonder coomb
Our childhood used to know,'
I should go with him in gloom,
Hoping it might be so.

Old Mrs Chundle tells with gentle comedy of a kind-hearted curate's troubles with an ignorant old woman. He shows concern for her spiritual welfare, persuading her to come to Church. When unforeseen inconveniences arise, the curate, who, though well-meaning is rather out of touch with his parishioners, cools in his zeal. The pleasant and urbane rector confirms him in his new, more practical attitude to the woman. She sends messages asking him to visit her, but he puts it off. When he eventually arrives, she has died. 'Two or three times' a neighbour explains 'she said she hoped you would come soon, as you'd promised to, and you were so staunch and faithful in wishing to do her good, that she knew't was not by your own wish you didn't arrive.' The curate leaves the scene 'like Peter at the cock-crow'. When he reaches a lonely place in the lane, he kneels and prays. Trying to be good by his own efforts has led him to disaster. Niceness is not enough. We must allow ourselves to be guided by God.

More explicitly, John Cheever's *The Lowboy* shows the inadequacy of a materialistic view of life. It is the story of a man in danger because he tries to store up earthly riches for himself. He looks to possessions for security, and, of course, he finds none. A particular possession, the lowboy, spoils his life. He has feared fiscal bankruptcy more than spiritual bankruptcy, and now he is judged. The story ends with this emphatic declaration, which, though it has an apocalyptic ring, makes its meaning clear enough:

Out they go – the Roman coins, the sea horse from Venice, and the Chinese fan. We can cherish nothing less than our random understanding of death and the earth-shaking love that draws us to one another. Down with the stuffed owl in the upstairs hall and the statue of Hermes on the newel post! Hock the ruby necklace, throw away the invitation to Buckingham Palace, jump up and down on the perfume atomizer from Murano and the Canton fish plates. Dismiss whatever molests us and challenges our purpose, sleeping or waking. Cleanliness and valor will be our watchwords. Nothing less will get us past the armed sentry and over the mountainous border.

Some short stories are intended, like the stories often included in sermons, to illustrate and to bring to life a biblical text. *A Child's Dream of a Star*, for example, might have been written to illustrate the text 'In my father's house are many rooms' (John c.14 v.2) and *The Lowboy* 'Provide purses for yourselves that will not wear out, a treasure in heaven that will not be exhausted' (Luke c.12 v.33). Frank Harris's *The Holy Man* is a story on the theme of Paul's teaching on natural religious feeling: 'When the Gentiles who have not the law do by nature what the law requires. . . . They show that what the law requires is written on their hearts' (Romans c.2 vs.14–15). A young bishop is shown to be a true follower of Jesus in his enthusiasm, which takes no account of the 'dignity and state' of the Church. When he and his cavilling helpers sail to an isolated fishing village, where the Gospel has never been preached, they meet a bearded old holy man whom the bishop recognizes as having an instinctive response to the spirit of Jesus that is in some details superior to that of the Church, as represented by his companions. The bishop is back on his boat and out to sea when the Jesus-like humility of the man is proven by his walking on water to reach them because he wants to be reminded of the words of 'that beautiful prayer, the prayer Jesus taught his disciples'.

T. S. Eliot called G. K. Chesterton's fiction 'propaganda' for Christianity. His avowed aim was to show that the Christian point of view is the right one. His stories are sermonizing in the sense that they contain the same mixture of example and teaching as a sermon, though, of course, the proportions are different. Chesterton's detective, Father Brown, is a modern Sir Galahad. Like the boy knight he looks too puny for conflict, (a villain calls him 'a celibate little simpleton'), but, because he is inspired and protected by God, he triumphs. His Christianity gives him an understanding of the deeper laws of the universe, which in turn gives him a crucial advantage over his adversaries and rivals, the evil-doers and the sceptics.

Chesterton is the greatest writer of Christian short stories. He can tell a tale in a prose style that mixes evanescent beauty with robust wit in a way which is unmatched in twentieth-century fiction, even by Evelyn Waugh. The reader is amused and intrigued by an entertainment which at the end turns out to have been teaching something very serious. Concluding *The Blue Cross*, Chesterton openly preaches, but even then with a rhetorical flourish which makes it not dull (as preaching so often is) but wonderful:

'I know that people charge the Church with lowering reason, but it is just the other way. Alone on earth, the Church makes reason really supreme. Alone on earth, the Church affirms that God Himself is bound by reason. . . . '

'Reason and justice grip the remotest and the loneliest star. Look at those stars. Don't they look as if they were single diamonds and sapphires? Well, you can imagine any mad botany or geology you please. Think of forests of adamant with leaves of brilliants. Think the moon is a blue moon, a single elephantine sapphire. But don't fancy that all that frantic astronomy would make the smallest difference to the reason and justice of conduct. On plains of opal, under cliffs cut out of pearl, you would still find a noticeboard, "Thou shalt not steal".'

James Hogg's *The Cameronian Preacher's Tale* begins '. . . what I am about to say is far better than man's preaching, it is one of those terrible sermons which God preaches to mankind. . . .' Rough-hewn out of Scottish folk-tradition, and charged, both in its phrasing and in its tribal setting, with something of the harshness of the Old Testament, this 'sermon' is a reminder of what God's justice will mean for the unrighteous. When one proud and haughty highlander murders his rival in business, God miraculously intervenes, and 'vengeance is the Lord's.' More miraculous intervention brings consolation to the dead man's widow both in this life and 'where the blessed alone are admitted.' The Cameronian Preacher has retold God's sermon that people might 'know there is a God who ruleth this world by wise and invisible means, and punisheth the wicked, and cheereth the humble of heart and the lowly minded'.

An important feature of the Christian short story, and one which distinguishes it from the traditional sermon, is that it can show, with all the refined techniques of fiction, how God's punishment overtakes the wicked, how people turn their backs on God, how they delude themselves into believing that their godless way of life is godly. A short story can investigate what it feels like to be touched by Grace, and by what process of thought and emotion people accept Jesus.

Oscar Wilde's fairy story *The Selfish Giant* has a power, perhaps rivalled only by Dickens's *A Christmas Carol*, to reduce readers to tears. The story shows how selfishness is its own punishment. Readers feel with the Giant the rush of happy feelings that are his rewards as he accepts the love of Jesus, and as he loves in turn his fellow creatures. After reading *The Selfish Giant* we long to live better.

If the sermon is a public form of narration, the short story's is personal, being addressed by one person to one another. Its quiet tone is therefore fitted to explore an individual's intimate relations with God: the small affirmations and evasions of his soul in response to God's call. As Chekov observed, something the short story does well is to portray venial sins, those petty habits of selfishness and self-deception that can mar a life as much as any mortal sin. The religious snobbism of Jemima Gam is her besetting venial sin, that of Hardy's curate is the self-reliant nature of his charity, and in the case of the man damned by his lowboy, it is an overkeen interest in interior decoration.

'I follow sins beyond the moment of their acting' says the sinister, devil-like figure who appears to Markheim in Robert Louis Stevenson's story: 'I find in all that the last consequence is death; and to my eyes the pretty maid who thwarts her mother with such taking graces on a question of a ball, drips no less visibly with human gore than such a murderer as yourself'. Markheim is basically a good and generous-spirited man, but because he has deceived himself into thinking that he is an 'unwilling sinner', a victim of circumstances, he has fallen gradually, insensibly into degradation, and now, having finally descended to murder, (in a scene which in its horror rivals its parallel in *Crime and Punishment*), Divine retribution closes in on him 'as if the gallows itself was striding through the Christmas streets'.

Many short stories are charitable in the sense that they openly plead for love (e.g. *The Man in Black* and *The Selfish Giant*), but the genre as a whole is also charitable in the less obvious sense that it specializes, as the critic Valerie Shaw has noted, in 'discovering the hidden beauty of obscure lives'. Short stories have a rich history of drawing attention to the unostentatious goodness of the poor, the unimportant and the unimpressive. To a Christian writer like

Elizabeth Gaskell, the world may appear an oppressively secular place where Christians are underdogs whose apparently dreary lives are nevertheless quietly illumined by Grace. Her *The Three Eras of Libbie Marsh* is for this reason the story in the anthology which is most imbued with the spirit of Jesus.

Libbie Marsh is a lonely working girl forced to board with unsympathetic strangers in the slums of Victorian Manchester. Grace comes into her life when from her window she notices a crippled boy who is confined to bed in a room on the opposite side of the street. She buys him a present of a bird in a cage, and so becomes acquainted with the boy and his bad-tempered mother. The theme of Mrs Gaskell's story is the redemptive power of pain. Libbie finds relief from her own sufferings in charitable acts to relieve another's. It is only when the boy's mother finds an opportunity to help Libby in her suffering that she feels able to thank her for the happiness she has brought her boy, and so a bond of friendship is forged between the two women. Through his suffering the boy learns a 'most true and holy patience'. And grieving on the death of the boy, Libbie Marsh finds her holy vocation and peace of mind. Mrs Gaskell has recently been taken up by feminists, and, indeed, Libbie Marsh might be adopted as a model for modern Christian feminists. Like many Christians she is misunderstood as a spoilsport and a killjoy, but as a Christian she finds real joy in her God-given work.

Francis Bret Harte's *The Outcasts of Poker Flat* is also a story about someone low, even despicable, in the world's estimation who finds other-worldly glory in suffering. Mr John Oakhurst, a small-time gambler at war with himself and his better nature, is expelled with several other misfits from a small town, Poker Flat. Harte's beautiful image for God's miraculous intervention in fallen Creation is a snow storm that cuts the outcasts off from civilization. 'Feathery drifts of snow, shaken from the long pine boughs, flew like white-winged birds, and settled about them as they slept. The moon through the rifted clouds looked down upon what had been the camp. But all human stain, all trace of earthly travail, was hidden beneath the spotless mantle mercifully flung from above.' Grace is gentle yet painful. The situation of the outcasts becomes desperate, guiding Oakhurst to an act of martyrdom through which he finds salvation.

Like the romantic poem, the short story tends to concentrate on a moment of revelation and decision that changes the meaning and the course of a life. Unlike the romantic poem the short story is well adapted to set this moment in its context of mundane reality. In what is perhaps the most powerful but also in some ways the most deft story in the collection, *The Artificial Nigger*, Flannery O'Connor depicts a world which, because it is fallen, is squalid and petty.

Mr Head and his grandson, Nelson, make what is for them a momentous trip to the city. Nelson is worried that they will get lost, but Mr Head, trusting in his own common-sense, dismisses his fears. When they do get lost, their predicament takes on a metaphysical dimension. 'I never said I wanted to come' complains the boy. 'I only said I was born here and I never had nothing to do with that. I want to go home. I never wanted to come in the first place.' The boy's feelings about the city in that moment are his feelings about life. Later he accidentally knocks over an old lady, and when a policeman arrives to investigate the commotion, his grandfather denies that he knows the boy. Nelson's reproaches bring Mr Head to despair: 'He knew now that he was wandering into a black strange place where nothing was like it had ever been before, a long old age without respect and an end that would be welcome because it would be the end.' Mr Head is deep in sin and, in an absolute sense, helpless. In recognition of this he cries out 'Oh Gawd I'm lost! Oh hep me Gawd I'm lost'; and it is only then, when he discards complacency, that he opens up to Grace. In a bizarre incident Mr Head and Nelson are brought back together, and we know that God has again miraculously intervened to tip the balance in favour of salvation.

> 'Mr Head stood very still and felt the action of mercy touch him again but this time he knew that there were no words in the world that could name it. He understood that it grew out of agony, which is not denied to any man and which is given in strange ways to children. He understood it was all a man could carry into death to give his Maker and he suddenly burned with shame that he had so little of it to take with him. He stood appalled, judging himself with the thoroughness of God, while the action of mercy covered his pride like a flame and consumed it. He had never thought himself a great sinner before but he saw now that his true depravity had been hidden from him lest it cause him despair. He realized that he was forgiven for sins from the beginning of time, when he had conceived in his own heart the sin of Adam, until the present, when he had denied poor Nelson. He saw that no sin was too monstrous for him to claim as

his own, and since God loved in proportion as He forgave, he felt ready at that instant to enter Paradise.'

Flannery O'Connor's *The Artificial Nigger* epitomizes what the short story does better than any other literary genre; it describes the impinging of the divine on the mundane. She brilliantly elucidates the insufficiency of common sense when it comes to dealing with the everyday. Like the other writers featured in this anthology she holds a microscope to apparently insignificant corners of a decaying world to show it to be a battleground of good and evil. The reader is shown God's purpose for the world working itself out in miniature. In Christian short stories religion and fiction help each other to do the special work that distinguishes them. They revivify a world that has become dead to us. They re-expose us to life's mysteries, and remind us of its terrible dangers and its equally terrible beauties. We are drawn back into life by being reminded of what is at stake. In the expanding maelstrom of the printed words of men, we may look to short stories and occasionally glimpse there the Word of God.

Mark Booth

'To see a World in a Grain of Sand
And a Heaven in a Wild Flower.
Hold Infinity in the palm of your hand
And Eternity in an hour.'

Sir Galahad and the Holy Grail
Traditional

Now the time that had been foretold by Merlin drew near. He had prophesied that, with the coming of Arthur, the island of Britain should grow in strength and fame, and her knights should be more valiant and more pure in word and deed than the knights of any other land. But that, in a little while, they would become proud, and finding that none could withstand them, they would use their strength evilly.

To the court of King Arthur, as he sat in London, came tidings of how his barons warred with each other in remoter parts of his dominions, seizing castles, killing, forsaking the ways of the Holy Church of Christ and turning to the idolatry of the old British pagans, some of whom still lurked and performed their evil rites in the desolate and secret places of the forests and hills.

At the feast of Pentecost all the court went to the Minster to hear the service; and when they returned to the palace the king ordered that dinner should be prepared in the hall of the Round Table, for this was one of the days when it was his custom to assemble all his knights at a great feast of knighthood.

While they waited for the horn to sound, signalling that the meal was ready, one came running to the king, saying that a miracle had happened. And Arthur went to the hall of the Round Table with his knights. The seats about the great circular board had originally been inscribed by Merlin with the letters of gold that spelt out 'Here should sit Sir Bedevere' or 'Here should sit Sir Gawaine'. The name of a knight was thus written in every seat except the one named by Merlin the Siege Perilous, which had been without inscription. Twice reckless knights had dared to sit, but only to be struck dead by a sudden flashing blow of mystery. Now an inscription had miraculously appeared: 'In the four-hundred-and-fifty-fourth year after the passion of our Lord, shall he that shall fill this seat come among ye'.

When they saw this marvel the knights looked at each other in wonder. 'It seems to me,' said Lancelot 'that this is the very day on which this seat shall be filled by whom it is appointed, for this is the four-hundred-and-fifty-fourth winter since Christ died on the cross.'

Then the horn was sounded to dinner, and each knight took the seat appointed for him, and young knights served them. All the seats round the table were filled except the Siege Perilous. Men ate and drank soberly, for they felt that an adventure strange and marvellous would happen that day, and so indeed it turned out.

A lady came to the hall and asked Sir Lancelot to ride with her into the forest nearby. Lancelot consenting, they rode together until they came to a nunnery hidden deep in the forest; and there the lady told Lancelot to dismount, and led him into a great and stately room. Presently twelve nuns entered and with them a youth, the fairest that Lancelot had ever seen. 'Sir,' said the nuns, 'we have brought up this child in our midst and now that he is grown to manhood, we pray you to make him a knight, for of none worthier could he receive the honour.' 'Is this your wish?' Lancelot asked the young squire; and when he said that it was, Lancelot promised to make him a knight after the great festival had been celebrated in the church the next day.

So in the morning after they had worshipped, Lancelot knighted Galahad – for that was the youth's name – and asked him if he would ride at once with him to the king's court; but the young knight excusing himself, Sir Lancelot rode back alone to Camelot, where all rejoiced that he had returned in time to keep the feast with the whole Order of the Round Table.

Now, according to custom, King Arthur was waiting for some marvel to befall before he and his knights sat down to the banquet. Presently a squire entered the hall and said: 'Sir King, a great wonder has appeared. There floats on the river a mighty stone, a block of red marble, and it is thrust through with a sword, the hilt of which is set thick with precious stones.' On hearing this, the King and all his knights went forth to view the stone and found it as the squire had said; moreover, looking closer, they read these words: 'None shall draw me hence, but only he who by whose side I must hang; and he shall be the best knight in the world.' Immediately, all bade Lancelot draw forth the sword, but he refused, saying that the sword was not for him. Then, at the king's command, Sir Gawaine made the attempt and failed, as did Sir Perceval after him. So the knights knew the adventure was not for them, and, returning to the hall, took their places about the Round Table.

No sooner were they seated than an aged man clothed all in white entered the hall, followed by a young knight in red armour, by whose side hung an empty scabbard. The old man approached King Arthur and bowing low before him said: 'Sir, I bring you a young knight of the house and lineage of Joseph of Arimathea, and through him shall great glory be won for all the land of Britain.' Greatly did King Arthur rejoice to hear this, and welcomed the two heartily. Then when the young knight had saluted the King, the old man led him to the Siege Perilous; and all the knights were amazed, for they saw that where the other words had been engraved, was written now in shining gold: 'This is the Siege of the noble prince, Sir Galahad.' Straightway the young man seated himself there, where none other had ever sat without losing his life; and all who saw it said to one another: 'Surely this is he that shall find the Holy Grail.'

Now the Holy Grail was the blessed dish from which Our Lord had eaten the Last Supper, and it had been brought to the land of Britain by Joseph of Arimathea, but because of men's sinfulness it had been withdrawn from human sight, only that, from time to time, it appeared to the pure in heart.

When all had partaken of the royal banquet, King Arthur told Sir Galahad to come with him to the river's brink; and showing him the floating stone with the sword thrust through it, told him how his knights had failed to draw forth the sword. 'Sir' said Galahad, 'it is no marvel that they failed, for the adventure was meant for me, as my empty scabbard shows.' So saying he lightly drew the sword from the heart of the stone and lightly he slid it into the scabbard at his side. While all yet wondered at this adventure of the sword, there came riding to them a lady on a white palfrey who, saluting King Arthur, said: 'Sir King, Nacien the hermit sends you word that this day shall great honour be shown to you and all your house, for the Holy Grail shall appear in your hall to you and your fellowship. And to Lancelot she said: 'Sir Knight, you have always been the best knight of all the world; but another has come to whom you must yield precedence.' Then Lancelot answered humbly: 'I know well I was never the best.' 'Ay, truly, you were and are still of sinful men,' said she, and rode away before any could question her further.

So that evening, when all were gathered about the Round Table, each knight in his own seat, suddenly there was a crash of thunder so mighty that the hall trembled, and there flashed into the hall a sunbeam brighter than any that had ever been seen before; and then, draped all in white samite, there glided through the air what none might see, yet all knew to be the Holy Grail. And all the air was filled with sweet odours, and on every one was shed a light in which he looked fairer and nobler than ever before. So they sat in an amazed silence, till presently King Arthur rose and gave thanks to God for the grace given to him and his court.

Then up sprang Sir Gawaine, who was a faithful knight and true man to his king, though a proud one and hasty. 'Now I do here avow', he said 'that tomorrow, without fail, I shall set forth, and I shall labour with all the strength of my body and my soul to go in quest of the Holy Grail, so that if I be fit to see it and to bring it hither, this dear land may be saved from woe.'

So hot were his words that many of the better knights rose also, and raising their right hands made a like avowal; and those that cared not for the quest felt that they must seem to do so as the others did, and so made avowal also, though in their hearts they thought more of pride and earthly power.

Then King Arthur was grieved, for he foresaw the ruin of his noble Order. And turning to Sir Gawaine, he said: 'Nephew, you have done ill, for through you I am bereft of the noblest company of knights that ever brought honour to any realm in Christendom. Well I know that never again shall all of you gather in this hall, and it grieves me to lose men I have loved as my life and through whom I have won peace and righteousness for all my realm.' So the king mourned and his knights with him, but they could not recall their oaths.

Great woe was there in Camelot next day when, after worship in the Cathedral, the knights who had vowed themselves to the Quest of the Holy Grail mounted their horses and rode away. A good company it was that passed through the streets, the townsfolk weeping to see them go: Sir Lancelot du Lac and his kin Sir Galahad, of whom all expected great deeds, Sir Bors and Sir Perceval, and many others scarcely less famous than they. So they rode together to the Castle of Vagon, where they were entertained hospitably, and the next day they separated, each to ride his own way to see what adventures should happen to him.

Now Sir Galahad was without a shield, and he rode for days without adventure. At evensong on the fourth day he came to an abbey of white monks, and there was made great cheer. He found two other knights of the Round Table at that abbey, one King Bagdemagus and the other Sir Ulfin. When they had greeted each other Sir Galahad asked King Bagdemagus what adventure had brought him there. 'Sir,' said Bagdemagus, 'I was told that in this abbey was preserved a wondrous shield which none but the best knight in the world might bear without grievous harm to himself. And though I know well that there are better knights than I, tomorrow I intend to make the attempt. But, I pray you, stay at this monastery a while until you hear from me; and if I fail, take the adventure upon yourself.' 'So be it', said Sir Galahad.

The next day, at their request, Sir Galahad and King Bagdemagus were led into the church by a monk, and shown where, behind the altar, hung the wondrous shield, whiter than snow except for the blood-red cross in its midst. Then the monk warned them of the danger to any who, being unworthy, should dare to bear the shield. But King Bagdemagus answered 'I know well that I am not the best knight in the world, yet I will try and discover if I may bear it.' So he hung it about his neck, and, saying farewell, rode away with his squire.

The two had not journeyed for long before they saw a knight approach armed all in white mail and mounted upon a white horse. Immediately he couched spear and, charging King Bagdemagus, pierced him through the shoulder, and carried him from his horse; and standing over the wounded knight, he said: 'Knight, you have shown great folly, for none shall bear this shield save the peerless knight, Sir Galahad.' Then, taking the shield, he gave it to the squire and said: 'Carry this shield to the good knight Sir Galahad and greet him from me.' 'What is your name?' asked the squire. 'That is not for you or any other to know.' 'One thing, I pray you,' said the squire, 'why may this shield be borne by none but Sir Galahad without danger?' 'Because it belongs to him only,' answered the stranger knight, and vanished.

Then the squire took the shield, and, setting Bagdemagus on his horse, carried him back to the abbey, where he lay long sick unto death. To Galahad the squire gave the shield, and told him all that had befallen. So Galahad hung the shield about his neck, and rode the way that Bagdemagus had gone the day before; and presently he met the White Knight, whom he greeted courteously, asking that he would explain to him the marvels of the red-cross shield. 'That I will gladly,' answered the White Knight.

'You must know, Sir Knight, that this shield was made and given by Joseph of Arimathea to the good King Evelake of Sarras, so that, by the might of the holy symbol, he should overthrow the heathen who threatened his kingdom. But afterwards, King Evelake followed

Joseph to this land of Britain where they taught the true faith to the people who before were heathen. Then when Joseph lay dying, he bade King Evelake set the shield in the monastery where you lay last night, and foretold that none should wear it without loss until that day when it should be taken by the knight, ninth and last in descent from him, who should come to that place the fifteenth day after receiving the degree of knighthood. Even so it has been with you, Sir Knight,' So saying, the unknown knight disappeared.

Now Sir Galahad rode back to the abbey, where the monks were glad to see him again. 'We have need of a pure knight' they said, as they took him to a tomb in the churchyard. A pitiful noise was heard, and a voice from the tomb cried 'Galahad, servant of God, do not come near me.' But the young knight went towards the tomb, and raised the stone. Then a thick smoke arose, and through the smoke a figure uglier than any man leapt from the tomb, shouting 'Angels are round thee, Galahad, servant of God, I can do you no harm.'

The knight stooped down, and saw a body all dressed in armour lying there, and a sword lay by its side. 'This was a false knight', said Sir Galahad, 'let us carry his body away from this place.'

The monks entreated Sir Galahad to stay and live with them in the abbey, but, spurred on by the hope of seeing again the light that was brighter than any sunbeam, he rode on.

It was Galahad's custom to pray to God every day for counsel and guidance in his great undertaking. Not long after he had left the abbey, he turned aside at a wayside chapel to perform his devotions, and while he was kneeling before the altar he suddenly heard a voice that said: 'Rise, Sir Galahad, and go now to the Castle of Maidens which is near at hand, and there do away with the wicked custom that you will find.'

The young knight was overjoyed on hearing this summons, for here was an adventure to his taste. Mounting once more, he rode on asking his way from all he met. The castle was well known, for its ill-repute had spread far and wide, and many of those he encountered tried to deter him from journeying thither. But Galahad laughed, and, looking to his arms, spurred his horse boldly to the castle gates. Scarcely had he reined up, when seven knights, all brothers, dashed out to meet him. 'Now guard thee, knight,' they cried, 'for we promise you nothing but death.' 'What, then,' returned Galahad, 'will you all set upon me at once?' 'Even so,' cried the others, and couching their spears they charged down upon him. Then Galahad spurred forward to meet them, and with a mighty thrust of his own lance he sent the foremost of the brothers headlong to the ground. The other six fell upon him with their swords and spears, but receiving their blows on his shield the young knight escaped unscathed. Casting aside his lance, Galahad now drew forth his great sword, and dashed fiercely at his adversaries.

So quick and strong were his strokes that the knights were forced to give way before him. At last they one and all turned and fled, Galahad pursuing them for some distance. At the entrance to the castle an old monk awaited him with the keys in his hands. The young knight took these, and at once opened the gates to the great joy of all those within, who had been held captive by the seven brothers.

Galahad now learned how the castle had come to gain its evil name. It had formerly belonged to the Duke Lianoir, the lord of the surrounding country, but the seven brothers had overcome him by treachery, and killed him, making his beautiful daughter a prisoner. The maiden had then prophesied that for their wickedness they should not hold the castle for many years, for by one knight alone should they all be overthrown. The brothers then vowed that no lady or knight should pass by the castle alive until that knight of whom she spake appeared. And thus the castle had come by its name, for a great number of maidens had fallen into their hands.

With many other adventures did Galahad meet, and in all of them he carried himself as became a brave and valiant knight. Once he encountered Sir Lancelot and Sir Perceval, but they knew him not, for he was in different armour, and they had never seen the shield with the red cross before. And so great was his prowess that even the skilled Sir Lancelot, the victor of a hundred tourneys, went down before him, while Sir Perceval received so mighty a stroke that his head was near cleft in twain.

Besides adventures such as these, the young knight was assailed by divers temptations, but through all he passed unharmed, his soul as pure as when he left the nuns' good care to enter into the world of men.

Sir Lancelot, Sir Gawaine and the rest of the company of Round Table knights who had set out on the search for the Holy Grail, fared equally ill in their enterprise. There was not one who was worthy to achieve the quest, not one but who was stained with sin and unfit to see the sacred vessel.

Sir Lancelot, indeed, came nearest to finding the Holy Grail, for he eventually found himself outside the room wherein it was kept. A voice forbade him to enter, but Lancelot determined to venture in, for which he was struck down. And for many days and nights he lay as one dead, after which, having recovered his strength, he returned home.

Now as Galahad was nearing the end of his quest, he sought shelter at a little hermitage. Thither there came in the night a damsel who desired speech with Sir Galahad, so he rose, and went to her. 'Galahad,' said she, 'arm yourself and mount your horse and follow me, for I have come to guide you in your quest.' So they rode together until they came to the seashore, and there the damsel showed Galahad a great ship into which he had to board. Then she bade him farewell and, he, going on to the ship, found there already the good knights Sir Bors and Sir Perceval, who made much joy of the meeting. They sailed in that ship until they came to the castle of King Pelles, who welcomed them gladly. Then as they all sat at supper that night, suddenly the hall was filled with a great light, and the holy vessel appeared in their midst covered in white samite. While they all rejoiced, there came a voice saying: 'My Knights whom I have chosen, ye have seen the holy vessel dimly. Continue your journey to the city of Sarras and there the Perfect Vision shall be yours.'

Joseph of Arimathea had lived in the city of Sarras teaching its people the true faith, before he came into the land of Britain; but when Sir Galahad and his fellows came there after a long voyage, they found it ruled by a heathen king named Estorause, who cast them into a deep dungeon. There they were kept a year, but at the end of that time the tyrant died. Then the great men of the land gathered together to consider who should be their king. While they were in council, a voice came bidding them take as their king the youngest of the three knights whom King Estorause had thrown in prison, and, releasing the three knights, they made Galahad king as the voice had told them.

Thus Sir Galahad became king of the famous city of Sarras in Babylon. He had reigned a year, wisely and well, when, early one morning, he and the other two knights, his fellows, went into the chapel, and there they saw, kneeling in prayer, a marvellously aged man robed as a bishop. He turned to them, and said: 'Come forth, Galahad, thou servant of Christ, for now shalt thou see that which thou has so long desired. I am Joseph of Arimathea, and I am come to show you the Perfect Vision of the Holy Grail.' Seeing their looks of perplexity, the bishop smiled sweetly upon them, and said, 'Marvel not, O knights, for though I am now a spirit, I know thy weakness, and have come to aid thee.'

On the instant there appeared before them, without veil or cover, the holy vessel in a radiance of light such as almost blinded them. Sir Bors and Sir Perceval, when at length they recovered from the brightness of that glory, looked up to find that the holy Joseph and the wondrous vessel had passed from their sight. Then they went to Sir Galahad where he still knelt in prayer, and, behold, he was dead; for what he had been praying for had happened; in the moment when he had seen the vision, his soul had gone back to God.

And since then there has never been a man so holy as to say that he had seen the Holy Grail.

A Curious Inconsistency of the Man in Black

Oliver Goldsmith

Though fond of many acquaintances, I desire an intimacy only with a few. The Man in Black, whom I have often mentioned, is one whose friendship I could wish to acquire, because he possesses my esteem. His manners, it is true, are tinctured with some strange inconsistencies; and he may be justly termed a humorist in a nation of humorists. Though he is generous even to profusion, he affects to be thought a prodigy of parsimony and prudence; though his conversation be replete with the most sordid and selfish maxims, his heart is dilated with the most unbounded love. I have known him profess himself a man-hater, while his cheek was glowing with compassion; and, while his looks were softened into pity, I have heard him use the language of the most unbounded ill-nature. Some affect humanity and tenderness, others boast of having such dispositions from nature; but he is the only man I ever knew who seemed ashamed of his natural benevolence. He takes as much pains to hide his feelings as any hypocrite would to conceal his indifference; but on every unguarded moment the mask drops off, and reveals him to the most superficial observer.

In one of our late excursions into the country, happening to discourse upon the provision that was made for the poor in England, he seemed amazed how any of his countrymen could be so foolishly weak as to relieve occasional objects of charity, when the laws had made such ample provision for their support. 'In every parish-house,' says he, 'the poor are supplied with food, clothes, fire, and a bed to lie on; they want no more, I desire no more myself; yet still they seem discontented. I am surprised at the inactivity of our magistrates, in not taking up such vagrants, who are only a weight upon the industrious; I am surprised that the people are found to relieve them, when they must be at the same time sensible that it in some measure encourages idleness, extravagance,and imposture. Were I to advise any man for whom I had the least regard, I would caution him by all means not to be imposed upon by their false pretences: let me assure you, sir, they are impostors, every one of them, and rather merit a prison than relief.'

He was proceeding in this strain, earnestly to dissuade me from an imprudence of which I am seldom guilty, when an old man, who still had about him the remnants of tattered finery, implored our compassion. He assured us that he was no common beggar, but forced into the shameful profession to support a dying wife and five hungry children. Being prepossessed against such falsehoods, his story had not the least influence upon me; but it was quite otherwise with the Man in Black: I could see it visibly operate upon his countenance, and effectually interrupt his harangue. I could easily perceive that his heart burned to relieve the five starving children, but he seemed ashamed to discover his weakness to me. While he thus hesitated between compassion and pride, I pretended to look another way, and he seized this opportunity of giving the poor petitioner a piece of silver, bidding him at the same time, in order that I should hear, go work for his bread, and not tease passengers with such impertinent falsehoods for the future.

As he had fancied himself quite unperceived, he continued, as we proceeded, to rail against beggars with as much animosity as before: he threw in some episodes on his own amazing prudence and economy, with his profound skill in discovering impostors; he explained the manner in which he would deal with beggars were he a magistrate, hinted at enlarging some of the prisons for their reception, and told two stories of ladies that were robbed by beggar-men. He was beginning a third to the same purpose, when a sailor with a wooden leg once more crossed our walks, desiring our pity, and blessing our limbs. I was for going on without taking any notice, but my friend, looking wistfully upon the poor petitioner, bid me stop, and he would show me with how much ease he could at any time detect an impostor.

He now, therefore, assumed a look of importance, and in an angry tone began to examine the sailor, demanding in what engagement he was thus disabled and rendered unfit for service. The sailor replied, in a tone as angrily as he, that he had been an officer on board a private ship of war, and that he had lost his leg abroad, in defence of those who did nothing at home. At this reply, all my friend's importance vanished in a moment; he had not a single question more to ask; he now only studied what method he should take to relieve him unobserved. He had, however, no easy part to act, as he was obliged to preserve the appearance of ill-nature before me, and yet relieve himself by relieving the sailor. Casting, therefore, a furious look upon some bundles of chips which the fellow carried in a string at his back, my friend demanded how he sold his matches; but, not waiting for a reply, desired, in a surly tone, to have a shilling's worth. The sailor seemed at first surprised at his demand, but soon recollecting himself, and presenting his whole bundle, 'Here, master,' says he, 'take all my cargo, and a blessing into the bargain.'

It is impossible to describe with what an air of triumph my friend marched off with his new purchase: he assured me that he was firmly of opinion that those fellows must have stolen their goods, who could thus afford to sell them for half value. He informed me of several different uses to which those chips might be applied; he expatiated largely upon the savings that would result from lighting candles with a match instead of thrusting them into the fire. He averred that he would as soon have parted with a tooth as his money to those vagabonds, unless for some valuable consideration. I cannot tell how long this panegyric upon frugality and matches might have continued, had not his attention been called off by another object more distressful than either of the former. A woman in rags, with one child in her arms, and another on her back, was attempting to sing ballads, but with such a mournful voice that it was difficult to determine whether she was singing or crying. A wretch, who in the deepest distress still aimed at good-humour, was an object my friend was by no means capable of withstanding: his vivacity and his discourse were instantly interrupted; upon this occasion his very dissimulation had forsaken him. Even in my presence he immediately applied his hands to his pockets in order to relieve her; but guess his confusion when he found he had already given away all the money he carried about him to former abjects. The misery painted in the woman's visage was not half so strongly expressed as the agony in his. He continued to search for some time, but to no purpose, till, at length recollecting himself, with a face of ineffable good-nature, as he had no money, he put into her hands his shilling's worth of matches.

As there appeared something reluctantly good in the character of my companion, I must own it surprised me what could be his motives for thus concealing virtues which others take such pains to display. I was unable to repress my desire of knowing the history of a man who thus seemed to act under continual restraint, and whose benevolence was rather the effect of appetite than reason.

It was not, however, till after repeated solicitations he thought it proper to gratify my curiosity. 'If you are fond,' says he, 'of hearing hairbreadth 'scapes, my history must certainly please; for I have been for twenty years upon the very verge of starving, without ever being starved.'

'My father, the younger son of a good family, was possessed of a small living in the church. His education was above his fortune, and his generosity greater than his education. Poor as he was, he had his flatterers, still poorer than himself; for every dinner he gave them they returned an equivalent in praise, and this was all he wanted. The same ambition that actuates a monarch at the head of an army influenced my father at the head of his table: he told the story of the ivy-tree, and that was laughed at; he repeated the jest of the two scholars and one pair of breeches, and the company laughed at that; but the story of Taffy in the sedan-chair was sure to set the table in a roar: thus his pleasure increased in proportion to the pleasure he gave; he loved all the world, and he fancied all the world loved him.

'As his fortune was but small, he lived up to the very extent of it; he had no intentions of leaving his children money, for that was dross; he was resolved they should have learning; for learning, he used to observe, was better than silver or gold. For this purpose, he undertook to instruct us himself; and took as much pains to form our morals as to improve our understanding. We were told that universal benevolence was what first cemented society: we were taught to consider all the wants of mankind as our own; to regard the human face divine with affection and esteem; he wound us up to be mere machines of pity, and rendered us incapable of withstanding the slightest impulse made either by real or fictitious distress: in a word, we were perfectly instructed in the art of giving away thousands before we were taught the more necessary qualifications of getting a farthing.

'I cannot avoid imagining, that thus refined by his lessons out of all my suspicion, and divested of even all the little cunning which nature had given me, I resembled, upon my first entrance into the busy and insidious world, one of those gladiators who were exposed without armour in the amphitheatre at Rome. My father, however, who had only seen the world on one side, seemed to triumph in my superior discernment; though my whole stock of wisdom consisted in being able to talk like himself upon subjects that once were useful, but that now were utterly useless, because connected with the busy world no longer.

'The first opportunity he had of finding his expectations disappointed was in the very middling figure I made in the university; he had flattered himself that he should soon see me rising into the foremost rank in literary reputation, but was mortified to find me utterly unnoticed and unknown. His disappointment might have been partly ascribed to his having overrated my talents, and partly to my dislike of mathematical reasonings, at a time when my imagination and memory, yet unsatisfied, were more eager after new objects than desirous of reasoning upon those I knew. This did not, however, please my tutor, who observed, indeed, that I was a little dull; but at the same time allowed that I seemed to be very good-natured and had no harm in me.

'After I had resided at college seven years, my father died, and left me – his blessing. Thus shoved from shore without ill-nature to protect, or cunning to guide, or proper stores to subsist me in so dangerous a voyage, I was obliged to embark in the wide world at twenty-two. But, in order to settle in life, my friends advised (for they always advise when they begin to despise us), they advised me, I say, to go into orders.

'To be obliged to wear a long wig, when I liked a short one, or a black coat, when I generally dressed in brown, I thought was such a restraint upon my liberty that I absolutely rejected the proposal. A priest in England is not the same mortified creature with a bonze in China: with us, not he that fasts best, but eats best, is reckoned the best liver; yet I rejected a life of luxury, indolence, and ease from no other consideration but that boyish one of dress. So that my friends were now perfectly satisfied I was undone; and yet they thought it a pity for one who had not the least harm in him and was so very good-natured.

'Poverty naturally begets dependence, and I was admitted as flatterer to a great man. At first, I was surprised that the situation of a flatterer at a great man's table could be thought disagreeable: there was no great trouble in listening attentively when his lordship spoke, and laughing when he looked round for applause. This even good manners might have obliged me to perform. I found, however, too soon, that his lordship was a greater dunce than myself; and from that very moment my power of flattery was at an end. I now rather aimed at setting him right than at receiving his absurdities with submission: to flatter those we do not know is an easy task; but to flatter our intimate acquaintances, all whose foibles are strongly in our eye, is drudgery insupportable. Every time I now opened my lips in praise, my falsehood went to my conscience; his lordship soon perceived me to be unfit for service; I was therefore discharged; my patron at the same time being graciously pleased to observe that he believed I was tolerably good-natured, and had not the least harm in me.

'Disappointed in ambition, I had recourse to love. A young lady, who lived with her aunt, and was possessed of a pretty fortune in her own disposal, had given me, as I fancied, some reason to expect success. The symptoms by which I was guided were striking. She had always laughed with me at her awkward acquaintances, and at her aunt among the number; she always observed that a man of sense would make a better husband than a fool, and I as constantly applied the observation in my own favour. She continually talked, in my company, of friendship and the beauties of the mind, and spoke of Mr Shrimp my rival's high-heeled shoes with detestation. These were circumstances which I thought strongly in my favour; so, after resolving and resolving, I had courage enough to tell her my mind. Miss heard my proposal with serenity, seeming at the same time to study the figures of her fan. Out at last it came. There was but one small objection to complete our happiness, which was no more than – that she was married three months before to Mr Shrimp, with high-heeled shoes! By way of consolation, however, she observed, that, though I was disappointed in her, my addresses to her aunt would probably kindle her into sensibility; as the old lady always allowed me to be very good-natured, and not to have the least share of harm in me.

'Yet still I had friends, numerous friends, and to them I was resolved to apply. O friendship! thou fond soother of the human breast, to thee we fly in every calamity; to thee the wretched seek for succour; on thee the care-tired son of misery fondly relies: from thy kind assistance the unfortunate always hopes relief, and may be ever sure of – disappointment. My first application was to a city scrivener, who had frequently offered to lend me money, when he knew I did not want it. I informed him, that now was the time to put his friendship to the test; that I wanted to borrow a couple of hundred for a certain occasion, and was resolved to take it up from him. 'And pray, sir,' cried my friend, 'do you want all this money?' – 'Indeed, I never wanted it more,' returned I. – 'I am sorry for that,' cries the scrivener, 'with all my heart; for they who want money when they come to borrow will always want money when they should come to pay.'

'From him I flew, with indignation, to one of the best friends I had in the world, and made the same request. 'Indeed, Mr Drybone,' cries my friend, 'I always thought it would come to this. You know, sir, I would not advise you but for your own good; but your conduct has hitherto been ridiculous in the highest degree, and some of your acquaintance always thought you a very silly fellow. Let me see – you want two hundred pounds. Do you only want two hundred, sir, exactly?' – 'To confess a truth,' returned I, 'I shall want three hundred; but then, I have another friend, from whom I can borrow the rest.' – 'Why, then,' replied my friend, 'if you would take my advice, (and you know I should not presume to advise you but for your own good,) I would recommend it to you to borrow the whole sum from that other friend; and then one note will serve for all, you know.'

'Poverty now began to come fast upon me; yet instead of growing more provident or cautious as I grew poor, I became every day more indolent and simple. A friend was arrested for fifty pounds; I was unable to extricate him, except by becoming his bail. When at liberty, he fled from his creditors, and left me to take his place. In prison I expected greater satisfactions than I enjoyed at large. I hoped to converse with men in this new world, simple and believing like myself; but I found them as cunning and as cautious as those in the world I had left behind. They spunged up my money while it lasted, borrowed my coals and never paid for them, and cheated me when I played at cribbage. All this was done because they believed me to be very good-natured, and knew that I had no harm in me.

'Upon my first entrance into this mansion, which is to some the abode of despair, I felt no sensations different from those I experienced abroad. I was now on one side of the door, and those who were unconfined were on the other: this was all the difference between us. At first, indeed, I felt some uneasiness, in considering how I should be able to provide this week for the wants of the week ensuing; but after some time, if I found myself sure of eating one day, I never troubled my head how I was to be supplied another. I seized every precarious meal with the utmost good-humour; indulged no rants of spleen at my situation; never called down Heaven and all the stars to behold me dining upon a halfpenny-worth of radishes; my very companions were taught to believe that I liked salad better than mutton. I contented myself with thinking that all my life I should either eat white bread or brown; considered that all that happened was best; laughed when I was not in pain, took the world as it went, and read Tacitus often for want of more books and company.

'How long I might have continued in this torpid state of simplicity I cannot tell, had I not been roused by seeing an old acquaintance whom I knew to be a prudent blockhead, preferred to a place in the government. I now found that I had pursued a wrong track, and that the true way of being able to relieve others was first to aim at independence myself: my immediate care, therefore, was to leave my present habitation and make an entire reformation in my conduct and behaviour. For a free, open, undesigning deportment, I put on that of closeness, prudence, and economy. One of the most heroic actions I ever performed, and for which I shall praise myself as long as I live, was the refusing half-a-crown to an old acquaintance at the time when he wanted it, and I had it to spare: for this alone I deserve to be decreed an ovation.

'I now therefore pursued a course of uninterrupted frugality, seldom wanted a dinner, and was consequently invited to twenty. I soon began to get the character of a saving hunks that had money, and insensibly grew into esteem. Neighbours have asked my advice in the disposal of their daughters; and I have always taken care not to give any. I have contracted a friendship with an alderman, only by observing that if we take a farthing from a thousand pounds, it will be a thousand pounds no longer. I have been invited to a pawnbroker's table, by pretending to hate gravy; and am now actually upon treaty of marriage with a rich widow, for only having observed that the bread was rising. If ever I am asked a question, whether I know it or not, instead of answering, I only smile and look wise. If a charity is proposed, I go about with the hat, but put nothing in myself. If a wretch solicits my pity, I observe that the world is filled with impostors, and take a certain method of not being deceived by never relieving. In short, I now find the truest way of finding esteem, even from the indigent, is to give away nothing, and thus have much in our power to give.'

The Cameronian Preacher's Tale
James Hogg

S it near me, my children, and come nigh, all ye who are not of my kindred, though of my flock; for my days and hours are numbered; death is with me dealing, and I have a sad and a wonderful story to relate. I have preached and ye have profited; but what I am about to say is far better than man's preaching, it is one of those terrible sermons which God preaches to mankind, of blood unrighteously shed, and most wondrously avenged. The like has not happened in these our latter days. His presence is visible in it; and I reveal it that its burthen may be removed from my soul, so that I may die in peace; and I disclose it, that you may lay it up in your hearts and tell it soberly to your children, that the warning memory of a dispensation so marvellous may live and not perish. Of the deed itself, some of you have heard a whispering; and some of you know the men of whom I am about to speak; but the mystery which covers them up as with a cloud I shall remove; listen, therefore, my children, to a tale of truth, and may you profit by it!

On Dryfe Water, in Annandale, lived Walter Johnstone, a man open hearted and kindly, but proud withal and warm tempered; and on the same water lived John Macmillan, a man of a nature grasping and sordid, and as proud and hot tempered as the other. They were strong men, and vain of their strength; lovers of pleasant company, well to live in the world, extensive dealers in corn and cattle; married too, and both of the same age – five and forty years. They often met, yet they were not friends; nor yet were they companions, for bargain making and money seeking narroweth the heart and shuts up generosity of soul. They were jealous, too, of one another's success in trade, and of the fame they had each acquired for feats of personal strength and agility, and skill with the sword – a weapon which all men carried, in my youth, who were above the condition of a peasant. Their mutual and growing dislike was inflamed by the whisperings of evil friends, and confirmed by the skilful manner in which they negotiated bargains over each other's heads. When they met, a short and surly greeting was exchanged, and those who knew their natures looked for a meeting between them, when the sword or some other dangerous weapon would settle for ever their claims for precedence in cunning and in strength.

They met at the fair of Longtown, and spoke, and no more – with them both it was a busy day, and mutual hatred subsided for a time, in the love of turning the penny and amassing gain. The market rose and fell, and fell and rose; and it was whispered that Macmillan, through the superior skill or good fortune of his rival, had missed some bargains which were very valuable, while some positive losses touched a nature extremely sensible of the importance of wealth. One was elated and the other depressed – but not more depressed than moody and incensed, and in this temper they were seen in the evening in the back room of a public inn, seated apart and silent, calculating losses and gains, drinking deeply, and exchanging dark looks of hatred and distrust. They had been observed, during the whole day, to watch each other's movements, and now when they were met face to face, the labours of the day over, and their natures inflamed by liquor as well as by hatred, their companions looked for personal strife between them, and wondered not a little when they saw Johnstone rise, mount on his horse, and ride homewards, leaving his rival in Longtown. Soon afterwards Macmillan started up from a moody fit, drank off a large draught of brandy, threw down a half-guinea, nor waited for change – a thing uncommon with him; and men said, as his horse's feet struck fire from the pavement, that if he overtook Johnstone, there would be a living soul less in the land before sunrise.

Before sunrise next morning the horse of Walter Johnstone came with an empty saddle to his stable door. The bridle was trampled to pieces amongst its feet, and its saddle and sides were splashed over with blood as if a bleeding body had been carried across its back. The cry arose in the country, an instant search was made, and on the side of the public road was found a place where a deadly contest seemed to have happened. It was in a small green field, bordered by a wood, in the farm of Andrew Pattison. The sod was dinted deep with men's feet, and trodden down and trampled and sprinkled over with blood as thickly as it had ever been with dew. Blood drops, too, were traced to some distance, but nothing more was discovered; the body could not be found, though every field was examined and every pool dragged. His money and bills, to the amount of several thousand pounds, were gone, so was his sword – indeed nothing of him could be found on earth save his blood, and for its spilling a strict account was yet to be sought.

Suspicion instantly and naturally fell on John Macmillan, who denied all knowledge of the deed. He had arrived at his own house in due course of time, no marks of weapon or warfare were on him, he performed family worship as was his custom, and he sang the psalm as loudly and prayed as fervently as he was in the habit of doing. He was apprehended and tried, and saved by the contradictory testimony of the witnesses against him, into whose hearts the spirit of falsehood seemed to have entered in order to perplex and confound the judgment of men – or rather that man might have no hand in the punishment, but that God should bring it about in his own good time and way. 'Revenge is mine, saith the Lord,' which meaneth not because it is too sweet a morsel for man, as the scoffer said, but because it is too dangerous. A glance over this conflicting testimony will show how little was then known of this foul offence, and how that little was rendered doubtful and dark by the imperfections of human nature.

Two men of Longtown were examined. One said that he saw Macmillan insulting and menacing Johnstone, laying his hand on the hilt of his sword with a look dark and ominous; while the other swore that he was present at the time, but that it was Johnstone who insulted and menaced Macmillan, and laid his hand on the hilt of his sword and pointed to the road homewards. A very expert and searching examination could make no more of them; they were both respectable men with characters above suspicion. The next witnesses were of another stamp, and their testimony was circuitous and contradictory. One of them was a shepherd – a reluctant witness. His words were these: 'I was frae hame on the night of the murder, in the thick of the wood, no just at the place which was bloody and trampled, but gaye and near hand it. I canna say I can just mind what I was doing; I had somebody to see I jalouse, but wha it was is naebody's business but my ain. There was maybe ane forbye myself in the wood, and maybe twa; there was ane at ony rate, and I am no sure but it was an auld acquaintance. I see nae use there can be in questioning me. I saw nought, and therefore can say nought. I canna but say that I heard something – the trampling of horses, and a rough voice saying, 'Draw and defend yourself.' Then followed the clashing of swords and half smothered sort of work, and then the sound of horses' feet was heard again, and that's a' I ken about it; only I thought the voice was Walter Johnstone's, and so thought Kate Pennie, who was with me and kens as meikle as me.' The examination of Katherine Pennie, one of the Pennies of Pennieland, followed, and she declared that she had heard the evidence of Dick Purdie with surprise and anger. On that night she was not over the step of her father's door for more than five minutes, and that was to look at the sheep in the fauld; and she neither heard the clashing of swords nor the word of man or woman. And with respect to Dick Purdie, she scarcely knew him even by sight; and if all tales were true that were told of him, she would not venture into a lonely wood with him, under the cloud of night, for a gown of silk with pearls on each sleeve. The shepherd, when recalled, admitted that Kate Pennie might be right, 'For after a',' said he, 'it happened in the dark, when a man like me, no that gleg of the uptauk, might confound persons. Somebody was with me, I am gaye and sure, frae what took place – if it was nae Kate, I kenna wha it was, and it couldna weel be Kate either, for Kate's a douce quean, and besides is married.' The judge dismissed the witnesses with some indignant words, and turning to the prisoner, said, 'John Macmillan, the prevarications of these witnesses have saved you; mark my words – saved you be from man, but not from God. On the murderer, the Most High will lay his hot right hand, visibly and before men, that we may know that blood unjustly shed will be avenged. You are at liberty to depart.' He left the bar and resumed his station and his pursuits as usual; nor did he appear sensible to the feeling of the country, which was strong against him.

A year passed over his head, other events happened, and the murder of Walter Johnstone began to be dismissed from men's minds. Macmillan went to the fair of Longtown, and when evening came he was seated in the little back room which I mentioned before, and in company with two men of the names of Hunter and Hope. He sat late, drank deeply, but in the midst of the carousal a knock was heard at the door, and a voice called sharply, 'John Macmillan.' He started up, seemed alarmed, and exclaimed, 'What in Heaven's name can *he* want with me?' and opening the door hastily, went into the garden, for he seemed to dread another summons lest his companions should know the voice. As soon as he was gone, one said to the other, 'If that was not the voice of Walter Johnstone, I never heard it in my life; he is either come back in the flesh or in the spirit, and in either way John Macmillan has good cause to dread him.' They listened – they heard Macmillan speaking in great agitation; he was answered only by a low sound, yet he appeared to understand what was said, for his concluding words were, 'Never! never! I shall rather submit to His judgment who cannot err.' When he returned he was pale and shaking, and he sat down and seemed buried in thought. He spread his palms on his knees, shook his head often, then, starting up, said, 'The judge was a fool and no prophet – to mortal man is not given the wisdom of God – so neighbours let us ride.' They mounted their horses and rode homewards into Scotland at a brisk pace.

The night was pleasant, neither light nor dark; there were few travellers out, and the way winded with the hills and with the streams, passing through a pastoral and beautiful country. Macmillan rode close by the side of his companions, closer than was desirable or common; yet he did not speak, nor make answer when he was spoken to; but looked keenly and earnestly before and behind him, as if he expected the coming of someone, and every tree and bush seemed to alarm and startle him. Day at last dawned, and with the growing light his alarm subsided, and he began to converse with his companions, and talk with a levity which surprised them more than his silence had done before. The sun was all but risen when they approached the farm of Andrew Pattison, and here and there the top of a high tree and the summit of a hill had caught light upon them. Hope looked to Hunter silently, when they came nigh the bloody spot where it was believed the murder had been committed. Macmillan sat looking resolutely before him, as if determined not to look upon it; but his horse stopt at once, trembled violently, and then sprung aside, hurling its rider headlong to the ground. All this passed in a moment; his companions sat astonished; the horse rushed forward, leaving him on the ground, from whence he never rose in life, for his neck was broken by the fall, and with a convulsive shiver or two he expired. Then did the prediction of the judge, the warning voice and summons of the preceding night, and the spot and the time, rush upon their recollection; and they firmly believed that a murderer and robber lay dead beside them. 'His horse saw something,' said Hope to Hunter; 'I never saw such flashing eyes in a horse's head;' – 'and *he* saw something too,' replied Hunter, 'for the glance that he gave to the bloody spot, when his horse started, was one of terror. I never saw such a look, and I wish never to see such another again.'

When John Macmillan perished, matters stood thus with his memory. It was not only loaded with the sin of blood and the sin of robbery, with the sin of making a faithful woman a widow and her children fatherless, but with the grievous sin also of having driven a worthy family to ruin and beggary. The sum which was lost was large, the creditors were merciless; they fell upon the remaining substance of Johnstone, sweeping it wholly away; and his widow sought shelter in a miserable cottage among the Dryfesdale hills, where she supported her children by gathering and spinning wool. In a far different state and condition remained the family of John Macmillan. He died rich and unencumbered, leaving an evil name and an only child, a daughter, wedded to one whom many knew and esteemed, Joseph Howatson by name, a man sober and sedate; a member, too, of our own broken remnant of Cameronians.

Now, my dear children, the person who addresses you was then, as he is yet, God's preacher for the scattered kirk of Scotland, and his tent was pitched among the green hills of Annandale. The death of the transgressor appeared unto me the manifest judgment of God, and when my people gathered around me I rejoiced to see so great a multitude, and, standing in the midst of them, I preached in such a wise that they were deeply moved. I took for my text these words, 'Hath there been evil in the land and the Lord hath not known it?' I discoursed on the wisdom of Providence in guiding the affairs of men. How he permitted our evil passions to acquire the mastery over us, and urge us to deeds of darkness; allowing us to flourish for a season, that he might strike us in the midst of our splendour in a way so visible and awful that the wildest would cry out, 'Behold the finger of God.' I argued the matter home to the heart; I named no names, but I saw Joseph Howatson hide his face in his hands, for he felt and saw from the eyes which were turned towards him that I alluded to the judgment of God upon his relative.

Joseph Howatson went home heavy and sad of heart, and somewhat touched with anger at God's servant for having so pointedly and publicly alluded to his family misfortune; for he believed his father-in-law was a wise and a worthy man. His way home lay along the banks of a winding and beautiful stream, and just where it entered his own lands there was a rustic gate, over which he leaned for a little space, ruminating upon earlier days, on his wedded wife, on his children, and finally his thoughts settled on his father-in-law. He thought of his kindness to himself and to many others, on his fulfilment of all domestic duties, on his constant performance of family worship, and on his general reputation for honesty and fair dealing. He then dwelt on the circumstances of Johnstone's disappearance, on the singular summons his father-in-law received in Longtown, and the catastrophe which followed on the spot and on the very day of the year that the murder was supposed to be committed. He was sore in perplexity, and said aloud, 'Would to God I knew the truth; but the doors of eternity, alas! are shut on the secret for ever.' He looked up and John Macmillan stood before him – stood with all the calmness and serenity and meditative air which a grave man wears when he walks out on a sabbath eve.

'Joseph Howatson,' said the apparition, 'on no secret are the doors of eternity shut – of whom were you speaking?' – 'I was speaking,' answered he, 'of one who is cold and dead, and to whom you bear a strong resemblance,' 'I am he,' said the shape; 'I am John Macmillan.' 'God of heaven!' replied Joseph Howatson, 'how can that be; did I not lay his head in the grave; see it closed over him; how, therefore, can it be? Heaven permits no such visitations.' 'I entreat you my son,' said the shape, 'to believe what I say; the end of man is not when his body goes to dust; he exists in another state, and from that state am I permitted to come to you; waste not time, which is brief, with vain doubts, I am John Macmillan.' 'Father, father,' said the young man, deeply agitated, 'answer me, did you kill and rob Walter Johnstone?' 'I did,' said the Spirit, 'and for that have I returned to earth; listen to me.' The young man was so much overpowered by a revelation thus fearfully made, that he fell insensible on the ground; and when he recovered, the moon was shining, the dews of night were upon him, and he was alone.

Joseph Howatson imagined that he had dreamed a fearful dream; and conceiving that Divine Providence had presented the truth to his fancy, he began to consider how he could secretly make reparation to the wife and children of Johnstone for the double crime of his relative. But on more mature reflection he was impressed with the belief that a spirit had appeared to him, the spirit of his father-in-law, and that his own alarm had hindered him from learning fully the secret of his visit to earth; he therefore resolved to go to the same place next sabbath night, seek rather than avoid an interview, acquaint himself with the state of bliss or woe in which the spirit was placed, and learn if by acts of affection and restitution he could soften his sufferings or augment his happiness. He went accordingly to the little rustic gate by the side of the lonely stream; he walked up and down; hour passed after hour, but he heard nothing and saw nothing save the murmuring of the brook and the hares running among the wild clover. He had resolved to return home, when something seemed to rise from the ground, as shapeless as a cloud at first, but moving with life. It assumed a form, and the appearance of John Macmillan was once more before him. The young man was nothing daunted, but looking on the spirit, said, 'I thought you just and upright and devout, and incapable of murder and robbery.' The spirit seemed to dilate as it made its answer. 'The death of Walter Johnstone sits lightly upon me. We had crossed each other's purposes, we had lessened each other's gains, we had vowed revenge, we met on fair terms, tied our horses to a gate, and fought fairly and long; and when I slew him, I but did what he sought to do to me. I threw him over his horse, carried him far into the country, sought out a deep quagmire on the north side of the Snipe Knowe, in Crake's Moss, and having secured his bills and other perishable property, with the purpose of returning all to his family, I buried him in the moss, leaving his gold in his purse, and laying his cloak and his sword above him.

'Now listen, Joseph Howatson. In my private desk you will find a little key tied with red twine; take it and go to the house of Janet Mathieson in Dumfries, and underneath the hearthstone in my sleeping room you will get my strong-box, open it, it contains all the bills and bonds belonging to Walter Johnstone. Restore them to his widow. I would have restored them but for my untimely death. Inform her privily and covertly where she will find the body of her husband, so that she may bury him in the churchyard with his ancestors. Do these things, that I may have some assuagement of misery; neglect them, and you will become a world's wonder.' The spirit vanished with these words, and was seen no more.

Joseph Howatson was sorely troubled. He had communed with a spirit, he was impressed with the belief that early death awaited him; he felt a sinking of soul and a misery of body, and he sent for me to help him with counsel, and comfort him in his unexampled sorrow. I loved him and hastened to him; I found him weak and woe-begone, and the hand of God seemed to be sore upon him. He took me out to the banks of the little stream where the shape appeared to him, and having desired me to listen without interrupting him, told me how he had seen his father-in-law's spirit, and related the revelations which it had made and the commands it had laid upon him. 'And now,' he said, 'look upon me. I am young, and ten days ago I had a body strong and a mind buoyant, and gray hairs and the honours of old age seemed to await me. But ere three days pass I shall be as the clod of the valley, for he who converses with a spirit, a spirit shall he soon become. I have written down the strange tale I have told you and I put it into your hands, perform for me and for my wretched parent, the instructions which the grave yielded up its tenant to give; and may your days be long in the land, and may you grow gray-headed among your people.' I listened to his words with wonder and with awe, and I promised to obey him in all his wishes with my best and most anxious judgment. We went home together; we spent the evening in prayer. Then he set his house in order, spoke to all his children cheerfully and with a mild voice, and falling on the neck of his wife, said, 'Sarah Macmillan, you were the choice of my young heart, and you have been a wife to me kind, tender, and gentle.' He looked at his children and he looked at his wife, for his heart was too full for more words, and retired to his chamber. He was found next morning kneeling by his bedside, his hands held out as if repelling some approaching object, horror stamped on every feature, and cold and dead.

Then I felt full assurance of the truth of his communications; and as soon as the amazement which his untimely death occasioned had subsided, and his wife and little ones were somewhat comforted, I proceeded to fulfil his dying request. I found the small key tied with red twine, and I went to the house of Janet Mathieson in Dumfries, and I held up the key and said, 'Woman, knowest thou that?' and when she saw it she said, 'Full well I know it, it belonged to a jolly man and a douce, and mony a merry hour has he whiled away wi' my servant maidens and me.' And when she saw me lift the hearthstone, open the box, and spread out the treasure which it contained, she held up her hands, 'Eh! what o'gowd! what o'gowd! but half's mine, be ye saint or sinner; John Macmillan, douce man, aye said he had something there which he considered as not belonging to him but to a quiet friend; weel I wot he meant me, for I have been a quiet friend to him and his.' I told her I was commissioned by his daughter to remove the property, that I was the minister of that persecuted remnant of the kirk called Cameronians, and she might therefore deliver it up without fear. 'I ken weel enough wha ye are,' said this worthless woman, 'd'ye think I dinna ken a minister of the kirk; I have seen meikle o' their siller in my day, frae eighteen to fifty and aught have I caroused with divines, Cameronians, I trow, as well as those of a freer kirk. But touching this treasure, give me twenty gowden pieces, else I'se gar three stamps of my foot bring in them that will see me righted, and send you awa to the mountains bleating like a sheep shorn in winter.' I gave the imperious woman twenty pieces of gold, and carried away the fatal box.

Now, when I got free of the ports of Dumfries, I mounted my little horse and rode away into the heart of the country, among the pastoral hills of Dryfesdale. I carried the box on the saddle before me, and its contents awakened a train of melancholy thoughts within me. There were the papers of Walter Johnstone, corresponding to the description which the spirit gave, and marked with his initials in red ink by the hand of the man who slew him. There were two gold watches and two purses of gold, all tied with red twine, and many bills and much money to which no marks were attached. As I rode along pondering on these things, and casting about in my own mind how and by what means I should make restitution, I was aware of a morass, broad and wide, which with all its quagmires glittered in the moonlight before me. I knew I had penetrated into the centre of Dryfesdale, but I was not well acquainted with the country; I therefore drew my bridle, and looked around to see if any house was nigh, where I could find shelter for the night. I saw a small house built of turf and thatched with heather, from the window of which a faint light glimmered. I rode up, alighted, and there I found a woman in widow's weeds, with three sweet children, spinning yarn from the wool which the shepherds shear in spring from the udders of the ewes. She welcomed me, spread bread and placed milk before me. I asked a blessing, and ate and drank, and was refreshed.

Now it happened that, as I sat with the solitary woman and her children, there came a man to the door, and with a loud yell of dismay burst it open and staggered forward crying, 'There's a corse candle in Crake's Moss, and I'll be a dead man before the morning,' 'Preserve me! piper', said the widow, 'ye're in a piteous taking; here is a holy man who will speak comfort to you, and tell you how all these are but delusions of the eye or exhalations of nature.' 'Delusions and exhalations, Dame Johnstone,' said the piper, 'd'ye think I dinna ken a corse light from an elf candle, an elf candle from a will-o'-wisp, and a will-o'-wisp from all other lights of this wide world.' The name of the morass and the woman's name now flashed upon me, and I was struck with amazement and awe. I looked on the widow, and I looked on the wandering piper, and I said, 'Let me look on those corse lights, for God creates nothing in vain; there is a wise purpose in all things, and a wise aim.' And the piper said, 'Na, na; I have nae wish to see ony mair on't, a dead light bodes the living nae gude; and I am sure if

I gang near Crake's Moss it will lair me amang the hags and quags.' And I said, 'Foolish old man, you are equally safe every where; the hand of the Lord reaches round the earth, and strikes and protects according as it was foreordained, for nothing is hid from his eyes – come with me.' And the piper looked strangely upon me and stirred not a foot; and I said, 'I shall go by myself,' and the woman said, 'Let me go with you, for I am sad of heart, and can look on such things without fear; for, alas! since I lost my own Walter Johnstone, pleasure is no longer pleasant: and I love to wander in lonesome places and by old churchyards.' 'Then,' said the piper, 'I darena bide my lane with the bairns; I'll go also; but O! let me strengthen my heart with ae spring on pipes before I venture.' 'Play,' I said, 'Clavers and his Highlandmen, it is the tune to cheer ye and keep your heart up.' 'Your honour's no cannie,' said the old man; 'that's my favourite tune.' So he played it and said, 'Now I am fit to look on lights of good or evil.' And we walked into the open air.

All Crake's Moss seemed on fire; not illumined with one steady and uninterrupted light, but kindled up by fits like the northern sky with its wandering streamers. On a little bank which rose in the centre of the morass, the supernatural splendour seemed chiefly to settle; and having continued to shine for several minutes, the whole faded and left but one faint gleam behind. I fell on my knees, held up my hands to heaven, and said, 'This is of God; behold in that fearful light the finger of the Most High. Blood has been spilt, and can be no longer concealed; the point of the mariner's needle points less surely to the north than yon living flame points to the place where man's body has found a bloody grave. Follow me,' and I walked down to the edge of the moss and gazed earnestly on the spot. I knew now that I looked on the long hidden resting place of Walter Johnstone, and considered that the hand of God was manifest in the way that I had been thus led blindfold into his widow's house. I reflected for a moment on these things; I wished to right the fatherless, yet spare the feelings of the innocent; the supernatural light partly showed me the way, and the words which I now heard whispered by my companions aided in directing the rest.

'I tell ye, Dame Johnstone,' said the piper, 'the man's no cannie; or what's waur, he may belong to the spirit world himself, and do us a mischief. Saw ye ever mortal man riding with ae spur and carrying a silver-headed cane for a whip, wi' sic a fleece of hair about his haffets and sic a wild ee in his head; and then he kens a' things in the heavens aboon and the earth beneath. He kenned my favourite tune Clavers; I'se uphaud he's no in the body, but ane of the souls made perfect of the auld Covenanters whom Grahame or Grierson slew; we're daft to follow him'. 'Fool body,' I heard the widow say, 'I'll follow him; there's something about that man, be he in the spirit or in the flesh, which is pleasant and promising. O! could he but, by prayer or other means of lawful knowledge, tell me about my dear Walter Johnstone; thrice has he appeared to me in dream or vision with a sorrowful look, and weel ken I what that means.' We had now reached the edge of the morass, and a dim and uncertain light continued to twinkle about the green knoll which rose in its middle. I turned suddenly round and said, 'For a wise purpose am I come; to reveal murder; to speak consolation to the widow and the fatherless, and to soothe the perturbed spirits of those whose fierce passions ended in untimely death. Come with me; the hour is come, and I must not do my commission negligently.' 'I kenned it, I kenned it,' said the piper, 'he's just one of the auld persecuted worthies risen from his red grave to right the injured, and he'll do't discreetly; follow him, Dame, follow him.' 'I shall follow,' said the widow, 'I have that strength given me this night which will bear me through all trials which mortal flesh can endure.'

When we reached the little green hillock in the centre of the morass, I looked to the north and soon distinguished the place described by my friend Joseph Howatson, where the body of Walter Johnstone was deposited. The moon shone clear, the stars aided us with their light, and some turfcutters having left their spades standing near, I ordered the piper to take a spade and dig where I placed my staff. 'O dig carefully,' said the widow, 'do not be rude with mortal dust.' We dug and came to a sword; the point was broken and the blade hacked. 'It is the sword of my Walter Johnstone,' said his widow, 'I could swear to it among a thousand.' 'It is my father's sword,' said a fine dark haired boy who had followed us unperceived, 'it is my father's sword, and were he living who wrought this, he should na be lang in rueing it.' 'He is dead, my child,' I said, 'and beyond your reach, and vengeance is the Lord's.' 'O, Sir,' cried his widow, in a flood of tears, 'ye ken all things; tell me, is this my husband or no?' 'It is the body of Walter Johnstone,' I answered, 'slain by one who is passed to his account, and buried here by the hand that slew him, with his gold in his purse and his watch in his pocket.' So saying we uncovered the body, lifted it up, laid it on the grass; the embalming nature of the morass had preserved it from decay, and mother and child, with tears and with cries, named his name and lamented over him. His gold watch and his money, his cloak and his dress, were untouched and entire, and we bore him to the cottage of his widow, where with clasped hands she sat at his feet and his children at his head till the day drew nigh the dawn; I then rose and said, 'Woman, thy trials have been severe and manifold; a good wife, a good mother, and a good widow hast thou been, and thy reward will be where the blessed alone are admitted. It was revealed to me by a mysterious revelation that thy husband's body was where we found it; and I was commissioned by a voice, assuredly not of this world, to deliver thee this treasure, which is thy own, that thy children may be educated, and that bread and raiment may be thine.' And I delivered her husband's wealth into her hands, refused gold which she offered, and mounting my horse, rode over the hills and saw her no more. But I soon heard of her, for there rose a strange sound in the land, that a Good Spirit had appeared to the widow of Walter Johnstone, had disclosed where her husband's murdered body lay, had enriched her with all his lost wealth, had prayed by her side till the blessed dawn of day, and then vanished with the morning light. I closed my lips on the secret till now; and I reveal it to you, my children, that you may know there is a God who ruleth this world by wise and invisible means, and punisheth the wicked, and cheereth the humble of heart and the lowly minded.

Such was the last sermon of the good John Farley, a man whom I knew and loved. I think I see him now, with his long white hair and his look mild, eloquent, and sagacious. He was a giver of good counsel, a sayer of wise sayings, with wit at will, learning in abundance, and a gift in sarcasm which the wildest dreaded.

Dennis Haggarty's Wife
William Makepeace Thackeray

There was an odious Irishwoman and her daughter who used to frequent the 'Royal Hotel' at Leamington some years ago, and who went by the name of Mrs. Major Gam. Gam had been a distinguished officer in his Majesty's service, whom nothing but death and his own amiable wife could overcome. The widow mourned her husband in the most becoming bombazeen she could muster, and had at least half-an-inch of lampblack round the immense visiting tickets which she left at the houses of the nobility and gentry her friends.

Some of us, I am sorry to say, used to call her Mrs. Major Gammon; for if the worthy widow had a propensity, it was to talk largely of herself and family (of her own family, for she held her husband's very cheap), and of the wonders of her paternal mansion, Molloyville, county of Mayo. She was of the Molloys of that county; and though I never heard of the family before, I have little doubt, from what Mrs. Major Gam stated, that they were the most ancient and illustrious family of that part of Ireland. I remember there came down to see his aunt a young fellow with huge red whiskers and tight nankeens, a green coat and an awful breastpin, who, after two days' stay at the Spa, proposed marriage to Miss S— or, in default, a duel with her father; and who drove a flash curricle with a bay and a grey, and who was presented with much pride by Mrs. Gam as Castlereagh Molloy of Molloyville. We all agreed that he was the most insufferable snob of the whole season, and were delighted when a bailiff came down in search of him.

Well, this is all I know personally of the Molloyville family; but at the house if you met the widow Gam, and talked on any subject in life, you were sure to hear of it. If you asked her to have pease at dinner, she would say, 'Oh, sir, after the pease at Molloyville, I really don't care for any others, – do I, dearest Jemima? We always had a dish in the month of June, when my father gave his head gardener a guinea (we had three at Molloyville), and sent him with his compliments and a quart of pease to our neighbour, dear Lord Marrowfat. What a sweet place Marrowfat Park is! isn't it, Jemima?' If a carriage passed by the window, Mrs. Major Gammon would be sure to tell you that there were three carriages at Molloyville, 'the barouche, the chawiot, and the covered cyar.' In the same manner she would favour you with the number and names of the footmen of the establishment; and on a visit to Warwick Castle (for this bustling woman made one in every party of pleasure that was formed from the hotel), she gave us to understand that the great walk by the river was altogether inferior to the principal avenue of Molloyville Park. I should not have been able to tell so much about Mrs. Gam and her daughter, but that, between ourselves, I was particularly sweet upon a young lady at the time, whose papa lived at the 'Royal,' and was under the care of Dr. Jephson.

The Jemima appealed to by Mrs. Gam in the above sentence was, of course, her daughter, apostrophized by her mother, 'Jemima, my soul's darling!' or, 'Jemima, my blessed child!' or, 'Jemima, my own love!' The sacrifices that Mrs. Gam had made for that daughter were, she said, astonishing. The money she had spent in masters upon her, the illnesses through which she had nursed her, the ineffable love the mother bore her, were only known to heaven, Mrs. Gam said. They used to come into the room with their arms round each other's waists: at dinner between the courses the mother would sit with one hand locked in her daughter's; and if only two or three young men were present at the time, would be pretty sure to kiss Jemima more than once during the time whilst the bohea was poured out.

As for Miss Gam, if she was not handsome, candour forbids me to say she was ugly. She was neither one nor t'other. She was a person who wore ringlets and a band round her forehead; she knew four songs, which became rather tedious at the end of a couple of months' acquaintance; she had excessively bare shoulders; she inclined to wear numbers of cheap ornaments, rings, brooches, *ferronnières*, smelling-bottles, and was always, we thought, very smartly dressed: though old Mrs. Lynx hinted that her gowns and her mother's were turned over and over again, and that her eyes were almost put out by darning stockings.

These eyes Miss Gam had very large, though rather red and weak, and used to roll them about at every eligible unmarried man in the place. But though the widow subscribed to all the balls, though she hired a fly to go the meet of the hounds, though she was constant at church, and Jemima sang louder than any person there except the clerk, and though, probably, any person who made her a happy husband would be invited down to enjoy the three footmen, gardeners and carriages at Molloyville, yet no English gentleman was found sufficiently audacious to propose. Old Lynx used to say that the pair had been at Tunbridge, Harrogate, Brighton, Ramsgate, Cheltenham, for this eight years past; where they had met, it seemed, with no better fortune. Indeed, the widow looked rather high for her blessed child: and as she looked with the contempt which no small number of Irish people feel upon all persons who get their bread by labour or commerce; and as she was a person whose energetic manners, costume, and brogue were not much to the taste of quiet English country gentlemen, Jemima – sweet, spotless flower, – still remained on her hands, a thought withered, perhaps, and seedy.

Now, at this time, the 120th Regiment was quartered at Weedon Barracks, and with the corps was a certain Assistant-Surgeon Haggarty, a large, lean, tough, raw-boned man, with big hands, knock-knees, and carroty whiskers, and withal, as honest a creature as ever handled a lancet. Haggarty, as his name imports, was of the very same nation as Mrs. Gam, and, what is more, the honest fellow had some of the peculiarities which belonged to the widow, and bragged about his family almost as much as she did. I do not know of what particular part of Ireland they were kings, but monarchs they must have been, as have been the ancestors of so many thousand Hibernian families; but they had been men of no small consideration in Dublin, 'where my father,' Haggarty said, 'is as well known as King William's statue, and where he "rowls his carriage, too," let me tell ye.'

Hence, Haggarty was called by the wags 'Rowl the carriage,' and several of them made inquiries of Mrs. Gam regarding him: 'Mrs. Gam, when you use to go up from Molloyville to the Lord Lieutenant's balls, and had your town-house in Fitzwilliam Square, used you to meet the famous Doctor Haggarty in society?'

'Is it Surgeon Haggarty of Gloucester Street ye mean? The black Papist! D'ye suppose that the Molloys would sit down to table with a creature of that sort?'

'Why, isn't he the most famous physician in Dublin, and doesn't he rowl his carriage there?'

'The horrid wretch! He keeps a shop, I tell ye, and sends his sons out with the medicine. He's got four of them off into the army, Ulick and Phil, and Terence and Denny, and now it's Charles that takes out the physic. But how should I know about these odious creatures?

Their mother was a Burke, of Burke's Town, county Cavan, and brought Surgeon Haggarty two thousand pounds. She was a Protestant; and I am surprised how she could have taken up with a horrid, odious, Popish apothecary!'

From the extent of the widow's information, I am led to suppose that the inhabitants of Dublin are not less anxious about their neighbours than are the natives of English cities; and I think it is very probable that Mrs. Gam's account of the young Haggartys who carried out the medicine is perfectly correct, for a lad in the 120th made a caricature of Haggarty coming out of a chemist's shop with an oilcloth basket under his arm, which set the worthy surgeon in such fury that there would have been a duel between him and the ensign, could the fiery doctor have had his way.

Now, Dionysius Haggarty was of an exceedingly inflammable temperament, and it chanced that of all the invalids, the visitors, the young squires of Warwickshire, the young manufacturers from Birmingham, the young officers from the barracks – it chanced unluckily for Miss Gam and himself, that he was the only individual who was in the least smitten by her personal charms. He was very tender and modest about his love, however, for it must be owned that he respected Mrs. Gam hugely, and fully admitted, like a good simple fellow as he was, the superiority of that lady's birth and breeding to his own. How could he hope that he, a humble assistant-surgeon, with a thousand pounds his aunt Kitty left him for all his fortune, – how could he hope that one of the race of Molloyville would ever condescend to marry him?

Inflamed, however, by love, and inspired by wine, one day at a picnic at Kenilworth, Haggarty, whose love and raptures were the talk of the whole regiment, was induced by his waggish comrades to make a proposal in form.

'Are you aware, Mr. Haggarty, that you are speaking to a Molloy?' was all the reply majestic Mrs. Gam made when, according to the usual formula, the fluttering Jemima referred her suitor to 'mamma'. She left him with a look which was meant to crush the poor fellow to earth; she gathered up her cloak and bonnet, and precipitately called for her fly. She took care to tell every single soul in Leamington that the son of the odious Papist apothecary had had the audacity to propose for her daughter (indeed, a proposal, coming from whatever quarter it may, does no harm), and left Haggarty in a state of extreme depression and despair.

His down-heartedness, indeed, surprised most of his acquaintances in and out of the regiment, for the young lady was no beauty, and a doubtful fortune, and Dennis was a man outwardly of an unromantic turn, who seemed to have a great deal more liking for beaf-steak and whisky-punch than for women, however fascinating.

But there is no doubt this shy, uncouth, rough fellow had a warmer and more faithful heart hid within him than many a dandy who is as handsome as Apollo. I, for my part, never can understand why a man falls in love, and heartily give him credit for so doing, never mind with what or whom. *That* I take to be a point quite as much beyond an individual's own control as catching of the small-pox or the colour of his hair. To the surprise of all, Assistant-Surgeon Dionysius Haggarty was deeply and seriously in love; and I am told that one day he very nearly killed the before-mentioned young ensign with a carving-knife, for venturing to make a second caricature, representing Lady Gammon and Jemima in a fantastical park, surrounded by three gardeners, three carriages, three footmen, and the covered cyar. He would have no joking concerning them. He became moody and quarrelsome of habit. He was for some time much more in the surgery and hospital than in the mess. He gave up the eating, for the most part, of those vast quantities of beef and pudding, for which his stomach had used to afford such ample and swift accommodation; and when the cloth was drawn, instead of taking twelve tumblers, and singing Irish melodies, as he used to do, in a horrible cracked yelling voice, he would retire to his own apartment, or gloomily pace the barrack-yard, or madly whip and spur a grey mare he had on the road to Leamington, where his Jemima (although invisible for him) still dwelt.

The season at Leamington coming to a conclusion by the withdrawal of the young fellows who frequented that watering-place, the Widow Gam retired to her usual quarters for the other months of the year. Where these quarters were, I think we have no right to ask, for I believe she had quarrelled with her brother at Molloyville, and besides, was a great deal too proud to be a burden on anybody.

Not only did the widow quit Leamington, but very soon afterwards the 120th received its marching orders, and left Weedon and Warwickshire. Haggarty's appetite was by this time partially restored, but his love was not altered, and his humour was still morose and gloomy. I am informed that at this period of his life he wrote some poems relative to his unhappy passion; a wild set of verses of several lengths, and in his handwriting, being discovered upon a sheet of paper in which a pitch-plaster was wrapped up, which Lieutenant and Adjutant Wheezer was compelled to put on for a cold.

Fancy, then, three years afterwards, the surprise of all Haggarty's acquaintances on reading in the public papers the following announcement:–

'Married, at Monkstown on the 12th instant, Dionysius Haggarty, Esq., of H.M. 120th Foot, to Jemima Amelia Wilhelmina Molloy, daughter of the late Major Lancelot Gam, R.M., and granddaughter of the late, and niece of the present Burke Bodkin Blake Molloy, Esq., Molloyville, county Mayo.'

'Has the course of true love at last begun to run smooth?' thought I, as I laid down the paper; and the old times, and the old leering, bragging widow, and the high shoulders of her daughter, and the jolly days with the 120th, and Dr. Jephson's one-horse chaise, and the Warwickshire hunt, and – and Louisa S—, but never mind *her*, – came back to my mind. Has that good-natured, simple fellow at last met with his reward? Well, if he has not to marry the mother-in-law too, he may get on well enough.

Another year announced the retirement of Assistant-Surgeon Haggarty from the 120th, where he was replaced by Assistant-Surgeon Angus Rothsay Leech, a Scotchman, probably; with whom I have not the least acquaintance, and who has nothing whatever to do with this little history.

Still more years passed on, during which time I will not say that I kept a constant watch upon the fortunes of Mr. Haggarty and his lady, for, perhaps, if the truth were known, I never thought for a moment about them; until one day, being at Kingstown, near Dublin, dawdling on the beach, and staring at the Hill of Howth, as most people at that watering-place do, I saw coming towards me a tall gaunt man, with a pair of bushy red whiskers, of which I thought I had seen the like in former years, and a face which could be no other than Haggarty's. It was Haggarty, ten years older than when we last met, and greatly more grim and thin. He had on one shoulder a young gentleman in a dirty tartan costume, and a face exceedingly like his peeping from under a battered plume of black feathers, while with his other hand he was dragging a light green go-cart, in which reposed a female infant of some two years old. Both were roaring with great power of lungs.

As soon as Dennis saw me, his face lost the dull, puzzled expression which had seemed to characterize it; he dropped the pole of the go-cart from one hand, and his son from the other, and came jumping forward to greet me with all his might, leaving his progeny roaring in the road.

'Bless my sowl,' says he, 'sure it's Fitz-Boodle? Fitz, don't you remember me? Dennis Haggarty of the 120th? Leamington, you know? Molloy, my boy, hould your tongue, and stop your screeching, and Jemima's too; d'ye hear? Well, it does good to sore eyes to see an old face. How fat you're grown, Fitz; and were ye ever in Ireland before? and a'n't ye delighted with it? Confess, now isn't it beautiful?'

This question regarding the merits of their country, which I have remarked is put by most Irish persons, being answered in a satisfactory manner, and the shouts of the infants appeased from an apple-stall hard by, Dennis and I talked of old times; I congratulated him on his marriage with the lovely girl whom we all admired, and hoped he had a fortune with her, and so forth. His appearance, however, did not bespeak a great fortune: he had an old grey hat, short old trousers, an old waistcoat with regimental buttons, and patched Blucher boots, such as are not usually sported by persons in easy life.

'Ah!' says he, with a sigh, in reply to my queries, 'times are changed since them days, Fitz-Boodle. My wife's not what she was – the beautiful creature you knew her. Molloy my boy, run off in a hurry to your mamma, and tell her an English gentleman is coming home to dine; for you'll dine with me, Fitz, in course?' And I agreed to partake of that meal; though Master Molloy altogether declined to obey his papa's orders with respect to announcing the stranger.

'Well, I must announce you myself,' says Haggarty, with a smile. 'Come, it's just dinner-time, and my little cottage is not a hundred yards off.' Accordingly, we all marched in procession to Dennis's little cottage, which was one of a row and a half of one-storied houses, with little court-yards before them, and mostly with very fine names on the door-posts of each. 'Surgeon Haggarty' was emblazoned on Dennis's gate, on a stained green copper-plate; and, not content with this, on the door-post above the bell was an oval with the inscription of 'New Molloyville'. The bell was broken, of course; the court, or garden-path, was mouldy, weedy, seedy; there were some dirty rocks, by way of ornament, round a faded grass-plot in the centre, some clothes and rags hanging out of most part of the windows of New Molloyville, the immediate entrance to which was by a battered scraper, under a broken trellis-work, up which a withered creeper declined any longer to climb.

'Small, but snug,' says Haggarty: 'I'll lead the way, Fitz; put your hat on the flower-pot there, and turn to the left into the drawing-room.' A fog of onions and turf-smoke filled the whole of the house, and gave signs that dinner was not far off. Far off? You could hear it frizzling in the kitchen, where the maid was also endeavouring to hush the crying of a third refractory child. But as we entered, all three of Haggarty's darlings were in full war.

'Is it you Dennis?' cried a sharp raw voice, from a dark corner of the drawing-room to which we were introduced, and in which a dirty tablecloth was laid for dinner, some bottles of porter and a cold mutton-bone being laid out on a rickety grand-piano hard by. 'Ye're always late, Mr. Haggarty. Have you brought the whisky from the Nowlan's? I'll go bail ye've not now.'

'My dear, I've brought an old friend of yours and mine to take pot-luck with us to-day,' said Dennis.

'When is he to come?' said the lady. At which speech I was rather surprised, for I stood before her.

'Here he is Jemima my love,' answered Dennis, looking at me. 'Mr. Fitz-Boodle; don't you remember him in Warwickshire, darling?'

'Mr Fitz-Boodle! I am very glad to see him,' said the lady, rising curtseying with much cordiality.

Mrs. Haggarty was blind.

Mrs. Haggarty was not only blind, but it was evident that smallpox had been the cause of her loss of vision. Her eyes were bound with a bandage, her features were entirely swollen, scarred, and distorted by the horrible effects of the malady. She had been knitting in a corner when we entered, and was wrapped in a very dirty bed-gown. Her voice to me was quite different to that in which she addressed her husband. She spoke to Haggarty in broad Irish: she addressed me in that most odious of all languages – Irish-English, endeavouring to the utmost to disguise her brogue, and to speak with the true dawdling *distingué* English air.

'Are you long in I-a-land?' said the poor creature in this accent. 'You must faind it a sad ba'ba'ous place, Mr. Fitz-Boodle, I'm shu-ah! It was vary kaind of you to come upon us *en famille*, and accept a dinner *sans cérémonie*. Mr. Haggarty, I hope you'll put the waine into aice, Mr. Fitz-Boodle must be melted with this hot weathah.'

For some time she conducted the conversation in this polite strain, and I was obliged to say, in reply to a query of hers, that I did not find her the least altered, though I should never have recognized her but for this rencontre. She told Haggarty with a significant air to get the wine from the cellah, and whispered to me that he was his own butlah; and the poor fellow, taking the hint, scudded away into the town for a pound of veal cutlets and a couple of bottles of wine from the tavern.

'Will the childhren get their potatoes and butther here?' said a barefoot girl, with long black hair flowing over her face, which she thrust in at the door.

'Let them sup in the nursery, Elizabeth, and send – ah! Edwards to me.'

'Is it cook you mane, ma'am?' said the girl.
'Send her at once!' shrieked the unfortunate woman; and the noise of frying presently ceasing, a hot woman made her appearance, wiping her brows with her apron, and asking, with an accent decidedly Hibernian, what the misthress wanted.

'Lead me up to my dressing-room, Edwards: I really am not fit to be seen in this dishabille by Mr. Fitz-Boodle.'

'Fait' I can't!' says Edwards; 'sure the masther's out at the butcher's, and can't look to the kitchen-fire!'

'Nonsense, I must go!' cried Mrs. Haggarty; and so Edwards, putting on a resigned air, and giving her arm and face a further rub with her apron, held out her arm to Mrs. Dennis, and the pair went upstairs.

She left me to indulge my reflections for half-an-hour, at the end of which period she came downstairs dressed in an old yellow satin, with the poor shoulders exposed just as much as ever. She had mounted a tawdry cap, which Haggarty himself must have selected for her. She had all sorts of necklaces, bracelets, and earrings in gold, in garnets, in mother-of-pearl, in ormolu. She brought in a furious savour of musk, which drove the odours of onions and turf-smoke, before it; and she waved across her wretched, angular, scarred features, an old cambric handkerchief with a yellow-lace border.

'And so you would have known me anywhere, Mr. Fitz-Boodle?' said she, with a grin that was meant to be most fascinating. 'I was sure you would; for though my dreadful illness deprived me of my sight, it is a mercy that it did not change my features or complexion at all!'

This mortification had been spared the unhappy woman: but I

don't know whether, with all her vanity, her infernal pride, folly, and selfishness, it was charitable to leave her in her error.

Yet why correct her? There is a quality in certain people which is above all advice, exposure, or correction. Only let a man or woman have DULLNESS sufficient, and they need bow to no extant authority. A dullard recognizes no betters; a dullard can't see that he is in the wrong; a dullard has no scruples of conscience, no doubts of pleasing, or succeeding, or doing right; no qualms for other people's feelings, no respect but for the fool himself. How can you make a fool perceive that he is a fool? Such a personage can no more see his own folly than he can see his own ears. And the great quality of dullness is to be unalterably contented with itself. What myriads of souls are there of this admirable sort – selfish, stingy, ignorant, passionate, brutal; bad sons, mothers, fathers, never known to do kind actions!

To pause, however, in this disquisition which was carrying us far off Kingstown, New Molloyville, Ireland, – nay, into the wide world wherever Dullness inhabits, let it be stated that Mrs. Haggarty, from my brief acquaintance with her and her mother, was of the order of persons just mentioned. There was an air of conscious merit about her, very hard to swallow along with the infamous dinner poor Dennis managed, after much delay, to get on the table. She did not fail to invite me to Molloyville, where she said her cousin would be charmed to see me; and she told me almost as many anecdotes about that place as her mother used to impart in former days. I observed, moreover, that Dennis cut her the favourite pieces of the beefsteak, that she ate thereof with great gusto, and that she drank with similar eagerness of the various strong liquors at table. 'We Irish ladies are all fond of a leetle glass of punch,' she said, with a playful air, and Dennis mixed her a powerful tumbler of such violent grog as I myself could swallow only with some difficulty. She talked of her suffering a great deal, of her sacrifices, of the luxuries to which she had been accustomed before marriage, – in a word, of a hundred of those themes on which some ladies are in the custom of enlarging when they wish to plague some husbands.

But honest Dennis, far from being angry at this perpetual, wearisome, impudent recurrence to her own superiority, rather encouraged the conversation than otherwise. It pleased him to hear his wife discourse about her merits and family splendours. He was so thoroughly beaten down and henpecked, that he, as it were, gloried in his servitude, and fancied that his wife's magnificence reflected credit on himself. He looked towards me, who was half sick of the woman and her egotism, as if expecting me to exhibit the deepest sympathy, and flung me glances across the table as much as to say, 'What a gifted creature my Jemima is, and what a fine fellow I am to be in possession of her!' When the children came down she scolded them, of course, and dismissed them abruptly (for which circumstance, perhaps, the writer of these pages was not in his heart very sorry), and, after having sat a preposterously long time, left us, asking whether we would have coffee there or in her boudoir.

'Oh! here, of course,' said Dennis, with rather a troubled air, and in about ten minutes the lovely creature was led back to us again by 'Edwards,' and the coffee made its appearance. After coffee her husband begged her to let Mr. Fitz-Boodle hear her voice: 'He longs for some of his old favourites.'

'No! *do* you?' said she; and was led in triumph to the jingling old piano, and with a screechy, wiry voice, sung those very abominable old ditties which I had heard her sing at Leamington ten years back.

Haggarty, as she sang, flung himself back in the chair delighted. Husbands always are, and with the same song, one that they have heard when they were nineteen years old, probably; most Englishmen's tunes have that date, and it is rather affecting, I think, to hear an old gentleman of sixty or seventy quavering the old ditty that was fresh when *he* was fresh and in his prime. If he has a musical wife, depend on it he thinks her old songs of 1788 are better than any he has heard since: in fact he has heard *none* since. When the old couple are in high good-humour the old gentleman will take the old lady round the waist, and say, 'My dear, do sing me one of your own songs,' and she sits down and sings with her old voice, and, as she sings, the roses of her youth bloom again for a moment, Ranelagh resuscitates, and she is dancing a minuet in powder and a train.

This is another digression. It was occasioned by looking at poor Dennis's face while his wife was screeching (and, believe me, the former was the more pleasant occupation). Bottom tickled by the fairies could not have been in greater ecstacies. He thought the music was divine; and had further reason for exulting in it, which was, that his wife was always in a good humour after singing, and never would sing but in that happy frame of mind. Dennis had hinted so much in our little colloquy during the ten minutes of his lady's absence in the 'boudoir'; so, at the conclusion of each piece, we shouted 'Bravo!' and clapped our hands like mad.

Such was my insight into the life of Surgeon Dionysius Haggarty and his wife; and I must have come upon him at a favourable moment too, for poor Dennis has spoken, subsequently, of our delightful evening at Kingstown, and evidently thinks to this day that his friend was fascinated by the entertainment there. His inward economy was as follows: he had his half-pay, a thousand pounds, about a hundred a year that his father left, and his wife had sixty pounds a year from the mother; which the mother, of course, never paid. He had no practice, for he was absorbed in attention to his Jemima and the children, whom he used to wash, to dress, to carry out, to walk, or to ride, as we have seen, and who could not have a servant, as their dear blind mother could never be left alone. Mrs. Haggarty, a great invalid, used to lie in bed till one, and have breakfast and hot luncheon there. A fifth part of his income was spent in having her wheeled about in a chair, by which it was his duty to walk daily for an allotted number of hours. Dinner would ensue, and the amateur clergy, who abound in Ireland, and of whom Mrs. Haggarty was a great admirer, lauded her everywhere as a model of resignation and virtue, and praised beyond measure the admirable piety with which she bore her sufferings.

Well, every man to his taste. It did not certainly appear to me that *she* was the martyr of the family.

'The circumstances of my marriage with Jemima,' Dennis said to me, in some after conversations we had on this interesting subject, 'were the most romantic and touching you can conceive. You saw what an impression the dear girl had made upon me when we were at Weedon; for from the first day I set eyes on her, and heard her sing her delightful song of "Dark-eyed Maiden of Araby," I felt, and said to Turniquet of ours, that every night, that *she* was the dark-eyed maid of Araby for *me*, – not that she was, you know, for she was born in Shropshire. But I felt that I had seen the woman who was to make me happy or miserable for life. You know how I proposed for her at Kenilworth, and how I was rejected, and how I almost shot myself in consequence, – no, you don't know that, for I said nothing about it to any one, but I can tell you it was a very near thing; and a very lucky thing for me I didn't do it: for, – would you believe it? – the dear girl was in love with me all the time.'

'Was she really?' said I, who recollected that Miss Gam's love of those days showed itself in a very singular manner; but the fact is, when women are most in love they most disguise it.

'Over head and ears in love with poor Dennis,' resumed that

worthy fellow, 'who'd ever have thought it? But I have it from the best authority, from her own mother, with whom I'm not over and above good friends now; but of this fact she assured me, and I'll tell you when and how.

'We were quartered at Cork three years after we were at Weedon, and it was our last year at home; and a great mercy that my dear girl spoke in time, or where should we have been *now?* Well, one day, marching home from parade, I saw a lady seated at an open window by another who seemed an invalid, and the lady at the window, who was dressed in the profoundest mourning, cried out, with a scream, "Gracious heavens! it's Mr. Haggarty of the 120th."

' "Sure I know that voice," says I to Whiskerton.

' "It's a great mercy you don't know it a deal too well," says he: "it's Lady Gammon. She's on some husband-hunting scheme, depend on it, for that daughter of hers. She was at Bath last year on the same errand, and at Cheltenham the year before, where heaven bless you! she's as well known as the 'Hen and Chickens.' "

' "I'll thank you not to speak disrespectfully of Miss Jemima Gam," said I to Whiskerton; "she's of one of the first families in Ireland, and whoever says a word against a woman I once proposed for, insults me – do you understand?"

' "Well, marry her, if you like," says Whiskerton, quite peevish: "marry her, and be hanged!"

'Marry her! the very idea of it set my brain a-whirling, and made me a thousand times more mad than I am by nature.

'You may be sure I walked up the hill to the parade-ground that afternoon, and with a beating heart too. I came to the widow's house. It was called "New Molloyville," as this is. Wherever she takes a house for six months, she calls it "New Molloyville;" and has had one in Mallow, in Bandon, in Sligo, in Castlebar, in Fermoy, in Drogheda, and the deuce knows where besides: but the blinds were down, and though I thought I saw somebody behind 'em, no notice was taken of poor Denny Haggarty, and I paced up and down all mess-time in hopes of catching a glimpse of Jemima, but in vain. The next day I was on the ground again; I was just as much in love as ever, that's the fact. I'd never been in that way before, look you; and when once caught, I knew it was for life.

'There's no use in telling you how long I beat about the bush, but when I *did* get admittance to the house (it was through the means of young Castlereagh Molloy, whom you may remember at Leamington, and who was at Cork for the regatta, and used to dine at our mess, and had taken a mighty fancy to me) – when I *did* get into the house, I say, I rushed *in medias res*, at once; I couldn't keep myself quiet, my heart was too full.

'Oh, Fitz! I shall never forget the day, – the moment I was inthrojuiced into the dthrawing-room' (as he began to be agitated, Dennis's brogue broke out with greater richness than ever; but though a stranger may catch, and repeat from memory, a few words, it is next to impossible for him to *keep up a conversation* in Irish, so that we had best give up all attempts to imitate Dennis). 'When I saw old Mother Gam,' said he, 'my feelings overcame me all at once. I rowled down on the ground, sir, as if I'd been hit by a musket-ball. "Dearest madam," says I, "I'll die if you don't give me Jemima."

'"Heavens, Mr. Haggarty!" says she, "how you seize me with surprise! Castlereagh, my dear nephew, had you not better leave us?" and away he went, lighting a cigar, and leaving me still on the floor.

'"Rise, Mr. Haggarty," continued the widow. "I will not attempt to deny that this constancy towards my daughter is extremely affecting, however sudden your present appeal may be. I will not attempt to deny that, perhaps, Jemima may have a similar feeling; but, as I said, I never could give my daughter to a Catholic."

'"I'm as good a Protestant as yourself, ma'am," says I; "my mother was an heiress, and we were all brought up her way."

'"That makes the matter very different," says she, turning up the whites of her eyes. "How could I ever have reconciled it to my conscience to see my blessed child married to a Papist? How could I ever have taken him to Molloyville? Well, this obstacle being removed, *I* must put myself no longer in the way between two young people. *I* must sacrifice myself; as I always have when my darling girl was in question. You shall see her, the poor dear, lovely, gentle sufferer, and learn your fate from her own lips."

'"The sufferer, ma'am," says I; "has Miss Gam been ill?"

'"What! haven't you heard?" cried the widow. "Haven't you heard of the dreadful illness which so nearly carried her from me? For nine weeks, Mr. Haggarty, I watched day and night, without taking a wink of sleep, – for nine weeks she lay trembling between death and life; and I paid the doctor eighty-three guineas. She is restored now; but she is the wreck of the beautiful creature she was. Suffering, and, perhaps, *another disappointment* – but we won't mention that *now* – have so pulled her down. But I will leave you, and prepare my sweet girl for this strange, this entirely unexpected visit."

'I won't tell you what took place between me and Jemima, to whom I was introduced as she sat in the darkened room, poor sufferer! nor describe to you with what a thrill of joy I seized (after groping about for it) her poor emaciated hand. She did not withdraw it; I came out of that room an engaged man, sir; and *now* I was enabled to show her that I had always loved her sincerely, for there was my will, made three years back, in her favour: that night she refused me, as I told you. I would have shot myself, but they'd have brought me in *non compos*, and my brother Mick would have contested the will, and so I determined to live, in order that she might benefit by my dying. I had but a thousand pounds then: since that my father has left me two more. I willed every shilling to her, as you may fancy, and settled it upon her when we married, as we did soon after. It was not for some time that I was allowed to see the poor girl's face, or, indeed, was aware of the horrid loss she had sustained. Fancy my agony, my dear fellow, when I saw that beautiful wreck!'

There was something not a little affecting to think, in the conduct of this brave fellow, that he never once, as he told his story, seemed to allude to the possibility of his declining to marry a woman who was not the same as the woman he loved; but that he was quite as faithful to her now, as he had been when captivated by the poor tawdry charms of the silly Miss of Leamington. It was hard that such a noble heart as this should be flung away upon yonder foul mass of greedy vanity. Was it hard, or not, that he should remain deceived in his obstinate humility, and continue to admire the selfish, silly being whom he had chosen to worship?

'I should have been appointed surgeon of the regiment,' continued Dennis 'soon after, when it was ordered abroad to Jamaica, where it now is. But my wife would not hear of going, and said she would break her heart if she left her mother. So I retired on half-pay, and took this cottage; and in case any practice should fall in my way – why, there is my name on the brass plate, and I'm ready for anything that comes. But the only case that ever *did* come was one day when I was driving my wife in the chaise, and another, one night, of a beggar with a broken head. My wife makes me a present of a baby every year, and we've no debts; and between you and me and the post, as long as my mother-in-law is out of the house, I'm as happy as I need be.'

'What! you and the old lady don't get on well?' said I.

'I can't say we do; it's not in nature, you know,' said Dennis, with a faint grin. 'She comes into the house, and turns it topsy-turvy. When she's here I'm obliged to sleep in the scullery. She's never paid her daughter's income since the first year, though she brags about her sacrifices as if she had ruined herself for Jemima; and besides, when she's here, there's a whole clan of the Molloys, horse, foot, and dragoons, that are quartered upon us, and eat me out of house and home.'

'And this Molloyville such a fine place as the widow described it?' asked I, laughing, and not a little curious.

'Oh, a mighty fine place entirely!' said Dennis, 'There's the oak park of two hundred acres, the finest land ye ever saw, only they've cut all the wood down. The garden in the old Molloy's time, they say, was the finest ever seen in the West of Ireland; but they've taken all the glass to mend the house windows: and small blame to them either. There's a clear rent-roll of three and fifty hundred a year, only it's in the hand of the receivers; besides other debts, on which there is no land security.'

'Your cousin-in-law, Castlereagh Molloy, won't come into a large fortune?'

'Oh, he'll do very well,' said Dennis. 'As long as he can get credit, he's not the fellow to stint himself. Faith, I was fool enough to put my name to a bit of paper for him, and as they could not catch him in Mayo, they laid hold of me at Kingstown here. And there was a pretty to do. Didn't Mrs. Gam say I was ruining her family, that's all! I paid it by instalments (for all my money is settle on Jemima); and Castlereagh, who's an honourable fellow, offered me any satisfaction in life. Anyhow, he couldn't do more than *that*.'

'Of course not, and now you're friends?'

'Yes, and he and his aunt have had a tiff, too; and he abuses her properly, I warrant ye. He says that she carried about Jemima from place to place, and flung her at the head of every unmarried man in England a'most, – my poor Jemima, and she all the while dying in love with me! As soon as she got over the small-pox – she took it at Fermoy – God bless her, I wish I'd been by to be her nurse-tender, – as soon as she was rid of it, the old lady said to Castlereagh, "Castlereagh, go the bar'cks, and find out in the Army List where the 120th is." Off she came to Cork hot foot. It appears that while she was ill, Jemima's love for me showed itself in such a violent way that her mother was overcome, and promised that, should the dear child recover, she would try and bring us together. Castlereagh says she would have gone after us to Jamaica.'

'I have no doubt she would,' said I.

'Could you have a stronger proof of love than that?' cried Dennis. My dear girl's illness and frightful blindness have, of course, injured her health and her temper. She cannot in her position look to the children, you know, and so they come under my charge for the most part; and her temper is unequal, certainly. But you see what a sensitive, refined, elegant creature she is, and may fancy that she's often put out by a rough fellow like me.'

Here Dennis left me, saying it was time to go and walk out the children; and I think his story has matter of some wholesome reflection in it for bachelors who are about to change their condition, or may console some who are mourning their celibacy. Marry, gentlemen, if you like; leave your comfortable dinner at the club for cold mutton and curl-papers at your home; give up your books or pleasures, and take to yourselves wives and children; but think well on what you do first, as I have no doubt you will after this advice and example. Advice is always useful in matters of love; men always take it; they always follow other people's opinions, not their own: they always profit by example. When they see a pretty woman, and feel the delicious madness of love coming over them, they always stop to calculate her temper, her money, their own money, or suitableness for the married life. . . . Ha, ha, ha! Let us fool in this way no more. I have been in love forty-three times with all ranks and conditions of women, and would have married every time if they would have let me. How many wives had King Solomon, the wisest of men? And is not that story a warning to us that Love is master of the wisest? Is it only fools who defy him.

I must come, however, to the last, and perhaps the saddest, part of poor Denny Haggarty's history. I met him once more, and in such a condition as made me determine to write this history.

In the month of June last I happened to be at Richmond, a delightful little place of retreat; and there, sunning himself upon the terrace, was my old friend of the 120th: he looked older, thinner, poorer, and more wretched than I had ever seen him. 'What! you have given up Kingstown?' said I, shaking him by the hand.

'Yes,' says he.

'And is my lady and your family here at Richmond?'

'No,' says he, with a sad shake of the head; and the poor fellow's hollow eyes filled with tears.

'Good heavens, Denny! what's the matter?' said I. He was squeezing my hand like a vice as I spoke.

'They've LEFT me!' he burst out with a dreadful shout of passionate grief – a horrible scream which seemed to be wrenched out of his heart. 'Left me!' said he, sinking down on a seat, and clenching his great fists, and shaking his lean arms wildly. 'I'm a wise man now, Mr. Fitz-Boodle. Jemima has gone away from me, and yet you know how I loved her, and how happy we were! I've got nobody now; but I'll die soon, that's one comfort: and to think it's she that'll kill me after all!'

The story, which he told with a wild and furious lamentation such as is not known among men of our cooler country, and such as I don't like now to recall, was a very simple one. The mother-in-law had taken possession of the house, and had driven him from it. His property at his marriage was settled on his wife. She had never loved him, and told him this secret at last, and drove him out of doors with her selfish scorn and ill-temper. The boy had died; the girls were better, he said, brought up among the Molloys than they could be with him; and so he was quite alone in the world, and was living, or rather dying, on forty pounds a year.

His troubles are very likely over by this time. The two fools who caused his misery will never read this history of him; *they* never read godless stories in magazines; and I wish, honest reader, that you and I went to church as much as they do. These people are not wicked *because* of their religious observances, but *in spite* of them. They are too dull to understand humility, too blind to see a tender and simple heart under a rough ungainly bosom. They are sure that all their conduct towards my poor friend here has been perfectly righteous, and that they have given proofs of the most Christian virtue. Haggarty's wife is considered by her friends as a martyr to a savage husband, and her mother is the angel that has come to rescue her. All they did was to cheat him and desert him. And safe in that wonderful self-complacency with which the fools of this earth are endowed, they have not a single pang of conscience for their villany towards him, and consider their heartlessness as a proof and consequence of their spotless piety and virtue.

The Three Eras of Libbie Marsh
Elizabeth Gaskell

St Valentine's Day

L ast November but one there was a flitting in our neighbourhood; hardly a flitting after all, for it was only a single person changing her place of abode, from one lodging to another; and instead of a comfortable cartload of drawers, and baskets, and dressers, and beds, with old king clock at the top of all, there was only one large wooden chest to be carried after the girl, who moved slowly and heavily along the streets, listless and depressed more from the state of her mind than of her body. It was Libbie Marsh, who had been obliged to quit her room in Dunn Street, because the acquaintances, with whom she had been living there, were leaving Manchester. She tried to think herself fortunate in having met with lodgings rather more out of the town, and with those who were known to be respectable; she did indeed try to be contented, but in spite of her reason, the old feeling of desolation came over her, as she was now about to be again thrown entirely among strangers.

No. 2, —— Court, Albemarle Street, was reached at last; and the pace, slow as it was, slackened, as she drew near the spot where she was to be left by the man who carried her box; for trivial as his acquaintance with her was, he was not quite a stranger, as every one else was, peering out of their open doors, and satisfying themselves it was only 'Dixon's new lodger.'

Dixon's house was the last on the left hand side of the court. A high brick wall connected it with its opposite neighbour. All the dwellings were of the same monotonous pattern, and one side of the court looked at its exact likeness opposite, as if it were seeing itself in a looking-glass.

Dixon's house was shut up, and the key left next door; but the woman in whose care it was knew that Libbie was expected, and came forwards to say a few explanatory words, to unlock the door, and stir the dull-grey ashes which were lazily burning in the grate, and then she returned to her own house; leaving poor Libbie standing alone with her great big chest on the middle of the house-place floor, with no one to say a word, (even a common-place remark would have been better than that dull silence), that could help her to repel the fast-coming tears.

Dixon and his wife, and their eldest girl, worked in factories and were absent all day from their house; the youngest child, (also a little girl), was boarded out for the week days at the neighbour's where the door-key was deposited; but, although busy making dirt-pies at the entrance to the court when Libbie came in, she was too young to care much about her parents' new lodger. Libbie knew she was to sleep with the elder girl in the front bed-room; but, as you may fancy, it seemed a liberty even to go upstairs to take off her things, when no one was at home to marshal the way up the ladder-like steps. So she could only take off her bonnet, and sit down, and gaze at the now blazing fire, and think sadly on the past, and on the lonely creature she was in this wide world.

Father and mother gone; her little brother long since dead; (he would have been more than nineteen, had he been alive, but she only thought of him as the darling baby); her only friends (to call friends) living far away at their new home; her employers, – kind enough people in their way, but too rapidly twirling round on this bustling earth to have leisure to think of the little work-woman, excepting when they wanted gowns turned, carpets mended, or household linen darned; and hardly even the natural, though hidden hope, of a young girl's heart, to cheer her on with bright visions of a home of her own at some future day, where, loving and beloved, she might fulfil a woman's dearest duties.

For Libbie was very plain, as she had known so long, that the consciousness of it had ceased to mortify her. You can hardly live in Manchester without having some idea of your personal appearance. The factory lads and lasses take good care of that, and if you meet them at the hours when they are pouring out of the mills, you are sure to hear a good number of truths, some of them combined with such a spirit of impudent fun, that you can scarcely keep from laughing even at the joke against yourself. Libbie had often and often been greeted by such questions as 'How long is it since your were a beauty?' 'What would you take a day to stand in a field to scare away the birds?' etc., for her to linger under any delusion as to her looks.

While she was thus musing, and quietly crying over the pictures her fancy conjured up, the Dixons came dropping in, and surprised her with wet cheeks and quivering lips.

She almost wished to have the stillness again she had felt so oppressive an hour ago, they talked and laughed so loudly and so much, and bustled about so noisily over every thing they did. Dixon took hold of one iron handle of her box, and helped her to bump it up stairs; while his daughter Anne followed to see the unpacking, and what sort of clothes 'little sewing-body had gotten.' Mrs Dixon rattled out the tea-things, and put the kettle on; fetched home her youngest child, which added to the commotion. Then she called Anne down-stairs and sent her off for this thing, and that. Eggs to put to the cream, it was so thin. Ham to give a relish to the bread and butter. Some new new bread (hot, if she could get it). Libbie heard all these orders given at full pitch of Mrs Dixon's voice, and wondered at their extravagance, so different to the habits of the place where she had last lodged. But they were fine spinners in the receipt of good wages; and confined all day to an atmosphere ranging from 75 to 80 degrees; they had lost all natural healthy appetite for simple food, and having no higher tastes, found their greatest enjoyment in their luxurious meals.

When tea was ready, Libbie was called downstairs with a rough but hearty invitation to share their meal; she sat mutely at the corner of the tea-table, while they went on with their own conversation about people and things she knew nothing about; till at length she ventured to ask for a candle to go and finish her unpacking before bed-time, as she had to go out sewing for several succeeding days. But once in the comparative peace of her bedroom her energy failed her, and she contented herself with locking her Noah's ark of a chest, and put out her candle, and went to sit by the window and gaze out at the night heavens; for ever and ever the 'blue sky that bends over all,' sheds down a feeling of sympathy with the sorrowful at the solemn hours, when the ceaseless stars are seen to pace its depths.

By and by her eye fell down to gazing at the corresponding window to her own on the opposite side of the court. It was lighted, but the blind was drawn down. Upon the blind she saw, at first unconsciously, the constant weary motion of a little, spectral shadow; a child's hand and arm, – no more; long, thin fingers hanging listlessly down from the wrist, while the arm moved up and down, as if keeping time to the heavy pulses of dull pain. She could not help hoping that sleep would soon come to still that incessant, feeble motion; and now and then it did cease, as if the little creature had dropped into a slumber from very weariness; but presently the arm jerked up with the fingers clenched, as if with a sudden start of agony. When Anne came up to bed, Libbie was still sitting watching the shadow; and she directly asked to whom it belonged.

'It will be Margaret Hall's lad. Last summer when it was so hot, there was no biding with the window shut at nights; and their'n were open too; and many's the time he waked me up with his moans. They say he's been better sin' cold weather came.'

'Is he always so bad? Whatten ails him?' asked Libbie.

'Summut's amiss wi' his back-bone, folks say; he's better and worse like. He's a nice little chap enough; and his mother's not that bad either; only my mother and her had words, so now we don't speak.'

Libbie went on watching, and when she next spoke to ask who and what his mother was, Anne Dixon was fast asleep.

Time passed away, and, as usual, unveiled the hidden things.

Libbie found out that Margaret Hall was a widow, who earned her living as a washerwoman; that this little suffering lad was her only child, her dearly beloved. That while she scolded pretty nearly every body else 'till her name was up' in the neighbourhood for a termagant, to him she was evidently most tender and gentle. He lay alone on his little bed near the window through the day, while she was away, toiling for a livelihood. But when Libbie had plain sewing to do at her lodgings instead of going out to sew, she used to watch from her bed-room window for the time when the shadows opposite, by their mute gestures, told that the mother had returned to bend over the child; to smooth his pillow, to alter his position, to get him his nightly cup of tea. And often in the night Libbie could not help rising gently from bed to see if the little arm was waving up and down, as was his accustomed habit when sleepless from pain.

Libbie had a good deal of sewing to do at home that winter, and whenever it was not so cold as to numb her fingers, she took it up stairs in order to watch the little lad in her few odd moments of pause. On his better days he could sit up enough to peep out of his window, and she found he liked to look at her. Presently she ventured to nod to him across the court, and his faint smile, and ready nod back again, showed that this gave him pleasure. I think she would have been encouraged by this smile to proceed to a speaking acquaintance, if it had not been for his terrible mother, to whom it seemed to be irritation enough to know that Libbie was a lodger at the Dixons', for her to talk *at* her whenever they encountered each other, and to live evidently in wait for some opportunity of abuse.

With her constant interest in him, Libbie soon discovered his great want of an object on which to occupy his thoughts, and which might distract his attention, when alone through the long day, from the pain he endured. He was very fond of flowers. It was November when she had first removed to her lodgings, but it had been very mild weather and a few flowers yet lingered in the gardens, which the country-people gathered into nosegays, and brought on market days into Manchester. His mother had bought him a bunch of Michaelmas daisies the very day that Libbie had become a neighbour, and she watched their history. He put them first in an old tea-pot, of which the spout was broken off, and the lid lost; and he daily replenished the tea-pot from the jug of water his mother left near him to quench his feverish thirst. By and by one or two out of the constellation of lilac stars faded, and then the time he had hitherto spent in admiring (almost caressing) them, was devoted to cutting off those flowers whose decay marred the beauty of his nosegay. It took him half the morning with his feeble languid motions, and his cumbrous old scissors, to trim up his diminishing darlings. Then at last he seemed to think he had better preserve the few that remained by drying them; so they were carefully put between the leaves of the old Bible; and then whenever a better day came, when he had strength enough to lift the ponderous book, he used to open its pages to look at his flower friends. In winter he could have no more living flowers to tend.

Libbie thought and thought, till at last an idea flashed upon her mind that often made a happy smile steal over her face as she stitched away, and which cheered her through that solitary winter – for solitary it continued to be, although the Dixons were very good sort of people; never pressed her for payment if she had had but little work that week; never grudged her a share of their extravagant meals, which were far more luxurious than she could have met with any where else for her previously agreed payment in case of working at home; and they would fain have taught her to drink rum in her tea, assuring her that she should have it for nothing, and welcome. But they were too loud, too prosperous, too much absorbed in themselves to take off Libbie's feeling of solitariness; not half as much as did the little face by day, and the shadow by night, of him with whom she had never yet exchanged a word.

Her idea was this: her mother came from the east of England, where, as perhaps you know, they have the pretty custom of sending presents on St Valentine's day, with the donor's name unknown and of course that mystery constitutes half the enjoyment. The 14th of February was Libbie's birthday too; and many a year in the happy days of old had her mother delighted to surprise her with some little gift, of which she more than half guessed the giver, although each Valentine's day the manner of its arrival was varied. Since then, the 14th of February had been the dreariest day of all the year, because the most haunted by memory of departed happiness. But now, this year, if she could not have the gladness of heart herself, she would try and brighten the life of another. She would save, and she would screw, but she would buy a canary and a cage for that poor little laddie opposite, who wore out his monotonous life with so few pleasures, and so much pain.

I doubt I may not tell you here of the anxieties, and the fears, of the hopes, and the self-sacrifices, – all perhaps small in tangible effect as the widow's mite, yet not the less marked by the viewless angels who go about continually among us, – which varied Libbie's life before she accomplished her purpose. It is enough to say, it was accomplished. The very day before the 14th she found time to go with her half-guinea to a barber's who lived near Albemarle Street, and who was famous for his stock of singing birds. There are enthusiasts about all sorts of things, both good and bad; and many of the weavers in Manchester know and care more about birds that any one would easily credit. Stubborn, silent, reserved men on many things, you have only to touch on the subject of birds to light up their faces with brightness. They will tell you who won the prizes at the last canary show, where the prize birds may be seen; and give you all the details of those funny though pretty and interesting mimicries of great people's cattle shows. Among these amateurs, Emanuel Morris the barber was an oracle.

He took Libbie into his little back room, used for private shaving of modest men, who did not care to be exhibited in the front shop, decked out in the full glories of lather; and which was hung round with birds in rude wicker cages, with the exception of those who had won prizes, and were consequently honoured with gilt wire prisons. The longer and thinner the body of the bird was, the more admiration it received as far as its external beauty went; and when in addition to this chance the colour was deep and clear, and its notes strong and varied, the more did Emanuel dwell upon their perfections. But these were all prize birds; and on inquiry Libbie heard, with a little sinking at her heart, that their price ran from one to two guineas.

'I'm not over-particular as to shape and colour,' said she. 'I should like a good singer, that's all.'

She dropped a little in Emanuel's estimation. However, he showed her his good singers, but all were above Libbie's means.

'After all, I don't think I care so much about the singing very loud, it's but a noise after all; and sometimes noises fidgets folks.'

'They must be nesh folk as is put out with the singing o' birds,' replied Emanuel, rather affronted.

'It's for one who is poorly,' said Libbie, deprecatingly.

'Well, said he, as if considering the matter, 'folk that are cranky take more to them as shows 'em love, than to them who is clever and gifted. Happen yo'd rather have this'n,' opening a cage-door, and calling to a dull-coloured bird, sitting moped up in a corner, 'Here! Jupiter, Jupiter!'

The bird smoothed its feathers in an instant, and uttering a little note of delight, flew to Emanuel, putting its beak to his lips as if kissing him, and then perching on his head, it began a gurgling warble of pleasure, not by any means so varied or so clear as the song of the others, but which pleased Libbie more (for she was always one to find out she liked the gooseberries that were accessible, better than the grapes which were beyond her reach). The price, too, was just right; so she gladly took possession of the cage, and hid it under her cloak, preparatory to carrying it home. Emanuel meanwhile was giving her directions as to its food, with all the minuteness of one loving his subject.

'Will it soon get to know any one?' asked she.

'Give him two days only, and you and he'll be as thick as him and me are now. You've only to open his door, and call him, and he'd follow you round the room; but he'd first kiss you, and then perch on your head. He only wants larning, (which I've no time to give him), to do many another accomplishment.'

'What's his name? I didn't rightly catch it.'

'Jupiter; it's not common, but the town is o'errun with Bobbys and Dickys, and my birds are thought a bit out o'the way, I like to have better names for 'em, so I just picked a few out o'my lad's school-books. It's just as ready, when you're used to it, to say Jupiter as Dicky.'

'I could bring my tongue round to Peter better; would he answer to Peter?' asked Libbie, now on the point of departure.

'Happen he might; but I think he'd come readier to the three syllables.'

On Valentine's day, Jupiter's cage was decked round with ivy leaves, making quite a pretty wreath on the wicker-work; and to one of them was pinned a slip of paper, with these words written in Libbie's best round hand:–

'From your faithful Valentine. Please take notice: His name is Peter, and he will come if you call him, after a bit.'

But little work did Libbie do that afternoon, she was so engaged in watching for the messenger who was to bear her present to her little Valentine, and run away as soon as he had delivered up the canary, and explained for whom it was sent.

At last he came, then there was a pause before the woman of the house was at leisure to take it up stairs. Then Libbie saw the little face flush into a bright colour, the feeble hands tremble with delighted eagerness, the head bent down to try and make out the writing, (beyond his power, poor lad, to read), the rapturous turning round of the cage in order to see the canary in every point of view, head, tail, wings and feet; an intention which Jupiter, in his uneasiness at being again among strangers, did not second, for he hopped round so as continually to present a full front to the boy. It was a source of never-wearying delight to the little fellow till daylight closed in; he evidently forgot to wonder who had sent it him, in his gladness at the possession of such a treasure; and when the shadow of his mother darkened on the blind, and the bird had been exhibited, Libbie saw her do what, with all her tenderness, seemed rarely to have entered into her thoughts – she bent down, and kissed her boy in a mother's sympathy with the joy of her child.

The canary was placed for the night between the little bed and window, and when Libbie rose to take her accustomed peep, she saw the little arm put fondly round the cage, as if embracing his new treasure even in his sleep. How Jupiter slept that first night is quite another thing.

So ended the first day of Libbie's three eras in last year.

Whitsuntide

The brightest, fullest daylight poured down into No. 2, —— Court Albemarle Street, and the heat, even at the early hour of five, was almost as great as at the noontide on the June days of many years past.

The court seemed alive, and merry with voices and laughter. The bed-room windows were open wide, (and had been so all night on account of the heat), and every now and then you might see a head and a pair of shoulders, simply encased in shirt sleeves, popped out, and you might hear the inquiry passed from one to the other:–

'Well, Jack, and where art thou bound to?'

'Dunham!'

'Why what an old-fashioned chap thou be'st. Thy grandad afore thee went to Dunham; but thou wert always a slow coach. I'm off to Alderley, – me, and my missus.'

'Aye, that's because there's only thee and thy missus; wait till thou hast gotten four childer like me, and thou'lt be glad enough to take 'em to Dunham, oud-fashioned way, for four-pence a-piece.'

'I'd still go to Alderley; I'd not be bothered with my childer; they should keep house at home.'

A pair of hands (the person to whom they belonged invisible behind her husband) boxed his ears at this last speech, in a very spirited, although a playful manner, and the neighbours all laughed at the surprized look of the speaker, at this assault from an unseen foe; the man who had been holding the conversation with him, cried out,

'Sarved him right, Mrs Slater; he knows nought about it yet, but when he gets them, he'll be as loth to leave the babbies at home on a Whitsuntide, as any on us. We shall live to see him in Dunham park yet, wi' twins in his arms, and another pair on 'em clutching at daddy's coat tails, let alone your share of youngsters, missus.'

At this moment our friend Libbie appeared at her window, and Mrs Slater, who had taken her discomfited husband's place, called out,

'Elizabeth Marsh, where are Dixons and you bound to?'

'Dixons are not up yet; he said last night he'd take his holiday out in lying in bed. I'm going to th' old-fashioned place, – Dunham.'

'Thou art never going by thyself, moping?'

'No! I'm going with Margaret Hall and her lad,' replied Libbie, hastily withdrawing from the window in order to avoid hearing any remarks on the associates she had chosen for her day of pleasure – the scold of the neighbourhood, and her sickly, ailing child!

But Jupiter might have been a dove, and his ivy-leaves an olive-branch, for the peace he had brought, the happiness he had caused, to three individuals at least. For of course it could not long be a mystery who had sent little Frank Hall his Valentine; nor could his mother long maintain her hard manner towards one who had given her child a new pleasure. She was shy, and she was proud, and for some time she struggled against the natural desire of manifesting her gratitude; but one evening, when Libbie was returning home with a bundle of work half as large as herself, as she dragged herself along through the heated street she was overtaken by Margaret Hall, her burden gently pulled from her, and her way home shortened, and her weary spirits soothed and cheered by the outpourings of Margaret's heart; for her barrier of reserve once broken down, she had much to say, to thank her for days of amusement and happy employment for her lad, to speak of his gratitude, to tell of her hopes and fears – the hopes and fears which made up the dates of her life. From that time Libbie lost her awe of the termagant in interest for the mother, whose all was ventured in so frail a bark. From that time Libbie was a fast friend with both mother and son; planning mitigations to the sorrowful days of the latter, as eagerly as poor Margaret Hall, and with far more resources. His life had flickered up under the charm and the excitement of the last few months. He even seemed strong enough to undertake the journey to Dunham, which Libbie had arranged as a Whitsuntide treat, and for which she and his mother had been hoarding up for several weeks. The canal-boat left Knott-Mill at six, and it was now past five; so Libbie let herself out very gently, and went across to her friends. She knocked at the door of their lodging room, and without waiting for an answer entered.

Franky's face was flushed, and he was trembling with excitement, partly from pleasure, but partly from some eager wish not yet granted.

'He wants sore to take Peter with him,' said his mother, as if referring the matter to Libbie. The boy looked imploringly at her.

'He would so like it, I know. For one thing, he'd miss me sadly, and chirp for me all day long, he'd be so lonely. I could not be half so happy, a-thinking on him, left alone here by himself. Then Libbie, he's just like a Christian, so fond of flowers, and green leaves, and them sort of things. He chirrups to me so when mother brings me a pennyworth of wall-flowers to put round his cage. He would talk if he could, you know, but I can tell what he means quite as well as if he spoke. Do let Peter go, Libbie! I'll carry him in my own arms.'

So Jupiter was allowed to be of the party. Now Libbie had overcome the great difficulty of conveying Franky to the boat by offering to 'slay' for a coach, and the shouts and exclamations of the neighbours told them that their conveyance awaited them at the bottom of the court. His mother carried Franky, light in weight, though heavy in helplessness; and he would hold the cage, believing that he was thus redeeming his promise that Peter should be a trouble to no one. Libbie preceded to arrange the bundle containing their dinner, as a support in the corner of the coach. The neighbours came out with many blunt speeches, and more kindly wishes, and one or two of them would have relieved Margaret of her burden, if she would have allowed it. The presence of that little crippled fellow seemed to obliterate all the angry feelings which had existed between his mother and her neighbours, and which had formed the politics of that little court for many a day.

And now they were fairly off! Franky bit his lips in attempted endurance of the pain the motion caused him, but winced and shrunk, until they were fairly on a macadamized thoroughfare, when he closed his eyes, and seemed desirous of a few minutes' rest. Libbie felt very shy, and very much afraid of being seen by her employers 'set up in a coach;' and so she hid herself in a corner, and made herself as small as possible; while Mrs Hall had exactly the opposite feeling, and was delighted to stand up, stretching out of the window, and nodding to pretty nearly every one they met, or passed, on the footpaths; and they were not a few, for the streets were quite gay, even at that early hour, with parties going to this or that railway station; or to the boats which crowded the canals in this bright holiday week. And almost every one they met seemed to enter into Mrs Hall's exhilaration of feeling, and had a smile or a nod in return. At last she plumped down by Libbie and exclaimed,

'I never was in a coach but once afore, and that was when I was a going to be married. It's like heaven; and all done over with such beautiful gimp, too,' continued she, admiring the lining of the vehicle. Jupiter did not enjoy it so much.

As if the holiday time, the lovely weather, and the 'sweet hour of prime' had a genial influence (as no doubt they have), everybody's heart seemed softened towards poor Franky. The driver lifted him out with the gentleness of strength, and bore him tenderly down to the boat; the people there made way, and gave him up the best seat in their power; or rather, I should call it a couch, for they saw he was weary, and insisted on his lying down – an attitude he would have been ashamed to assume without the protection of his mother and Libbie, who now appeared, bearing their tickets, and carrying Peter.

Away the boat went to make room for others; for every conveyance both by land and by water is in requisition in Whitsun-week to give the hard-worked crowds an opportunity of tasting the charms of the country. Even every standing place in the canal packets was occupied; and as they glided along, the banks were lined by people, who seemed to find it object enough to watch the boats go by, packed close and full with happy beings brimming with anticipation of a day's pleasure. The country through which they passed is as uninteresting as can well be imagined, but still it is country; and the screams of delight from the children, and the low laughs of pleasure from the parents, at every blossoming tree which trailed its wreaths against some cottage-wall, or at the tufts of late primroses which lingered in the cool depths of grass along the canal banks, the thorough relish of everything, as if dreading to let the least circumstance on this happy day pass over without its due appreciation, made the time seem all too short, although it took two hours to arrive at a place only eight miles distant from Manchester. Even Franky, with all his impatience to see Dunham woods, (which I think he confused with London, believing both to be paved with gold), enjoyed the easy motion of the boat as much, floating along, while pictures moved before him, that he regretted when the time came for landing among the soft green meadows that come sloping down to the dancing water's brim. His fellow passengers carried him to the park, and refused all payment; although his mother had laid by sixpence on purpose, as a recompense for this service.

'Oh, Libbie, how beautiful! Oh, mother, mother! Is the whole world out of Manchester as beautiful as this! I did not know trees were like this. Such green homes for birds! Look, Peter! would not you like to be there, up among those boughs? But I can't let you go, you know, because you're my little bird-brother, and I should be quite lost without you.'

They spread a shawl upon the fine mossy turf at the root of a beech tree, which made a sort of natural couch, and there they laid him, and bade him rest in spite of the delight which made him believe himself capable of any exertion. Where he lay, (always holding Jupiter's cage, and often talking to him as to a playfellow), he was on the verge of a green area shut in by magnificent trees, in all the glory of their early foliage before the summer heats have deepened their verdure into one rich monotonous tint. And hither came party after party; old men and maidens, young men and children – whole families trooped along after the guiding fathers, who bore the youngest in their arms, or astride upon their backs, while they turned round occasionally to the wives, with whom they shared some fond local remembrance. For years has

Dunham park been the favourite resort of the Manchester workpeople; for more years than I can tell; probably ever since 'The Duke,' by his canals, opened out the system of cheap travelling. It is scenery, too, which presents such a complete contrast to the whirl and turmoil of Manchester; so thoroughly woodland, with its ancestral trees, (here and there lightning-blanched), its 'verdurous walls,' its grassy walks leading far away into some glade where you start at the rabbit, rustling among the last year's fern, and where the wood-pigeon's call seems the only fitting and accordant sound. Depend upon it, this complete sylvan repose, this accessible depth of quiet, this lapping the soul in green images of the country, forms the most complete contrast to a townsperson, and consequently has over such the greatest power to charm.

Presently Libbie found out she was very hungry. Now they were but provided with dinner, which was of course to be eaten as near twelve o'clock as might be; and Margaret Hall, in her prudence, asked a working man near, to tell her what o'clock it was?

'Nay!' said he; 'I'll ne'er look at clock or watch to-day. I'll not spoil my pleasure by finding out how fast it's going away. If thou'rt hungry, eat. I make my own dinner hour, and I've eaten mine an hour ago.'

So they had their veal pies, and then found out it was only about half-past ten o'clock, by so many pleasurable events had that morning been marked. But such was their buoyancy of spirts that they only enjoyed their mistake, and joined in the general laugh against the man who had eaten his dinner somewhere about nine. He laughed most heartily of all, till suddenly stopping, he said,

'I must not go on at this rate; laughing gives me such an appetite.'

'Oh, if that's all,' said a merry-looking man, lying at full length, and crushing the fresh scent out of the grass, while two or three little children tumbled over him, and crept about him, as kittens or puppies frolic with their parents; 'if that's all, we'll have a subscription of eatables for them improvident folk as have eaten their dinner for their breakfast. Here's a sausage pasty and a handful of nuts for my share. Bring round a hat, Bob, and see what the company will give.'

Bob carried out the joke, much to little Franky's amusement, and no one was so churlish as to refuse, although the contributions varied from a peppermint drop up to a veal-pie, and a sausage pasty.

'It's a thriving trade,' said Bob, as he emptied his hatful of provisions on the grass by Libbie's side. 'Besides, it's tip-top too to live on the public. Hark! what is that?'

The laughter and the chat were suddenly hushed, and mothers told their little ones to listen, as far away in the distance, now sinking and falling, now swelling and clear, came a ringing peal of children's voices, blended together in one of those psalm tunes which we are all of us familiar with, and which bring to mind the old, old days when we, as wondering children, were first led to worship 'Our Father,' by those beloved ones who have since gone to the more perfect worship. Holy was that distant choral praise even to the most thoughtless; and when it in fact was ended, in the instant's pause during which the ear awaited the repetition of the air, they caught the noon-tide hum and buzz of the myriads of insects, who danced away their lives in that glorious day; they heard the swaying of the mighty woods in the soft, yet resistless breeze; and then again once more burst forth the merry jests and the shouts of childhood; and again the elder ones resumed their happy talk, as they lay or sat 'under the greenwood tree.' Fresh parties came dropping in; some loaded with wild flowers, almost with branches of hawthorn indeed; while one or two had made prize of the earliest dog-roses, and had cast away campion, stitchwort, ragged robin, all, to keep the lady of the hedges from being obscured or hidden among the commonalty.

One after another drew near to Franky, and looked on with interest as he lay, sorting the flowers given to him. Happy parents stood by, with their household bands around them in health and comeliness, and felt the sad prophecy of those shrivelled limbs, those wasted fingers, those lamp-like eyes, with their bright dark lustre. His mother was too eagerly watching his happiness to read the meaning of the grave looks, but Libbie saw them, and understood them, and a chill shudder went through her even on that day, as she thought on the future.

'Aye! I thought we should give you a start!'

A start they did give, with their terrible slap on Libbie's back, as she sat, idly grouping flowers, and following out her sorrowful thoughts. It was the Dixons! Instead of keeping their holiday by lying in bed, they and their children had roused themselves, and had come by the omnibus to the nearest point. For an instant the meeting was an awkward one on account of the feud between Margaret Hall and Mrs Dixon; but there was no long resisting of kindly Mother Nature's soothings at that holiday time, and in that lovely tranquil spot; or if they could have been unheeded, the sight of Franky would have awed every angry feeling into rest, so changed was he since the Dixons had last seen him; since he had been the Puck, or Robin-goodfellow of the neighbourhood, whose marbles were always rolling themselves under people's feet, and whose top strings were always hanging in nooses to catch the unwary. Yes! he, the feeble, mild, almost girlish-looking lad, had once been a merry, happy rogue, and as such often cuffed by Mrs Dixon, the very Mrs Dixon who now stood gazing with the tears in her eyes. Could she, in sight of him, the changed, the fading, keep up a quarrel with his mother?

'How long hast thou been here?' asked Dixon.

'Welly on for all day.' answered Libbie.

'Hast never been to see the deer, or the king and queen oaks? Lord! how stupid!'

His wife pinched his arm, to remind him of Franky's helpless condition, which of course tethered the otherwise willing feet.

But Dixon had a remedy. He called Bob, and one or two others, and each taking a corner of the strong plaid shawl, they slung Franky as in a hammock, and thus carried him merrily along down the wood-paths, over the soft grassy turf, while the glimmering shine and shadow fell on his upturned face. The women walked behind, talking, loitering along, always in sight of the hammock, now picking up some green treasure from the ground, now catching at the low-hanging branches of the horse-chestnut. The soul grew much on that day, and in those woods, and all unconsciously, as souls do grow. They followed Franky's hammockbearers up a grassy knoll, on the top of which stood a group of pine-trees, whose stems looked like dark red gold in the sunbeams. They had taken Franky there to show him Manchester, far away in the blue plain, against which the woodland foreground cut with a soft clear line. Far, far away in the distance on that flat plain you might see the motionless cloud of smoke hanging over a great town; and that was Manchester, old, ugly, smoky Manchester! dear, busy, earnest, working, noble Manchester; where their children had been born, (and perhaps where some lay buried), where their homes were, where God had cast their lives, and told them to work out their destiny.

'Hurrah for oud smoke-jack!' cried Bob, putting Franky softly down on the grass, before he whirled his hat round, preparatory for a cheer. 'Hurrah! hurrah!' from all the men.

'There's the rim of my hat lying like a quoit yonder,' observed Bob quietly, as he replaced his brimless hat on his head, with the gravity of a judge.

'Here's the Sunday-school childer a-coming to sit on this shady side, and have their buns and milk. Hark! they're singing the Infant School grace.'

They sat close at hand, so that Franky could hear the words they sang, in rings of children, making (in their gay summer prints, newly donned for that week) garlands of little faces, all happy and bright upon the green hill side. One little 'Dot' of a girl came shyly near Franky, whom she had long been watching, and threw her half bun at his side, and then ran away and hid herself, in very shame at the boldness of her own sweet impulse. She kept peeping behind her screen at Franky all the time; and he, meanwhile, was almost too much pleased and happy to eat: the world was so beautiful; and men, and women, and children, all so tender and kind; so softened, in fact, by the beauty of that earth; so unconsciously touched by the Spirit of Love which was the Creator of that lovely earth. But the day drew to an end; the heat declined; the birds once more began their warblings; the fresh scents again hung about plant, and tree, and grass, betokening the fragrant presence of the reviving dew; and – the boat time was near. As they trod the meadow path once more, they were joined by many a party they had encountered during the day, all abounding in happiness, all full of the day's adventures. Long-cherished quarrels had been forgotten, new friendships formed. Fresh tastes and higher delights had been imparted that day. We have all of us one look, now and then, called up by some noble or loving thought, (our highest on earth), which will be our likeness in Heaven. I can catch the glance on many a face; the glancing light of the cloud of glory from Heaven, 'which is our home.' That look was present on numbers of hard-worked, wrinkled countenances, as they turned backwards to cast a longing, lingering look at Dunham woods, fast deepening into the blackness of night, but whose memory was to haunt in greenness and freshness many a loom, and workshop, and factory, with images of peace and beauty.

That night, as Libbie lay awake, revolving the incidents of the day, she caught Franky's voice through the open windows. Instead of the frequent moan of pain, he was trying to recall the burden of one of the children's hymns:

'Here we suffer grief and pain,
Here we meet to part again,
In Heaven we part no more.
Oh! that will be joyful,' etc.

She recalled his question, his whispered question, to her in the happiest part of the day. He asked, 'Libbie, is Dunham like Heaven? The people here are as kind as angels; and I don't want Heaven to be more beautiful than this place. If you and mother would but die with me, I should like to die, and live always there.' She had checked him, for she had feared he was impious; but now the young child's craving for some definite idea of the land to which his inner wisdom told him he was hastening, had nothing in it wrong or even sorrowful, for

'In Heaven we part no more.'

Michaelmas

The church clocks had struck three; the crowds of gentlemen returning to business after their early dinners had disappeared within offices and warehouses; the streets were comparatively clear and quiet, and ladies were venturing to sally forth for their afternoon's shopping, and their afternoon calls.

Slowly, slowly along the streets, elbowed by life at every turn, a little funeral wound its quiet way. Four men bore along a child's coffin; two women, with bowed heads, followed meekly.

I need not tell you whose coffin it was, or who were these two mourners. All was now over with little Frank Hall; his romps, his games, his sickening, his suffering, his death. All was now over, but the Resurrection and the Life!

His mother walked as in a stupor. Could it be that he was dead? If he had been less of an object to her thoughts, less of a motive for her labours, she could sooner have realized it. As it was, she followed his poor, cast-off, worn-out body, as if she were borne along by some oppressive dream. If he were really dead, how could *she* be alive?

Libbie's mind was far less stunned, and consequently far more active than Margaret Hall's. Visions, as in a phantasmagoria, came rapidly passing before her, – recollections of the time (which seemed now so long ago) when the shadow of the feebly-waving arm first caught her attention; of the bright, strangely isolated day at Dunham Park, where the world had seemed so full of enjoyment, and beauty, and life; of the long-continued heat, through which poor Franky had panted his strength away in the little close room, where there was no escaping the hot rays of the afternoon sun; of the long nights, when his mother and she had watched by his side, as he moaned continually, whether awake or asleep; of the fevered moaning slumber of exhaustion; of the pitiful little self-upbraidings for his own impatience of suffering, (only impatience to his own eyes, – most true and holy patience in the sight of others); and then the fading away of life, the loss of power, the increased unconsciousness, the lovely look of angelic peace which followed the dark shadow on the countenance, – where was he – what was he now?

And so they laid him in his grave; and heard the solemn funeral words; but far off, in the distance – as if not addressed to them.

Margaret Hall bent over the grave to catch one last glance – she had not spoken, or sobbed, or done aught but shiver now and then, since the morning; but now her weight bore more heavily on Libbie's arm, and without sigh or sound she fell, an unconscious heap on the piled-up gravel. They helped Libbie to bring her round; but long after her half-opened eyes and altered breathings showed that her senses were restored, she lay, speechless and motionless, without attempting to rise from her strange bed, as if earth now contained nothing worth even that trifling exertion.

At last Libbie and she left that holy consecrated spot, and bent their steps back to the only place more consecrated still; where he had rendered up his spirit; and where memories of him haunted each common, rude piece of furniture that their eyes fell upon. As the woman of the house opened the door, she pulled Libbie on one side, and said,

'Anne Dixon has been across to see you; she wants to have a word with you.'

'I cannot go now,' replied Libbie, as she pushed hastily along in order to enter the room (*his* room), at the same time with the childless mother. For, as she anticipated, the sight of that empty spot, the glance at the uncurtained open window, letting in the fresh air, and the broad rejoicing light of day, where all had so long been darkened and subdued, unlocked the waters of the fountain, and long and shrill were the cries for her boy, that the poor woman uttered.

'Oh! dear Mrs Hall,' said Libbie, herself drenched in tears, 'do not take on so badly; I'm sure it would grieve *him* sore, if he was alive, – and you know he is, – Bible tells us so; and may be he's here, watching how we go on without him, and hoping we don't fret over-much.'

Mrs Hall's sobs grew worse, and more hysterical.

'Oh! listen!' said Libbie, once more struggling against her own increasing agitation. 'Listen! there's Peter chirping as he always does when he's put about, frightened like; and, you know, he that's gone could never abide to hear the canary chirp in that shrill way.'

Margaret Hall did check herself, and curb her expression of agony, in order not to frighten the little creature he had loved; and as her outward grief subsidised, Libbie took up the old large Bible, which fell open at the never-failing comfort of the 14th chapter of St John's Gospel. How often those large family Bibles do fall open at that chapter! as if, unused in more joyous and prosperous times, the soul went home to its words of loving sympathy when weary and sorrowful, just as the little child seeks the tender comfort of its mother in all its griefs and cares.

And Margaret put back her wet, ruffled, grey hair from her heated, tear-stained, woeful face, and listened with such earnest eyes; trying to form some idea of the 'Father's House,' where her boy had gone to dwell.

They were interrupted by a low tap at the door. Libbie went.

'Anne Dixon has watched you home, and wants to have a word with you,' said the woman of the house in a whisper. Libbie went back, and closed the book with a word of explanation to Margaret Hall, and then ran down stairs to learn the reason of Anne's anxiety to see her.

'Oh, Libbie!' she burst out with, and then checking herself, into the remembrance of Libbie's last solemn duty; 'how's Margaret Hall? But of course, poor thing, she'll fret a bit at first; she'll be some time coming round, mother says, seeing it's as well that poor lad is taken; for he'd always ha'been a cripple, and a trouble to her – he was a fine lad once, too.'

She had come full of another and a different subject; but the sight of Libbie's sad weeping face, and the quiet subdued tone of her manner, made her feel it awkward to begin on any other theme than the one which filled up her companion's mind. To her last speech, Libbie answered sorrowfully,

'No doubt, Anne, it's ordered for the best; but oh! don't call him, don't think he could ever ha' been a trouble to his mother, though he were a cripple. She loved him all the more for each thing she had to do for him, – I'm sure I did.' Libbie cried a little behind her apron. Anne Dixon felt still more awkward at introducing her discordant subject.

'Well! – Flesh is grass, Bible says!' and having fulfilled the etiquette of quoting a text if possible, if not, of making a moral observation on the fleeting nature of earthly things, she thought she was at liberty to pass on to her real errand.

'You must not go on moping yourself, Libbie Marsh. What I wanted special for to see you this afternoon, was to tell you, you must come to my wedding to-morrow. Nancy Dawson has fallen sick, and there's none I should like to have bridesmaid in her place so well as you.'

'To-morrow! Oh, I cannot; indeed I cannot.'

'Why not?'

Libbie did not answer, and Anne Dixon grew impatient.

'Surely in the name o' goodness, you're never going to baulk yourself of a day's pleasure for the sake of yon little cripple that's dead and gone?'

'No, – it's not baulking myself of, – don't be angry Anne Dixon, with me please, but I don't think it would be pleasure to me – I don't feel as if I could enjoy it; thank you all the same, but I did love that little lad very dearly, – I did,' (sobbing a little), 'and I can't forget him, and make merry so soon.'

'Well, I never!' exclaimed Anne, almost angrily.

'Indeed, Anne, I feel your kindness, and you and Bob have my best wishes, – that's what you have, – but even if I went, I should be thinking all day of him, and of his poor, poor mother, and they say it's bad to think over-much on them that is dead, at a wedding!'

'Nonsense!' said Anne, 'I'll take the risk of the ill-luck. After all, what is marrying? just a spree, Bob says. He often says he does not think I shall make him a good wife, for I know nought about house-matters wi' working in a factory; but he says he'd rather be uneasy wi' me, than easy wi' any one else. There's love for you! And I tell him I'd rather have him tipsy than any one else sober.'

'Oh, Anne Dixon, hush! you don't know yet what it is to have a drunken husband! I have seen something of it; father used to get fuddled: and in the long run it killed mother, let alone – Oh, Anne, God above only knows what the wife of a drunken man has to bear. Don't tell,' said she, lowering her voice, 'but father killed our little baby in one of his bouts; mother never looked up again, nor father either, for that matter, only his was in a different way. Mother will have gotten to little Jeannie now, and they'll be so happy together, – and perhaps Franky too. Oh!' said she, recovering herself from her train of thought, 'never say aught lightly of the wife's lot whose husband is given to drink.'

'Dear! what a preachment! I tell you what, Libbie! you're as born an old maid as ever I saw. You'll never be married, to either drunken or sober.'

Libbie's face went rather red, but without losing its meek expression.

'I know that as well as you can tell me. And more reason, therefore, that as God has seen fit to keep me out o' woman's natural work, I should try and find work for myself. I mean,' said she, seeing Anne Dixon's puzzled look, 'that as I know I'm never like for to have a home of my own, or a husband, who would look to me to make all straight, or children to watch over and care for, all which I take to be woman's natural work, I must not lose time in fretting and fidgeting after marriage, but just look about me for somewhat else to do. I can see many a one misses it in this. They will hanker after what is ne'er likely to be theirs, instead of facing it out, and settling down to be old maids; and as old maids, just looking round for the odd jobs God leaves in the world for such as old maids to do, – there's plenty of such work, – and there's the blessing of God on them as does it.' Libbie was almost out of breath at this outpouring of what had long been her inner thoughts.

'That's all very true, I make no doubt, for them as is to be old maids; but as I'm not, (please God, to-morrow comes), you might have spared your breath to cool your porridge. What I want to know is, whether you'll be bridesmaid to-morrow or not. Come now, do! it will do you good, after all your watching, and working, and slaving yourself for that poor Franky Hall.'

'It was one of my odd jobs,' said Libbie, smiling, though her eyes were brimming over with tears. 'But, dear Anne,' continued she, recovering herself, 'I could not do it to-morrow; indeed I could not!'

'And I can't wait,' said Anne Dixon, almost sulkily. 'Bob and I put if off from to-day because of the funeral, and Bob had set his heart on its being on Michaelmas-day; and mother says the goose won't keep beyond tomorrow. Do come! father finds eatables, and Bob finds drink, and we shall be so jolly! And after we've been to church, we're to walk round the town in pairs; white satin ribbon in our bonnets, and refreshment at any public-house we like, Bob says. And after dinner, there's to be a dance. Don't be a fool; you can do no good by staying. Margaret Hall will have to go out washing, I'll be bound.'

'Yes! she must go to Mrs Wilkinson's, and for that matter I must go working too. Mrs Williams has been after me to make her girl's winter things ready; only I could not leave Franky, he clung so to me.'

'Then you won't be bridesmaid! Is that your last word?'

'It is; you must not be angry with me, Anne Dixon,' said Libbie, deprecatingly.

But Anne was gone without a reply.

With a heavy heart Libbie mounted the little staircase. For she felt how ungracious her refusal of Anne's kindness must appear to one, who understood so little the feelings which rendered her acceptance of it a moral impossibility.

On opening the door, she saw Margaret Hall, with the Bible open on the table before her. For she had puzzled out the place where Libbie was reading, and with her finger under the line, was spelling out the words of consolation, piecing the syllables together aloud, with the earnest anxiety of comprehension with which a child first learns to read. So Libbie took the stool by her side, before she was aware that any one had entered the room.

'What did she want you for?' asked Margaret. 'But I can guess: she wanted you to be at th'wedding as is to come off this week, they say. Ay! they'll marry, and laugh, and dance, all as one as if my boy was alive,' said she, bitterly; 'well, he was neither kith nor kin of yours, so I maun try and be thankful for what you've done for him, and not wonder at your forgetting him afore he's well settled in his grave.'

'I never can forget him, and I'm not going to the wedding,' said Libbie, gently, for she understood the mother's jealousy of her dead child's claims.

'I must go work at Mrs Williams's to-morrow,' she said in explanation, for she was unwilling to boast of the tender fond regret which had been her principal motive for declining Anne's invitation.

'And I mun go washing, just as if nothing had happened,' sighed forth Mrs Hall. 'And I mun come home at night, and find his place empty, and all still where I used to be sure of hearing his voice, ere ever I got up the stair. No one will ever call me mother again!'

She fell a-crying pitifully, and Libbie could not speak for her own emotion for some time. But during this silence she put the key stone in the arch of thoughts she had been building up for many days; and when Margaret was again calm in her sorrow, Libbie said, 'Mrs Hall, I should like – would you like me to come for to live here altogether?'

Margaret Hall looked up with a sudden light on her countenance, which encouraged Libbie to go on.

'I could sleep with you, and pay half, you know; and we should be together in the evenings, and her as was home first would watch for the other, – and' (dropping her voice) 'we could talk of him at nights you know.'

She was going on, but Mrs Hall interrupted her.

'Oh! Libbie Marsh! and can you really think of coming to live wi me! I should like it above – But no! it must not be; you've no notion o what a creature I am at times. More like a mad one, when I'm in rage; and I can't keep it down. I seem to get out of bed wrong side i the morning, and I must have my passion out with the first person meet. Why, Libbie,' said she, with a doleful look of agony on her face 'I even used to fly out on him, poor sick lad as he was, and you ma judge how little I can keep it down frae that. No! you must not come. must live alone now,' sinking her voice into the low tones of despair

But Libbie's resolution was brave and strong:

'I'm not afraid,' said she, smiling. 'I know you better than yo know yourself, Mrs Hall. I've seen you try of late to keep it down when you've been boiling over, and I think you'll go on a-doing so And at any rate, when you've had your fit out you're very kind; and can forget if you have been a bit put out. But I'll try not to put you out. Do let me come; I think *he* would like us to keep together. I'll d my very best to make you comfortable.'

'It's me! It's me as will be making your life miserable with m temper, or else, God knows how my heart clings to you. You and me i folk alone in the world, for we both loved one who is dead, and wh had none else to love him. If you will live with me, Libbie, I'll try as never did afore, to be gentle and quiet-tempered. Oh! will you try me Libbie Marsh?'

So, out of the little grave, there sprang a hope and a resolution which made life an object to each of the two.

When Elizabeth Marsh returned home the next evening from he day's labours, Anne (Dixon no longer) crossed over, all in her brida finery, to endeavour to induce her to join the dance going on in he father's house.

'Dear Anne! this is good of you, a-thinking of me to-night,' said Libbie, kissing her. 'And though I cannot come, (I've promised Mr Hall to be with her), I shall think on you, and trust you'll be happy; have got a little needle-case, I looked out for your, – stay, here it is – wish it were more, only –'

'Only – I know what – you've been a-spending all your money i nice things for poor Franky. Thou'rt a real good 'un, Libbie, and I' keep your needle-book to my dying day, that I will.'

Seeing Anne in such a friendly mood emboldened Libbie to tell her of her change of place; of her intention of lodging henceforward with Margaret Hall.

'Thou never will! Why, father and mother are as fond of thee as can be, – they'll lower thy rent, if that's what it is; and thou know'st they never grudge thee bit or drop. And Margaret Hall of all folk to lodge wi'! She's such a Tartar! Sooner than not have a quarrel, she'd fight right hand against left. Thou'lt have no peace of thy life. What on earth can make you think of such a thing, Libbie Marsh?'

'She'd be so lonely without me,' pleaded Libbie. 'I'm sure I could make her happier (even if she does scold me a bit now and then) than she'd be living alone. And I'm not afraid of her; and I mean to do my best not to vex her; and it will ease her heart, may be, to talk to me at times about Franky. I shall often see your father and mother, and I shall always thank them for their kindness to me. But they have you, and little Mary, and poor Mrs Hall has no one.'

Anne could only repeat 'Well! I never!' and hurry off to tell the news at home.

But Libbie was right. Margaret Hall is a different woman to the scold of the neighbourhood she once was; touched and softened by the two purifying angels, Sorrow and Love. And it is beautiful to see her affection, her reverence for Libbie Marsh. Her dead mother could hardly have cared for her more tenderly than does the hard-featured washerwoman, not long ago so fierce and unwomanly. Libbie herself has such peace shining on her countenance, as almost makes it beautiful, as she renders the services of a daughter to Franky's mother – no longer the desolate, lonely orphan, a stranger on the earth.

Do you ever read the moral concluding sentence of a story? I never do; but I once (in the year 1811, I think) heard of a deaf old lady living by herself, who did; and as she may have left some descendants with the same amiable peculiarity, I will put in for their benefit what I believe to be the secret of Libbie's peace of mind, the real reason why she no longer feels oppressed at her own loneliness in the world.

She has a purpose in life, and that purpose is a holy one.

A Child's Dream of a Star
Charles Dickens

There was once a child, and he strolled about a good deal, and thought of a number of things. He had a sister, who was a child too, and his constant companion. These two used to wonder all day long. They wondered at the beauty of the flowers; they wondered at the height and blueness of the sky; they wondered at the depth of the bright water; they wondered at the goodness and the power of God who made the lovely world.

They used to say to one another, sometimes, Supposing all the children upon earth were to die, would the flowers, and the water, and the sky, be sorry? They believed they would be sorry. For, said they, the buds are the children of the flowers, and the little playful streams that gambol down the hill-sides are the children of the water; and the smallest bright specks playing at hide-and-seek in the sky all night must surely be the children of the stars; and they would all be grieved to see their playmates, the children of men, no more.

There was one clear shining star that used to come out in the sky before the rest, near the church spire, above the graves. It was larger and more beautiful, they thought, than all the others, and every night they watched for it, standing hand in hand at a window. Whoever saw it first, cried out, 'I see the star!' And often they cried out both together, knowing so well when it would rise, and where. So they grew to be such friends with it, that, before lying down in their beds, they always looked out once again, to bid it good night; and when they were turning round to sleep, they used to say, 'God bless the star!'

But while she was still very young – oh, very, very young! – the sister drooped, and came to be so weak that she could no longer stand in the window at night; and then the child looked sadly out by himself, and when he saw the star, turned round and said to the patient pale face on the bed, 'I see the star!' and then a smile would come upon the face, and a little weak voice used to say, 'God bless my brother and the star!'

And so the time came all too soon when the child looked out alone, and when there was no face on the bed, and when there was a little grave among the graves, not there before; and when the star made long rays down towards him, as he saw it through his tears. '

Now, these rays were so bright, and they seemed to make such a shining way from earth to Heaven, that when the child went to his solitary bed, he dreamed about the star; and dreamed that, lying where he was, he saw a train of people taken up that sparkling road by angels. And the star, opening, showed him a great world of light, where many more such angels waited to receive them.

All these angels, who were waiting, turned their beaming eyes upon the people who were carried up into the star; and some came out from the long rows in which they stood, and fell upon the people's necks, and kissed them tenderly, and went away with them down avenues of light, and were so happy in their company, that lying in his bed he wept for joy.

But, there were many angels who did not go with them, and among them one he knew. The patient face that once had lain upon the bed was glorified and radiant, but his heart found out his sister among all the host.

His sister's angel lingered near the entrance of the star, and said to the leader among those who had brought the people thither, 'Is my brother come?'

And he said, 'No.'

She was turning hopefully away, when the child stretched out his arms and cried, 'Oh, sister, I am here! Take me!' and then she turned her beaming eyes upon him, and it was night; and the star was shining into the room, making long rays down towards him as he saw it through his tears.

From that hour forth, the child looked out upon the star as on the home he was to go to, when his time should come; and he thought that he did not belong to the earth alone, but to the star too, because of his sister's angel gone before.

There was a baby born to be a brother to the child; and while he was so little that he never yet had spoken a word, he stretched his tiny form out on his bed, and died.

Again the child dreamed of the opened star, and of the company of angels, and the train of people, and the rows of angels with their beaming eyes all turned upon those people's faces.

Said his sister's angel to the leader, 'Is my brother come?'

And he said, 'Not that one, but another.'

As the child beheld his brother's angel in her arms, he cried, 'Oh, sister, I am here! Take me!' And she turned and smiled upon him, and the star was shining.

He grew to be a young man, and was busy at his books when an old servant came to him and said, 'Thy mother is no more. I bring her blessing on her darling son!'

Again at night he saw the star, and all that former company. Said his sister's angel to the leader, 'Is my brother come?'

And he said, 'Thy mother!'

A mighty cry of joy went forth through all the star, because the mother was reunited to her two children. And he stretched out his arms and cried, 'Oh, mother, sister, and brother, I am here! Take me!' And they answered him, 'Not yet,' and the star was shining.

He grew to be a man, whose hair was turning grey, and he was sitting in his chair by the fireside, heavy with grief, and with his face bedewed with tears, when the star opened once again.

Said his sister's angel to the leader, 'Is my brother come?'

And he said, 'Nay, but his maiden daughter.'

And the man who had been the child saw his daughter, newly lost to him, a celestial creature among those three, and he said, 'My daughter's head is on my sister's bosom, and her arm is round my mother's neck, and at her feet there is the baby of old time, and I can bear the parting from her, God be praised!'

And the star was shining.

Thus the child came to be an old man, and his once smooth face was wrinkled, and his steps were slow and feeble, and his back was bent. And one night as he lay upon his bed, his children standing round, he cried, as he had cried so long ago, 'I see the star!'

They whispered one another, 'He is dying.'

And he said, 'I am. My age is falling from me like a garment, and I move towards the star as a child. And oh, my Father, now I thank thee that it has so often opened to receive those dear ones who await me!'

And the star was shining; and it shines upon his grave.

The Outcasts of Poker Flat
Francis Bret Harte

As Mr John Oakhurst, gambler, stepped into the main street of Poker Flat on the morning of the twenty-third of November 1850, he was conscious of a change in its moral atmosphere since the preceding night. Two or three men, conversing earnestly together, ceased as he approached, and exchanged significant glances. There was a Sabbath lull in the air, which, in a settlement unused to Sabbath influences, looked ominous.

Mr Oakhurst's calm, handsome face betrayed small concern of these indications. Whether he was conscious of any predisposing cause, was another question. 'I reckon they're after somebody,' he reflected; 'likely it's me.' He returned to his pocket the handkerchief with which he had been whipping away the red dust of Poker Flat from his neat boots, and quietly discharged his mind of any further conjecture.

In point of fact, Poker Flat was 'after somebody'. It had lately suffered the loss of several thousand dollars, two valuable horses, and a prominent citizen. It was experiencing a spasm of virtuous reaction, quite as lawless and ungovernable as any of the acts that had provoked it. A secret committee had determined to rid the town of all improper persons. This was done permanently in regard of two men who were then hanging from the boughs of a sycamore in the gulch, and temporarily in the banishment of certain other objectionable characters. I regret to say that some of these were ladies. It is but due to the sex, however, to state that their impropriety was professional, and it was only in such easily established standards of evil that Poker Flat ventured to sit in judgement.

Mr Oakhurst was right in supposing that he was included in this category. A few of the committee had urged hanging him as a possible example, and a sure method of reimbursing themselves from his pockets of the sums he had won from them, 'It's agin justice,' said Jim Wheeler, 'to let this yer young man from Roaring Camp – an entire stranger – carry away our money.' But a crude sentiment of equity residing in the breasts of those who had been fortunate enough to win from Mr Oakhurst overruled this narrower local prejudice.

Mr Oakhurst received his sentence with philosophic calmness, none the less coolly that he was aware of the hesitation of his judges. He was too much of a gambler not to accept Fate. With him life was at best an uncertain game, and he recognized the usual percentage in favor of the dealer.

A body of armed men accompanied the deported wickedness of Poker Flat to the outskirts of the settlement. Besides Mr Oakhurst, who was known to be a coolly desperate man, and for whose intimidation the armed escort was intended, the expatriated party consisted of a young woman familiarly known as 'The Duchess'; another, who had gained the infelicitous title of 'Mother Shipton'; and 'Uncle Billy,' a suspected sluice-robber and confirmed drunkard. The cavalcade provoked no comments from the spectators, nor was any word uttered by the escort. Only, when the gulch which marked the uttermost limit of Poker Flat was reached, the leader spoke briefly and to the point. The exiles were forbidden to return at the peril of their lives.

As the escort disappeared, their pent-up feelings found vent in a few hysterical tears from the Duchess, some bad language from Mother Shipton, and a Parthian volley of expletives from Uncle Billy. The philosophic Oakhurst alone remained still. He listened calmly to Mother Shipton's desire to cut somebody's heart out, to the repeated statements of the Duchess that she would die on the road, and to the alarming oaths that seemed to be bumped out of Uncle Billy as he rode forward. With the easy good humour characteristic of his class, he insisted upon exchanging his own riding-horse, Five Spot, for the sorry mule which the Duchess rode. But even this act did not draw the party into any closer sympathy. The young woman readjusted her somewhat draggled plumes with a feeble, faded coquetry; Mother Shipton eyed the possessor of Five Spot with malevolence, and Uncle Billy included the whole party in one sweeping anathema.

The road to Sandy Bar – a camp that, not having as yet experienced the regenerating influences of Poker Flat, consequently seemed to offer some invitation to the emigrants – lay over a steep mountain range. It was distant a day's severe journey. In that advanced season, the party soon passed out of the moist, temperate regions of the foothills into the dry, cold, bracing air of the Sierras. The trail was narrow and difficult. At noon the Duchess, rolling out of her saddle upon the ground, declared her intention of going no farther, and the party halted.

The spot was singularly wild and impressive. A wooded ampitheatre, surrounded on three sides by precipitous cliffs of naked granite, sloped gently toward the crest of another precipice that overlooked the valley. It was undoubtedly the most suitable spot for a camp, had camping been advisable. But Mr Oakhurst knew that scarcely half the journey to Sandy Bar was accomplished, and the party were not equipped or provisioned for delay. This fact he pointed out to his companions curtly, with a philosophic commentary on the folly of 'throwing up their hand before the game was played out'. But they were furnished with liquor, which in this emergency stood them in place of food, fuel, rest, and prescience. In spite of his remonstrances, it was not long before they were more or less under its influence. Uncle Billy passed rapidly from a bellicose state into one of stupor, the Duchess became maudlin, and Mother Shipton snored. Mr Oakhurst alone remained erect, leaning against a rock, calmly surveying them.

Mr Oakhurst did not drink. It interfered with a profession which required coolness, impassiveness, and presence of mind, and, in his own language, he 'couldn't afford it'. As he gazed at his recumbent fellow-exiles, the loneliness begotten of his pariah-trade, his habits of life, his very vices, for the first time seriously oppressed him. He bestirred himself in dusting his black clothes, washing his hands and face, and other acts characteristic of his studiously neat habits, and for a moment forgot his annoyance. The thought of deserting his weaker and more pitiable companions never perhaps occurred to him. Yet he could not help feeling the want of that excitement which, singularly enough, was most conducive to the calm equanimity for which he was notorious. He looked at the gloomy walls that rose a thousand feet sheer above the circling pines around him; at the sky, ominously clouded; at the valley below, already deepening into shadow. And, doing so, suddenly he heard his own name called.

A horseman slowly ascended the trail. In the fresh, open face of the new-comer Mr Oakhurst recognized Tom Simson, otherwise known as 'The Innocent' of Sandy Bar. He had met him some months before over a 'little game', and had, with perfect equanimity, won the entire fortune – amounting to some forty dollars – of that guileless youth. After the game was finished, Mr Oakhurst drew the youthful speculator behind the door and thus addressed him: 'Tommy, you're a good

little man, but you can't gamble worth a cent. Don't try it over again.'
He then handed him his money back, pushed him gently from the
room, and so made a devoted slave of Tom Simson.

There was a remembrance of this in his boyish and enthusiastic
greeting of Mr Oakhurst. He had started, he said, to go to Poker Flat
to seek his fortune. 'Alone?' No, not exactly alone; in fact – a giggle –
he had run away with Piney Woods. Didn't Mr Oakhurst remember
Piney? She that used to wait on the table at the Temperance House?
They had been engaged a long time, but old Jake Woods had
objected, and so they had run away, and were going to Poker Flat to
be married, and here they were. And they were tired out, and how
lucky it was they had found a place to camp and company. All this the
Innocent delivered rapidly, while Piney – a stout, comely damsel of
fifteen – emerged from behind the pine-tree, where she had been
blushing unseen, and rode to the side of her lover.

Mr Oakhurst seldom troubled himself with sentiment, still less with
propriety; but he had a vague idea that the situation was not
felicitous. He retained, however, his presence of mind sufficiently to
kick Uncle Billy, who was about to say something, and Uncle Billy
was sober enough to recognize in Mr Oakhurst's kick a superior
power that would not bear trifling. He then endeavoured to dissuade
Tom Simson from delaying further, but in vain. He even pointed out
the fact that there was no provision, nor means of making a camp.
But, unluckily, the Innocent met this objection by assuring the party
that he was provided with an extra mule loaded with provisions, and
by the discovery of a rude attempt at a log-house near the trail. 'Piney
can stay with Mrs Oakhurst,' said the Innocent, pointing to the
Duchess, 'and I can shift for myself.'

Nothing but Mr Oakhurst's admonishing foot saved Uncle Billy
from bursting into a roar of laughter. As it was, he felt compelled to
retire up the canyon until he could recover his gravity. There he
confided the joke to the tall pine-trees, with many slaps of his leg,
contortions of his face, and the usual profanity. But when he returned
to the party, he found them seated by a fire – for the air had grown
strangely chill and the sky overcast – in apparently amicable conversation. Piney was actually talking in an impulsive, girlish fashion
to the Duchess, who was listening with an interest and animation she
had not shown for many days. The Innocent was holding forth
apparently with equal effect, to Mr Oakhurst and Mother Shipton,
who was actually relaxing into amiability. 'Is this yer a d–d picnic?'

said Uncle Billy, with inward scorn, as he surveyed the sylvan group, the glancing fire-light, and the tethered animals in the foreground. Suddenly an idea mingled with the alcoholic fumes that disturbed his brain. It was apparently of a jocular nature, for he felt impelled to slap his leg again and cram his fist into his mouth.

As the shadows crept slowly up the mountain, a slight breeze rocked the tops of the pine-trees, and moaned through their long and gloomy aisles. The ruined cabin, patched and covered with pine boughs, was set apart for the ladies. As the lovers parted, they unaffectedly exchanged a kiss, so honest and sincere that it might have been heard above the swaying pines. The frail Duchess and the malevolent Mother Shipton were probably too stunned to remark upon the last evidence of simplicity, and so turned without a word to the hut. The first was replenished, the men lay down before the door, and in a few minutes were asleep.

Mr Oakhurst was a light sleeper. Toward morning he awoke benumbed and cold. As he stirred the dying fire, the wind, which was now blowing strongly, brought to his cheek that which caused the blood to leave it – snow!

He started to his feet with the intention of awakening the sleepers, for there was no time to lose. But turning to where Uncle Billy had been lying, he found him gone. A suspicion leaped to his brain and a curse to his lips. He ran to the spot where the mules had been tethered; they were no longer there. The tracks were already rapidly disappearing in the show.

The momentary excitement brought Mr Oakhurst back to the fire with his usual calm. He did not waken the sleepers. The Innocent slumbered peacefully, with a smile on his good humoured, freckled face; the virgin Piney slept beside her frailer sisters as sweetly as though attended by celestial guardians, and Mr Oakhurst, drawing his blanket over his shoulders, stroked his mustachios and waited for the dawn. It came slowly in the whirling mist of snowflakes, that dazzled and confused the eye. What could be seen of the landscape appeared magically changed. He looked over the valley, and summed up the present and future in two words – 'Snowed in!'

A careful inventory of the provisions, which, fortunately for the party, had been stored within the hut, and so escaped the felonious fingers of Uncle Billy, disclosed the fact that with care and prudence they might last ten days longer. 'That is,' said Mr Oakhurst, *sotto voce* to the Innocent, 'if you're willing to board us. If you ain't – and perhaps you'd better not – you can wait till Uncle Billy gets back with provisions.' For some occult reason, Mr Oakhurst could not bring himself to disclose Uncle Billy's rascality, and so offered the hypothesis that he had wandered from the camp and had accidentally stampeded the animals. He dropped a warning to the Duchess and Mother Shipton, who of course knew the facts of their associate's defection. 'They'll find out the truth about us *all*, when they find out anything,' he added, significantly, 'and there's no good frightening them now.'

Tom Simson not only put all his worldly store at the disposal of Mr Oakhurst, but seemed to enjoy the prospect of their enforced seclusion. 'We'll have a good camp for a week, and then the snow'll melt, and we'll all go back together.' The cheerful gaiety of the young man and Mr Oakhurst's calm infected the others. The Innocent, with the aid of pine boughs, extemporized a thatch for the roofless cabin, and the Duchess directed Piney in the rearrangement of the interior with a taste and tact that opened the blue eyes of that provincial maiden to their fullest extent.

'I reckon now you're used to fine things at Poker Flat,' said Piney. The Duchess turned away sharply to conceal something that reddened her cheek through its professional tint, and Mother Shipton requested Piney not to 'chatter'. But when Mr Oakhurst returned from a weary search for the trail, he heard the sound of happy laughter echoed from the rocks. He stopped in some alarm, and his thoughts first naturally reverted to the whisky, which he had prudently *cached*. 'And yet it don't somehow sound like whisky,' said the gambler. It was not until he caught sight of the blazing fire through the still blinding storm, and the group around it, that he settled to the conviction that it was 'square fun'.

Whether Mr Oakhurst had *cached* his cards with the whisky as something debarred the free access of the community, I cannot say. It was certain that, in Mother Shipton's words, he 'didn't say cards once' during the evening. Haply the time was beguiled by an accordion, produced somewhat ostentatiously by Tom Simson, from his pack. Notwithstanding some difficulties attending the manipulation of this instrument, Piney Woods managed to pluck several reluctant melodies from its keys, to an accompaniment by the Innocent on a pair of bone castinets. But the crowning festivity of the evening was reached in a rude camp-meeting hymn, which the lovers, joining hands, sang with great earnestness and vociferation. I fear that a certain defiant tone and Covenanter's swing to its chorus, rather than any devotional quality, caused it speedily to infect the others who at last joined in the refrain:

I'm proud to live in the service of the Lord,
And I'm bound to die in His army.

The pines rocked, the storm eddied and whirled above the miserable group, and the flames of their altar leaped heavenward, as if in token of the vow.

At midnight the storm abated, the rolling clouds parted, and the stars glittered keenly above the sleeping camp. Mr Oakhurst, whose professional habits had enabled him to live on the smallest possible amount of sleep, in dividing the watch with Tom Simson, somehow managed to take upon himself the greatest part of that duty. He excused himself to the Innocent, by saying that he had 'often been a week without sleep'. 'Doing what?' asked Tom. 'Poker!' replied Oakhurst, sententiously, 'when a man gets a streak of luck – nigger-luck – he don't get tired. The luck gives in first. Luck,' continued the gambler, reflectively, 'is a mighty queer thing. All you know about it for certain is that it's bound to change. And it's finding out when it's going to change that makes you. We've had a streak of bad luck since we left Poker Flat – you came along, and slap you get into it, too. If you can hold your cards right along you're all right. For,' added the gambler, with cheerful irrelevance,

'I'm proud to live in the service of the Lord,
And I'm bound to die in His army.'

The third day came, and the sun, looking through the white-curtained valley, saw the outcasts divide their slowly decreasing store of provisions for the morning meal. It was one of the peculiarities of that mountain climate that its rays diffused a kindly warmth over the wintry landscape, as if in regretful commiseration of the past. But it revealed drift on drift of snow piled high around the hut; a hopeless, uncharted, trackless sea of white lying below the rocky shores to which the castaways still clung. Through the marvelously clear air, the smoke of the pastoral village of Poker Flat rose miles away. Mother Shipton saw it, and from a remote pinnacle of her rocky fastness, hurled in that direction a final malediction. It was her last vituperative attempt, and perhaps for that reason was invested with a certain degree of sublimity. It did her good, she privately informed the

Duchess. 'Just to go out there and cuss, and see.' She then set herself to the task of amusing 'the child', as she and the Duchess were pleased to call Piney. Piney was no chicken, but it was a soothing and ingenious theory of the pair thus to account for the fact that she didn't swear and wasn't improper.

When night crept up again through the gorges, the reedy notes of the accordion rose and fell in fitful spasms and longdrawn gasps by the flickering camp-fire. But music failed to fill entirely the aching void left by insufficient food, and a new diversion was proposed by Piney – story-telling. Neither Mr Oakhurst nor his female companions caring to relate their personal experiences, this plan would have failed, too, but for the Innocent. Some months before he had chanced upon a stray copy of Mr Pope's ingenious translation of the Iliad. He now proposed to narrate the principal incidents of that poem – having thoroughly mastered the argument and fairly forgotten the words – in the current vernacular of Sandy Bar. And so for the rest of that night the Homeric demi-gods again walked the earth. Trojan bully and wily Greek wrestled in the winds, and the great pines in the canyon seemed to bow to the wrath of the son of Peleus. Mr Oakhurst listened with quiet satisfaction. Most especially was he interested in the fate of 'Ash-heels', as the Innocent persisted in denominating the 'swift-footed Achilles'.

So with small food and much of Homer and the accordion, a week passed over the heads of the outcasts. The sun again forsook them, and again from leaden skies the snowflakes were sifted over the land. Day by day closer around them drew the snowy circle, until at last they looked from their prison over drifted walls of dazzling white, that towered twenty feet above their heads. It became more and more difficult to replenish their fires, even from the fallen trees beside them, now half-hidden in the drifts. And yet no one complained. The lovers turned from the dreary prospect and looked into each other's eyes, and were happy. Mr Oakhurst settled himself coolly to the losing game before him. The Duchess, more cheerful than she had been, assumed the care of Piney, Only Mother Shipton – once the strongest of the party – seemed to sicken and fade. At midnight on the tenth day she called Oakhurst to her side. 'I'm going,' she said, in a voice of querulous weakness, 'but don't say anything about it. Don't waken the kids. Take the bundle from under my head and open it.' Mr Oakhurst did so. It contained Mother Shipton's rations for the last week, untouched. 'Give 'em to the child,' she said, pointing to the sleeping Piney. 'You've starved yourself,' said the gambler. 'That's what they call it,' said the woman, querulously, as she lay down again, and turning her face to the wall, passed quietly away.

The accordion and the bones were put aside that day, and Homer was forgotten. When the body of Mother Shipton had been committed to the snow, Mr Oakhurst took the Innocent aside, and showed him a pair of snowshoes, which he had fashioned from the old pack-saddle. 'There's one chance in a hundred to save her yet,' he said, pointing to Piney; 'but it's there,' he added, pointing toward Poker Flat. 'If you reach there in two days she's safe.' 'And you?' asked Tom Simson. 'I'll stay here,' was the curt reply.

The lovers parted with a long embrace. 'You are not going, too?' said the Duchess, as she saw Mr Oakhurst apparently waiting to accompany him. 'As far as the canyon,' he replied. He turned suddenly, and kissed the Duchess, leaving her pallid face aflame, and her trembling limbs rigid with amazement.

Night came, but not Mr Oakhurst. It brought the storm again and the whirling snow. Then the Duchess, feeding the fire, found that someone had quietly piled beside the hut enough fuel to last them a few days longer. The tears rose to her eyes, but she hid them from Piney.

The women slept but little. In the morning, looking into each other's faces, they read their fate. Neither spoke; but Piney, accepting the position of the stronger, drew near and placed her arm around the Duchess's waist. They kept this attitude for the rest of the day. That night the storm reached its greatest fury, and, rending asunder the protecting pines, invaded the very hut.

Toward morning they found themselves unable to feed the fire, which gradually died away. As the embers slowly blackened, the Duchess crept closer to Piney, and broke the silence of many hours: 'Piney, can you pray?' 'No, dear,' said Piney, simply. The Duchess without knowing exactly why, felt relieved, and putting her head upon Piney's shoulder, spoke no more. And so reclining, the younger and purer pillowing the head of her soiled sister upon her virgin breast, they fell asleep.

The wind lulled as if it feared to waken them. Feathery drifts of snow, shaken from the long pine boughs, flew like whitely winged birds, and settled about them as they slept. The moon through the rifted clouds looked down upon what had been the camp. But all human stain, all trace of earthly travail, was hidden beneath the spotless mantle flung from above.

They slept all that day and the next, nor did they waken when voices and footsteps broke the silence of the camp. And when pitying fingers brushed the snow from their wan faces, you could scarcely have told from the equal peace that dwelt upon them, which was she that had sinned. Even the Law of Poker Flat recognized this, and turned away, leaving them still locked in each other's arms.

But at the head of the gulch, on one of the largest pine trees, they found the deuce of clubs pinned to the bark with a bowie knife. It bore the following, written in pencil, in a firm hand:

†

BENEATH THIS TREE
LIES THE BODY
OF
JOHN OAKHURST,
WHO STRUCK A STREAK OF BAD LUCK
ON THE 23RD OF NOVEMBER, 1850,
AND
HANDED IN HIS CHECKS
ON THE 7TH OF DECEMBER, 1850.

†

And pulseless and cold, with a Derringer by his side and a bullet in his heart, though still calm as in life, beneath the snow lay he who was at once the strongest and yet the weakest of the outcasts of Poker Flat.

The Requiem

Anton Chekov

(translated by R. E. C. Long)

At the church of the Odigitriefi Virgin in Verchniye Zaprudni village the service had just ended. The worshippers moved from their places and left the church; and soon no one remained save the shopkeeper, Andrei Andreitch, one of the oldest residents, and a member of the local 'Intelligentsia'. Andrei Andreitch leaned on his elbow on the rail of the choir and waited. On his face, well shaven, fat, and marked with traces of old pimples, were two inimical expressions: resignation to inscrutable destiny, and unlimited, dull contempt for his fellow-worshippers in their cheap overcoats and gaudy handkerchiefs. As it was Sunday, he was dressed in his best. He wore a cloth overcoat with yellow bone buttons, blue trousers outside his top-boots, and solid goloshes, such big, awkward goloshes as are worn only by people positive, deliberate, and convinced in their faith.

His greasy, idle eyes were bent on the iconostasis. Familiar to him were the lengthy faces of the saints, the watchman Matvei, who puffed out his cheeks and blew out the candles, the tarnished candelabra, the threadbare carpet, the clerk Lopukhoff, who ran anxiously from the altar carrying the host to the sexton. All these things he had seen long ago, and again and again, as often as his five fingers. But one thing was unfamiliar. At the north door stood Father Grigori, still in priestly vestments, and angrily twitching his bushy eyebrows.

'What is he frowning at, God be with him?' thought the shopkeeper. 'Yes, and he shakes his hand! And stamps his foot! Tell me what that means, please. What does it all mean, Heavenly Mother? Whom is he glaring at?'

Andrei Andreitch looked around, and saw that the church was already deserted. At the door thronged a dozen men, but their backs were turned to the altar.

'Come at once when you are called! Why do you stand there, looking like a statue?' came Father Grigori's angry voice. 'I am calling *you!*'

The shopkeeper looked at Father Grigori's red, wrathful face, and for the first time realised that the frowning eyebrows and twitching fingers were directed at himself. He started, walked away from the choir, and resolutely, in his creaking goloshes, went up to the altar.

'Andrei Andreitch, was it you who handed this in during oblation, for the repose of Marya?' asked the priest, looking furiously at the shopkeeper's fat, perspiring face.

'Yes.'

'So . . . and that means that you wrote it too? You?'

And Father Grigori wrathfully pushed a slip of paper under the shopkeeper's eyes. On this paper, given in by Andrei Andreitch during oblation, in a big, wandering hand, was written –

'Pray for the soul of God's slave, the Adulteress Marya.'

'Exactly; I wrote it . . .' answered the shopkeeper.

'How dare you write such a thing?' whispered the priest slowly, and his hoarse whisper expressed indignation and horror.

The shopkeeper looked at him with dull amazement and doubt, and felt frightened; from the day of his birth, Father Grigori had never spoken so angrily to a member of the Verchniye Zaprudni 'Intelligentsia.' For a moment the two men faced each other in silence. The tradesman's surprise was so great that his fat face seemed to melt on all sides, as wet dough.

'How dare you?' repeated the priest.

'I don't understand,' said Andrei Andreitch doubtfully.

'So you don't understand,' whispered Father Grigori, receding in amazement, and flourishing his arms. 'What have you got on your shoulders? A head, is it, or some other object? You hand a paper across the altar with a word which even in the street is regarded as improper! Why do you stick out your eyes? Is it possible you do not know the meaning of this word?'

'This, I suppose, is all about the word "adulteress,"' stammered the shopkeeper, reddening and blinking his eyes. 'I see nothing wrong. Our Lord, in His mercy, this same thing . . . forgave an adulteress . . . prepared a place for her; yes, and the life of the blessed Mary of Egypt shows in what sense this word, excuse. . . .'

The shopkeeper was about to adduce some other defence, but he lost the thread, and rubbed his lips with his cuff.

'So that's how you understand it!' The priest again flourished his hand impatiently. 'You forget that our Lord forgave her – understand that – but you condemn her, you call her an improper name! And who is it? Your own daughter! Not merely in the sacred Scriptures, even in the profane, you will never read of such an act! I repeat to you, Andrei, don't try to be clever! Don't play the philosopher, brother! If God gave you a speculative head, and you don't know how to manage it, then better not speculate. . . . Don't try and be too clever – be silent!'

'Yes, but, you know, she . . . excuse my using the word, she was an actress,' protested the shopkeeper.

'An actress! No matter what her career, it is your duty, once she's dead, to forget it, and not to write it on paper!'

'I understand . . .' consented the shopkeeper.

'You should be forced to do penance,' growled the deacon from behind the altar, looking derisively at Andrei Andreitch's guilty face. 'Then you'd soon drop your clever words. Your daughter was a well-known actress. Even in the newspapers they mentioned her death. . . . Philosopher!'

'I understand, of course . . . really,' stammered the shopkeeper. 'It was an unsuitable word, but I used it not in condemnation, Father Grigori; I wished to express myself scripturally . . . in short, to make you understand who it was you were to pray for. People always hand in some description, for instance: the infant John, the drowned woman Pelageya, the soldier Yegor, murdered Paul, and so on. . . . That is all I wanted.'

'You are wrong, Andrei! God will forgive you, but take care the next time! And the chief thing is this; don't be too clever, and think like others. Abase yourself ten times and begone!'

'Yes,' said the shopkeeper, rejoiced that the ordeal was over. His face again resumed its expression of dignified self-importance. 'Ten adorations! I understand. But now, *batiushka*, allow me to make a request. Because I, after all, was her father . . . you yourself know; in spite of everything she was my daughter. I should like to ask you to say the mass for her soul to-day. And I venture to ask you also, father deacon!'

'That is right!' said Father Grigori, taking off his surplice. 'I praise you for that. I can approve of it. . . . Now begone! We will come out at once.'

Andrei Andreitch walked heavily from the altar, and, red-faced, with a solemn memorial-service expression, stood in the middle of the church. The watchman Matvei set before him a table with a crucifixion; and after a brief delay the mass began.

The church was still. Audible only were the censer's metallic ring and the droning voices. Near Andrei Andreitch stood the watchman Matvei, the midwife Makarievna, and her little son Mitka, with the paralysed hand. No one else attended. The clerk sang badly in an ugly, dull bass, but his words were so mournful that the shopkeeper gradually lost his pompous expression, and felt real grief. He remembered his little Mashutka. . . . He remembered the day she was born, when he served as footman at Verchniye Zaprudni Hall; remembered how in the rush of his footman's existence, he never noticed that his little girl was growing up. Those long years during which she changed into a graceful girl, fair-haired, with eyes as big as copecks, sped away unobserved. He remembered that she was brought up, as the children of all the favoured servants, with the young ladies of the house; how the squire's family, merely from lack of other work, taught her to read, to write, and to dance; and how he, Andrei, took no part in her training. Only when at long intervals he met her at the gate, or on the landing, he would remember that she was his daughter and begin, as far as time allowed, to teach her her prayers and read from the Bible. Yes, and what fame he gained for knowledge of the rubric and the Holy Scriptures! And the little girl, however rigid and pompous her father's face, listened with delight. She yawned, it is true, as she repeated the prayers; but when, stammering and doing his best to speak magniloquently, he told her Bible stories she was all ears. And at Esau's lentils, the doom of Sodom, and the woes of little Joseph she turned pale, and opened wide her big blue eyes.

And then, when he retired from his post as footman, and with his savings opened a shop in the village, the family took Mashutka away to Moscow.

He remembered how three years before her death she came to him on a visit. She was already a young woman, graceful and well built, with the dress and manners of a gentlewoman. And she spoke so cleverly, as if out of a book, smoked cigarettes, and slept till midday. Andrei Andreitch asked her what was her business; and she, looking him straight in the face, said boldly, 'I am an actress!' And this frank avowal seemed to the retired footman the height of immodesty. Mashutka began to tell her father of her stage triumphs and of her stage life; but seeing her father's purple face, she stopped suddenly. In silence, without exchanging a glance, they had spent three weeks together until it was time for Mashutka to go. Before leaving, she begged her father to walk with her along the river bank. And, shameful as it was to appear in daylight before honest people with a daughter who was a vagrant play-actress, he conceded her prayer.

'What glorious country you have!' she said ecstatically as they walked. 'What ravines, what marshes! Heavens, how beautiful is my native land!'

And she began to cry.

'Such things only take up space,' thought Andrei Andreitch, with a dull look at the ravines. He understood nothing of his child's delight. 'There is as much use from them as milk from a goat!'

And she continued to cry, inhaling the air greedily, as if she knew that her breaths were already numbered. . . .

Andrei Andreitch shook his head as a bitten horse, and to quench these painful memories, began to cross himself vigorously.

'Remember, Lord,' he muttered, 'thy dead slave, the Adulteress Marya, and forgive her all her sins!'

Again the improper word burst from his lips; but he did not notice it; what was set so deeply in his mind was not to be uprooted with a spade, much less by the admonitions of Father Grigori. Makarievna sighed, and whispered something, and paralysed Mitka seemed lost in thought.

' . . . where there is neither sorrow, nor sickness, nor sighing!' droned the clerk, covering his face with his right hand.

From the censer rose a pillar of blue smoke and swam in the broad, oblique sun-ray which cut the obscure emptiness of the church. And it seemed that with the smoke there floated in the sun-ray the soul of the dead girl. Eddies of smoke, like infants' curls, were swept upwards to the window; and the grief and affliction with which this poor soul was full seemed to pass away.

Markheim

Robert Louis Stevenson

'Yes,' said the dealer, 'our windfalls are of various kinds. Some customers are ignorant, and then I touch a dividend on my superior knowledge. Some are dishonest,' and here he held up the candle, so that the light fell strongly on his visitor, 'and in that case,' he continued, 'I profit by my virtue.'

Markheim had but just entered from the daylight streets, and his eyes had not yet grown familiar with the mingled shine and darkness in the shop. At these pointed words, and before the near presence of the flame, he blinked painfully and looked aside.

The dealer chuckled. 'You come to me on Christmas Day,' he resumed, 'when you know that I am alone in my house, put up my shutters, and make a point of refusing business. Well, you will have to pay for that; you will have to pay for my loss of time, when I should be balancing my books; you will have to pay, besides, for a kind of manner that I remark in you today very strongly. I am the essence of discretion, and ask no awkward questions; but when a customer cannot look me in the eye, he has to pay for it.' The dealer once more chuckled; and then, changing to his usual business voice, though still with a note of irony, 'You can give, as usual, a clear account of how you came into the possession of the object?' he continued. 'Still your uncle's cabinet? A remarkable collector, sir!'

And the little pale, round-shouldered dealer stood almost on tip-toe, looking over the top of his gold spectacles, and nodding his head with every mark of disbelief. Markheim returned his gaze with one of infinite pity, and a touch of horror.

'This time,' said he, 'you are in error. I have not come to sell, but to buy. I have no curios to dispose of; my uncle's cabinet is bare to the wainscot; even were it still intact, I have done well on the Stock Exchange, and should more likely add to it than otherwise, and my errand today is simplicity itself. I seek a Christmas present for a lady,' he continued, waxing more fluent as he struck into the speech he had prepared; 'and certainly I owe you every excuse for thus disturbing you upon so small a matter. But the thing was neglected yesterday; I must produce my little compliment at dinner; and, as you very well know, a rich marriage is not a thing to be neglected.'

There followed a pause, during which the dealer seemed to weigh this statement incredulously. The ticking of many clocks among the curious lumber of the shop, and the faint rushing of the cabs in a near thoroughfare, filled up the interval of silence.

'Well, sir,' said the dealer, 'be it so. You are an old customer after all; and if, as you say, you have the chance of a good marriage, far be it from me to be an obstacle. Here is a nice thing for a lady now,' he went on, 'this hand glass – fifteenth century, warranted; comes from a good collection, too; but I reserve the name, in the interests of my customer, who was just like yourself, my dear sir, the nephew and sole heir of a remarkable collector.'

The dealer, while he thus ran on in his dry and biting voice, had stooped to take the object from its place; and, as he had done so, a shock had passed through Markheim, a start both of hand and foot, a sudden leap of many tumultuous passions to the face. It passed as swiftly as it came, and left no trace beyond a certain trembling of the hand that now received the glass.

'A glass,' he said hoarsely, and then paused, and repeated it more clearly. 'A glass? For Christmas? Surely not?'

'And why not?' cried the dealer. 'Why not a glass?'

Markheim was looking upon him with an indefinable expression. 'You ask me why not?' he said. 'Why, look here – look in it – look at yourself! Do you like to see it? No! nor I – nor any man.'

The little man had jumped back when Markheim had so suddenly confronted him with the mirror; but now, perceiving there was nothing worse on hand, he chuckled. 'Your future lady, sir, must be pretty hard favoured,' said he.

'I ask you,' said Markheim, 'for a Christmas present, and you give me this – this damned reminder of years, and sins and follies – this hand-conscience! Did you mean it? Had you a thought in your mind? Tell me. It will be better for you if you do. Come, tell me about yourself. I hazard a guess now, that you are in secret a very charitable man?'

The dealer looked closely at his companion. It was very odd, Markheim did not appear to be laughing; there was something in his face like an eager sparkle of hope, but nothing of mirth.

'What are you driving at?' the dealer asked.

'Not charitable?' returned the other gloomily. 'Not charitable; not pious; not scrupulous; unloving, unbeloved; a hand to get money, a safe to keep it. Is that all? Dear God, man, is that all?'

'I will tell you what it is,' began the dealer, with some sharpness, and then broke off again into a chuckle. 'But I see this is a love match of yours, and you have been drinking the lady's health.'

'Ah!' cried Markheim, with a strange curiosity. 'Ah, have you been in love? Tell me about that.'

'I,' cried the dealer. 'I in love! I never had the time, nor have I the time today for all this nonsense. Will you take the glass?'

'Where is the hurry?' returned Markheim. 'It is very pleasant to stand here talking; and life is so short and insecure that I would not hurry away from any pleasure – no, not even from so mild a one as this. We should rather cling, cling to what little we can get, like a man at a cliff's edge. Every second is a cliff, if you think upon it – a cliff a mile high – high enough, if we fall, to dash us out of every feature of humanity. Hence it is best to talk pleasantly. Let us talk of each other: why should we wear this mask? Let us be confidential. Who knows, we might become friends?'

'I have just one word to say to you,' said the dealer. 'Either make your purchase, or walk out of my shop!'

'True, true,' said Markheim. 'Enough fooling. To business. Show me something else.'

The dealer stooped once more, this time to replace the glass upon the shelf, his thin blond hair falling over his eyes as he did so. Markheim moved a little nearer, with one hand in the pocket of his greatcoat; he drew himself up and filled his lungs; at the same time many different emotions were depicted together on his face – terror, horror, and resolve, fascination and a physical repulsion; and through a haggard lift of his upper lip, his teeth looked out.

'This, perhaps, may suit,' observed the dealer: and then, as he began to re-arise, Markheim bounded from behind upon his victim. The long, skewer-like dagger flashed and fell. The dealer struggled like a hen, striking his temple on the shelf, and then tumbled on the floor in a heap.

Time had some score of small voices in that shop, some stately and slow as was becoming to their great age; others garrulous and hurried. All these told out the seconds in an intricate chorus of tickings. Then the passage of a lad's feet, heavily running on the pavement, broke in upon these smaller voices and startled Markheim into the consciousness of his surroundings. He looked about him awfully. The candle stood on the counter, its flame solemnly wagging in a draught; and by that inconsiderable movement, the whole room was filled with noiseless bustle and kept heaving like a sea: the tall shadows nodding, the gross blots of darkness swelling and dwindling as with respiration, the faces of the portraits and the china gods changing and wavering like images in water. The inner door stood ajar, and peered into that leaguer of shadows with a long slit of daylight like a pointing finger.

From these fear-stricken rovings, Markheim's eyes returned to the body of his victim, where it lay both humped and sprawling, incredibly small and strangely meaner than in life. In these poor, miserly clothes, in that ungainly attitude, the dealer lay like so much sawdust. Markheim had feared to see it, and, lo! it was nothing. And yet, as he gazed, this bundle of old clothes and pool of blood began to find eloquent voices. There it must lie; there was none to work the cunning hinges or direct the miracle of locomotion – there it must lie till it was found. Found! ay, and then? Then would this dead flesh lift up a cry that would ring over England, and fill the world with the echoes of pursuit. Ay, dead or not, this was still the enemy. 'Time was that when the brains were out,' he thought; and the first word struck into his mind. Time, now that the deed was accomplished – time, which had closed for the victim, had become instant and momentous for the slayer.

The thought was yet in his mind, when, first one and then another, with every variety of pace and voice – one deep as the bell from a cathedral turret, another ringing on its treble notes the prelude of a waltz – the clocks began to strike the hour of three in the afternoon.

The sudden outbreak of so many tongues in that dumb chamber staggered him. He began to bestir himself, going to and fro with the candle, beleaguered by moving shadows, and startled to the soul by chance reflections. In many rich mirrors, some of home design, some from Venice or Amsterdam, he saw his face repeated and repeated, as it were an army of spies; his own eyes met and detected him; and the sound of his own steps, lightly as they fell, vexed the surrounding quiet. And still, as he continued to fill his pockets, his mind accused him with a sickening iteration, of the thousand faults of his design. He should have chosen a more quiet hour; he should have prepared an alibi; he should not have used a knife; he should have been more cautious, and only bound and gagged the dealer, and not killed him; he should have been more bold, and killed the servant also; he should have done all things otherwise: poignant regrets, weary, incessant toiling of the mind to change what was unchangeable, to plan what was now useless, to be the architect of the irrevocable past. Meanwhile, and behind all this activity, brute terrors, like the scurrying of rats in a deserted attic, filled the more remote chambers of his brain with riot; the hand of the constable would fall heavy on his shoulder, and his nerves would jerk like a hooked fish; or he beheld, in galloping defile, the dock, the prison, the gallows, and the black coffin.

Terror of the people in the street sat down before his mind like a besieging army. It was impossible, he thought, but that some rumour of the struggle must have reached their ears and set on edge their curiosity; and now, in all the neighbouring houses, he divined them sitting motionless and with uplifted ear – solitary people, condemned to spend Christmas dwelling alone on memories of the past, and now startingly recalled from that tender exercise; happy family parties, struck into silence round the table, the mother still with raised finger: every degree and age and humour, but all, by their own hearths, prying and hearkening and weaving the rope that was to hang him. Sometimes it seemed to him he could not move too softly; the clink of the tall Bohemian goblets rang out loudly like a bell; and alarmed by the bigness of the ticking, he was tempted to stop the clocks. And then, again, with a swift transition of his terrors, the very silence of the place appeared a source of peril, and a thing to strike and freeze the passer-by; and he would step more boldly, and bustle aloud among the contents of the shop, and imitate, with elaborate bravado, the movements of a busy man at ease in his own house.

But he was now so pulled about by different alarms that, while one portion of his mind was still alert and cunning, another trembled on the brink of lunacy. One hallucination in particular took a strong hold on his credulity. The neighbour hearkening with white face beside his window, the passer-by arrested by a horrible surmise on the pavement – these could at worst suspect, they could not know; through the brick walls and shuttered windows only sounds could penetrate. But here, within the house, was he alone? He knew he was; he had watched the servant set forth sweet-hearting, in her poor best, 'out for the day' written in every ribbon and smile. Yes, he was alone, of course; and yet, in the bulk of empty house above him, he could surely hear a stir of delicate footing – he was surely conscious, inexplicably conscious of some presence. Ay, surely; to every room and corner of the house his imagination followed it; and now it was a faceless thing, and yet had eyes to see with; and again it was a shadow of himself; and yet again behold the image of the dead dealer, reinspired with cunning and hatred.

At times, with a strong effort, he would glance at the open door which still seemed to repel his eyes. The house was tall, the skylight small and dirty, the day blind with fog; and the light that filtered down to the ground story was exceedingly faint, and showed dimly on the threshold of the shop. And yet, in that strip of doubtful brightness, did there not hang wavering a shadow?

Suddenly, from the street outside, a very jovial gentleman began to beat with a staff on the shop-door, accompanying his blows with shouts and railleries in which the dealer was continually called upon by name. Markheim, smitten into ice, glanced at the dead man. But no! he lay quite still; he was fled away far beyond earshot of these blows and shoutings; he was sunk beneath seas of silence; and his name, which would once have caught his notice above the howling of a storm, had become an empty sound. And presently the jovial gentleman desisted from his knocking and departed.

Here was a broad hint to hurry what remained to be done, to get forth from this accusing neighbourhood, to plunge into a bath of London multitudes, and to reach, on the other side of day, that haven of safety and apparent innocence – his bed. One visitor had come: at any moment another might follow and be more obstinate. To have done the deed, and yet not to reap the profit, would be too abhorrent a failure. The money, that was now Markheim's concern; and as a means to that, the keys.

He glanced over his shoulder at the open door, where the shadow was still lingering and shivering; and with no conscious repugnance of the mind, yet with a tremor of the belly, he drew near the body of his victim. The human character had quite departed. Like a suit half-stuffed with bran, the limbs lay scattered, the trunk doubled, on the floor; and yet the thing repelled him. Although so dingy and inconsiderable to the eye, he feared it might have more significance to the touch. He took the body by the shoulders, and turned it on its back. It was strangely light and supple, and the limbs, as if they had been broken, fell into the oddest postures. The face was robbed of all expression; but it was as pale as wax, and shockingly smeared with blood about one temple. That was, for Markheim, the one displeasing circumstance. It carried him back, upon the instant, to a certain fair-day in a fishers' village: a gray day, a piping wind, a crowd upon

117

the street, the blare of brasses, the booming of drums, the nasal voice of a ballad singer; and a boy going to and fro, buried over head in the crowd and divided between interest and fear, until, coming out upon the chief place of concourse, he beheld a booth and a great screen with pictures, dismally designed, garishly coloured: Brownrigg with her apprentice; the Mannings with their murdered guest; Weare in the death-grip of Thurtell; and a score besides of famous crimes. The thing was as clear as an illusion; he was once again that little boy; he was looking once again, and with the same sense of physical revolt, at these vile pictures; he was still stunned by the thumping of the drums. A bar of that day's music returned upon his memory; and at that, for the first time, a qualm came over him, a breath of nausea, a sudden weakness of the joints, which he must instantly resist and conquer.

He judged it more prudent to confront than to flee from these considerations; looking the more hardily in the dead face, bending his mind to realise the nature and greatness of his crime. So little a while ago that face had moved with every change of sentiment, that pale mouth had spoken, that body had been all on fire with governable energies; and now, and by his act, that piece of life had been arrested, as the horologist, with interjected finger, arrests the beating of the clock. So he reasoned in vain; he could rise to no more remorseful consciousness; the same heart which had shuddered before the painted effigies of crime, looked on its reality unmoved. At best, he felt a gleam of pity for one who had been endowed in vain with all those faculties that can make the world a garden of enchantment, one who had never lived and who was now dead. But of penitence, no, not a tremor.

With that, shaking himself clear of these considerations, he found the keys and advanced towards the open door of the shop. Outside, it had begun to rain smartly; and the sound of the shower upon the roof had banished silence. Like some dripping cavern, the chambers of the house were haunted by an incessant echoing, which filled the ear and mingled with the ticking of the clocks. And, as Markheim approached the door, he seemed to hear, in answer to his own cautious tread, the steps of another foot withdrawing up the stair. The shadow still palpitated loosely on the threshold. He threw a ton's weight of resolve upon his muscles, and drew back the door.

The faint, foggy daylight glimmered dimly on the bare floor and stairs; on the bright suit of armour posted, halbert in hand, upon the landing; and on the dark wood-carvings, and framed pictures that hung against the yellow panels of the wainscot. So loud was the beating of the rain through all the house that, in Markheim's ears, it began to be distinguished into many different sounds. Footsteps and sighs, the tread of regiments marching in the distance, the chink of money in the counting, and the creaking of doors held stealthily ajar, appeared to mingle with the patter of the drops upon the cupola and the gushing of the water in the pipes. The sense that he was not alone grew upon him to the verge of madness. On every side he was haunted and begirt by presences. He heard them moving in the upper chambers; from the shop, he heard the dead man getting to his legs; and as he began with a great effort to mount the stairs, feet fled quietly before him and followed stealthily behind. If he were but deaf, he thought, how tranquilly he would possess his soul! And then again, and hearkening with ever fresh attention, he blessed himself for that unresting sense which held the outposts and stood a trusty sentinel upon his life. His head turned continually on his neck; his eyes, which seemed starting from their orbits, scouted on every side, and on every side were half-rewarded as with the tail of something nameless vanishing. The four-and-twenty steps to the first floor were four-and-twenty agonies.

On that first storey, the doors stood ajar, three of them like three ambushes, shaking his nerves like the throats of cannon. He could never again, he felt, be sufficiently immured and fortified from men's observing eyes; he longed to be home, girt in by walls, buried among bedclothes, and invisible to all but God. And at that thought he wondered a little, recollecting tales of other murderers and the fear they were said to entertain of heavenly avengers. It was not so, at least, with him. He feared the laws of nature, lest, in their callous and immutable procedure, they should preserve some damning evidence of his crime. He feared tenfold more, with a slavish, superstitious terror, some scission in the continuity of man's experience, some wilful illegality of nature. He played a game of skill, depending on the rules, calculating consequence from cause; and what if nature, as the defeated tyrant overthrew the chess-board, should break the mould of their succession? The like had befallen Napoleon (so writers said) when the winter changed the time of its appearance. The like might befall Markheim: the solid walls might become transparent and reveal his doings like those of bees in a glass hive; the stout planks might yield under his foot like quicksands and detain him in their clutch; ay, and there were soberer accidents that might destroy him: if, for instance, the house should fall and imprison him beside the body of his victim; or the house next door should fly on fire, and the firemen invade him from all sides. These things he feared; and, in a sense, these things might be called the hands of God reached forth against sin. But about God Himself he was at ease; his act was doubtless exceptional, but so were his excuses, which God knew; it was there, and not among men, that he felt sure of justice.

When he had got safe into the drawing-room, and shut the door behind him, he was aware of a respite from alarms. The room was quite dismantled, uncarpeted besides, and strewn with packing cases and incongruous furniture; several great pier-glasses, in which he beheld himself at various angles, like an actor on a stage; many pictures, framed and unframed, standing, with their faces to the wall; a fine Sheraton sideboard, a cabinet of marquetry, and a great old bed, with tapestry hangings. The windows opened to the floor; but by great good fortune the lower part of the shutters had been closed, and this concealed him from the neighbours. Here, then, Markheim drew in a packing case before the cabinet, and began to search among the keys. It was a long business, for there were many; and it was irksome, besides; for, after all, there might be nothing in the cabinet, and time was on the wing. But the closeness of the occupation sobered him. With the tail of his eye he saw the door – even glanced at it from time to time directly, like a besieged commander pleased to verify the good estate of his defences. But in truth he was at peace. The rain falling in the street sounded natural and pleasant. Presently, on the other side, the notes of a piano were wakened to the music of a hymn, and the voices of many children took up the air and words. How stately, how comfortable was the melody! How fresh the youthful voices! Markheim gave ear to it smilingly, as he sorted out the keys; and his mind was thronged with answerable ideas and images; church-going children and the pealing of the high organ; children afield, bathers by the brookside, ramblers on the brambly common, kite-flyers in the windy and cloud-navigated sky; and then, at another cadence of the hymn, back again to church, and the somnolence of summer Sundays, and the high genteel voice of the parson (which he smiled a little to recall) and the painted Jacobean tombs, and the dim lettering of the Ten Commandments in the chancel.

And as he sat thus, at once busy and absent, he was startled to his feet. A flash of ice, a flash of fire, a bursting gush of blood, went over him, and then he stood transfixed and thrilling. A step mounted the stair slowly and steadily, and presently a hand was laid upon the knob, and the lock clicked, and the door opened.

Fear held Markheim in a vice. What to expect he knew not, whether the dead man walking, or the official ministers of human justice, or some chance witness blindly stumbling in to consign him to the gallows. But when a face was thrust into the aperture, glanced round the room, looked at him, nodded and smiled as if in friendly recognition, and then withdrew again, and the door closed behind it, his fear broke loose from his control in a hoarse cry. At the sound of this the visitant returned.

'Did you call me?' he asked pleasantly, and with that he entered the room and closed the door behind him.

Markheim stood and gazed at him with all his eyes. Perhaps there was a film upon his sight, but the outlines of the newcomer seemed to change and waver like those of the idols in the wavering candlelight of the shop; and at times he thought he knew him; and at times he thought he bore a likeness to himself; and always, like a lump of living terror, there lay in his bosom the conviction that this thing was not of the earth and not of God.

And yet the creature had a strange air of the commonplace, as he stood looking on Markheim with a smile; and when he added: 'You are looking for the money, I believe?' it was in the tones of everyday politeness.

Markheim made no answer.

'I should warn you,' resumed the other, 'that the maid has left her sweetheart earlier than usual and will soon be here. If Mr. Markheim be found in this house, I need not describe to him the consequences.'

'You know me?' cried the murderer.

The visitor smiled. 'You have long been a favourite of mine,' he said; 'and I have long observed and often sought to help you.'

'What are you?' cried Markheim: 'the devil?'

'What I may be,' returned the other, 'cannot affect the service I propose to render you.'

'It can,' cried Markheim; 'it does! Be helped by you? No, never; not by you! You do not know me yet; thank God, you do not know me!'

'I know you,' replied the visitant, with a sort of kind severity or rather firmness. 'I know you to the soul.'

'Know me!' cried Markheim. 'Who can do so? My life is but a travesty and slander on myself. I have lived to belie my nature. All men do; all men are better than this disguise that grows about and stifles them. You see each dragged away by life, like one whom bravos have seized and muffled in a cloak. If they had their own control – if you could see their faces, they would be altogether different, they would shine out for heroes and saints! I am worse than most; myself is more overlaid; my excuse is known to me and God. But, had I the time, I could disclose myself.'

'To me?' inquired the visitant.

'To you before all,' returned the murderer. 'I supposed you were intelligent. I thought – since you exist – you would prove a reader of the heart. And yet you would propose to judge me by my acts! Think of it; my acts! I was born and I have lived in a land of giants; giants have dragged me by the wrists since I was born out of my mother – the giants of circumstance. And you would judge me by my acts! But can you not look within? Can you not understand that evil is hateful to me? Can you not see within me the clear writing of conscience, never blurred by any wilful sophistry, although too often disregarded? Can you not read me for a thing that surely must be common as humanity – the unwilling sinner?'

'All this is very feelingly expressed,' was the reply, 'but it regards me not. These points of consistency are beyond my province, and I care not in the least by what compulsion you may have been dragged away, so as you are but carried in the right direction. But time flies; the servant delays, looking in the faces of the crowd and at the pictures on the hoardings, but still she keeps moving nearer; and remember, it is as if the gallows itself was striding towards you through the Christmas streets! Shall I help you; I, who know all? Shall I tell you where to find the money?'

'For what price?' asked Markheim.

'I offer you the service for a Christmas gift,' returned the other.

Markheim could not refrain from smiling with a kind of bitter triumph. 'No,' said he, 'I will take nothing at your hands; if I were dying of thirst, and it was your hand that put the pitcher to my lips, I should find the courage to refuse. It may be credulous, but I will do nothing to commit myself to evil.'

'I have no objection to a deathbed repentance,' observed the visitant.

'Because you disbelieve their efficacy!' Markheim cried.

'I do no say so,' returned the other; 'but I look on these things from a different side, and when the life is done my interest falls. The man has lived to serve me, to spread black looks under colour of religion, or to sow tares in the wheat-field, as you do, in a course of weak compliance with desire. Now that he draws so near to his deliverance, he can add but one act of service – to repent, to die smiling, and thus to build up in confidence and hope the more timorous of my surviving followers. I am not so hard a master. Try me. Accept my help. Please yourself in life as you have done hitherto; please yourself more amply, spread your elbows at the board; and when the night begins to fall and the curtains to be drawn, I tell you, for your greater comfort, that you will find it even easy to compound your quarrel with your conscience, and to make a truckling peace with God. I came but now from such a deathbed, and the room was full of sincere mourners, listening to the man's last words: and when I looked into that face, which had been set as a flint against mercy, I found it smiling with hope'.

'And do you, then, suppose me such a creature?' asked Markheim. 'Do you think I have no more generous aspirations than to sin, and sin, and sin, and, at the last, sneak into heaven? My heart rises at the thought. Is this, then, your experience of mankind? or is it because you find me with red hands that you presume such baseness? and is this crime of murder indeed so impious as to dry up the very springs of good?'

'Murder is to me no special category,' replied the other. 'All sins are murder, even as all life is war. I behold your race, like starving mariners on a raft, plucking crusts out of the hands of famine and feeding on each other's lives. I follow sins beyond the moment of their acting; I find in all that the last consequence is death; and to my eyes, the pretty maid who thwarts her mother with such taking graces on a question of a ball, drips no less visibly with human gore than such a murderer as yourself. Do I say that I follow sins? I follow virtues also; they differ not by the thickness of a nail, they are both scythes for the reaping angel of Death. Evil, for which I live, consists not in action but in character. The bad man is dear to me; not the bad act, whose fruits, if we could follow them far enough down the hurtling cataract of the ages, might yet be found more blessed than those of the rarest virtues. And it is not because you have killed a dealer, but because you are Markheim, that I offer to forward your escape.'

'I will lay my heart open to you,' answered Markheim. 'This crime on which you find me is my last. On my way to it I have learned many lessons; itself is a lesson, a momentous lesson. Hitherto I have been driven with revolt to what I would not; I was a bond-slave to poverty, driven and scourged. There are robust virtues that can stand in these temptations; mine was not so: I had a thirst of pleasure. But today, and out of this deed, I pluck both warning and riches – both the power and fresh resolve to be myself. I become in all things a free actor in the world; I begin to see myself all changed, these hands the agents of good, this heart at peace. Something comes over me out of the past; something of what I have dreamed on Sabbath evenings to the sound of the church organ, of what I forecast when I shed tears over noble books, or talked, an innocent child, with my mother. There lies my life; I have wandered a few years, but now I see once more my city of destination.'

'You are to use this money on the Stock Exchange, I think?' remarked the visitor; 'and there, if I mistake not, you have already lost some thousands?'

'Ah,' said Markheim, 'but this time I have a sure thing.'

'This time, again, you will lose,' replied the visitor quietly.

'Ah, but I keep back the half!' cried Markheim.

'That also you will lose,' said the other.

The sweat started upon Markheim's brow. 'Well, then, what matter?' he exclaimed. 'Say it be lost, say I am plunged again in poverty, shall one part of me, and that the worse, continue until the end to override the better? Evil and good run strong in me, haling me both ways. I do not love the one thing, I love all. I can conceive great deeds, renunciations, martyrdoms; and though I be fallen to such a crime as murder, pity is no stranger to my thoughts. I pity the poor; who knows their trials better than myself? I pity and help them; I prize love, I love honest laughter; there is no good thing nor true thing on earth but I love it from my heart. And are my vices only to direct my life, and my virtues to lie without effect, like some passive lumber of the mind? Not so; good, also, is a spring of acts.'

But the visitant raised his finger. 'For six-and-thirty years that you have been in this world,' said he, 'through many changes of fortune and varieties of humour, I have watched you steadily fall. Fifteen years ago you would have started at a theft. Three years back you would have blenched at the name of murder. Is there any crime, is there any cruelty or meanness, from which you still recoil? – five years from now I shall detect you in the fact! Downward, downward, lies your way; nor can anything but death avail to stop you.'

'It is true,' Markheim said huskily, 'I have in some degree complied with evil. But it is so with all: the very saints, in the mere exercise of living, grow less dainty, and take on the tone of their surroundings.'

'I will propound to you one simple question,' said the other; 'and as you answer, I shall read to you your moral horoscope. You have grown in many things more lax; possibly you do right to be so; and at any account, it is the same with all men. But granting that, are you in any one particular, however trifling, more difficult to please with your own conduct, or do you go in all things with a looser rein?'

'In any one?' repeated Markheim, with an anguish of considera-tion. 'No,' he added, with despair, 'in none! I have gone down in all.'

'Then,' said the visitor, 'content yourself with what you are, for you will never change; and the words of your part on this stage are irrevocably written down.'

Markheim stood for a long while silent, and indeed it was the visitor who first broke the silence. 'That being so,' he said, 'shall I show you the money?'

'And grace?' cried Markheim.

'Have you not tried it?' returned the other. 'Two or three years ago, did I not see you on the platform of revival meetings, and was not your voice the loudest in the hymn?'

'It is true,' said Markheim; 'and I see clearly what remains for me by way of duty. I thank you for these lessons from my soul; my eyes are opened, and I behold myself at last for what I am.'

At this moment, the sharp note of the door-bell rang through the house; and the visitant, as though this were some concerted signal for which he had been waiting, changed at once in his demeanour.

'The maid!' he cried. 'She has returned, as I forewarned you, and there is now before you one more difficult passage. Her master, you must say, is ill; you must let her in, with an assured but rather serious countenance – no smiles, no overacting, and I promise you success! Once the girl within, and the door closed, the same dexterity that has already rid you of the dealer will relieve you of this last danger in your path. Thenceforward you have the whole evening – the whole night, if needful – to ransack the treasures of the house and to make good your safety. This is help that comes to you with the mask of danger. Up!' he cried, 'up, friend; your life hangs trembling in the scales: up, and act!'

Markheim steadily regarded his counsellor. 'If I be condemned to evil acts,' he said, 'there is still one door of freedom open – I can cease from action. If my life be an ill thing, I can lay it down. Though I be, as you say truly, at the beck of every small temptation, I can yet, by one decisive gesture, place myself beyond the reach of all. My love of good is damned to barrenness; it may, and let it be! But I have still my hatred of evil; and from that, to your galling disappointment, you shall see that I can draw both energy and courage."

The features of the visitor began to undergo a wonderful and lovely change: they brightened and softened with a tender triumph, and, even as they brightened, faded and dislimned. But Markheim did not pause to watch or understand the transformation. He opened the door and went downstairs very slowly, thinking to himself. His past went soberly before him; he beheld it as it was, ugly and strenuous like a dream, random as chance-medley – a scene of defeat. Life, as he thus reviewed it, tempted him no longer; but on the farther side he perceived a quiet haven for his bark. He paused in the passage, and looked into the shop, where the candle still burned by the dead body. It was strangely silent. Thoughts of the dealer swarmed into his mind, as he stood gazing. And then the bell once more broke out into impatient clamour.

He confronted the maid upon the threshold with something like a smile.

'You had better go for the police,' said he: 'I have killed your master.'

The Selfish Giant
Oscar Wilde

Every afternoon, as they were coming from school, the children used to go and play in the Giant's garden.

It was a large lovely garden, with soft green grass. Here and there over the grass stood beautiful flowers like stars, and there were twelve peach-trees that in the spring-time broke out into delicate blossoms of pink and pearl, and in the autumn bore rich fruit. The birds sat on the trees and sang so sweetly that the children used to stop their games in order to listen to them. 'How happy we are here!' they cried to each other.

One day the giant came back. He had been to visit his friend the Cornish ogre, and had stayed with him for seven years. After the seven years were over he had said all that he had to say, for his conversation was limited, and he determined to return to his own castle. When he arrived he saw the children playing in the garden.

'What are you doing there?' he cried in a very gruff voice, and the children ran away.

'My own garden is my own garden,' said the Giant; 'any one can understand that, and I will allow nobody to play in it but myself.' So he built a high wall all round it, and put up a notice-board.

TRESPASSERS

WILL BE

PROSECUTED

He was a very selfish Giant.

The poor children had now nowhere to play. They tried to play on the road, but the road was very dusty and full of hard stones, and they did not like it. They used to wander round the high wall when their lessons were over, and talk about the beautiful garden inside. 'How happy we were there,' they said to each other.

Then the Spring came, and all over the country there were little blossoms and little birds. Only in the garden of the Selfish Giant it was still winter. The birds did not care to sing in it as there were no children, and the trees forgot to blossom. Once a beautiful flower put its head out from the grass, but when it saw the notice-board it was so sorry for the children that it slipped back into the ground again, and went off to sleep. The only people who were pleased were the Snow and the Frost. 'Spring has forgotten this garden,' they cried, 'so we will live here all the year round.' The Snow covered up the grass with her great white cloak, and the Frost painted all the trees silver. Then they invited the North Wind to stay with them, and he came. He was wrapped in furs, and he roared all day about the garden, and blew the chimney-pots down. 'This is a delightful spot,' he said, 'we must ask the Hail on a visit.' So the Hail came. Every day for three hours he rattled on the roof of the castle till he broke most of the slates, and then he ran round and round the garden as fast as he could go. He was dressed in grey, and his breath was like ice.

'I cannot understand why the Spring is so late in coming,' said the Selfish Giant, as he sat at the window and looked out at his cold white garden; 'I hope there will be a change in the weather.'

But the Spring never came, nor the Summer. The Autumn gave gold fruit to every garden, but to the Giant's garden she gave none. 'He is too selfish,' she said. So it was always Winter there and the North Wind and the Hail, and the Frost, and the Snow danced about through the trees.

One morning the Giant was lying awake in bed when he heard some lovely music. It sounded so sweet to his ears that he thought it must be the King's musicians passing by. It was really only a little linnet singing outside his window, but it was so long since he had heard a bird sing in his garden that it seemed to him to be the most beautiful music in the world. Then the Hail stopped dancing over his head, and the North Wind ceased roaring, and a delicious perfume came to him through the open casement. 'I believe the spring has come at last,' said the Giant; and he jumped out of bed and looked out.

What did he see?

He saw a most wonderful sight. Through a little hole in the wall the children had crept in, and they were sitting in the branches of the trees. In every tree that he could see there was a little child. And the trees were so glad to have the children back again that they had covered themselves with blossoms, and were waving their arms gently above the children's heads. The birds were flying about and twittering with delight, and the flowers were looking up through the green grass and laughing. It was a lovely scene, only in one corner it was still winter. It was the farthest corner of the garden, and in it was standing a little boy. He was so small that he could not reach up to the branches of the tree, and he was wandering all round it, crying bitterly. The poor tree was still quite covered with frost and snow, and the North Wind was blowing and roaring above it. 'Climb up! little boy,' said the Tree, and it bent its branches down as low as it could; but the boy was too tiny.

And the Giant's heart melted as he looked out. 'How selfish I have been!' he said; 'now I know why the Spring would not come here. I will put that poor little boy on the top of the tree, and then I will knock down the wall, and my garden shall be the children's play-ground for ever and ever.' He was really very sorry for what he had done.

So he crept downstairs and opened the front door quite softly, and went out into the garden. But when the children saw him they were so frightened that they all ran away, and the garden became winter again. Only the little boy did not run, for his eyes were so full of tears that he did not see the Giant coming. And the Giant stole up behind him and took him gently in his hand, and put him up into the tree. And the tree broke at once into blossom, and the birds came and sang on it, and the little boy stretched out his two arms and flung them round the Giant's neck, and kissed him. And the other children, when they saw that the Giant was not wicked any longer, came running back, and with them came the Spring. 'It is your garden now, little children,' said the Giant, and he took a great axe and knocked down the wall. And when the people were going to market at twelve o'clock they found the Giant playing with the children in the most beautiful garden they had ever seen.

All day long they played, and in the evening they came to the Giant to bid him good-bye.

'But where is your little companion?' he said: 'the boy I put into the tree.' The Giant loved him the best because he had kissed him.

'We don't know,' answered the children; 'he has gone away.'

'You must tell him to be sure and come here tomorrow,' said the Giant. but the children said that they did not know where he lived, and had never seen him before; and the Giant felt very sad.

Every afternoon, when school was over, the children came and played with the Giant. Bu the little boy whom the Giant loved was never seen again. The Giant was very kind to all the children, yet he longed for his first little friend, and often spoke of him. 'How I would like to see him!' he used to say.

Years went over, and the Giant grew very old and feeble. He could not play about any more, so he sat in a huge armchair, and watched the children at their games, and admired his garden. 'I have many beautiful flowers,' he said; 'but the children are the most beautiful flowers of all.'

One winter morning he looked out of his window as he was dressing. He did not hate the winter now, for he knew that it was merely the Spring asleep, and that the flowers were resting.

Suddenly he rubbed his eyes in wonder, and looked and looked. It certainly was a marvellous sight. In the farthest corner of the garden was a tree quite covered with lovely white blossoms. Its branches were all golden, and silver fruit hung down from them, and underneath it stood the little boy he had loved.

Downstairs ran the Giant in great joy, and out into the garden. He hastened across the grass, and came near to the child. And when he came quite close his face grew red with anger, and he said, 'Who hath dared to wound thee?' For on the palms of the child's hands were the prints of two nails, and the prints of two nails were on the little feet.

'Who hath dared to wound thee?' cried the Giant; 'tell me, that I may take my big sword and slay him.'

'Nay!' answered the child; 'but these are the wounds of Love.'

'Who art thou?' said the Giant, and a strange awe fell on him, and he knelt before the little child.

And the child smiled on the Giant, and said to him, You let me play once in your garden, today you shall come with me to my garden, which is Paradise.'

And when the children ran in that afternoon, they found the Giant lying dead under the tree, all covered with white blossoms.

Old Mrs Chundle
Thomas Hardy

The curate had not been a week in the parish, but the autumn morning proving fine, he thought he would make a little water-colour sketch, showing a distant view of the Corvsgate ruin two miles off, which he had passed on his way hither. The sketch occupied him a longer time than he had anticipated. The luncheon hour drew on, and he felt hungry.

Quite near him was a stone-built old cottage of respectable and substantial build. He entered it, and was received by an old woman.

'Can you give me something to eat, my good woman?' he said.

She held her hand to her ear.

'Can you give me something for lunch?' he shouted. 'Bread and cheese – anything will do.'

A sour look crossed her face, and she shook her head. 'That's unlucky,' murmured he. She reflected and said more urbanely, 'Well, I'm going to have my own bit o' dinner in no such long time hence. 'Tis taters and cabbage, boiled with a scantling o' bacon. Would ye like it? But I suppose 'tis the wrong sort, and that ye would sooner have bread and cheese.'

'No, I'll join you. Call me when it is ready. I'm just out here.'

'Ay, I've seen ye. Drawing the old stones, baint ye?'

'Yes, my good woman.'

'Sure 'tis well some folk have nothing better to do with their time. Very well, I'll call ye, when I've dished up.'

He went out and resumed his painting; till in about seven or ten minutes the old woman appeared at her door and held up her hand. The curate washed his brush, went to the brook, rinsed his hands and proceeded to the house.

'There's yours,' she said, pointing to the table. 'I'll have my bit here.' And she denoted the settle.

'Why not join me?'

'Oh, faith, I don't want to eat with my betters – not I.' And she continued firm in her resolution, and ate apart.

The vegetables had been well cooked over a wood fire – the only way to cook a vegetable properly – and the bacon was well boiled. The curate ate heartily: he thought he had never tasted such potatoes and cabbage in his life, which he probably had not, for they had been just brought in from the garden, so that the very freshness of the morning was still in them. When he had finished he asked her how much he owed for the repast, which he had much enjoyed.

'Oh, I don't want to be paid for that bit of snack 'a b'lieve!'

'But really you must take something. It was an excellent meal.'

''Tis all my own growing, that's true. But I don't take money for a bit o' victuals. I've never done such a thing in my life.'

'I should feel much happier if you would.'

She seemed unsettled by his feeling, and added as by compulsion, 'Well, then; I suppose twopence won't hurt ye?'

'Twopence?'

'Yes. Twopence.'

'Why my good woman, that's no charge at all. I am sure it is worth this, at least.' And he laid down a shilling.

'I tell 'ee 'tis *twopence*, and no more!' she said primly. 'Why, bless the man, it didn't cost me more than three halfpence, and that leaves me a fair quarter profit. The bacon is the heaviest item; that may perhaps be a penny. The taters I've got plenty of, and the cabbage is going to waste.'

He thereupon argued no further, paid the limited sum demanded, and went to the door. 'And where does that road lead?, he asked, by way of engaging her in a little friendly conversation before parting, and pointing to a white lane which branched from the direct highway near her door.

'They tell me that it leads to Enckworth.'

'And how far is Enckworth?'

'Three miles, they say. But God knows if 'tis true.'

'You haven't lived here long, then?'

'Five-and-thirty year come Martinmas.'

'And yet you have never been to Enckworth?'

'Not I. Why should I ever have been to Enckworth? I never had any business there – a great mansion of a place, holding people that I've no more doings with than with the people of the moon. No, there's on'y two places I ever go to from year's end to year's end: that's once a fortnight to Anglebury, to do my bit o' marketing, and once a week to my parish church.'

'Which is that?'

'Why, Kingscreech.'

'Oh – then you are in my parish?'

'Maybe. Just on the outskirts.'

'I didn't know the parish extended so far. I'm a newcomer. Well, I hope we may meet again. Good afternoon to you,'

When the curate was next talking to his rector he casually observed: 'By the way, that's a curious old soul who lives out towards Corvsgate – old Mrs – I don't known her name – A deaf old woman.'

'You mean old Mrs Chundle, I suppose.'

'She tells me she's lived there five-and-thirty years, and has never been to Enckworth, three miles off. She goes to two places only, from year's end to year's end – to the market town, and to church on Sundays.'

'To church on Sundays. H'm. She rather exaggerates her travels, to my thinking. I've been rector here thirteen years, and I have certainly never seen her at church in my time.'

'A wicked old woman. What can she think of herself for such deception!'

'She didn't know you belonged here when she said it, and could find out the untruth of her story. I warrant she wouldn't have said it to me!' And the rector chuckled.

On reflection the curate felt that this was decidedly a case for his ministrations, and on the first spare morning he strode across to the cottage beyond the ruin. He found its occupant of course at home.

'Drawing picters again?' she asked, looking up from the hearth, where she was scouring the fire-dogs.

'No, I come on a more important matter, Mrs Chundle. I am the new curate of this parish.'

'You said you was last time. And after you had told me and went away I said to myself, he'll be here again sure enough, hang me if I didn't. And here you be.'

'Yes. I hope you don't mind?'

'Oh, no. You find us a roughish lot, I make no doubt?'

'Well, I won't go into that. But I think it was a very culpable – unkind thing of you to tell me you came to church every Sunday, when I find you've not been seen there for years.'

'Oh, did I tell 'ee that?'

'You certainly did.'

'Now I wonder what I did that for?'

'I wonder too.'

'Well, you could ha' guessed, after all, that I didn't come to any service. Lord, what's the good o' my lumpering all the way to church and back again, when I'm as deaf as a plock? Your own commonsense ought to have told 'ee that 'twas but a figure o' speech, seeing you was a pa'son.'

'Don't you think you could hear the service if you were to sit close to the reading-desk and pulpit?'

'I'm sure I couldn't. Oh no – not a word. Why I couldn't hear anything even at that time when Isaac Coggs used to cry the Amens out loud beyond anything that's done nowadays, and they had the barrel-organ for the tunes – years and years agone, when I was stronger in my narves than now.'

'H'm – I'm sorry. There's one thing I could do, which I would with pleasure, if you'll use it. I could get you an ear-trumpet. Will you use it?'

'Ay, sure. That I woll. I don't care what I use – 'tis all the same to me.'

'And you'll come?'

'Yes. I may as well go there as bide here, I suppose.'

The ear-trumpet was purchased by the zealous young man, and the next Sunday, to the great surprise of the parishioners when they arrived, Mrs Chundle was discovered in the front seat of the nave of Kingscreech Church, facing the rest of the congregation with an unmoved countenance.

She was the centre of observation through the whole morning service. The trumpet, elevated at a high angle, shone and flashed in the sitters' eyes as the chief object in the sacred edifice.

The curate could not speak to her that morning, and called the next day to inquire the result of the experiment. As soon as she saw him in the distance she began shaking her head.

'No, no,' she said decisively as he approached. 'I knowed 'twas all nonsense.'

'What?'

''Twasn't a mossel o' good, and so I could have told 'ee before. A-wasting your money in jimcracks upon a' old 'ooman like me.'

'You couldn't hear? Dear me – how disappointing.'

'You might as well have been mouthing at me from the top o' Creech Barrow.'

'That's unfortunate.'

'I shall never come no more – never – to be made such a fool of as that again.'

The curate mused. 'I'll tell you what, Mrs Chundle. There's one thing more to try, and only one. If that fails I suppose we shall have to give it up. It is a plan I have heard of, though I have never myself tried it; it's having a sound tube fixed, with its lower mouth in the seat immediately below the pulpit, where you would sit, the tube running up inside the pulpit with its upper end opening in a bell-mouth just beside the book-board. The voice of the preacher enters the bell-mouth, and is carried down directly to the listener's ear. Do you understand?.

'Exactly.'

'And you'll come, if I put it up at may own expense?'

'Ay, I suppose, I'll try it, e'en though I said I wouldn't. I may as well do that as do nothing, I reckon.'

The kind-hearted curate, at great trouble to himself, obtained the tube and had it fixed vertically as described, the upper mouth being immediately under the face of whoever should preach, and on the following Sunday morning it was to be tried. As soon as he came from the vestry the curate perceived to his satisfaction Mrs Chundle in the seat beneath, erect and at attention, her head close to the lower orifice of the sound-pipe, and a look of great complacency that her soul required a special machinery to save it, while other people's could be saved in a commonplace way. The rector read the prayers from the desk on the opposite side, which part of the service Mrs Chundle could follow easily enough by the help of the prayer-book; and in due course the curate mounted the eight steps into the wooden octagon, gave out his text, and began to deliver his discourse.

It was a fine frosty morning in early winter, and he had not got far with his sermon when he became conscious of a steam rising from the bellmouth of the tube, obviously caused by Mrs Chundle's breathing at the lower end, and it was accompanied by a suggestion of onion-stew. However, he preached on a while, hoping it would cease, holding in his left hand his finest cambric handkerchief kept especially for Sunday morning services. At length, no longer able to endure the odour, he lightly dropped the handkerchief into the bell of the tube, without stopping for a moment the eloquent flow of his words; and he had the satisfaction of feeling himself in comparatively pure air.

He heard a fidgeting below; and presently there arose to him over the pulpit-edge a hoarse whisper: 'The pipe's chokt!'

'Now, as you will perceive, my brethren,' continued the curate, unheeding the interruption; 'by applying this test to ourselves, our discernment of –'

'The pipe's chokt!' came up in a whisper yet louder and hoarser.

'Our discernment of actions as morally good or indifferent will be much quickened, and we shall be materially helped in our –'

Suddenly came a violent puff of warm wind, and he beheld his handkerchief rising from the bell of the tube and floating to the pulpit floor. The little boys in the gallery laughed, thinking it a miracle. Mrs Chundle had, in fact, applied her mouth to the bottom end, blown with all her might, and cleared the tube. In a few seconds the atmosphere of the pulpit became as before, to the curate's great discomfiture. Yet stop the orifice again he dared not, lest the old woman should make a still greater disturbance and draw the attention of the congregation to this unseemly situation.

'If you carefully analyze the passage I have quoted,' he continued in somewhat uncomfortable accents, 'you will perceive that it naturally suggests three points for consideration –'

('It's not onions: it's peppermint,' he said to himself.)

'Namely, mankind in its unregenerate state –'

('And cider.')

'The incidence of the law, and loving-kindness or grace, which we will now severally consider –'

('And pickled cabbage. What a terrible supper she must have made!')

'Under the twofold aspect of external and internal consciousness.'

Thus the reverend gentlemen continued strenuously for perhaps five minutes longer; then he could stand it no more. Desperately thrusting his thumb into the hole, he drew the threads of his distracted discourse together, the while hearing her blow vigorously to dislodge the plug. But he stuck to the hole, and brought his sermon to a premature close.

He did not call on Mrs Chundle the next week, a slight cooling of his zeal for her spiritual welfare being manifest; but he encountered her at the house of another cottager whom he was visiting; and she immediately addressed him as a partner in the same enterprize.

'I could hear beautiful!' she said. 'Yes; every word! Never did I know such a wonderful machine as that there pipe. But you forgot what you was doing once or twice, and put your handkerchief on the top o' en, and stopped the sound a bit. Please not to do that again, for it makes me lose a lot. Howsomever, I shall come every Sunday morning reg'lar now, please God.'

The curate quivered internally.

'And will ye come to my house once in a while and read to me?'

'Of course.'

Surely enough the next Sunday the ordeal was repeated for him. In the evening he told his trouble to the rector. The rector chuckled.

'You've brought it upon yourself,' he said. 'You don't know this parish so well as I. You should have left the old woman alone.'

'I suppose I should!'

'Thank Heaven, she thinks nothing of my sermons, and doesn't come when I preach. Ha, ha!'

'Well,' said the curate somewhat ruffled, 'I must do something. I cannot stand this. I shall tell her not to come.'

'You can hardly do that.'

'And I've half-promised to go and read to her. But – I shan't go.'

'She's probably forgotten by this time that you promised.'

A vision of his next Sunday in the pulpit loomed horridly before the young man, and at length he determined to escape the experience. The pipe should be taken down. The next morning he gave directions, and the removal was carried out.

A day or two later a message arrived from her, saying that she wished to see him. Anticipating a terrific attack from the irate old woman, he put off going to her for a day, and when he trudged out towards her house on the following afternoon it was in a vexed mood. Delicately nurtured man as he was, he had determined not to re-erect the tube, and hoped he might hit on some new *modus vivendi*, even if any inconvenience to Mrs Chundle, in a situation that had become intolerable as it was last week.

'Thank Heaven, the tube is gone,' he said to himself as he walked; 'and nothing will make me put it up again!'

On coming near he saw to his surprise that the calico curtains of the cottage windows were all drawn. He went up to the door, which was ajar; and a little girl peeped through the opening.

'How is Mrs Chundle?' he asked blandly.

'She's dead, sir,' said the girl in a whisper.

'Dead? . . . Mrs Chundle dead?'

'Yes, sir.'

A woman now came. 'Yes, 'tis so, sir. She went off quite sudden-like about two hours ago. Well, you see, sir, she was over seventy years of age, and last Sunday she was rather late in starting for church, having to put her bit o' dinner ready before going out; and was very anxious to be in time. So she hurried overmuch, and runned up the hill, which at her time of life she ought not to have done. It upset her heart, and she's been poorly all the week since, and that made her send for 'ee. Two or three times she said she hoped you would come soon, as you'd promised to, and you were so staunch and faithful in wishing to do her good, that she knew 'twas not by your own wish you didn't arrive. But she would not let us send again, as it might trouble 'ee too much, and there might be other poor folks needing you. She worried to think she might not be able to listen to 'ee next Sunday, and feared you'd be hurt at it, and think her remiss. But she was eager to hear you again later on. However, 'twas ordained otherwise for the poor soul, and she was soon gone. "I've found a real friend at last," she said. "He's a man in a thousand. He's not ashamed of a' old woman, and he holds that her soul is worth saving as well as richer people's." She said I was to give you this.'

It was a small folded piece of paper, directed to him and sealed with a thimble. On opening it he found it to be what she called her will, in which she had left him her bureau, case-clock, four-post bedstead, and framed sampler – in fact all the furniture of any account that she possessed.

The curate went out, like Peter at the cock-crow. He was a meek young man, and as he went his eyes were wet. When he reached a lonely place in the lane he stood still thinking, and kneeling down in the dust of the road, rested his elbow in one hand and covered his face with the other.

Thus he remained some minutes or so, a black shape on the hot white of the sunned trackway; till he rose, brushed the knees of his trousers, and walked on.

The Song of the Minster
William Canton

When John of Fulda became Prior of Hethholme, says the old chronicle, he brought with him to the Abbey many rare and costly books – beautiful illuminated missals and psalters and portions of the Old and New Testament. And he presented rich vestments to the Minister; albs of fine linen, and copes embroidered with flowers of gold. In the west front he built two great arched windows filled with marvellous storied glass. The shrine of St. Egwin he repaired at vast outlay, adorning it with garlands in gold and silver, but the colour of the flowers was in coloured gems, and in like fashion the little birds in the nooks of the foliage. Stalls and benches of carved oak he placed in the choir; and many other noble works he had wrought in his zeal for the glory of God's house.

In all the western land was there no more fair or stately Minster than this of the Black Monks, with the peaceful township on one side, and on the other the sweet meadows and the acres of wheat and barley sloping down to the slow river, and beyond the river the clearings in the ancient forest.

But Thomas the Sub-prior was grieved and troubled in his mind by the richness and the beauty of all he saw about him, and by the Prior's eagerness to be ever adding some new work in stone, or oak, or metal, or jewels.

'Surely,' he said to himself, 'these things are unprofitable – less to the honour of God than to the pleasure of the eye and the pride of life and the luxury of our house! Had so much treasure not been wasted on these vanities of bright colour and carved stone, our dole to the poor of Christ might have been fourfold, and they filled with good things. But now let our almoner do what best he may, I doubt not many a leper sleeps cold, and many a poor man goes lean with hunger.'

This the Sub-prior said, not because his heart was quick with fellowship for the poor, but because he was of a narrow and gloomy and grudging nature, and he could conceive of no true service of God which was not one of fasting and praying, of joylessness and mortification.

Now you must know that the greatest of the monks and the hermits and the holy men were not of this kind. In their love of God they were blithe of heart, and filled with a rare sweetness and tranquillity of soul, and they looked on the goodly earth with deep joy, and they had a tender care for the wild creatures of wood and water. But Thomas had yet much to learn of the beauty of holiness.

Often in the bleak dark hours of the night he would leave his cell and steal into the Minster, to fling himself on the cold stones before the high altar; and there he would remain, shivering and praying, till his strength failed him.

It happened one winter night, when the thoughts I have spoken of had grown very bitter in his mind, Thomas guided his steps by the glimmer of the sanctuary lamp to his accustomed place in the choir. Falling on his knees, he laid himself on his face with the palms of his outstretched hands flat on the icy pavement. And as he lay there, taking a cruel joy in the freezing cold and the torture of his body, he became gradually aware of a sound of far-away yet most heavenly music.

He raised himself to his knees to listen, and to his amazement he perceived that the whole Minster was pervaded by a faint mysterious light, which was every instant growing brighter and clearer. And as the light increased the music grew louder and sweeter, and he knew that it was within the sacred walls. But it was no mortal minstrelsy.

The strains he heard were the minglings of angelic instruments, and the cadences of voices of unearthly loveliness. They seemed to proceed from the choir about him, and from the nave and transept and aisles; from the pictured windows and from the clerestory and from the vaulted roofs. Under his knees he felt that the crypt was throbbing and droning like a huge organ.

Sometimes the song came from one part of the Minster, and then all the rest of the vast building was silent; then the music was taken up, as it were in response, in another part; and yet again voices and instruments would blend in one indescribable volume of harmony, which made the huge pile thrill and vibrate from roof to pavement.

As Thomas listened, his eyes became accustomed to the celestial light which encompassed him, and he saw – he could scarce credit his senses that he saw – the little carved angels of the oak stalls in the choir clashing their cymbals and playing their psalteries.

He rose to his feet, bewildered and half terrified. At that moment the mighty roll of unison ceased, and from many parts of the church there came a concord of clear high voices, like a warbling of silver trumpets, and Thomas heard the words they sang. And the words were these:

Tibi omnes Angeli.
To Thee all Angels cry aloud.

So close to him were two of these voices that Thomas looked up to the spandrels in the choir, and he saw that it was the carved angels leaning out of the spandrels that were singing. And as they sang the breath came from their stone lips white and vaporous into the frosty air.

He trembled with awe and astonishment, but the wonder of what was happening drew him towards the altar. The beautiful tabernacle work of the altar screen contained a double range of niches filled with the statues of saints and kings; and these, he saw, were singing. He passed slowly onward with his arms outstretched, like a blind man who does not know the way he is treading.

The figures on the painted glass of the lancets were singing.

The winged heads of the baby angels over the marble memorial slabs were singing.

The lions and griffons and mythical beasts of the finials were singing.

The effigies of dead abbots and priors were singing on their tombs in bay and chantry.

The figures in the frescoes on the walls were singing.

On the painted ceiling westward of the tower the verses of the Te Deum, inscribed in letters of gold above the shields of kings and princes and barons, were visible in the divine light, and the very words of these verses were singing, like living things.

And the breath of all these as they sang turned to a smoke as of incense in the wintry air, and floated about the high pillars of the Minster.

Suddenly the music ceased, all save the deep organ-drone.

Then Thomas heard the marvellous antiphon repeated in the bitter darkness outside; and that music, he knew, must be the response of the galleries of stone kings and queens, of abbots and virgin martyrs, over the western portals, and of the monstrous gargoyles along the eaves.

When the music ceased in the outer darkness, it was taken up again in the interior of the Minster.

At last there came one stupendous united cry of all the singers, and in that cry even the organ-drone of the crypt, and the clamour of the brute stones of pavement and pillar, of wall and roof, broke into words articulate. And the words were these:

Per singulos dies, benedicimus Te.
Day by day; we magnify Thee,
And we worship Thy name; even world without end.

As the wind of the summer changes into the sorrowful wail of the yellowing woods, so the strains of joyous worship changed into a wail of supplication; and as he caught the words, Thomas too raised his voice in wild entreaty:

Miserere nostri, Domine, miserere nostri.
O Lord, have mercy upon us; have mercy upon us.

And then his senses failed him, and he sank to the ground in a long swoon.

When he came to himself all was still, and all was dark save for the little yellow flower of light in the sanctuary lamp.

As he crept back to his cell he saw with unsealed eyes how churlishly he had grudged God the glory of man's genius and the service of His dumb creatures, the metal of the hills, and the stone of the quarry, and the timber of the forest; for now he knew that at all seasons, and whether men heard the music or not, the ear of God was filled by day and by night with an everlasting song from each stone of the vast Minster:

We magnify Thee,
And we worship Thy name; ever world without end.

The Blue Cross

G. K. Chesterton

Between the silver ribbon of morning and the green glittering ribbon of sea, the boat touched Harwich and let loose a swarm of folk like flies, among whom the man we must follow was by no means conspicuous – nor wished to be. There was nothing notable about him, except a slight contrast between the holiday gaiety of his clothes and the official gravity of his face. His clothes included a slight, pale grey jacket, a white waistcoat, and a silver straw hat with a grey-blue ribbon. His lean face was dark by contrast, and ended in a curt black beard that looked Spanish and suggested an Elizabethan ruff. He was smoking a cigarette with the seriousness of an idler. There was nothing about him to indicate the fact that the grey jacket covered a loaded revolver, that the white waistcoat covered a police card, or that the straw hat covered one of the most powerful intellects in Europe. For this was Valentin himself, the head of the Paris police and the most famous investigator of the world; and he was coming from Brussels to London to make the greatest arrest of the century.

Flambeau was in England. The police of three countries had tracked the great criminal at last from Ghent to Brussels, from Brussels to the Hook of Holland; and it was conjectured that he would take some advantage of the unfamiliarity and confusion of the Eucharistic Congress, then taking place in London. Probably he would travel as some minor clerk or secretary connected with it; but, of course, Valentin could not be certain; nobody could be certain about Flambeau.

It is many years now since this colossus of crime suddenly ceased keeping the world in a turmoil; and when he ceased, as they said after the death of Roland, there was a great quiet upon the earth. But in his best days (I mean, of course, his worst) Flambeau was a figure as statuesque and international as the Kaiser. Almost every morning the daily paper announced that he had escaped the consequences of one extraordinary crime by committing another. He was a Gascon of gigantic stature and bodily daring; and the wildest tales were told of his outbursts of athletic humour; how he turned the *juge d'instruction* upside down and stood him on his head, 'to clear his mind'; how he ran down the Rue de Rivoli with a policeman under each arm. It is due to him to say that his fantastic physical strength was generally employed in such bloodless though undignified scenes; his real crimes were chiefly those of ingenious and wholesale robbery. But each of his thefts was almost a new sin, and would make a story by itself. It was he who ran the great Tyrolean Dairy Company in London, with no dairies, no cows, no carts, no milk, but with some thousand subscribers. These he served by the simple operation of moving the little milk-cans outside people's doors to the doors of his own customers. It was he who had kept up an unaccountable and close correspondence with a young lady whose whole letter-bag was intercepted, by the extraordinary trick of photographing his messages infinitesimally small upon the slides of a microscope. A sweeping simplicity, however, marked many of his experiments. It is said he once repainted all the numbers in a street in the dead of night merely to divert one traveller into a trap. It is quite certain that he invented a portable pillar-box, which he put up at corners in quiet suburbs on the chance of strangers dropping postal orders into it. Lastly he was known to be a startling acrobat; despite his huge figure, he could leap like a grasshopper and melt into the treetops like a monkey. Hence the great Valentin, when he set out to find Flambeau, was perfectly well aware that his adventures would not end when he had found him.

But how was he to find him? On this the great Valentin's ideas were still in process of settlement.

There was one thing which Flambeau, with all his dexterity of disguise, could not cover, and that was his singular height. If Valentin's quick eye had caught a tall apple-woman, a tall grenadier, or even a tolerably tall duchess, he might have arrested them on the spot. But all along his train there was nobody that could be a disguised Flambeau, any more than a cat could be a disguised giraffe. About the people on the boat he had already satisfied himself; and the people picked up at Harwich or on the journey limited themselves with certainty to six. There was a short railway official travelling up to the terminus, three fairly short market-gardeners picked up two stations afterwards, one very short widow lady going up from a small Essex town, and a very short Roman Catholic priest going up from a small Essex village. When it came to the last case, Valentin gave it up and almost laughed. The little priest was so much the essence of those

Eastern flats: he had a face as round and dull as a Norfolk dumpling; he had eyes as empty as the North Sea; he had several brown-paper parcels which he was quite incapable of collecting. The Eucharistic Congress had doubtless sucked out of their local stagnation many such creatures, blind and helpless, like moles disinterred. Valentin was a sceptic in the severe style of France, and could have no love for priests. But he could have pity for them, and this one might have provoked pity in anybody. He had a large, shabby umbrella, which constantly fell on the floor. He did not seem to know which was the right end of his return ticket. He explained with a moon-calf simplicity to everybody in the carriage that he had to be careful, because he had something made of real silver 'with blue stones' in one of his brown-paper parcels. His quaint blending of Essex flatness with saintly simplicity continuously amused the Frenchman till the priest arrived (somehow) at Stratford with all his parcels, and came back for his umbrella. When he did the last, Valentin even had the good nature to warn him not to take care of the silver by telling everybody about it. But to whomever he talked, Valentin kept his eye open for someone else; he looked out steadily for anyone, rich or poor, male or female, who was well up to six feet; for Flambeau was four inches above it.

He alighted at Liverpool Street, however, quite conscientiously secure that he had not missed the criminal so far. He then went to Scotland Yard to regularize his position and arrange for help in case of need; he then lit another cigarette and went for a long stroll in the streets of London. As he was walking in the streets and squares beyond Victoria, he paused suddenly and stood. It was a quaint, quiet square, very typical of London, full of an accidental stillness. The tall, flat houses round looked at once prosperous and uninhabited; the square of shrubbery in the centre looked as deserted as a green Pacific islet. One of the four sides was much higher than the rest, like a dais; and the line of this side was broken by one of London's admirable accidents – a restaurant that looked as if it had strayed from Soho. It was an unreasonably attractive object, with dwarf plants in pots and long, striped blinds of lemon yellow and white. It stood specially high above the street, and in the usual patchwork way of London, a flight of steps from the street ran up to meet the front door almost as a fire-escape might run up to a first-floor window. Valentin stood and smoked in front of the yellow-white blinds and considered them long.

The most incredible thing about miracles is that they happen. A few clouds in heaven do come together into the staring shape of one human eye. A tree does stand up in the landscape of a doubtful journey in the exact and elaborate shape of a note of interrogation. I have seen both these things myself within the last few days. Nelson does die in the instant of victory; and a man named Williams does quite accidentally murder a man named Williamson; it sounds like a sort of infanticide. In short, there is in life an element of elfin coincidence which people reckoning on the prosaic may perpetually miss. As it has been well expressed in the paradox of Poe, wisdom should reckon on the unforeseen.

Aristide Valentin was unfathomably French; and the French intelligence is intelligence specially and solely. He was not 'a thinking machine'; for that is a brainless phrase of modern fatalism and materialism. A machine only *is* a machine because it cannot think. But he was a thinking man, and a plain man at the same time. All his wonderful successes, that looked like conjuring, had been gained by plodding logic, by clear and commonplace French thought. The French electrify the world not by starting any paradox, they electrify it by carrying out a truism. They carry a truism so far – as in the French Revolution. But exactly because Valentin understood reason, he understood the limits of reason. Only a man who knows nothing of motors talks of motoring without petrol; only a man who knows nothing of reason talks of reasoning without strong, undisputed first principles. Here he has no strong first principles. Flambeau had been missed at Harwich; and if he was in London at all, he might be anything from a tall tramp on Wimbledon Common to a tall toast-master at the Hôtel Métropole. In such a naked state of nescience, Valentin had a view and a method of his own.

In such cases he reckoned on the unforeseen. In such cases, when he could not follow the train of the reasonable, he coldly and carefully followed the train of the unreasonable. Instead of going to the right places – banks, police-stations, rendezvous – he systematically went to the wrong places; knocked at every empty house, turned down every *cul de sac*, went up every lane blocked with rubbish, went round every crescent that led him uselessly out of the way. He defended this crazy course quite logically. He said that if one had a clue this was the worst way; but if one had no clue at all it was the best, because there was just the chance that any oddity that caught the eye of the pursuer might be the same that had caught the eye of pursued. Somewhere a man must begin, and it had better be just where another man might stop. Something about that flight of steps up to the shop, something about the quietude and quaintness of the restaurant, roused all the detective's rare romantic fancy and made him resolve to strike at random. He went up the steps, and, sitting down by the window, asked for a cup of black coffee.

It was half-way through the morning, and he had not breakfasted; the slight litter of other breakfasts stood about on the table to remind him of his hunger; and adding a poached egg to his order, he proceeded musingly to shake some white sugar into his coffee, thinking all the time about Flambeau. He remembered how Flambeau had escaped, once by a pair of nail scissors, and once by a house on fire; once by having to pay for an unstamped letter, and once by getting people to look through a telescope at a comet that might destroy the world. He thought his detective brain as good as the criminal's, which was true. But he fully realized the disadvantage. 'The criminal is the creative artist; the detective only the critic,' he said with a sour smile, and lifted his coffee cup to his lips slowly, and put it down very quickly. He had put salt in it.

He looked at the vessel from which the silvery powder had come; it was certainly a sugar-basin; as unmistakably meant for sugar as a champagne-bottle for champagne. He wondered why they should keep salt in it. He looked to see if there were any more orthodox vessels. Yes, there were two salt-cellars quite full. Perhaps there was some speciality in the condiment in the salt-cellars. He tasted it; it was sugar. Then he looked round the restaurant with a refreshed air of interest, to see if there were any other traces of that singular artistic taste which puts the sugar in the salt-cellars and the salt in the sugar-basin. Except for an odd splash of some dark fluid on one of the white-papered walls, the whole place appeared neat, cheerful, and ordinary. He rang the bell for the waiter.

When that official hurried up, fuzzy-haired and somewhat blear-eyed at that early hour, the detective (who was not without an appreciation of the simpler forms of humour) asked him to taste the sugar and see if it was up to the high reputation of the hotel. The result was that the waiter yawned suddenly and woke up.

'Do you play this delicate joke on your customers every morning?' inquired Valentin. 'Does changing the salt and sugar never pall on you as a jest?'

The waiter, when this irony grew clearer, stammeringly assured him that the establishment had certainly no such intention; it must be a most curious mistake. He picked up the sugar-basin and looked at it; he picked up the salt-cellar and looked at that, his face growing more and more bewildered. At last he abruptly excused himself, and hurrying away, returned in a few seconds with the proprietor. The proprietor also examined the sugar-basin and then the salt-cellar; the proprietor also looked bewildered.

Suddenly the waiter seemed to grow inarticulate with a rush of words.

'I zink,' he stuttered eagerly, 'I zink it is those two clergymen.'

'What two clergymen?'

'The two clergymen,' said the waiter, 'that threw soup at the wall.'

'Threw soup at the wall?' repeated Valentin, feeling sure this must be some Italian metaphor.

'Yes, yes,' said the attendant excitedly, and pointing at the dark splash on the white paper; 'threw it over there on the wall.'

Valentin looked his query at the proprietor, who came to his rescue with fuller reports.

'Yes, sir,' he said, 'it's quite true, though I don't suppose it has anything to do with the sugar and salt. Two clergymen came in and drank soup here very early, as soon as the shutters were taken down. They were both very quiet, respectable people; one of them paid the bill and went out; the other, who seemed a slower coach altogether, was some minutes longer getting his things together. But he went at last. Only, the instant before he stepped into the street he deliberately picked up his cup, which he had only half emptied, and threw the soup slap on the wall. I was in the back room myself, and so was the waiter; so I could only rush out in time to find the wall splashed and the shop empty. It didn't do any particular damage, but it was confounded cheek; and I tried to catch the men in the street. They were too far off though; I only noticed they went round the corner into Carstairs Street.'

The detective was on his feet, hat settled and stick in hand. He had already decided that in the universal darkness of his mind he could only follow the first odd finger that pointed; and this finger was odd enough. Paying his bill and clashing the glass doors behind him, he was soon swinging round into the other street.

It was fortunate that even in such fevered moments his eye was cool and quick. Something in a shop-front went by him like a mere flash; yet he went back to look at it. The shop was a popular greengrocer and fruiterer's, an array of goods set out in the open air and plainly ticketed with their names and prices. In the two most prominent compartments were two heaps, of oranges and of nuts respectively. On the heap of nuts lay a scrap of cardboard, on which was written in bold, blue chalk, 'Best tangerine oranges, two a penny.' On the oranges was the equally clear and exact description, 'Finest Brazil nuts, 4d. a lb.' M. Valentin looked at these two placards and fancied he had met this highly subtle form of humour before, and that somewhat recently. He drew the attention of the red-faced fruiterer, who was looking rather sullenly up and down the street, to this inaccuracy in his advertisements. The fruiterer said nothing, but sharply put each card into its proper place. The detective, leaning elegantly on his walking-cane, continued to scrutinize the shop. At last he said: 'Pray excuse my apparent irrelevance, my good sir, but I should like to ask you a question in experimental psychology and the association of ideas.'

The red-faced shopman regarded him with an eye of menance; but he continued gaily, swinging his cane. 'Why,' he pursued, 'why are two tickets wrongly placed in a greengrocer's shop like a shovel hat that has come to London for a holiday? Or in case I do not make myself clear, what is the mystical association which connects the idea of nuts marked as oranges with the idea of two clergymen, one tall and the other short?'

The eyes of the tradesman stood out of his head like a snail's; he really seemed for an instant likely to fling himself upon the stranger. At last he stammered angrily: 'I don't know what you 'ave to do with it, but if you're one of their friends, you can tell 'em from me that I'll knock their silly 'eads off, parsons or no parsons, if they upset my apples again.'

'Indeed?' asked the detective, with great sympathy. 'Did they upset your apples?'

'One of 'em did,' said the heated shopman; 'rolled 'em all over the street. I'd 'ave caught the fool but for havin' to pick 'em up.'

'Which way did these parsons go?' asked Valentin.

'Up that second road on the left-hand side, and then across the square,' said the other promptly.

'Thanks,' said Valentin, and vanished like a fairy. On the other side of the second square he found a policeman, and said: 'This is urgent, constable; have you seen two clergymen in shovel hats?'

The policeman began to chuckle heavily. 'I 'ave, sir; and if you arst me, one of 'em was drunk. He stood in the middle of the road that bewildered that – '

'Which way did they go?' snapped Valentin.

'They took one of them yellow buses over there,' answered the man; 'them that go to Hampstead.'

Valentin produced his official card and said very rapidly: 'Call up two of your men to come with me in pursuit,' and crossed the road with such contagious energy that the ponderous policeman was moved to almost agile obedience. In a minute and a half the French detective was joined on the opposite pavement by an inspector and a man in plain clothes.

'Well, sir,' began the former, with smiling importance, 'and what may – ?'

Valentin pointed suddenly with his cane. 'I'll tell you on the top of that omnibus,' he said, and was darting and dodging across the tangle of the traffic. When all three sank panting on the top seats of the yellow vehicle, the inspector said: 'We could go four times as quick in a taxi.'

'Quite true,' replied their leader placidly, 'if we only had an idea of where we were going.'

'Well, where *are* you going?' asked the other, staring.

Valentin smoked frowningly for a few seconds; then, removing his cigarette, he said: 'If you *know* what a man's doing, get in front of him; but if you want to guess what he's doing, keep behind him. Stray when he strays; stop when he stops; travel as slowly as he. Then you may see what he saw and may act as he acted. All we can do is to keep our eyes skinned for a queer thing.'

'What sort of a queer thing do you mean?' asked the inspector.

'Any sort of queer thing,' answered Valentin, and relapsed into obstinate silence.

The yellow omnibus crawled up the northern roads for what seemed like hours on end; the great detective would not explain further, and perhaps his assistants felt a silent and growing doubt of his errand. Perhaps, also, they felt a silent and growing desire for lunch, for the hours crept long past the normal luncheon hour, and the long roads of the North London suburbs seemed to shoot out into length after length like an infernal telescope. It was one of those journeys on which a man perpetually feels that now at last he must have come to the end of the universe, and then finds he has only come to the beginning of Tufnell Park. London died away in draggled taverns and dreary scrubs, and then was unaccountably born again in blazing high streets and blatant hotels. It was like passing through thirteen separate vulgar cities all just touching each other. But though the winter twilight was already threatening the road ahead of them, the Parisian detective still sat silent and watchful, eyeing the frontage of the streets that slid by on either side. By the time they had left Camden Town behind, the policeman were nearly asleep; at least, they gave something like a jump as Valentin leapt erect, struck a hand on each man's shoulder, and shouted to the driver to stop.

They tumbled down the steps into the road without realizing why they had been dislodged; when they looked round for enlightenment they found Valentin triumphantly pointing his finger towards a window on the left side of the road. It was a large window, forming part of the long façade of a gilt and palatial public-house; it was the part reserved for respectable dining, and labelled 'Restaurant'. This window, like all the rest along the frontage of the hotel, was of frosted and figured glass, but in the middle of it was a big, black smash, like a star in the ice.

'Our cue at last,' cried Valentin, waving his stick; 'the place with the broken window.'

'What window? What cue?' asked his principal assistant: 'Why, what proof is there that this has anything to with them?'

Valentin almost broke his bamboo stick with rage.

'Proof! he cried. 'Good God! the man is looking for proof! Why, of course, the chances are twenty to one that it has *nothing* to do with them. But what else can we do? Don't you see we must either follow one wild possibility or else go home to bed?' He banged his way into the restaurant, followed by his companions, and they were soon seated at a late luncheon at a little table, and looking at the star of smashed glass from the inside. Not that it was very informative to them even then.

'Got your window broken, I see,' said Valentin to the waiter, as he paid his bill.

'Yes, sir,' answered the attendant, bending busily over the change, to which Valentin silently added an enormous tip. The waiter straightened himself with mild but unmistakable animation.

'Ah, yes sir,' he said. 'Very odd thing, that, sir.'

'Indeed? Tell us about it,' said the detective with careless curiosity.

'Well, two gents in black came in,' said the waiter; 'two of those foreign parsons that are running about. They had a cheap and quite little lunch, and one of them paid for it and went out. The other was just going out to join him when I looked at my change again and found he'd paid me more than three times too much. "Here," I says to the chap who was nearly out of the door, "you've paid too much." "Oh," he says, very cool, "have we?" "Yes," I says, and picks up the bill to show him. Well, that was a knockout.'

'What do you mean?' asked his interlocutor.

'Well, I'd have sworn on seven Bibles that I'd put 4s. on that bill. But now I saw I'd put 14s., as plain as paint.'

'Well?' cried Valentin, moving slowly, but with burning eyes, 'and then?'

'The parson at the door he says, all serene, "Sorry to confuse your accounts, but it'll pay for the window." "What window?" I says. "The one I'm going to break," he says, and smashed that blessed pane with his umbrella.'

All the inquirers made an exclamation; and the inspector said under his breath: 'Are we after escaped lunatics?' The waiter went on with some relish for the ridiculous story:

'I was so knocked silly for a second, I couldn't do anything. The man marched out of the place and joined his friend just round the corner. Then they went so quick up Bullock Street that I couldn't catch them, though I ran round the bars to do it.'

'Bullock Street,' said the detective, and shot up that thoroughfare as quickly as the strange couple he pursued.

Their journey now took them through bare brick ways like tunnels; streets with few lights and even with few windows; streets that seemed built out of the blank backs of everything and everywhere. Dusk was deepening, and it was not easy even for the London policemen to guess in what exact direction they were treading. The inspector, however, was pretty certain that they would eventually strike some part of Hampstead Heath. Abruptly one bulging and gas-lit window broke the blue twilight like a bull's-eye lantern; and Valentin stopped an instant before a little garish sweet-stuff shop. After an instant's hesitation he went in; he stood amid the gaudy colours of the confectionery with entire gravity and brought thirteen chocolate cigars with a certain care. He was clearly preparing an opening; but he did not need one.

An angular, elderly young woman in the shop had regarded his elegant appearance with a merely automatic inquiry; but when she saw the door behind him blocked with the blue uniform of the inspector, her eyes seemed to wake up.

'Oh,' she said, 'if you've come about that parcel, I've sent it off already.'

'Parcel!' repeated Valentin; and it was his turn to look inquiring.

'I mean the parcel the gentleman left – the clergyman gentleman.'

'For goodness' sake,' said Valentin, leaning forward with his first real confession of eagerness, 'for Heaven's sake tell us what happened exactly.'

'Well,' said the woman, a little doubtfully, 'the clergymen came in about half an hour ago and bought some peppermints and talked a bit, and then went off towards the Heath. But a second after, one of them runs back into the shop and says, "Have I left a parcel?" Well, I looked everywhere and couldn't see one; so he says, "Never mind; but if it should turn up, please post it to this address," and he left me the address and a shilling for my trouble. And sure enough, though I thought I'd looked everywhere, I found he'd left a brown-paper parcel, so I posted it to the place he said. I can't remember the address now; it was somewhere in Westminster. But as the thing seemed so important, I thought perhaps the police had come about it.'

'So they have,' said Valentin shortly. 'Is Hampstead Heath near here?'

'Straight on for fifteen minutes,' said the woman, 'and you'll come right out on the open.' Valentin sprang out of the shop and began to run. The other detectives followed him at a reluctant trot.

The street they threaded was so narrow and shut in by shadows that when they came out unexpectedly into the void common and vast sky they were startled to find the evening still so light and clear. A perfect dome of peacock-green sank into gold amid the blackening trees and the dark violet distances. The glowing green tint was just deep enough to pick out in points of crystal one or two stars. All that was left of the daylight lay in a golden glitter across the edge of Hampstead and that popular hollow which is called the Vale of Health. The holiday-makers who roam this region had not wholly dispersed: a few couples sat shapelessly on benches; and here and there a distant girl still shrieked in one of the swings. The glory of heaven deepened and darkened around the sublime vulgarity of man; and standing on the slope and looking across the valley, Valentin beheld the thing which he sought.

Among the black and breaking groups in that distance was one especially black which did not break – a group of two figures clerically clad. Though they seemed as small as insects, Valentin could see that one of them was much smaller than the other. Though the other had a student's stoop and an inconspicuous manner, he could see that the man was well over six feet high. He shut his teeth and went forward, whirling his stick impatiently. By the time he had substantially diminished the distance and magnified the two black figures as in a vast microscope, he had perceived something else; something which startled him, and yet which he had somehow expected. Whoever was the tall priest, there could be no doubt about the identity of the short one. It was his friend of the Harwich train, the stumpy little *curé* of Essex whom he had warned about his brown-paper parcels.

Now, so far as this went, everything fitted in finally and rationally enough. Valentin had learned by his inquiries that morning that a Father Brown from Essex was bringing up a silver cross with sapphires, a relic of considerable value, to show some of the foreign priests at a congress. This undoubtedly was the 'silver with blue stones'; and Father Brown undoubtedly was the little greenhorn in the train. Now there was nothing wonderful about the fact that what Valentin had found out Flambeau had also found out; Flambeau found out everything. Also there was nothing wonderful in the fact that when Flambeau heard of a sapphire cross he should try to steal it; that was the most natural thing in all natural history. And most certainly there was nothing wonderful about the fact that Flambeau should have it all his own way with such a silly sheep as the man with the unbrella and the parcels. He was the sort of man whom anybody could lead on a string to the North Pole; it was not surprising that an actor like Flambeau, dressed as another priest, could lead him to Hampstead Heath. So far the crime seemed clear enough; and while the detective pitied the priest for his helplessness, he almost despised Flambeau for condescending to so gullible a victim. But when Valentin thought of all that had happened in between, of all that had led him to his triumph, he racked his brains for the smallest rhyme or reason in it. What had the stealing of a blue-and-silver cross from a priest from Essex to do with chucking soup at wallpaper? What had it to do with calling nuts oranges, or with paying for windows first and breaking them afterwards? He had come to the end of his chase; yet somehow he had missed the middle of it. When he failed (which was seldom), he had usually grasped the clue, but nevertheless missed the criminal. Here he had grasped the criminal, but still could not grasp the clue.

The two figures that they followed were crawling like black flies across the huge green contour of a hill. They were evidently sunk in conversation, and perhaps did not notice where they were going; but they were certainly going to the wilder and more silent heights of the Heath. As their pursuers gained on them, the latter had to use the undignified attitudes of the deer-stalker, to crouch behind clumps of trees and even to crawl prostrate in deep grass. By these ungainly ingenuities the hunters even came close enough to the quarry to hear the murmur of the discussion, but no word could be distinguished except the word 'reason' recurring frequently in a high and almost childish voice. Once, over an abrupt dip of land and a dense tangle of thickets, the detectives actually lost the two figures they were following. They did not find the trail again for an agonizing ten minutes, and then it led round the brow of a great dome of hill overlooking an amphitheatre of rich and desolate sunset scenery. Under a tree in this commanding yet neglected spot was an old ramshackle wooden seat. On this seat sat the two priests still in serious speech together. The gorgeous green and gold still clung to the darkening horizon; but the dome above was turning slowly from peacock-green to peacock-blue, and the stars detached themselves more and more like solid jewels. Mutely motioning to his followers, Valentin contrived to creep up behind the big branching tree, and, standing there in deathly silence, heard the words of the strange priests for the first time.

After he had listened for a minute and a half, he was gripped by a devilish doubt. Perhaps he had dragged the two English policemen to the wastes of a nocturnal heath on an errand no saner than seeking figs on thistles. For the two priests were talking exactly like priests, piously with learning and leisure, about the most aerial enigmas of theology. The little Essex priest spoke the more simply, with his round face turned to the strengthening stars; the other talked with his head bowed, as if he were not even worthy to look at them. But no more innocently clerical conversation could have been heard in any white Italian cloister or black Spanish cathedral.

The first he heard was the tail of one of Father Brown's sentences, which ended: '. . . what they really meant in the Middle Ages by the heavens being incorruptible.'

The taller priest nodded his bowed head and said:

'Ah, yes, these modern infidels appeal to their reason; but who can look at those millions of worlds and not feel that there may well be wonderful universes above us where reason is utterly unreasonable?'

'No,' said the other priest; 'reason is always reasonable, even in the last limbo, in the lost borderland of things. I know that people charge the Church with lowering reason, but it is just the other way. Alone on earth, the Church makes reason really supreme. Alone on earth, the Church affirms that God Himself is bound by reason.'

The other priest raised his austere face to the spangled sky and said: 'Yet who knows if in that infinite universe – ?'

'Only infinite physically,' said the little priest, turning sharply in his seat, 'not infinite in the sense of escaping from the laws of truth.'

Valentin behind his tree was tearing his finger-nails with silent fury. He seemed almost to hear the sniggers of the English detectives whom he had brought so far on a fantastic guess only to listen to the metaphysical gossip of two mild old parsons. In his impatience he lost the equally elaborate answer of the tall cleric, and when he listened again it was again Father Brown who was speaking:

'Reason and justice grip the remotest and the loneliest star. Look at those stars. Don't they look as if they were single diamonds and sapphires? Well, you can imagine any mad botany or geology you please. Think of forests of adamant with leaves of brilliants. Think the moon is a blue moon, a single elephantine sapphire. But don't fancy that all that frantic astronomy would make the smallest difference to the reason and justice of conduct. On plains of opal, under cliffs cut out of pearl, you would still find a noticeboard, "Thou shalt not steal."'

Valentin was just in the act of rising from his rigid and crouching attitude and creeping away as softly as might be, felled by the one great folly of his life. But something in the very silence of the tall priest made him stop until the latter spoke. When at last he did speak, he said simply, his head bowed and his hands on his knees:

'Well, I still think that other worlds may perhaps rise higher than our reason. The mystery of heaven is unfathomable, and I for one can only bow my head.'

Then, with brow yet bent and without changing by the faintest shade his attitude or voice, he added:

'Just hand over the sapphire cross of yours, will you? We're all alone here, and I could pull you to pieces like a straw doll.'

The utterly unaltered voice and attitude added a strange violence to that shocking change of speech. But the guarder of the relic only seemed to turn his head by the smallest section of the compass. He seemed still to have a somewhat foolish face turned to the stars.

Perhaps he had not understood. Or, perhaps, he had understood and sat rigid with terror.

'Yes,' said the tall priest, in the same low voice and in the same still posture, 'yes, I am Flambeau.'

Then, after a pause, he said:

'Come, will you give me that cross?'

'No,' said the other, and the monosyllable had an odd sound.

Flambeau suddenly flung off all his pontifical pretensions. The great robber leaned back in his seat and laughed low but long.

'No,' he cried; 'you won't give it me, you proud prelate. You won't give it me, you little celibate simpleton. Shall I tell you why you won't give it me? Because I've got it already in my own breast-pocket.'

The small man from Essex turned what seemed to be a dazed face in the dusk, and said, with the timid eagerness of 'The Private Secretary':

'Are – are you sure?'

Flambeau yelled with delight.

'Really, you're as good as a three-act farce,' he cried. 'Yes, you turnip, I am quite sure. I had the sense to make a duplicate of the right parcel, and now, my friend, you've got the duplicate, and I've got the jewels. An old dodge, Father Brown – a very old dodge.'

'Yes,' said Father Brown, and passed his hand through his hair with the same strange vagueness of manner. 'Yes, I've heard of it before.'

The colossus of crime leaned over to the little rustic priest with a sort of sudden interest.

'*You* have heard of it?' he asked. 'Where have *you* heard of it?'

'Well, I mustn't tell you his name, of course,' said the little man simply. 'He was a penitent, you know. He had lived prosperously for about twenty years entirely on duplicate brown-paper parcels. And so, you see, when I began to suspect you, I thought of this poor chap's way of doing it at once.'

'Began to suspect me,' repeated the outlaw with increased intensity. 'Did you really have the gumption to suspect me just because I brought you up to this bare part of the heath?'

'No, no,' said Brown with an air of apology. 'You see, I suspected you when we first met. It's that little bulge up the sleeve where you people have the spiked bracelet.'

'How in Tartarus,' cried Flambeau, 'did you ever hear of the spiked bracelet?'

'Oh, one's little flock, you know!' said Father Brown, arching his eyebrows rather blankly. 'When I was a curate in Hartlepool, there were three of them with spiked bracelets. So, as I suspected you from the first, don't you see, I made sure that the cross should go safe, anyhow. I'm afraid I watched you, you know. So at last I saw you change the parcels. Then, don't you see, I changed them back again. And then I left the right one behind.'

'Left it behind?' repeated Flambeau, and for the first time there was another note in his voice beside his triumph.

'Well, it was like this,' said the little priest, speaking in the same unaffected way. 'I went back to that sweet-shop and asked if I'd left a parcel, and gave them a particular address if it turned up. Well, I knew I hadn't; but when I went away again I did. So, instead of running after me with that valuable parcel, they have sent it flying to a friend of mine in Westminster.' Then he added rather sadly: 'I learnt that, too, from a poor fellow in Hartlepool. He used to do it with handbags he stole at railway stations, but he's in a monastery now. Oh, one gets to know, you know,' he added, rubbing his head again with the same sort of desperate apology. 'We can't help it, being priests. People come and tell us these things.'

Flambeau tore a brown-paper parcel out of his inner pocket and rent it in pieces. There was nothing but paper and sticks of lead inside it. He sprang to his feet with a gigantic gesture, and cried:

'I don't believe you. I don't believe a bumpkin like you could manage all that. I believe you've still got the stuff on you, and if you don't give it up – why, we're all alone, and I'll take it by force!'

'No,' said Father Brown simply, and stood up also; 'you won't take it by force. First, because I really haven't still got it. And, second, because we are not alone.'

Flambeau stopped in his stride forward.

'Behind that tree,' said Father Brown, pointing, 'are two strong policemen and the greatest detective alive. How did they come here, do you ask? Why, I brought them, of course! How did I do it? Why, I'll tell you if you like! Lord bless you, we have to know twenty such things when we work among the criminal classes! Well, I wasn't sure you were a thief, and it would never do to make a scandal against one of our own clergy. So I just tested you to see if anything would make you show yourself. A man generally makes a small scene if he finds salt in his coffee; if he doesn't he has some reason for keeping quiet. I changed the salt and sugar, and *you* kept quiet. A man generally objects if his bill is three times too big. If he pays it, he has some motive for passing unnoticed. I altered your bill, and *you* paid it.'

The world seemed waiting for Flambeau to leap like a tiger. But he was held back as by a spell; he was stunned with the utmost curiosity.

'Well,' went on Father Brown, with lumbering lucidity, 'as you wouldn't leave any tracks for the police, of course somebody had to. At every place we went to, I took care to do something that would get us talked about for the rest of the day. I didn't do much harm – a splashed wall, spilt apples, a broken window; but I saved the cross, as the cross will always be saved. It is at Westminster by now. I rather wonder you didn't stop it with the Donkey's Whistle.'

'With the what?' asked Flambeau.

'I'm glad you've never heard of it,' said the priest, making a face. 'It's a foul thing. I'm sure you're too good a man for a Whistler. I couldn't have countered it even with the Spots myself; I'm not strong enough in the legs.'

'What on earth are you talking about?' asked the other.

'Well, I did think you'd know the Spots,' said Father Brown, agreeably surprised. 'Oh, you can't have gone so very wrong yet!

'How in blazes do you know all these horrors?' cried Flambeau.

The shadow of a smile crossed the round, simple face of his clerical opponent.

'Oh, by being a celibate simpleton, I suppose,' he said. 'Has it never struck you that a man who does next to nothing but hear men's real sins is not likely to be wholly unaware of human evil? But, as a matter of fact, another part of my trade, too, made me sure you weren't a priest,'

'What?' asked the thief, almost gaping.

'You attacked reason,' said Father Brown. 'It's bad theology.'

And even as he turned away to collect his property, the three policemen came out from under the twilight trees. Flambeau was an artist and a sportsman. He stepped back and swept Valentin a great bow.

'Do not bow to me, *mon ami*,' said Valentin, with silver clearness. 'Let us both bow to our master.'

And they both stood an instant uncovered, while the little Essex priest blinked about for his umbrella.

The Holy Man (after Tolstoy)

Frank Harris

Paul, the eldest son of Count Stroganoff, was only thirty-two when he was made a Bishop: he was the youngest dignitary in the Church, yet his diocese was among the largest: it extended for hundreds of miles along the shore of the Caspian. Even as a youth Paul had astonished people by his sincerity and gentleness, and the honours paid to him seemed to increase his lovable qualities.

Shortly after his induction he set out to visit his whole diocese in order to learn the needs of the people. On this pastoral tour he took with him two older priests in the hope that he might profit by their experience. After many disappointments he was forced to admit that they could only be used as aids to memory, or as secretaries; for they could not even understand his passionate enthusiasm. The life of Christ was the model the young Bishop set before himself, and he took joy in whatever pain or fatigue his ideal involved. His two priests thought it unbecoming in a Bishop to work so hard and to be so careless of 'dignity and state', by which they meant ease and good living. At first they grumbled a good deal at the work and with apparent reason, for, indeed, the Bishop forgot himself in his mission, and as the tour went on his body seemed to waste away in the fire of his zeal.

After he had come to the extreme southern point of his diocese he took ship and began to work his way north along the coast, in order to visit all the fishing villages.

One afternoon, after a hard morning's work, he was seated on deck resting. The little ship lay becalmed a long way from the shore, for the water was shallow and the breeze had died down in the heat of the day.

There had been rain-clouds over the land, but suddenly the sun came out hotly and the Bishop caught sight of some roofs glistening rosy-pink in the sunshine a long way off.

'What place is that?' he asked the Captain.

'Krasnavodsk, I think it is called,' replied the Captain after some hesitation, 'a little nest between the mountains and the sea; a hundred souls perhaps in all.'

(Men are commonly called 'souls' in Russia as they are called 'hands' in England.)

'One hundred souls,' repeated the Bishop, 'shut away from the world; I must visit Krasnavodsk.'

The priests shrugged their shoulders but said nothing; they knew it was no use objecting or complaining. But this time the Captain came to their aid.

'It's twenty-five versts away,' he said, 'and the sailors are done up. You'll be able to get in easily enough, but coming out against the sea-breeze will take hard rowing.'

'To-morrow is Sunday,' rejoined the Bishop, 'and the sailors will be able to rest all day. Please, Captain, tell them to get out the·boat. I wouldn't ask for myself,' he added in a low voice.

The Captain understood; the boat was got out, and under her little lug-sail reached the shore in a couple of hours.

Lermontoff, the big helmsman, stepped at once into the shallow water and carried the Bishop on his back up the beach so that he shouldn't get wet. The two priests got to land as best they could.

At the first cottage the Bishop asked an old man, who was cutting sticks, where the church was.

'Church,' repeated the peasant, 'there isn't one.'

'Haven't you any pope, any priest here?' inquired the Bishop.

'What's that?'

'Surely,' replied the Bishop, 'you have some one here who visits the dying and prays with them, some one who attends to the sick women and children?'

'Oh, yes,' cried the old man, straightening himself; 'we have a holy man.'

'Holy man?' repeated the Bishop, 'who is he?'

'Oh, a good man, a saint,' replied the old peasant, 'he does everything for any one in need.'

'Is he a Christian?'

'I don't think so,' the old man rejoined, shaking his head, 'I've never heard that name.'

'Do you pay him for his services?' asked the Bishop.

'No, no,' was the reply, 'he would not take anything.'

'How does he live?' the Bishop probed farther.

'Like the rest of us he works in his little garden.'

'Show me where he lives: will you?' said the Bishop gently, and at once the old man put down his axe and led the way among the scattered huts.

In a few moments they came to the cottage standing in a square of cabbages. It was just like the other cottages in the village, poverty-stricken and weatherworn, wearing its patches without thought of concealment.

The old man opened the door:

'Some visitors for you, Ivanushka,' he said, standing aside to let the Bishop and his priests pass in.

The Bishop saw before him a broad, thin man of about sixty, dressed half like a peasant, half like a fisherman; he wore the usual sheepskin and high fisherman's boots. The only noticeable thing in his appearance was the way his silver hair and beard contrasted with the dark tan of his skin; his eyes were clear, blue, and steady.

'Come in, Excellency,' he said, 'come in,' and he hastily dusted a stool with his sleeve for the Bishop and placed it for him with a low bow.

'Thank you,' said the Bishop, taking the seat, 'I am somewhat tired, and the rest will be grateful. But be seated, too,' he added, for the 'holy man' was standing before him bowed in an attitude of respectful attention. Without a word Ivan drew up a stool and sat down.

'I was surprised,' the Bishop began, 'to find you have no church here, and no priest; the peasant who showed us the way did not even know what "Christian" meant.'

The holy man looked at him with his patient eyes, but said nothing, so the Bishop went on:

'You're a Christian: are you not?'

'I have not heard that name before,' said the holy man.

The Bishop lifted his eyebrows in surprise.

'Why then do you attend to the poor and ailing in their need?' he argued; 'why do you help them?'

The holy man looked at him for a moment, and then replied quietly:

'I was helped when I was young and needed it.'

'But what religion have you?' asked the Bishop.

'Religion,' the old man repeated, wonderingly, 'what is religion?'

'We call ourselves Christians,' the Bishop began, 'because Jesus, the founder of our faith, was called Christ. Jesus was the Son of God, and came down from heaven with the Gospel of Good Tidings; He taught men that they were the children of God, and that God is love.'

The face of the old man lighted up and he leaned forward eagerly:

'Tell me about Him, please.'

The Bishop told him the story of Jesus, and when he came to the end the old man cried:

'What a beautiful story! I've never heard or imagined such a story.'

'I intend,' said the Bishop, 'as soon as I get home again, to send you a priest, and he will establish a church here where you can worship God, and he will teach you the whole story of the suffering and death of the divine Master.'

'That will be good of you,' cried the old man, warmly, 'we shall be very glad to welcome him.'

The Bishop was touched by the evident sincerity of his listener.

'Before I go,' he said, 'and I shall have to go soon, because it will take us some hours to get out to the ship again, I should like to tell you the prayer that Jesus taught His disciples.'

'I should like very much to hear it,' the old man said quietly.

'Let us kneel down then,' said the Bishop, 'as a sign of reverence, and repeat it after me, for we are all brethren together in the love of the Master;' and saying this he knelt down, and the old man immediately knelt down beside him and clasped his hands as the Bishop clasped his and repeated the sentences as they dropped from the Bishop's lips.

'Our Father, which art in heaven, hallowed by Thy name.'

When the old man had repeated the words, the Bishop went on:

'Thy kingdom come. Thy will be done in earth as it is in heaven.'

The fervour with which the old man repeated the words 'Thy will be done in earth, as it is in heaven' was really touching.

The Bishop continued:

'Give us this day our daily bread. And forgive us our debts,[1] as we forgive our debtors.'

'Give . . . give ——,' repeated the old man, having apparently forgotten the words.

'Give us this day our daily bread,' repeated the Bishop, 'and forgive us our debts as we forgive our debtors.'

'Give and forgive,' said the old man at length . . . 'Give and forgive,' and the Bishop seeing that his memory was weak took up the prayer again:

[1] This form of the Lord's Prayer is evidently taken from Matthew.

'And lead us not into temptation, but deliver us from evil.'

Again the old man repeated the words with an astonishing fervour, 'And lead us not into temptation, but deliver us from evil.'

And the Bishop concluded:

'For Thine is the kingdom, and the power, and the glory, for ever. Amen.'

The old man's voice had an accent of loving and passionate sincerity as he said 'For thine is the kingdom, and the power and the beauty, for ever and ever. Amen.'

The Bishop rose to his feet and his host followed his example, and when he held out his hand the old man clasped it in both his, saying:

'How can I ever thank you for telling me that beautiful story of Christ; how can I ever thank you enough for teaching me His prayer?'

As one in an ecstasy he repeated the words: 'Thy kingdom come. Thy will be done in earth as it is in heaven. . . .'

Touched by his reverent, heartfelt sincerity, the Bishop treated him with great kindness; he put his hand on his shoulder and said:

'As soon as I get back I will send you a priest, who will teach you more, much more than I have had time to teach you; he will indeed tell you all you want to know of our religion – the love by which we live, the hope in which we die.' Before he could stop him the old man had bent his head and kissed the Bishop's hand; the tears stood in his eyes as he did him reverence.

He accompanied the Bishop to the water's edge, and, seeing the Bishop hesitate on the brink waiting for the steersman to carry him to the boat, the 'holy man' stooped and took the Bishop in his arms and strode with him through the water and put him gently on the cushioned seat in the sternsheets as if he had been a little child, much to the surprise of the Bishop and of Lermontoff, who said as if to himself:

'That fellow's as strong as a young man.'

For a long time after the boat had left the shore the old man stood on the beach waving his hands to the Bishop and his companions; but when they were well out to sea, on the second tack, he turned and went up to his cottage and disappeared from their sight.

A little later the Bishop, turning to his priests, said:

'What an interesting experience! What a wonderful old man! Didn't you notice how fervently he said the Lord's Prayer?'

'Yes,' replied the younger priest indifferently, 'he was trying to show off, I thought.'

'No, no,' cried the Bishop, 'His sincerity was manifest and his goodness too. Did you notice that he said "give and forgive" instead of just repeating the words? And if you think of it, "give us this day our daily bread and forgive us our debts as we forgive our debtors" seems a little like a bargain. I'm not sure that the simple word "give and forgive" is not better, more in the spirit of Jesus?'

The younger priest shrugged his shoulders as if the question had no interest for him.

'Perhaps that's what the old man meant?' questioned the Bishop after a pause.

But as neither of the priests answered him, he went on, as if thinking aloud:

'At the end again he used the word "beauty" for "glory". I wonder was that unconscious? In any case an extraordinary man and good, I am sure, out of sheer kindness and sweetness of nature, as many men are good in Russia. No wonder our *moujiks* call it "Holy Russia"; no wonder, when you can find men like that.'

'They are as ignorant as pigs,' cried the other priests, 'not a soul in the village can either read or write: they are heathens, barbarians. They've never even heard of Christ and don't know what religion means.'

The Bishop looked at them and said nothing; seemingly he preferred his own thoughts.

It was black night when they came to the ship, and at once they all went to their cabins to sleep; for the day had been very tiring.

The Bishop had been asleep perhaps a couple of hours when he was awakened by the younger priest shaking him and saying:

'Come on deck quickly, quickly, Excellency, something extraordinary's happening, a light on the sea and no one can make out what it is!'

'A light,' exclaimed the Bishop, getting out of bed and beginning to draw on his clothes.

'Yes, a light on the water,' repeated the priest; 'but come quickly, please; the Captain sent me for you.'

When the Bishop reached the deck, the Captain was standing with his night-glass to his eyes, looking over the waste of water to leeward, where, indeed, a light could be seen flickering close to the surface of the sea; it appeared to be a hundred yards or so away.

'What is it?' cried the Bishop, astonished by the fact that all the sailors had crowded round and were staring at the light.

'What is it?' repeated the Captain gruffly, for he was greatly moved; 'it's a man with a grey beard; he has a lantern in his right hand, and he's walking on the water.'

'But no one can walk on the water,' said the Bishop gently. 'It would be a miracle,' he added, in a tone of remonstrance.

'Miracle or not,' retorted the Captain, taking the glass from his eyes, 'that's what I see, and the man'll be here soon, for he's coming towards us. Look, you,' and he handed the glass to one of the sailors as he spoke.

The light still went on swaying about as if indeed it were being carried in the hand of a man. The sailor had hardly put the night-glass to his eyes, when he cried out:

'That's what it is! – a man walking on the water . . . it's the 'holy man' who carried your Excellency on board the boat this afternoon.'

'God help us!' cried the priests, crossing themselves.

'He'll be here in a moment or two,' added the sailor, 'he's coming quickly,' and, indeed, almost at once the old man came to them from the water and stepped over the low bulwark on to the deck.

At this the priests went down on their knees, thinking it was some miracle, and the sailors, including the Captain, followed their example, leaving the Bishop standing awe-stricken and uncertain in their midst.

The 'holy man' came forward, and, stretching out his hands, said:

'I'm afraid I've disturbed you, Excellency: but soon after you left me, I found I had forgotten part of that beautiful prayer and I could not bear you to go away and think me careless of all you had taught me, and so I came to ask you to help my memory just once more.'. . .

'I remember the first part of the prayer and the last words as if I had been hearing it all my life and knew it in my soul, but the middle has escaped me.'. . .

'I remember "Our Father, which art in heaven, Hallowed be Thy name. Thy kingdom come. Thy will be done in earth as it is in heaven," and then all I can remember is, "Give and forgive," and the end, "And lead us not into temptation, but deliver us from evil. For Thine is the kingdom, and the power and the beauty for ever and ever. Amen."

'But I've forgotten some words in the middle: won't you tell me the middle again?'

'How did you come to us?' asked the Bishop in awed wonderment. 'How did you walk on the water?'

'Oh, that's easy,' replied the old man, 'any one can do that; whatever you love and trust in this world loves you in return. We love the water that makes everything pure and sweet for us, and is never tired of cleansing, and the water loves us in return; any one can walk on it; but won't you teach me that beautiful prayer, the prayer Jesus taught His disciples?'

The Bishop shook his head, and in a low voice, as if to himself, said:

'I don't think I can teach you anything about Jesus the Christ. You know a great deal already. I only wish –.'

The Second Death

Graham Greene

She found me in the evening under the trees that grew outside the village. I had never cared for her and would have hidden myself if I'd seen her coming. She was to blame, I'm certain, for her son's vices. If they were vices, but I'm very far from admitting that they were. At any rate he was generous, never mean, like others in the village I could mention if I chose.

I was staring hard at a leaf or she would never have found me. It was dangling from the twig, its stalk torn across by the wind or else by a stone one of the village children had flung. Only the green tough skin of the stalk held it there suspended. I was watching closely, because a caterpillar was crawling across the surface making the leaf sway to and fro. The caterpillar was aiming at the twig, and I wondered whether it would reach it in safety or whether the leaf would fall with it into the water. There was a pool underneath the trees, and the water always appeared red, because of the heavy clay in the soil.

I never knew whether the caterpillar reached the twig, for, as I've said, the wretched woman found me. The first I knew of her coming was her voice just behind my ear.

'I've been looking in all the pubs for you,' she said in her old shrill voice. It was typical of her to say 'all the pubs' when there were only two in the place. She always wanted credit for the trouble she hadn't really taken.

I was annoyed and I couldn't help speaking a little harshly. 'You might have saved yourself the trouble,' I said, 'you should have known I wouldn't be in a pub on a fine night like this.'

The old vixen became quite humble. She was always smooth enough when she wanted anything. 'It's for my poor son,' she said. That meant that he was ill. When he was well I never heard her say anything better than 'that dratted boy'. She'd make him be in the house by midnight every day of the week, as if there were any serious mischief a man could get up to in a little village like ours. Of course we soon found a way to cheat her, but it was the principle of the thing I objected to – a grown man of over thirty ordered about by his mother, just because she hadn't a husband to control. But when he was ill, though it might be with only a small chill, it was 'my poor son'.

'He's dying,' she said, 'and God knows what I shall do without him.'

'Well, I don't see how I can help you,' I said. I was angry, because he'd been dying once before and she'd done everything but actually bury him. I imagined it was the same sort of dying this time, the sort a man gets over. I'd seen him about the week before on his way up the hill to see the big-breasted girl at the farm. I'd watched him till he was like a little black dot, which stayed suddenly by a square box in a field. That was the barn where they used to meet. I have very good eyes and it amuses me to try how far and how clearly they can see. I met him again some time after midnight and helped him get into the house without his mother knowing, and he was well enough then – only a little sleepy and tired.

The old vixen was at it again. 'He's been asking for you,' she shrilled at me.

'If he's as ill as you make out,' I said, 'it would be better for him to ask for a doctor.'

'Doctor's there, but he can't do anything.' That startled me for a moment, I'll admit it, until I thought, 'the old devil's malingering. He's got some plan or other.' He was quite clever enough to cheat a doctor. I had seen him throw a fit that would have deceived Moses.

'For God's sake come,' she said, 'he seems frightened.' Her voice broke quite genuinely, for I suppose in her way she was fond of him. I couldn't help pitying her a little, for I knew that he had never cared a mite for her and had never troubled to disguise the fact.

I left the trees and the red pool and the struggling caterpillar, for I knew that she would never leave me alone, now that her 'poor boy' was asking for me. Yet a week ago there was nothing she wouldn't have done to keep us apart. She thought me responsible for his ways, as though any mortal man could have kept him off a likely woman when his appetite was up.

I think it must have been the first time I had entered their cottage by the front door, since I came to the village ten years ago. I threw an amused glance at his window. I thought I could see the marks on the wall of the ladder we'd used the week before. We'd had a little difficulty in putting it straight, but his mother slept sound. He had brought the ladder down from the barn, and when he'd got safely in, I carried it up there again. But you could never trust his word. He'd lie to his best friend, and when I reached the barn I found the girl had gone. If he couldn't bribe you with his mother's money, he'd bribe you with other people's promises.

I began to feel uneasy directly I got inside the door. It was natural that the house should be quiet, for the pair of them never had any friends to stay, although the old woman had a sister-in-law living only a few miles away. But I didn't like the sound of the doctor's feet, as he came downstairs to meet us. He'd twisted his face into a pious solemnity for our benefit, as though there was something holy about death, even about the death of my friend.

'He's conscious,' he said, 'but he's going. There's nothing I can do. If you want him to die in peace, better let his friend go along up. He's frightened about something.'

The doctor was right. I could tell that as soon as I bent under the lintel and entered my friend's room. He was propped up on a' pillow, and his eyes were on the door, waiting for me to come. They were very bright and frightened, and his hair lay across his forehead in sticky stripes. I'd never realized before what an ugly fellow he was. He had got sly eyes that looked at you too much out of the corners, but when he was in ordinary health, they held a twinkle that made you forget the slyness. There was something pleasant and brazen in the twinkle, as much as to say, 'I know I'm sly and ugly. But what does that matter? I've got guts.' It was that twinkle, I think, some women found attractive and stimulating. Now when the twinkle was gone, he looked a rogue and nothing else.

I thought it my duty to cheer him up, so I made a small joke out of the fact that he was alone in bed. He didn't seem to relish it, and I was beginning to fear that he, too, was taking a religious view of his death, when he told me to sit down, speaking quite sharply.

'I'm dying,' he said, talking very fast, 'and I want to ask you something. That doctor's no good – he'd think me delirious. I'm frightened, old man. I want to be reassured,' and then after a long pause, 'someone with common sense.' He slipped a little further down in his bed.

'I've only once been badly ill before,' he said. 'That was before you settled here. I wasn't much more than a boy. People tell me that I was even supposed to be dead. They were carrying me out to burial, when a doctor stopped them just in time.'

I'd heard plenty of cases like that, and I saw no reason why he should want to tell me about it. And then I thought I saw his point. His mother had not been too anxious once before to see if he were properly dead, though I had little doubt that she made a great show of grief – 'My poor boy. I don't know what I shall do without him.' And I'm certain that she believed herself then, as she believed herself now. She wasn't a murderess. She was only inclined to be premature.

'Look here, old man,' I said, and I propped him a little higher on his pillow, 'you needn't be frightened. You aren't going to die, and anyway I'd see that the doctor cut a vein or something before they moved you. But that's all morbid stuff. Why, I'd stake my shirt that you've got plenty more years in front of you. And plenty more girls too,' I added to make him smile.

'Can't you cut out all that?' he said, and I knew then that he had turned religious. 'Why,' he said, 'if I lived, I wouldn't touch another girl. I wouldn't, not one.'

I tried not to smile at that, but it wasn't easy to keep a straight face. There's always something a bit funny about a sick man's morals. 'Anyway,' I said, 'you needn't be frightened.'

'It's not that,' he said. 'Old man, when I came round that other time, I thought that I'd been dead. It wasn't like sleep at all. Or rest in peace. There was someone there all round me, who knew everything. Every girl I'd ever had. Even that young one who hadn't understood. It was before your time. She lived a mile down the road, where Rachel lives now, but she and her family went away afterwards. Even the money I'd taken from mother. I don't call that stealing. It's in the family. I never had a chance to explain. Even the thoughts I'd had. A man can't help his thoughts.'

'A nightmare,' I said.

'Yes, it must have been a dream, mustn't it? The sort of dream people do get when they are ill. And I saw what was coming to me too. I can't bear being hurt. It wasn't fair. And I wanted to faint and I couldn't, because I was dead.'

'In the dream,' I said. His fear made me nervous. 'In the dream,' I said again.

'Yes, it must have been a dream – mustn't it? – because I woke up. The curious thing was I felt quite well and strong. I got up and stood in the road, and a little farther down, kicking up the dust, was a small crowd, going off with a man – the doctor who had stopped them burying me.'

'Well?' I said.

'Old man,' he said, 'suppose it was true. Suppose I had been dead. I believed it then, you know, and so did my mother. But you can't trust her. I went straight for a couple of years. I thought it might be a sort of second chance. Then things got fogged and somehow. . . It didn't seem really possible. It's not possible. Of course it's not possible. You know it isn't, don't you?'

'Why, no,' I said. 'Miracles of that sort don't happen nowadays. And anyway, they aren't likely to happen to you, are they? And here of all places under the sun.'

'It would be so dreadful,' he said 'if it had been true, and I'd got to go through all that again. You don't know what things were going to happen to me in that dream. And they'd be worse now.' He stopped and then, after a moment, he added as though he were stating a fact: 'When one's dead there's no unconsciousness any more for ever.'

'Of course it was a dream,' I said, and squeezed his hand. He was frightening me with his fancies. I wished that he'd die quickly, so that I could get away from his sly, bloodshot and terrified eyes and see something cheerful and amusing, like the Rachel he had mentioned, who lived a mile down the road.

'Why,' I said, 'if there had been a man about working miracles like that, we should have heard of others, you may be sure. Even poked away in this God-forsaken spot,' I said.

'There were some others,' he said. 'But the stories only went round among the poor, and they'll believe anything, won't they? There were lots of diseased and crippled they said he'd cured. And there was a man, who'd been born blind, and he came and just touched his eyelids and sight came to him. Those were all old wives' tales, weren't they?' he asked me, stammering with fear, and then lying suddenly still and bunched up at the side of the bed.

I began to say, 'Of course, they were all lies,' but I stopped, because there was no need. All I could do was to go downstairs and tell his mother to come up and close his eyes. I wouldn't have touched them for all the money in the world. It was a long time since I thought of that day, ages and ages ago, when I felt a cold touch like spittle on my lids and opening my eyes had seen a man like a tree surrounded by other trees walking away.

The Artificial Nigger
Flannery O'Connor

Mr Head awakened to discover that the room was full of moonlight. He sat up and stared at the floor boards – the colour of silver – and then at the ticking on his pillow, which might have been brocade, and after a second, he saw half of the moon five feet away in his shaving mirror, paused as if it were waiting for his permission to enter. It rolled forward and cast a dignifying light on everything. The straight chair against the wall looked stiff and attentive as if it were awaiting an order and Mr Head's trousers, hanging to the back of it, had an almost noble air, like the garment some great man had just flung to his servant; but the face on the moon was a grave one. It gazed across the room and out the window where it floated over the horse stall and appeared to contemplate itself with the look of a young man who sees his old age before him.

Mr Head could have said to it that age was a choice blessing and that only with years does a man enter into that calm understanding of life that makes him a suitable guide for the young. This, at least, had been his own experience.

He sat up and grasped the iron posts at the foot of his bed and raised himself until he could see the face on the alarm clock which sat on an overturned bucket beside the chair. The hour was two in the morning. The alarm on the clock did not work but he was not dependent on any mechanical means to awaken him. Sixty years had not dulled his responses; his physical reactions, like his moral ones, were guided by his will and strong character, and these could be seen plainly in his features. He had a long tube-like face with a long rounded open jaw and a long depressed nose. His eyes were alert but quiet, and in the miraculous moonlight they had a look of composure and of ancient wisdom as if they belonged to one of the great guides of men. He might have been Vergil summoned in the middle of the night to go to Dante, or better, Raphael, awakened by a blast of God's light to fly to the side of Tobias. The only dark spot in the room was Nelson's pallet, underneath the shadow of the window.

Nelson was hunched over on his side, his knees under his chin and his heels under his bottom. His new suit and hat were in the boxes that they had been sent in and these were on the floor at the foot of the pallet where he could get his hands on them as soon as he woke up. The slop jar, out of the shadow and made snow-white in the moonlight, appeared to stand guard over him like a small personal angel. Mr Head lay back down, feeling entirely confident that he could carry out the moral mission of the coming day. He meant to be up before Nelson and to have the breakfast cooking by the time he awakened. The boy was always irked when Mr Head was the first up. They would have to leave the house at four to get to the railroad junction by five-thirty. The train was to stop for them at five forty-five and they had to be there on time, for this train was stopping merely to accommodate them.

This would be the boy's first trip to the city though he claimed it would be his second because he had been born there. Mr Head had tried to point out to him that when he was born he didn't have the intelligence to determine his whereabouts but this had made no impression on the child at all and he continued to insist that this was to be his second trip. It would be Mr Head's third trip. Nelson had said 'I will've already been there twice and I ain't but ten.'

Mr Head had contradicted him.

'If you ain't been there in fifteen years, how you know you'll be able to find your way about?' Nelson had asked. 'How you know it hasn't changed some?'

'Have you ever,' Mr Head had asked, 'seen me lost?'

Nelson certainly had not but he was a child who was never satisfied until he had given an impudent answer and he replied, 'It's nowhere around here to get lost at.'

'The day is going to come,' Mr Head prophesied, 'when you'll find you ain't as smart as you think you are.' He had been thinking about this trip for several months but it was for the most part in moral terms that he conceived it. It was to be a lesson that the boy would never forget. He was to find out from it that he had no cause for pride merely because he had been born in a city. He was to find out that the city is not a great place. Mr Head meant him to see everything there is to see in a city so that he would be content to stay at home for the rest of his life. He fell asleep thinking how the boy would at last find out that he was not as smart as he thought he was.

He was awakened at three-thirty by the smell of fatback frying and he leaped off his cot. The pallet was empty and the clothes boxes had been thrown open. He put on his trousers and ran into the other room. The boy had a corn pone on cooking and had fried the meat. He was sitting in the half-dark at the table, drinking cold coffee out of a can. He had on his new suit and his new gray hat pulled low over his eyes. It was too big for him but they had ordered it a size large because they expected his head to grow. He didn't say anything but his entire figure suggested satisfaction at having arisen before Mr Head.

Mr Head went to the stove and brought the meat to the table in the skillet. 'It's no hurry,' he said. 'You'll get there soon enough and it's no guarantee you'll like it when you do neither,' and he sat down across from the boy whose hat teetered back slowly to reveal a fiercely expressionless face, very much the same shape as the old man's. They were grandfather and grandson but they looked enough alike to be brothers not too far apart in age, for Mr Head had a youthful expression by daylight, while the boy's look was ancient, as if he knew everything already and would be pleased to forget it.

Mr Head had once had a wife and daughter and when the wife died, the daughter ran away and returned after an interval with Nelson. Then one morning, without getting out of bed, she died and left Mr Head with sole care of the year-old child. He had made the mistake of telling Nelson that he had been born in Atlanta. If he hadn't told him that, Nelson couldn't have insisted that this was going to be his second trip.

'You may not like it a bit,' Mr Head continued. 'It'll be full of niggers.'

The boy made a face as if he could handle a nigger.

'All right,' Mr Head said. 'You ain't ever seen a nigger.'

'You wasn't up very early,' Nelson said.

'You ain't ever seen a nigger,' Mr Head repeated. 'There hasn't been a nigger in this county since we run that one out twelve years ago and that was before you were born.' He looked at the boy as if he were daring him to say he had ever seen a Negro.

'How you know I never saw a nigger when I lived there before?' Nelson asked. 'I probably saw a lot of niggers.'

'If you seen one you didn't know what he was,' Mr Head said, completely exasperated. 'A six-month-old child don't know a nigger from anybody else.'

'I reckon I'll know a nigger if I see one,' the boy said and got up and straightened his slick sharply creased gray hat and went outside to the privy.

They reached the junction some time before the train was due to arrive and stood about two feet from the first set of tracks. Mr Head carried a paper sack with some biscuits and a can of sardines in it for their lunch. A coarse-looking orange-coloured sun coming up behind the east range of mountains was making the sky a dull red behind them, but in front of them it was still gray and they faced a gray transparent moon, hardly stronger than a thumbprint and completely without light. A small tin switch box and a black fuel tank were all there was to mark the place as a junction; the tracks were double and did not converge again until they were hidden behind the bends at either end of the clearing. Trains passing appeared to emerge from a tunnel of trees and, hit for a second by the cold sky, vanish terrified into the woods again. Mr Head had had to make special arrangements with the ticket agent to have this train stop and he was secretly afraid it would not, in which case, he knew Nelson would say, 'I never thought no train was going to stop for you.' Under the useless morning moon the tracks looked white and fragile. Both the old man and child stared ahead as if they were awaiting an apparition.

Then suddenly, before Mr Head could make up his mind to turn back, there was a deep warning bleat and the train appeared, gliding very slowly, almost silently around the bend of trees about two hundred yards down the track, with one yellow front light shining. Mr Head was still not certain it would stop and he felt it would make an even bigger idiot of him if it went by slowly. Both he and Nelson, however, were prepared to ignore the train if it passed them.

The engine charged by, filling their noses with the smell of hot metal and then the second coach came to a stop exactly where they were standing. A conductor with the face of an ancient bloated bulldog was on the step as if he expected them, though he did not look as if it mattered one way or the other to him if they got on or not. 'To the right,' he said.

Their entry took only a fraction of a second and the train was already speeding on as they entered the quiet car. Most of the travellers were still sleeping, some with their heads hanging off the chair arms, some stretched across two seats, and some sprawled out with their feet in the aisle. Mr Head saw two unoccupied seats and pushed Nelson toward them. 'Get in there by the winder,' he said in his normal voice which was very loud at this hour of the morning. 'Nobody cares if you sit there because it's nobody in it. Sit right there.'

'I heard you,' the boy muttered. 'It's no use in you yelling,' and he sat down and turned his head to the glass. There he saw a pale ghost-like face scowling at him beneath the brim of a pale ghost-like hat. His grandfather, looking quickly too, saw a different ghost, pale but grinning, under a black hat.

Mr Head sat down and settled himself and took out his ticket and started reading aloud everything that was printed on it. People began to stir. Several woke up and stared at him. 'Take off your hat,' he said to Nelson and took off his own and put it on his knee. He had a small amount of white hair that had turned tobacco-coloured over the years and this lay flat across the back of his head. The front of his head was bald and creased. Nelson took off his hat and put it on his knee and they waited for the conductor to come ask for their tickets.

The man across the aisle from them was spread out over two seats, his feet propped on the window and his head jutting into the aisle. He had on a light blue suit and a yellow shirt unbuttoned at the neck. His eyes had just opened and Mr Head was ready to introduce himself when the conductor come up from behind and growled, 'Tickets.'

When the conductor had gone, Mr Head gave Nelson the return half of his ticket and said, 'Now put that in your pocket and don't lose it or you'll have to stay in the city.'

'Maybe I will,' Nelson said as if this were a reasonable suggestion.

Mr Head ignored him. 'First time this boy has ever been on a train,' he explained to the man across the aisle, who was sitting up now on the edge of his seat with both feet on the floor.

Nelson jerked his hat on again and turned angrily to the window.

'He's never seen anything before,' Mr Head continued. 'Ignorant as the day he was born, but I mean for him to get his fill once and for all.'

The boy leaned forward, across his grandfather and toward the stranger. 'I was born in the city,' he said. 'I was born there. This is my second trip.' He said it in a high positive voice but the man across the aisle didn't look as if he understood. There were heavy purple circles under his eyes.

Mr Head reached across the aisle and tapped him on the arm. 'The thing to do with a boy,' he said sagely, 'is to show him all it is to show. Don't hold nothing back.'

'Yeah,' the man said. He gazed down at his swollen feet and lifted the left one about ten inches from the floor. After a minute he put it down and lifted the other. All through the car people began to get up and move about and yawn and stretch. Separate voices could be heard here and there and then a general hum. Suddenly Mr Head's serene expression changed. His mouth almost closed and a light, fierce and cautious both, came into his eyes. He was looking down the length of the car. Without turning, he caught Nelson by the arm and pulled him forward. 'Look,' he said.

A huge coffee-coloured man was coming slowly forward. He had on a light suit and a yellow satin tie with a ruby pin in it. One of his hands rested on his stomach which rode majestically under his buttoned coat, and in the other he held the head of a black walking stick that he picked up and set down with a deliberate outward motion each time he took a step. He was proceeding very slowly, his large brown eyes gazing over the heads of the passengers. He had a small white mustache and white crinkly hair. Behind him there were two young women, both coffee-coloured, one in a yellow dress and one in a green. Their progress was kept at the rate of his and they chatted in low throaty voices as they followed him.

Mr Head's grip was tightening insistently on Nelson's arm. As the procession passed them, the light from a sapphire ring on the brown hand that picked up the cane reflected in Mr Head's eye, but he did not look up nor did the tremendous man look at him. The group proceeded up the rest of the aisle and out of the car. Mr Head's grip on Nelson's arm loosened. 'What was that?' he asked.

'A man,' the boy said and gave him an indignant look as if he were tired of having his intelligence insulted.

'What kind of man?' Mr Head persisted, his voice expressionless.

'A fat man,' Nelson said. He was beginning to feel that he had better be cautious.

'You don't know what kind?' Mr Head said in a final tone.

'An old man,' the boy said and had a sudden foreboding that he was not going to enjoy the day.

'That was a nigger,' Mr Head said and sat back.

Nelson jumped up on the seat and stood looking backward to the end of the car but the Negro had gone.

'I'd of thought you'd know a nigger since you seen so many when you was in the city on your first visit,' Mr Head continued. 'That's his first nigger,' he said to the man across the aisle.

The boy slid down in the seat. 'You said they were black,' he said in an angry voice 'You never said they were tan. How do you expect me to know anything when you don't tell me right?'

'You're just ignorant is all,' Mr Head said and he got up and moved over in the vacant seat by the man across the aisle.

Nelson turned backward again and looked where the Negro had disappeared. He felt that the Negro had deliberately walked down the aisle in order to make a fool of him, and he hated him with a fierce raw fresh hate; and also, he understood now why his grandfather disliked them. He looked toward the window and the face there seemed to suggest that he might be inadequate to the day's exactions. He wondered if he would even recognize the city when they came to it.

After he had told several stories, Mr Head realized that the man he was talking to was asleep and he got up and suggested to Nelson that they walk over the train and see the parts of it. He particularly wanted the boy to see the toilet so they went first to the men's room and examined the plumbing. Mr Head demonstrated the ice-water cooler as if he had invented it and showed Nelson the bowl with the single spigot where the travellers brushed their teeth. They went through several cars and came to the diner.

This was the most elegant car in the train. It was painted a rich egg-yellow and had a wine-coloured carpet on the floor. There were wide windows over the tables and great spaces of the rolling view were caught in miniature in the sides of the coffee pots and in the glasses. Three very black Negroes in white suits and aprons were running up and down the aisle, swinging trays and bowing and bending over the travellers eating breakfast. One of them rushed up to Mr Head and Nelson and said, holding up two fingers, 'Space for two!' but Mr Head replied in a loud voice, 'We eaten before we left!'

The waiter wore large brown spectacles that increased the size of his eye whites. 'Stan' aside then please,' he said with an airy wave of the arm as if he were brushing aside flies.

Neither Nelson nor Mr Head moved a fraction of an inch. 'Look,' Mr Head said.

The near corner of the diner, containing two tables, was set off from the rest by a saffron-coloured curtain. One table was set but empty but at the other, facing them, his back to the drape, sat the tremendous Negro. He was speaking in a soft voice to the two women while he buttered a muffin. He had a heavy sad face and his neck bulged over his white collar on either side. 'They rope them off,' Mr Head explained. Then he said, 'Let's go see the kitchen,' and they walked the length of the diner but the black waiter was coming fast behind them.

'Passengers are not allowed in the kitchen!' he said in a haughty voice. 'Passengers are NOT allowed in the kitchen!'

Mr Head stopped where he was and turned. 'And there's good reason for that,' he shouted into the Negro's chest, 'because the cockroaches would run the passengers out!'

All the travellers laughed and Mr Head and Nelson walked out, grinning. Mr Head was known at home for his quick wit and Nelson felt a sudden keen pride in him. He realized the old man would be his only support in the strange place they were approaching. He would be entirely alone in the world if he were ever lost from his grandfather. A terrible excitement shook him and he wanted to take hold of Mr Head's coat and hold on like a child.

As they went back to their seats they could see through the passing windows that the countryside was becoming speckled with small houses and shacks and that a highway ran alongside the train. Cars sped by on it, very small and fast. Nelson felt that there was less breath in the air than there had been thirty minutes ago. The man across the aisle had left and there was no one near for Mr Head to hold a conversation with so he looked out of the window, through his own reflection, and read aloud the names of the buildings they were passing. 'The Dixie Chemical Corp!' he announced. 'Southern Maid Flour! Dixie Doors! Southern Belle Cotton Products! Patty's Peanut Butter! Southern Mammy Cane Syrup!'

'Hush up!' Nelson hissed.

All over the car people were beginning to get up and take their luggage off the overhead racks. Women were putting on their coats and hats. The conductor stuck his head in the car and snarled, 'Firstoppppmry,' and Nelson lunged out of his sitting position, trembling. Mr Head pushed him down by the shoulder.

'Keep your seat,' he said in dignified tones. 'The first stop is on the edge of town. The second stop is at the main railroad station.' He had come by this knowledge on his first trip when he had got off at the first stop and had had to pay a man fifteen cents to take him into the heart of the town. Nelson sat back down, very pale. For the first time in his life, he understood that his grandfather was indispensable to him.

The train stopped and let off a few passengers and glided on as if it had never ceased moving. Outside, behind rows of brown rickety houses, a line of blue buildings stood up, and beyond them a pale rose-gray sky faded away to nothing. The train moved into the railroad yard. Looking down, Nelson saw lines and lines of silver tracks multiplying and criss-crossing. Then before he could start counting them, the face in the window started out at him, gray but distinct, and he looked the other way. The train was in the station. Both he and Mr Head jumped up and ran to the door. Neither noticed that they had left the paper sack with the lunch in it on the seat.

They walked stiffly through the small station and came out of a heavy door into the squall of traffic. Crowds were hurrying to work. Nelson didn't know where to look. Mr Head leaned against the side of the building and glared in front of him.

Finally Nelson said, 'Well, how do you see what all it is to see?'

Mr Head didn't answer. Then as if the sight of people passing had given him the clue, he said, 'You walk,' and started off down the street. Nelson followed, steadying his hat. So many sights and sounds were flooding in on him that for the first block he hardly knew what he was seeing. At the second corner, Mr Head turned and looked behind him at the station they had left, a putty-coloured terminal with a concrete dome on top. He thought that if he could keep the dome always in sight, he would be able to get back in the afternoon to catch the train again.

As they walked along, Nelson began to distinguish details and take note of the store windows, jammed with every kind of equipment – hardware, drygoods, chicken feed, liquor. They passed one that Mr Head called his particular attention to where you walked in and sat on a chair with your feet upon two rests and let a Negro polish your shoes. They walked slowly and stopped and stood at the entrances so he could see what went on in each place but they did not go into any of them. Mr Head was determined not to go into any city store because on his first trip here, he had got lost in a large one and had found his way out only after many people had insulted him.

They came in the middle of the next block to a store that had a weighing machine in front of it and they both in turn stepped up on it and put in a penny and received a ticket. Mr Head's ticket said, 'You weigh 120 pounds. You are upright and brave and all your friends admire you.' He put the ticket in his pocket, surprised that the machine should have got his character correct but his weight wrong, for he had weighed on a grain scale not long before and knew he weighed 110. Nelson's ticket said, 'You weigh 98 pounds. You have a great destiny ahead of you but beware of dark women.' Nelson did not know any women and he weighed only 68 pounds but Mr Head pointed out that the machine had probably printed the number upsidedown, meaning the 9 for a 6.

They walked on and at the end of five blocks the dome of the terminal sank out of sight and Mr Head turned to the left. Nelson could have stood in front of every store window for an hour if there had not been another more interesting one next to it. Suddenly he said, 'I was born here!' Mr Head turned and looked at him with horror. There was a sweaty brightness about his face. 'This is where I come from!' he said.

Mr Head was appalled. He saw the moment had come for drastic action. 'Lemme show you one thing you ain't seen yet,' he said and took him to the corner where there was a sewer entrance. 'Squat down,' he said, 'and stick you head in there,' and he held the back of the boy's coat while he got down and put his head in the sewer. He drew it back quickly, hearing a gurgling in the depths under the sidewalk. Then Mr Head explained the sewer system, how the entire city was underlined with it, how it contained all the drainage and was full of rats and how a man could slide into it and be sucked along down endless pitchblack tunnels. At any minute any man in the city might be sucked into the sewer and never heard from again. He described it so well that Nelson was for some seconds shaken. He connected the sewer passages with the entrance to hell and understood for the first time how the world was put together in its lower parts. He drew away from the curb.

Then he said, 'Yes, but you can stay away from the holes,' and his face took on that stubborn look that was so exasperating to his grandfather. 'This is where I come from!' he said.

Mr Head was dismayed but he only muttered. 'You'll get your fill,' and they walked on. At the end of two more blocks he turned to the left, feeling that he was circling the dome; and he was correct for in a half-hour they passed in front of the railroad station again. At first Nelson did not notice that he was seeing the same stores twice but when they passed the one where you put your feet on the rests while the Negro polished your shoes, he perceived that they were walking in a circle.

'We done been here!' he shouted. 'I don't believe you know where you're at!'

'The direction just slipped my mind for a minute,' Mr Head said and they turned down a different street. He still did not intend to let the dome get too far away and after two blocks in their new direction, he turned to the left. This street contained two- and three-story wooden dwellings. Anyone passing on the sidewalk could see into the rooms and Mr Head, glancing through one window, saw a woman lying on an iron bed, looking out, with a sheet pulled over her. Her knowing expression shook him. A fierce-looking boy on a bicycle came driving down out of nowhere and he had to jump to the side to keep from being hit. 'It's nothing to them if they knock you down,' he said. 'You better keep closer to me.'

They walked on for some time on streets like this before he remembered to turn again. The houses they were passing now were all unpainted and the wood in them looked rotten; the street between was narrower. Nelson saw a colored man. Then another. Then another. 'Niggers live in these houses,' he observed.

'Well come on and we'll go somewheres else,' Mr Head said. 'We didn't come to look at niggers,' and they turned down another street but they continued to see Negroes everywhere. Nelson's skin began to prickle and they stepped along at a faster pace in order to leave the neighborhood as soon as possible. There were colored men in their undershirts standing in the doors and colored women rocking on sagging porches. Colored children played in the gutters and stopped what they were doing to look at them. Before long they began to pass rows of stores with colored customers in them but they didn't pause at the entrances of these. Black eyes in black faces were watching them from every direction. 'Yes,' Mr Head said, 'this is where you were born – right here with all these niggers.'

Nelson scowled. 'I think you done got us lost,' he said.

Mr Head swung around sharply and looked for the dome. It was nowhere in sight. 'I ain't got us lost either,' he said. 'You're just tired of walking.'

'I ain't tired, I'm hungry,' Nelson said. 'Give me a biscuit.'

They discovered then that they had lost the lunch.

'You were the one holding the sack,' Nelson said. 'I would have kepaholt of it.'

'If you want to direct this trip, I'll go on by myself and leave you right here,' Mr Head said and was pleased to see the boy turn white. However, he realized they were lost and drifting farther every minute from the station. He was hungry himself and beginning to be thirsty and since they had been in the colored neighborhood, they had both begun to sweat. Nelson had on his shoes and he was unaccustomed to them. The concrete sidewalks were very hard. They both wanted to find a place to sit down but this was impossible and they kept on walking, the boy muttering under his breath, 'First you lost the sack and then you lost the way,' and Mr Head growling from time to time, 'Anybody wants to be from this nigger heaven can be from it!'

By now the sun was well forward in the sky. The odor of dinners cooking drifted out to them. The Negroes were all at their doors to see them pass. 'Whyn't you ask one of these niggers the way?' Nelson said 'You got us lost.'

'This is where you were born,' Mr Head said. 'You can ask one yourself if you want to.'

Nelson was afraid of the colored men and didn't want to be laughed at by the colored children. Up ahead he saw a large colored woman leaning in a doorway that opened onto the sidewalk. He hair stood straight out from her head for about four inches all around and she was resting on bare brown feet that turned pink at the sides. She had on a pink dress that showed her exact shape. As they came abreast of her, she lazily lifted one hand to her head and her fingers disappeared into her hair.

Nelson stopped. He felt his breath drawn up by the woman's dark eyes. 'How do you get back to town?' he said in a voice that did not sound like his own.

After a minute she said, 'You in town now,' in a rich low tone that made Nelson feel as if a cool spray had been turned on him.

'How do you get back to the train?' he said in the same reed-like voice.

'You can catch you a car,' she said.

He understood she was making fun of him but he was too paralyzed even to scowl. He stood drinking in every detail of her. His eyes travelled up from her great knees to her forehead and then made a triangular path from the glistening sweat on her neck down and across her tremendous bosom and over her bare arm back to where her fingers lay hidden in her hair. He suddenly wanted her to reach down and pick him up and draw him against her and then he wanted to feel her breath on his face. He wanted to look down and down into her eyes while she held him tighter and tighter. He had never had such a feeling before. He felt as if he were reeling down through a pitchblack tunnel.

'You can go a block down yonder and catch you a car take you to the railroad station Sugarpie,' she said.

Nelson would have collapsed at her feet if Mr Head had not pulled him roughly away. 'You act like you don't have any sense!' the old man growled.

They hurried down the street and Nelson did not look back at the woman. He pushed his hat sharply forward over his face which was already burning with shame. The sneering ghost he had seen in the train window and all the foreboding feelings he had on the way returned to him and he remembered that his ticket from the scale had said to beware of dark women and that his grandfather's had said he was upright and brave. He took hold of the old man's hand, a sign of dependence that he seldom showed.

They headed down the street toward the car tracks where a long yellow rattling trolley was coming. Mr Head had never boarded a streetcar and he let that one pass. Nelson was silent. From time to time his mouth trembled slightly but his grandfather, occupied with his own problems, paid him no attention. They stood on the corner and neither looked at the Negroes who were passing, going about their business just as if they had been white, except that most of them stopped and eyed Mr Head and Nelson. It occurred to Mr Head that since the streetcar ran on tracks, they could simply follow the tracks. He gave Nelson a slight push and explained that they would follow the tracks on into the railroad station, walking, and they set off.

Presently to their great relief they began to see white people again and Nelson sat down on the sidewalk against the wall of a building. 'I got to rest myself some,' he said. 'You lost the sack and the direction. You can just wait on me to rest myself.'

'There's the tracks in front of us,' Mr Head said. 'All we got to do is keep them in sight and you could have remembered the sack as good as me. This is where you were born. This is your old home town. This is your second trip. You ought to know how to do,' and he squatted down and continued in this vein but the boy, easing his burning feet out of his shoes, did not answer.

'And standing there grinning like a chim-pan-zee while a nigger woman gives you directions. Great Gawd!' Mr Head said.

'I never said I was nothing but born here,' the boy said in a shaky voice. 'I never said I would or wouldn't like it. I never said I wanted to come. I only said I was born here and I never had nothing to do with that. I want to go home. I never wanted to come in the first place. It was all your big idea. How you know you ain't following the tracks in the wrong direction?'

This last had occurred to Mr Head too. 'All these people are white,' he said.

'We ain't passed here before,' Nelson said. This was a neighborhood of brick buildings that might have been lived in or might not. A few empty automobiles were parked along the curb and there was an occasional passerby. The heat of the pavement came up through Nelson's thin suit. His eyelids began to droop, and after a few minutes his head tilted forward. His shoulders twitched once or twice and then he fell over on his side and lay sprawled in an exhausted fit of sleep.

Mr Head watched him silently. He was very tired himself but they could not both sleep at the same time and he could not have slept anyway because he did not know where he was. In a few minutes Nelson would wake up, refreshed by his sleep and very cocky, and would begin complaining that he had lost the sack and the way. You'd have a mighty sorry time if I wasn't here, Mr Head thought; and then another idea occurred to him. He looked at the sprawled figure for several minutes; presently he stood up. He justified what he was going to do on the grounds that it is sometimes necessary to teach a child a lesson he won't forget, particularly when the child is always reasserting his position with some new impudence. He walked without a sound to the corner about twenty feet away and sat down on a covered garbage can in the alley where he could look out and watch Nelson wake up alone.

The boy was dozing fitfully, half conscious of vague noises and black forms moving up from some dark part of him into the light. His face worked in his sleep and he had pulled his knees up under his chin. The sun shed a dull dry light on the narrow street; everything looked like exactly what it was. After a while Mr Head, hunched like an old monkey on the garbage can lid, decided that if Nelson didn't wake up soon, he would make a loud noise by bamming his foot against the can. He looked at his watch and discovered that it was two o'clock. Their train left at six and the possibility of missing it was too awful for him to think of. He kicked his foot backwards on the can and a hollow boom reverberated in the alley.

Nelson shot up onto his feet with a shout. He looked where his grandfather should have been and stared. He seemed to whirl several times and then, picking up his feet and throwing his head back, he dashed down the street like a wild maddened pony. Mr Head jumped off the can and galloped after but the child was almost out of sight. He saw a streak of gray disappearing diagonally a block ahead. He ran as fast as he could, looking both ways down every intersection, but without sight of him again. Then as he passed the third intersection, completely winded, he saw about half a block down the street a scene that stopped him altogether. He crouched behind a trash box to watch and get his bearings.

Nelson was sitting with both legs spread out and by his side lay an elderly woman, screaming. Groceries were scattered about the sidewalk. A crowd of women had already gathered to see justice done and Mr Head distinctly heard the old woman on the pavement shout, 'You've broken my ankle and your daddy'll pay for it! Every nickel! Police! Police!' Several of the women were plucking at Nelson's shoulder but the boy seemed too dazed to get up.

Something forced Mr Head from behind the trash box and forward, but only at a creeping pace. He had never in his life been accosted by a policeman. The women were milling around Nelson as if they might suddenly all dive on him at once and tear him to pieces, and the old woman continued to scream that her ankle was broken and to call for an officer. Mr Head came on so slowly that he could have been taking a backward step after each forward one, but when he was about ten feet away, Nelson saw him and sprang. The child caught him around the hips and clung panting against him.

The women all turned on Mr Head. The injured one sat up and shouted, 'You sir! You'll pay every penny of my doctor's bill that your boy has caused. He's a juve-nile delinquent! Where is an officer? Somebody take this man's name and address!'

Mr Head was trying to detach Nelson's fingers from the flesh in the back of his legs. The old man's head had lowered itself into his collar like a turtle's; his eyes were glazed with fear and caution.

'Your boy has broken my ankle!' the old woman shouted. 'Police!'

Mr Head sensed the approach of the policeman from behind. He stared straight ahead at the women who were massed in their fury like a solid wall to block his escape. 'This is not my boy,' he said. 'I never seen him before.'

He felt Nelson's fingers fall out of his flesh.

The women dropped back staring at him with horror, as if they were so repulsed by a man who would deny his own image and likeness that they could not bear to lay hands on him. Mr Head walked on, through a space they silently cleared, and left Nelson behind. Ahead of him he saw nothing but a hollow tunnel that had once been the street.

The boy remained standing where he was, his neck craned forward and his hands hanging by his sides. His hat was jammed on his head so that there were no longer any creases in it. The injured woman got up and shook her fist at him and the others gave him pitying looks, but he didn't notice any of them. There was no policeman in sight.

In a minute he began to move mechanically, making no effort to catch up with his grandfather but merely following at about twenty paces. They walked on for five blocks in this way. Mr Head's shoulders were sagging and his neck hung forward at such an angle that it was not visible from behind. He was afraid to turn his head. Finally he cut a short hopeful glance over his shoulder. Twenty feet behind, he saw two small eyes piercing into his back like pitchfork prongs.

The boy was not of a forgiving nature but this was the first time he had ever had anything to forgive. Mr Head had never disgraced himself before. After two more blocks, he turned and called over his shoulder in a high desperately gay voice, 'Let's us go get us a Co' Cola somewheres!'

Nelson, with a dignity he had never shown before, turned and stood with his back to his grandfather.

Mr Head began to feel the depth of his denial. His face as they walked on became all hollows and bare ridges. He saw nothing they were passing but he perceived that they had lost the car tracks. There was no dome to be seen anywhere and the afternoon was advancing. He knew that if dark overtook them in the city, they would be beaten and robbed. The speed of God's justice was only what he expected for himself, but he could not stand to think that his sins would be visited upon Nelson and that even now, he was leading the boy to his doom.

They continued to walk on block after block through an endless section of small brick houses until Mr Head almost fell over a water spigot sticking up about six inches off the edge of a grass plot. He had not had a drink of water since early morning but he felt he did not deserve it now. Then he thought that Nelson would be thirsty and they would both drink and be brought together. He squatted down and put his mouth to the nozzle and turned a cold stream of water into his throat. Then he called out in the high desperate voice, 'Come on and getcher some water!'

This time the child stared through him for nearly sixty seconds. Mr Head got up and walked on as if he had drunk poison. Nelson, though he had not had water since some he had drunk out of a paper cup on the train, passed by the spigot, disdaining to drink where his grandfather had. When Mr Head realized this, he lost all hope. His face in the waning afternoon light looked ravaged and abandoned. He could feel the boy's steady hate, travelling at an even pace behind him and he knew that (if by some miracle they escaped being murdered in the city) it would continue just that way for the rest of his life. He knew that now he was wandering into a black strange place where nothing was like it had ever been before, a long old age without respect and an end that would be welcome because it would be the end.

As for Nelson, his mind had frozen around his grandfather's treachery as if he were trying to preserve it intact to present at the final judgment. He walked without looking to one side or the other, but every now and then his mouth would twitch and this was when he felt, from some remote place inside himself, a black mysterious form reach up as if it would melt his frozen vision in one hot grasp.

The sun dropped down behind a row of houses and hardly noticing, they passed into an elegant suburban section where mansions were set back from the road by lawns with birdbaths on them. Here everything was entirely deserted. For blocks they didn't pass even a dog. The big white houses were like partially submerged icebergs in the distance. There were no sidewalks, only drives, and these wound around and around in endless ridiculous circles. Nelson made no move to come nearer to Mr Head. The old man felt that if he saw a sewer entrance he would drop down into it and let himself be carried away; and he could imagine the boy standing by, watching with only a slight interest, while he disappeared.

A loud bark jarred him to attention and he looked up to see a fat man approaching with two bulldogs. He waved both arms like someone shipwrecked on a desert island. 'I'm lost!' he called. 'I'm lost and can't find my way and me and this boy have got to catch this train and I can't find the station. Oh Gawd I'm lost! Oh hep me Gawd I'm lost!'

The man, who was bald-headed and had on golf knickers, asked him what train he was trying to catch and Mr Head began to get out his tickets, trembling so violently he could hardly hold them. Nelson had come up to within fifteen feet and stood watching.

'Well,' the fat man said, giving him back the tickets, 'you won't have time to get back to town to make this but you can catch it at the suburb stop. That's three blocks from here,' and he began explaining how to get there.

Mr Head stared as if he were slowly returning from the dead and when the man had finished and gone off with the dogs jumping at his heels, he turned to Nelson and said breathlessly, 'We're going to get home!'

The child was standing about ten feet away, his face bloodless under the gray hat. His eyes were triumphantly cold. There was no light in them, no feeling, no interest. He was merely there, a small figure, waiting. Home was nothing to him.

Mr Head turned slowly. He felt he knew now what time would be like without seasons and what heat would be like without light and what man would be like without salvation. He didn't care if he never made the train and if it had not been for what suddenly caught his attention, like a cry out of the gathering dusk, he might have forgotten there was a station to go to.

He had not walked five hundred yards down the road when he saw, within reach of him, the plaster figure of a Negro sitting bent over on a low yellow brick fence that curved around a wide lawn. The Negro was about Nelson's size and he was pitched forward at an unsteady angle because the putty that held him to the wall had cracked. One of his eyes was entirely white and he held a piece of brown watermelon.

Mr Head stood looking at him silently until Nelson stopped at a little distance. Then as the two of them stood there, Mr Head breathed, 'An artificial nigger!'

It was not possible to tell if the artificial Negro were meant to be young or old; he looked too miserable to be either. He was meant to look happy because his mouth was stretched up at the corners but the chipped eye and the angle he was cocked at gave him a wild look of misery instead.

'An artificial nigger!' Nelson repeated in Mr Head's exact tone.

The two of them stood there with their necks forward at almost the same angle and their shoulders curved in almost exactly the same way and their hands trembling identically in their pockets. Mr Head looked like an ancient child and Nelson like a miniature old man. They stood gazing at the artificial Negro as if they were faced with some great mystery, some monument to another's victory that brought them together in their common defeat. They could both feel it dissolving their differences like an action of mercy. Mr Head had never known before what mercy felt like because he had been too good to deserve any, but he felt he knew now. He looked at Nelson and understood that he must say something to the child to show that he was still wise and in the look the boy returned he saw a hungry need for that assurance. Nelson's eyes seemed to implore him to explain once and for all the mystery of existence.

Mr Head opened his lips to make a lofty statement and heard himself say, 'They ain't got enough real ones here. They got to have an artificial one.'

After a second, the boy nodded with a strange shivering about his mouth, and said, 'Let's go home before we get ourselves lost again.'

Their train glided into the suburb stop just as they reached the station and they boarded it together, and ten minutes before it was due to arrive at the junction, they went to the door and stood ready to jump off if it did not stop; but it did, just as the moon, restored to its full splendor, sprang from a cloud and flooded the clearing with light. As they stepped off, the sage grass was shivering gently in shades of silver and the clinkers under their feet glittered with a fresh black light. The treetops, fencing the junction like the protecting walls of a garden, were darker than the sky which was hung with gigantic white clouds illuminated like lanterns.

Mr Head stood very still and felt the action of mercy touch him again but this time he knew that there were no words in the world that could name it. He understood that it grew out of agony, which is not denied to any man and which is given in strange ways to children. He understood it was all a man could carry into death to give his Maker and he suddenly burned with shame that he had so little of it to take with him. He stood appalled, judging himself with the thoroughness of God, while the action of mercy covered his pride like a flame and consumed it. He had never thought himself a great sinner before but he saw now that his true depravity had been hidden from him lest it cause him despair. He realized that he was forgiven for sins from the beginning of time, when he had conceived in his own heart the sin of Adam, until the present, when he had denied poor Nelson. He saw that no sin was too monstrous for him to claim as his own, and since God loved in proportion as He forgave, he felt ready at that instant to enter Paradise.

Nelson, composing his expression under the shadow of his hat brim, watched him with a mixture of fatigue and suspicion, but as the train glided past them and disappeared like a frightened serpent into the woods, even his face lightened and he muttered, 'I'm glad I've went once, but I'll never go back again!'

The Lowboy
John Cheever

O
h I hate small men and I will write about them no more but in passing I would like to say that's what my brother Richard is: small. He has small hands, small feet, a small waist, small children, a small wife, and when he comes to our cocktail parties he sits in a small chair. If you pick up a book of his, you will find his name, 'Richard Norton,' on the flyleaf in his very small handwriting. He emanates, in my opinion, a disgusting *aura* of smallness. He is also spoiled, and when you go to his house you eat *his* food from *his* china with *his* silver, and if you observe his capricious and vulgar house rules you may be lucky enough to get some of *his* brandy, just as thirty years ago one went into his room to play with *his* toys at *his* pleasure and to be rewarded with a glass of *his* ginger ale. Some people make less of an adventure than a performance of their passions. They do not seem to fall in love and make friends but to cast, with men, women, children, and dogs, some stirring drama that they were committed to producing at the moment of their birth. This is especially noticeable on the part of those whose casting is limited by a slender emotional budget. The clumsy performances draw our attention to the play. The ingénue is much too old. So is the leading lady. The dog is the wrong breed, the furniture is ill-matched, the costumes are threadbare, and when the coffee is poured there seems to be nothing in the pot. But the drama goes on with as much terror and pity as it does in more magnificent productions. Watching my brother, I feel that he has marshalled a second-rate cast and that he is performing, perhaps for eternity, the role of a spoiled child.

It is traditional in our family to display our greatest emotional powers over heirlooms – to appropriate sets of dishes before the will can be probated, to have tugs-of-war with carpets, and to rupture blood relationships over the subject of a rickety chair. Stories and tales that dwell on some wayward attachment to an object – a soup tureen or a lowboy – seem to narrow down to the texture of the object itself, the glare on the china or the finish on the wood, and to generate those feelings of frustration that I, for one, experience when I hear harpsichord music. My last encounter with my brother involved a lowboy. Because our mother died unexpectedly and there was an ambiguous clause in her will, certain of the family heirlooms were seized by Cousin Mathilda. No one felt strong enough at the time to contest her claims. She is now in her nineties, and age seems to have cured her rapacity. She wrote to Richard and me saying that if she had anything we wanted she would be happy to let us have it. I wrote to say that I would like the lowboy. I remembered it as a graceful, bowlegged piece of furniture with heavy brasses and a highly polished veneer the color of cordovan. My request was halfhearted. I did not really care, but it seemed that my brother did. Cousin Mathilda wrote him that she was giving the lowboy to me, and he telephoned to say that he wanted it – that he wanted it so much more than I did that there was no point in even discussing it. He asked if he could visit me on Sunday – we live about fifty miles apart – and, of course, I invited him.

It was not his house or his whiskey that day, but it was his charm that he was dispensing and in which I was entitled to bask, and, noticing some roses in the garden that he had given my wife many years back, he said, 'I see *my* roses are doing well.' We drank in the garden. It was a spring day – one of those green-gold Sundays that excite our incredulity. Everything was blooming, opening, burgeoning. There was more than one could see – prismatic lights, prismatic smells, something that set one's teeth on edge with pleasure – but it was the shadow that was most mysterious and exciting, the light one could not define. We sat under a big maple, its leaves not yet fully formed but formed enough to hold the light, and it was astounding in its beauty, and seemed not like a single tree but one of a million, a link in a long chain of leafy trees beginning in childhood.

'What about the lowboy?' Richard asked.

'What about it? Cousin Mathilda wrote to ask if I wanted anything, and it was the only thing I wanted.'

'You've never cared about those things.'

'I wouldn't say that.'

'But it's *my* lowboy!'

'Everything has always been yours, Richard.'

'Don't quarrel,' my wife said, and she was quite right. I had spoken foolishly.

'I'll be happy to buy the lowboy from you,' Richard said.

'I don't want your money.'

'What do you want?'

'I would like to know why you want the lowboy so much.'

'It's hard to say, but I do want it, and I want it terribly!' He spoke with unusual candor and feeling. This seemed more than his well-known possessiveness. 'I'm not sure why. I feel that it was the centre of our house, the centre of our life before Mother died. If I had one solid piece of furniture, one object I could point to, that would remind me of how happy we all were, of how we used to live. . .'

I understood him (who wouldn't?), but I suspected his motives. The lowboy was an elegant piece of furniture, and I wondered if he didn't want it for cachet, as a kind of family crest, something that would vouch for the richness of his past and authenticate his descent from the most aristocratic of the seventeenth-century settlers. I could see him standing proudly beside it with a drink in his hand. *My* lowboy. It would appear in the background of their Christmas card, for it was one of those pieces of cabinetwork that seem to have a countenance of the most exquisite breeding. It would be the final piece in the puzzle of respectability that he had made of his life. We had shared a checkered, troubled, and sometimes sorrowful past, and Richard had risen from this chaos into a dazzling and resplendent respectability, but perhaps this image of himself would be improved by the lowboy; perhaps the image would not be complete without it.

I said that he could have it, then, and his thanks were intense. I wrote to Mathilda, and Mathilda wrote to me. She would send me, as a consolation, Grandmother DeLancey's sewing box, with its interesting contents – the Chinese fan, the sea horse from Venice, and the invitation to Buckingham Palace. There was a problem of delivery. Nice Mr Osborn was willing to take the lowboy as far as my house but no farther. He would deliver it on Thursday, and then I could take it on to Richard's in my station wagon whenever this was convenient. I called Richard and explained these arrangements to him, and he was, as he had been from the beginning, nervous and intense. Was my station wagon big enough? Was it in good condition? And where would I keep the lowboy between Thursday and Sunday? I mustn't leave it in the garage.

When I came home on Thursday the lowboy was there, and it was in the garage. Richard called in the middle of dinner to see if it had arrived, and spoke revealingly, from the depths of his peculiar feelings.

'Of course you'll let me have the lowboy?' he asked.

'I don't understand.'

'You won't *keep* it?'

What was at the bottom of this? I wondered. Why should he endure jealousy as well as love for a stick of wood? I said that I would deliver it to him on Sunday, but he didn't trust me. He would drive up with Wilma, his small wife, on Sunday morning and accompany me back.

On Saturday my oldest son helped me carry the thing from the garage into the hall, and I had a good look at it. Cousin Mathilda had cared for it tenderly and the ruddy veneer had a polish of great depth, but on the top was a dark ring – it gleamed through the polish like something seen under water – where, for as long as I could remember, an old silver pitcher had stood, filled with apple blossoms or peonies or roses or, as the summer ended, chrysanthemums and coloured leaves. I remembered the contents of the drawers, gathered there like a precipitate of our lives: the dog leashes, the ribbons for the Christmas wreaths, golf balls and playing cards, the German angel, the paper knife with which Cousin Timothy had stabbed himself, the crystal inkwell, and the keys to many forgotten doors. It was a powerful souvenir.

Richard and Wilma came on Sunday, bringing a pile of soft blankets to protect the varnish from the crudities of my station wagon. Richard and the lowboy were united like true lovers, and, considering the possibilities of magnificence and pathos in love, it seemed tragic that he should have become infatuated with a chest of drawers. He must have had the same recollections as I when he saw the dark ring gleaming below the polish and looked into the ink-stained drawers. I have seen gardeners attached to their lawns, violinists to their instruments, gamblers to their good-luck pieces, and old ladies to their lace, and it was in this realm of emotion, as unsparing as love, that Richard found himself. He anxiously watched my son and me carrying the thing out to the station wagon, wrapped in blankets. It was a little too big. The carved claw feet extended a few inches beyond the tail gate. Richard wrung his hands, but he had no alternative. When the lowbody was tucked in, we started off. He did not urge me to drive carefully, but I knew this was on his mind.

When the accident occurred, I could have been blamed in spirit but not in fact. I don't see how I could have avoided it. We were stopped at a toll station, where I was waiting for my change, when a convertible, full of adolescents, collided with the back of my car and splintered one of the bowed legs.

'Oh, you crazy fools!' Richard howled. 'You crazy, thoughtless criminals!' He got out of the car, waving his hands and swearing. The damage did not look too great to me, but Richard was inconsolable. With tears in his eyes, he lectured the bewildered adolescents. The lowboy was of inestimable value. It was over two hundred years old. No amount of money, no amount of insurance could compensate for the damage. Something rare and beautiful had been lost to the world. While he raved, cars piled up behind us, horns began to blow, and the toll collector told us to move. 'This is *serious*,' Richard said to him. When we had got the name and the registration of the criminal in the driver's seat, we went along, but he was terribly shaken. At his house we carried the injured antique tenderly into the dining room and put it on the floor in its wrappings. His shock seemed to have given way now to a glimmer of hope, and when he fingered the splintered leg you could see that he had begun to think of a future in which the leg would be repaired. He gave me a correct drink, and talked about his garden, as any well-mannered man in the face of a personal tragedy will carry on, but you could feel that his heart was with the victim in the next room.

Richard and I do not see much of one another, and we did not meet for a month or so, and when we did meet it was over dinner in the Boston airport, where we both chanced to be waiting for planes. It was summer – midsummer, I guess, because I was on the way to Nantucket. It was hot. It was getting dark. There was a special menu that night involving flaming swords. The cooked food – shish kebab or calves' liver or half a broiler – was brought to a side table and impaled on a small sword. Then a waiter would put what looked like cotton wool on the tip of the sword, ignite this, and serve the food in a blaze of fire and chivalry. I mention this not because it seemed comical or vulgar but because it was affecting to see, in the summer dusk, how delighted the good and modest people of Boston were with this show. While the flaming swords went to and fro, Richard talked about the lowboy.

What an adventure! What a story! First he had checked all the cabinetmakers in the neighbourhood and found a man in Westport who could be relied upon to repair the leg, but when the cabinetmaker saw the lowboy he, too, fell in love. He wanted to buy it, and when Richard refused he wanted to know its history. When the thing was repaired, they had it photographed and sent the picture to an authority on eighteenth-century furniture. It was famous, it was notorious, it was the Barstow lowboy, made by the celebrated Sturbridge cabinetmaker in 1780 and thought to have been lost in a fire. It had belonged to the Pooles (our great-great-grandmother was a Poole) and appeared in their inventories until 1840, when their house was destroyed, but only the knowledge of its whereabouts had been lost. The piece itself had come down, safely enough, to us. And now it had been reclaimed, like a prodigal, by the most highminded antiquarians. A curator at the Metropolitan had urged Richard to let the Museum have it on loan. A collector had offered him ten thousand dollars. He was enjoying the delicious experience of discovering that what he adored and possessed was adored by most of mankind.

I flinched when he mentioned the ten thousand dollars – after all, I could have kept the thing – but I did not want it, I had never really wanted it, and I sensed in the airport dining room that Richard was in some kind of danger. We said goodbye then and flew off in different directions. He called me in the autumn about some business, and he mentioned the lowboy again. Did I remember the rug on which it had stood at home? I did. It was an old Turkey carpet, multicolored and scattered with arcane symbols. Well, he had found very nearly the same rug at a New York dealer's, and now the claw feet rested on the same geometric fields of brown and yellow. You could see that he was putting things together – he was completing the puzzle – and while he never told me what happened next, I could imagine it easily enough. He bought a silver pitcher and filled it with leaves and sat there alone one autumn evening drinking whiskey and admiring his creation.

It would have been raining on the night I imagined; no other sound transports Richard with such velocity backward in time. At last everything was perfect – the pitcher, the polish on the heavy brasses, the carpet. The chest of drawers would seem not to have been lifted into the present but to have moved the past with it into the room. Wasn't that what he wanted? He would admire the dark ring in the varnish and the fragrance of the empty drawers, and under the influence of two liquids – rain and whiskey – the hands of those who had touched the lowboy, polished it, left their drinks on it, arranged the flowers in the pitcher and stuffed odds and ends of string into the drawers would seem to reach out of the dark. As he watched, their dull fingerprints clustered on the polish, as if this were their means of clinging to life. By recalling them, by going a step further, he evoked

them, and they came down impetuously into the room – they flew – as
if they had been waiting in pain and impatience all those years for his
invitation.

First to come back from the dead was Grandmother DeLancey, all
dressed in black and smelling of ginger. Handsome, intelligent,
victorious, she had broken with the past, and the thrill of this had
borne her along with the force of a wave through all the days of her life
and, so far as one knew, had washed her up into the very gates of
heaven. Her education, she said scornfully, had consisted of learning
how to hem a pocket handkerchief and speak a little French, but she
had left a world where it was improper for a lady to hold an opinion
and come into one where she could express her opinions on a
platform, pound the lectern with her fist, walk alone in the dark, and
cheer (as she always did) the firemen when the red wagon came
helling up the street. Her manner was firm and oracular, for she had
travelled as far west as Cleveland lecturing on women's rights. A lady
could be anything! A doctor! A lawyer! An engineer! A lady could, like
Aunt Louisa, smoke cigars.

Aunt Louisa was smoking a cigar as she flew in to join the
gathering. The fringe of a Spanish shawl spread out behind her in the
air, and her hoop earrings rocked as she made, as always, a forceful, a
pressing entrance, touched the lowboy, and settled on the blue chair.
She was an artist. She had studied in Rome. Crudeness, flamboyance,
passion, and disaster attended her. She tackled all the big subjects –
the Rape of the Sabines, and the Sack of Rome. Naked men and
women thronged her huge canvases, but they were always out of
drawing, the colours were dim, and even the clouds above her
battlefields seemed despondent. Her failure was not revealed to her
until it was too late. She poured her ambitions onto her oldest son,
Timothy, who walked in sullenly from the grave, carrying a volume of
Beethoven sonatas, his face dark with rancour.

Timothy would be a great pianist. It was her decision. He was put
through every suffering, deprivation, and humiliation known to a
prodigy. It was a solitary and bitter life. He had his first recital when
he was seven. He played with an orchestra when he was twelve. He
went on tour the next year. He wore strange clothes, and used grease
on his long curls, and killed himself when he was fifteen. His mother
had pushed him pitilessly. And why should this passionate and
dedicated woman have made such a mistake? She may have meant to
heal or avenge a feeling that, through birth or misfortune, she had

been kept out of the blessed company of contented men and women. She may have believed that fame would end all this – that if she were a famous painter or he a famous pianist, they would never again taste loneliness or know scorn.

Richard could not have kept Uncle Tom from joining them if he had wanted to. He was powerless. He had been too late in realizing that the fascination of the lowboy was the fascination of pain, and he had committed himself to it. Uncle Tom came in with the grace of an old athlete. He was the amorous one. No one had been able to keep track of his affairs. His girls changed weekly – they sometimes changed in midweek. There were tens, there were hundreds, there may have been thousands. He carried in his arms his youngest son, Peter, whose legs were in braces. Peter had been crippled just before his birth, when, during a quarrel between his parents, Uncle Tom pushed Aunt Louisa down the stairs.

Aunt Mildred came stiffly through the air, drew her blue skirt down over her knees as she settled herself, and looked uneasily at Grandmother. The old lady had passed on to Mildred her emancipation, as if it were a nation secured by treaties and compacts, flags and anthems. Mildred knew that passivity, needlepoint, and housework were not for her. To decline into a contented housewife would have meant handing over to the tyrant those territories that her mother had won for eternity with the sword. She knew well enough what it was that she must not do, but she had never decided what it was that she should do. She wrote pageants. She wrote verse. She worked for six years on a play about Christopher Columbus. Her husband, Uncle Sidney, pushed the perambulator and sometimes the carpet sweeper. She watched him angrily at his housework. He had usurped her rights, her usefulness. She took a lover and, going for the first three or four times to the hotel where they met, she felt that she had found herself. This was not one of the opportunities that her mother had held out to her, but it was better than Christopher Columbus. Furtive love was the contribution she was meant to make. The affair was sordid and came to a sordid end, with disclosures, anonymous letters, and bitter tears. Her lover absconded, and Uncle Sidney began to drink.

Uncle Sidney staggered back from the grave and sat down on the sofa beside Richard, stinking of liquor. He had been drunk ever since he discovered his wife's folly. His face was swollen. His belly was so enlarged that it had burst a shirt button. His mind and his eyes were glazed. In his drunkenness he dropped a lighted cigarette onto the sofa, and the velvet began to smoke. Richard's position seemed confined to observation. He could not speak or move. Then Uncle Sidney noticed the fire and poured the contents of his whiskey glass onto the upholstery. The whiskey and the sofa burst into flame. Grandmother, who was sitting on the old pegged Windsor chair, sprang to her feet, but the pegs caught her clothing and tore the seat of her dress. The dogs began to bark, and Peter, the young cripple, began to sing in a thin voice – obscenely sarcastic – 'Joy to the world! the Lord is come. Let Heaven and nature sing,' for it was a Christmas dinner that Richard had reconstructed.

At some point – perhaps when he purchased the silver pitcher – Richard committed himself to the horrors of the past, and his life, like so much else in nature, took the form of an arc. There must have been some felicity, some clearness in his feeling for Wilma, but once the lowboy took a commanding position in his house, he seemed driven back upon his wretched childhood. We went there for dinner – it must have been Thanksgiving. The lowboy stood in the dining room, on its carpet of mysterious symbols, and the silver pitcher was full of chrysanthemums. Richard spoke to his wife and children in a tone of vexation that I had forgotten. He quarrelled with everyone; he even quarrelled with my children. Oh, why is it that life is for some an exquisite privilege and others must pay for their seats at the play with a ransom of cholers, infections, and nightmares? We got away as soon as we could.

When we got home, I took the green glass epergne that belonged to Aunt Mildred off the sideboard and smashed it with a hammer. Then I dumped Grandmother's sewing box into the ash can, burned a big hole in her lace tablecloth, and buried her pewter in the garden. Out they go – the Roman coins, the sea horse from Venice, and the Chinese fan. We can cherish nothing less than our random understanding of death and the earth-shaking love that draws us to one another. Down with the stuffed owl in the upstairs hall and the statue of Hermes on the newel post! Hock the ruby necklace, throw away the invitation to Buckingham Palace, jump up and down on the perfume atomizer from Murano and the Canton fish plates. Dismiss whatever molests us and challenges our purpose, sleeping or waking. Cleanliness and valour will be our watchwords. Nothing less will get us past the armed sentry and over the mountainous border.

INTRODUCING

Psychiatry

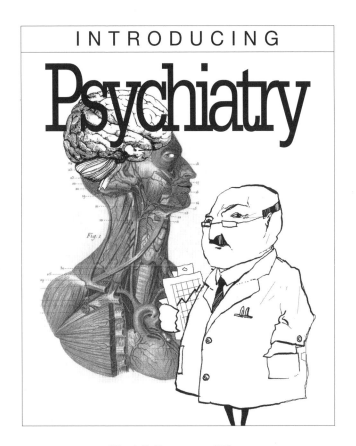

Nigel C. Benson and Piero

Edited by Richard Appignanesi

ICON BOOKS UK   TOTEM BOOKS USA

Published in the UK in 2004
by Icon Books Ltd., Grange Road,
Duxford, Cambridge CB2 4QF
E-mail: info@iconbooks.co.uk
www.iconbooks.co.uk

Sold in the UK, Europe, South Africa
and Asia by Faber and Faber Ltd.,
3 Queen Square, London WC1N 3AU
or their agents

Distributed in the UK, Europe, South Africa
and Asia by TBS Ltd., Frating Distribution
Centre, Colchester Road, Frating Green,
Colchester CO7 7DW

Published in Australia in 2004
by Allen & Unwin Pty. Ltd.,
PO Box 8500, 83 Alexander Street,
Crows Nest, NSW 2065

Published in the USA in 2004
by Totem Books
Inquiries to: Icon Books Ltd.,
Grange Road, Duxford,
Cambridge CB2 4QF, UK

Distributed to the trade in the USA by
National Book Network Inc.,
4720 Boston Way, Lanham,
Maryland 20706

Distributed in Canada by
Penguin Books Canada,
10 Alcorn Avenue, Suite 300,
Toronto, Ontario M4V 3B2

ISBN 1 84046 537 9

Originating editor: Richard Appignanesi

Printed and bound in Singapore
by Tien Wah Press

Human beings in crisis

What is psychiatry? Psychiatry is the branch of medicine that aims **to diagnose and treat mental illness.**

How common is mental illness?

To answer even basic questions about mental illness requires a context. A few simple statistics should give an immediate idea of the enormity of the problem.

Why don't more people seek psychiatric help?

According to some professionals, many disorders remain undetected and untreated because those affected are not seeking help. They are reluctant to become psychiatric patients.

Since ancient times, mental illness has often been associated with evil, witchcraft or the curse of sins! The mentally ill have been ostracized, ill-treated and at times deliberately killed or just left to die.

This is not all in the past. In the 21st century, there continue to be documented cases of mentally ill children being left to starve to death in some European and Asian countries.

What happened before psychiatry was invented?

Psychiatry in the modern sense dates from the period of Enlightenment, between 1730 and 1785. But there is a long history of dealing with mental disorders that goes back to the beginning of humankind.

Psychiatry can be traced back to the invention of so-called "primitive" diagnoses and treatments that are still in existence in some parts of the world today. "Primitive" here refers to the non-scientific nature of these therapies. But the word is misleading for two reasons.

> FIRST, THE UNDERLYING BELIEF SYSTEMS ARE NOT NECESSARILY SIMPLE AND ARE FREQUENTLY QUITE SOPHISTICATED.

> SECOND, THE CORRESPONDING TREATMENTS CAN BE EFFECTIVE, EVEN THOUGH THEY MAY BE DIFFICULT TO EXPLAIN BY CONVENTIONAL SCIENCE.

Primitive approaches to mental disorders mainly attributed them to physical disease or possession by evil spirits.

Examples of "primitive psychiatry"

Here are six examples of primitive theories about the causes of mental and physical illnesses, and their corresponding cures.

CAUSE OF ILLNESS	CURE
intrusion by a disease-object	extracting the disease-object (developed during the early Paleolithic period in the Old World)
loss of the soul	finding and restoring the lost soul (developed during the late Paleolithic period in Siberia)
possession by a spirit	exorcism, mechanical extraction or transferring to another living creature (developed during the late Pleistocene period in Western Asia)
breaking a taboo	confession (developed about 4,000 years ago in all three centres, along with the two below)
sorcery and witchcraft	counter-magic
frustration	gratification

POSSESSION AND EXORCISM STILL EXIST IN SOME PARTS OF THE WORLD TODAY.

Possession

A person, or group of people, is believed ill because an evil spirit has entered the body and "taken possession" of it. Possession is interesting because it is so widespread although, curiously, not universal. It was most common in Asia and Europe, especially around the Mediterranean, but less common on the American continent and (ironically) seems to be unknown among some of the most primitive tribes, e.g. the Australian Aborigines and the Pygmies of the Philippines.

There are generally two types of possession.

(a) The *somnambulic* – where the "possessed" is not aware of the possession.
(b) The *lucid* – where the individual remains aware of his or her own self, and of the intruding spirit.

Specialist **exorcists** speak not as themselves but in the name of a higher being. For example, today, Christian priests will still exorcize "in the name of Jesus". For exorcism to work, the exorcist must have absolute confidence in both himself and the higher being, and must totally believe in the reality of the possession by the evil spirit.

OFTEN THERE IS EXTENDED PREPARATION, INCLUDING FASTING AND PRAYER. THE EXORCISM ITSELF USUALLY CONSISTS OF A CEREMONY OR SERIES OF RITUALS.

EXORCISM CAN TAKE HOURS, DAYS, WEEKS, MONTHS OR EVEN YEARS BEFORE IT IS SUCCESSFUL.

Belief in possession (and related phenomena, such as witchcraft) gradually disappeared in Western societies through the rationalist influence of the Enlightenment. But it persisted among traditionalists, Romanticists and certain fundamentalist religious groups.

Healing through gratification of frustrations

The idea that frustrated wishes can cause disease has been known since ancient times.

The Bible, *Proverbs* XIII, 12, tells us: *"Hope deferred makes the heart sick, but the wish come true is a tree of life."*

And a Maori proverb says: *"There is a well of dissatisfaction in the heart of man, and hence vexation and anxiety."*

For centuries, until the 19th century, medical textbooks used to contain two illnesses that are almost forgotten today.

Romeo and Juliet

Lovesickness

YOUNG PEOPLE WOULD FADE AWAY AND DIE UNLESS THEY COULD BE WITH THE ONE PERSON THEY SECRETLY AND HOPELESSLY LOVED.

Homesickness (or nostalgia)

SOLDIERS, OR TRAVELLERS FAR FROM HOME, TALKED AND DREAMT INCESSANTLY ABOUT IT.

UNLESS THEY WERE ABLE TO RETURN HOME TO RECOVER, THEY COULD DIE OF THE MALADY.

Psychoanalysts today would readily understand these phenomena. Indeed, many aspects of primitive medicine would be recognized today.

Rational therapies in primitive psychiatry

Many of the practices of primitive therapy can be considered as precursors to present psychiatry or early examples of what we now call "alternative" or "complementary" therapies. For example, primitive approaches included the use of elementary surgery and drugs, baths, saunas and massage. Many modern medicines are connected to ancient wisdom.

THE COMMONLY USED ASPIRIN CONTAINS THE ACTIVE INGREDIENT SALICYLIC ACID WHICH IS IN WILLOW BARK.

G.W. Harley, who lived with the Mano tribe in Liberia, listed over 200 plants used by medicine men.

J. Qvistad studied the treatment of mental illness used by a native healer in Lapland and reported on a general recommendation: abstain from alcohol, tobacco and coffee; rise and retire early; keep occupied with light work; bathe twice a day (sea water in the morning and fresh water at night).

The primitive healer's creative illness

The primitive healer played a central role in the community. Patients often placed their confidence in the healer's *personality* much more than in the healing techniques. Part of the healer's training often involved an "initiatory illness" that mirrored experiences similar to those of their patients. The historian of psychiatry Henri Ellenberger classifies this in a group of experiences that he calls "creative illnesses".

Henri Ellenberger

Another important historical development occurred about 4000 BC when the first kingdoms and empires were founded in Asia …

Temple healing and philosophical psychotherapy

Early civilizations took over some aspects of primitive medicine, such as exorcism, and incorporated them into their religious and philosophical organizations. At the same time, physical diseases became separated from emotional conditions, with **physicians** and **lay healers** dealing more with the former, while **healing priests** dealt with the rest.

Religious and philosophical teachings also developed that included some forms of psychotherapy.

The Consolations of Philosophy

The Stoics learned the control of emotions and practised exercises in concentration and meditation. A topic such as "death" would be dissociated from personal fears, memories and established opinions, in order to cope with bereavement. Similarly, friendly discourses, called "consolations", were told or written for a person in sorrow.

Galen's Stoical approach

Galen (129–c.199 AD), a Greek physician in the Roman era, taught a method for mastering one's passions based on Stoicism. That was particularly important in his brutal times because the Greeks and Romans were apparently prone to fits of uncontrollable behaviour. In his *On the Passions of the Soul*, and *On the Errors of the Soul*, Galen describes many typical daily incidences.

Emperor Hadrian didn't exactly set a good example by piercing the eye of one of his slaves in a fit of anger. Galen put all this violence down to (in his terms) the "irascible" and "concupiscible" powers of the soul.

Galen's therapeutic methods

There are three steps for mastering one's passions …

1. Abstain from the crudest kind of emotional outbursts – kicking, biting, or in other ways wounding.

2. Find a mentor, a wise and older counsellor, who can point out your defects and dispense advice. (Galen stressed the paramount importance, and difficulty, of finding such a person.)

3. Engage, with the help of your mentor, in an unceasing effort to control your passions.

This method Galen considered feasible at any age, even 50, although it was best to start young. Other methods included reading aloud daily the maxims of the Greek sage Pythagoras and gradually reducing your standard of living until you had only the necessities of life …

The Roman Catholic Church and its "cures"

From about the third century AD, Galen and the other Graeco-Roman approaches to medicine were dismissed by the growing Christian Church for being undesirable pagan doctrines. In their place came the practices of prayers, vows, pilgrimages, and confessions made secretly to priests. The importance of the last activity can be seen in St Augustine's famous autobiography, the first in that genre, entitled *Confessions*.

Later Protestant "reformers" abolished compulsory confessions but introduced the practice of the "Cure of Souls" (*Seelsorge*). Confessions of disturbing secrets were obtained from distressed individuals in order to help them (similar to modern psychiatric therapies).

But there was also a much darker side to established Christianity.

The Witch Trials

Medieval belief in demonology and witchcraft persisted throughout Europe and pioneer America well into the 17th century. The trials of 250 people in 1691–2 in Salem, Massachusetts are well known. When anyone could be seized, accused of witchcraft, then tortured and burned alive, there must have been many cases of mentally ill people being caught up in the mass hysteria.

Execution of witches was eventually outlawed in Britain by the Witchcraft Act of 1736. The last person convicted was a medium imprisoned in WWII by a law not repealed until 1951! One of the last executions in Europe was in Switzerland in 1782.

Fortunately, a minority managed to keep alive the principles of "pagan" medicine – notably one individual …

Paracelsus

Paracelsus (1493–1541), a Swiss alchemist and visionary, was also an original and unconventional physician who cast scorn on the idea of "possession by demons".

MENTAL DISEASES HAVE NOTHING TO DO WITH EVIL SPIRITS OR DEVILS ...

ONE SHOULD NOT STUDY HOW TO EXORCIZE THE DEVIL BUT RATHER HOW TO CURE THE INSANE ... THE INSANE AND SICK ARE OUR BROTHERS AND SISTERS.

Paracelsus

Paracelsus, along with other brave souls – among them Juan Luis Vives, Cornelius Agrippa and Johann Weyer – paved the way for a scientific approach.

Scientific therapy

Modern science began at the end of the 16th century when measurement and experimentation were added to impartial observation as the means of increasing empirical knowledge. Medicine now became a branch of science and all therapies had to be "official". Primitive healing or popular cures were rejected. The contrast between primitive and scientific therapies can be summarized as follows …

Primitive therapy

The healer is something more than a physician: an important personality in the social group.

The healer uses his personality as a key part of the healing process.

The healer does not make a distinction between the physical and mental.

The healer's training often involves emotional or spiritual experiences.

Scientific therapy

The physician is a specialist among others.

The physician is impersonal and uses impersonal scientific techniques.

The physician concentrates on the strictly physical.

The training is purely rational, based on empirical laws.

THE HEALER USUALLY BELONGS TO A SCHOOL WHICH HAS ITS OWN TEACHINGS.

THE PHYSICIAN IS PART OF UNIFIED MEDICINE, UNIVERSALLY APPLICABLE.

The Enlightenment

Roughly speaking, the Enlightenment began in France in about 1730 and spread soon afterwards to England and Germany, before culminating around 1785. The birth of modern psychiatry can be traced to 1775, when the (new) physician Mesmer and the (old) exorcist Gassner clashed.

Johann Joseph Gassner (1727–79) was a popular, successful healer who attracted large crowds and exorcized many patients. But the authorities were not pleased with this and, in 1775, he was advised to confine his activities only to those patients sent to him by church ministers.

Animal Magnetism

Franz Anton Mesmer (1734–1815) was invited by an inquiry commission to investigate the work of Gassner and took the opportunity to display his new principle called "animal magnetism". He made various symptoms, such as convulsions and epilepsy, appear and disappear at a touch of his finger.

GASSNER WAS UNDOUBTEDLY AN HONEST MAN BUT WAS ACTUALLY USING "ANIMAL MAGNETISM" WITHOUT BEING AWARE OF IT.

MESMER WAS ABLE TO ESTABLISH HIMSELF AND DEFEAT HIS MAJOR RIVAL IN ONE BLOW. GASSNER DIED FOUR YEARS LATER.

Died 4 April 1779. Here lies the most celebrated exorcist of his time.

The rise of Mesmer

Mesmer became the Columbus of the new healing world and the founder of modern psychiatry. He travelled widely, performed his "magnetic" powers and cured many people. At first he used magnets and electricity in his cures but he dispensed with them by 1777.

Mesmer described his synthesized system, in 1779, under four basic principles.

(1) A fluid fills the universe and connects everything.
(2) Disease originates from the unequal distribution of this fluid in the human body.
(3) Using certain techniques, this fluid can be stored and channelled to others.
(4) In this way, "crises" can be provoked and diseases cured.

I SUMMARIZED THIS IN MY FAVOURITE APHORISM: "THERE IS ONLY ONE ILLNESS AND ONE HEALING."

To make healing possible, the "magnetizer" must establish a "**rapport**" – a kind of "tuning in" with the patient.

The end of Mesmer

Mesmer egocentrically believed his magnetism would cure or prevent all illnesses. His discovery would replace the whole history of medicine. He founded a successful Society (the "Société de l'Harmonie" – a sort of private school and masonic lodge) which people had to join in order to receive the secrets of magnetism. Mesmer was at the peak of his success when his activities received a series of setbacks from 1784 onwards.

Embarrassing incidents, such as failures to cure a blind musician and to demonstrate his powers to Prince Henry of Prussia, caused Mesmer to disappear from public view for the last 20 years of his life. He died in Switzerland in 1815.

Puységur's new magnetism

Mesmer's "magnetism" was continued by one of his disciples, the **Marquis de Puységur** (1751–1825). He developed a new type of treatment, **artificial somnambulism**, in which patients were apparently made to fall asleep, respond to instructions, and wake up cured with no memory of what had happened.

THE ENTIRE DOCTRINE OF ANIMAL MAGNETISM IS CONTAINED IN THE TWO WORDS: **BELIEVE** AND **WANT** ...

I BELIEVE I HAVE THE POWER WITHIN ME TO SET INTO ACTION THE VITAL PRINCIPLE OF MY FELLOW-MEN. I WANT TO MAKE USE OF IT ...

Later, in the 1840s, James Braid renamed artificial somnambulism "hypnosis" – the term we still use today.

The magnetic movement (along with many other things) was disrupted by the French Revolution of 1789 and it fell out of favour for about 25 years. However, the Romanticists resurrected it …

Romanticism

Romanticism originated in late 18th century Germany, and spread across England, France and other countries in the early 19th century. Romantic philosophers, poets and artists created a cult of the irrational and individual in reaction to the Enlightenment's over-emphasis on the values of reason and society. The German Romanticists were interested in animal magnetism for two reasons.

MESMER'S THEORY OF A UNIVERSAL, PHYSICAL "FLUID" FITS IN WITH OUR VIEW THAT THE UNIVERSE IS A LIVING ORGANISM WITH A SOUL THAT CONNECTS EVERYTHING.

EXTRA-LUCID MANIFESTATIONS, DESCRIBED BY MESMER AND PUYSÉGUR AS A "SIXTH SENSE", PROVIDE HUMANS WITH THE ABILITY TO DESCRIBE DISTANT EVENTS AND PREDICT THE FUTURE.

Magnetism and hypnotism once again fell into such disrepute by the 1860s that very few physicians would dare use them.

The Salpêtrière School

The Salpêtrière, an old and famous Paris hospital, was the site of a clinic in the 1860s led by **Jean-Martin Charcot** (1835–93). He was a neurologist who had become interested in mental phenomena. Charcot began using hypnotism in 1878, to treat cases of hysteria. During the 1880s, he demonstrated that conditions such as hysterical paralysis and mutism could be induced and removed under hypnosis.

HYSTERICS EXHIBIT "PARALYSIS" AND OTHER SYMPTOMS WITHOUT APPARENT CAUSE BY PHYSICAL DAMAGE ...

THE EXPLANATION MUST BE FOUND IN **MENTALLY INDUCED** DYSFUNCTION.

FREUD WAS PRESENT IN 1885 ...

SO, NEUROSES MAY BE CAUSED BY THE EXISTENCE OF UNCONSCIOUS IDEAS.

Freud

The Nancy School

The Nancy School, at another French hospital, was founded around 1880 by **Auguste Liébeault** (1823–1904), another who dared to use hypnotism openly. From 1886, this clinical school was led by **Hippolyte Bernheim** (1840–1919), who employed hypnotism to treat many organic diseases of the nervous system, rheumatism, gastrointestinal diseases and menstrual disorders.

I ALSO VISITED NANCY AND WAS IMPRESSED WITH BERNHEIM'S CONTENTION THAT POST-HYPNOTIC AMNESIA WAS NOT COMPLETE ...

THE PATIENT CAN BE PROMPTED TO RECALL WHAT HAPPENED UNDER HYPNOSIS.

Freud

Pierre Janet

Pierre Janet (1859–1947), already well known as a philosopher, began medical studies in 1889. He worked in Charcot's wards at the Salpêtrière until 1902. After that, Janet taught experimental psychology at the Collège de France.

Janet produced a massive and influential psychological system. His description of two main neuroses, hysteria and psychasthenia, was later used by Jung as the basis for his *extrovert* and *introvert* personalities.

Emil Kraepelin

Emil Kraepelin (1856–1926) is famous for his systematic classification of mental disorders, for instance, such concepts as "dementia praecox" (later called schizophrenia) and "manic-depressive illness". His system remains a basis for medical diagnosis today.

Kraepelin has been criticized for his formal, static and impersonal style of psychiatry. It is often claimed that he instigated the tendency of many psychiatrists to place over-hasty diagnostic labels on patients.

I TOOK THE GREATEST CARE THAT EVERY ONE OF MY PATIENTS SHOULD RECEIVE THE BEST TREATMENT AVAILABLE ...

HE WAS AN EXTREMELY HUMANE PERSON ...

YES, BUT TREATMENT USUALLY MEANT HOSPITALIZED INCARCERATION!

Janet, Kraepelin and other modern psychiatrists kept within the bounds of scientific *clinical* establishments. The next contributor to psychiatry was quite different ...

Sigmund Freud (1856–1939) studied medicine and neurology. He began private practice in neuropathology in 1886. By the mid-1890s, he was no longer interested in either hypnotism or conventional medicine. In 1895, Freud jointly published *Studies on Hysteria* with his colleague Josef Breuer, including the famous "Anna O" case study.

> IN *1896*, I COINED THE TERM "PSYCHOANALYSIS" FOR MY NEW THEORY AND METHOD OF TREATMENT ...

> I ALSO FELL INTO MY OWN DEEP NEUROSIS AND BEGAN **SELF-ANALYSIS** THROUGH **DREAMS** ...

Freud's *The Interpretation of Dreams*, published in 1900, came at the end of a period that Ellenberger calls Freud's "creative illness".

The essence of psychoanalytic theory

Freud's central psychoanalytic theory is that of the **unconscious mind** which contains all the secret wishes and fears kept by **repression** from the **conscious mind**. Normally this is a healthy situation, since it is best that the conscious mind remain untroubled to go about its daily business.

The role of the psychoanalyst

Unconscious repression of something profoundly disturbing and "unconfessable" will manifest itself in neurotic symptoms. The psychoanalyst's role is that of exorcist, confessor and midwife who coaxes the difficult "return of the repressed" into birth. Analysis relies on encouraging the patients' "free association", that is, saying whatever comes into their minds – memories, fantasies and bits of dream. Slowly, these will yield clues to *interpretation*.

Freud's influence

Freud was joined by **Carl Gustav Jung**, **Ludwig Binswanger** and
others to form a group that became, in 1910, the International
Psychoanalytic Association.

Many of those originally in the group, like Jung and Binswanger,
departed from Freud to develop their own theories and methods.

Jung's analytical psychology

Freud restricted his practice to neurotic patients. More gravely ill *psychotics* were unsuitable for psychoanalytic treatment. Jung instead had served his apprenticeship in psychiatry at the Burghölzli Mental Hospital, Zurich, under the eminent clinician Eugen Bleuler who coined the term "schizophrenia". He became senior doctor at the Burghölzli in 1905 and constantly faced "hard cases" of severe psychosis. Bleuler encouraged Jung's interest in Freud's theory of the unconscious …

Jung's famous split with Freud in 1913 and his subsequent formation of "analytical psychology" have greatly to do with an alternative or *dynamic approach* to psychosis.

Binswanger's existential analysis

Ludwig Binswanger (1881–1966), another Swiss psychiatrist inspired by Bleuler's refined work on schizophrenia, rebelled against the classic textbook descriptions of psychotic disorders. These failed to provide any real understanding of the psychotic's *subjective experiences*. Binswanger devised **existential analysis** in the 1920s and 30s, based on Freud, the philosophical phenomenology of Edmund Husserl and the existential system of his former pupil Martin Heidegger.

Edmund Husserl

Martin Heidegger

Ludwig Binswanger

THE POINT IS TO GRASP WHAT CONSCIOUSNESS INTENDS ...

EXISTENCE IS STRUCTURED BY ITS CONCERN FOR BEING ...

EXISTENTIAL ANALYSIS PROBES DYNAMICALLY INTO STATES OF CONSCIOUSNESS TO ACHIEVE UNDERSTANDING OF THE PATIENT'S INNER UNIVERSE.

WHAT IS IT LIKE TO BE THE PATIENT?

Dynamic versus organic psychiatry

Freud and his followers brought into psychiatry a *dynamic* element of the unconscious as originating source (or *psychogenesis*) of mental symptoms. The strictly *organic* view of mental illnesses assigns them to forms of brain pathology. Briefly, the clinical difference between them is that dynamic psychiatries take serious account of the patient's own *subjective expressions* in treatment; while organic types rely on neurophysiology, genetics and pharmacology for treatments.

Psychiatric hospitals

The organic and dynamic views of mental illness have not been satisfactorily reconciled. A crucial issue in organic treatment, in the past especially, meant hospitalization – in a word, *incarceration*. One of the oldest mental hospitals is England's Bethlehem Royal, founded in 1247. In the 17th century, after moving premises, inmates were exposed to the public for entertainment.

Should we close the hospitals?

The population inside British psychiatric hospitals reached a peak in the mid-1950s. Since the 1990s, there has been a policy of closing down hospitals.

Sounds ideal – but has that really improved the conditions of the mentally disturbed? That is one of the many issues we will encounter in our examination of psychiatry in actual practice.

What causes mental illness?

Ancient and primitive people often attributed mental illness to evil spirits – some agent "outside" the person – and this survives in some parts of the world today. Western science switched to causes "inside" the patient. The "nature-nurture debate" has been applied as much to mental illness as to other important aspects of human behaviour.

DURING THE 19TH AND EARLY 20TH CENTURIES, MOST MENTAL HEALTH PROFESSIONALS SPECIFIED THE GENETIC CAUSES OF MENTAL ILLNESS.

THEN, DURING THE MID-20TH CENTURY, EMPHASIS WAS PLACED ON THE SOCIAL RATHER THAN BIOLOGICAL CAUSES ...

Henri Ellenberger

... A TURN FROM ORGANIC TO DYNAMIC PSYCHOGENESIS.

However, the pendulum swung back by the end of the 20th century to highlight the possible genetic causes of many illnesses and behaviours – probably influenced by the success of the Human Genome Project. The causes of mental illness are now thought of as being a combination of social and biological factors.

Social causes of mental illness

Rates of mental illness are increased by the excessive stress experienced by both the employed and unemployed.

Some psychiatrists, and other researchers, believe much of mental illness is directly caused by modern, industrial living. The explanation can't be as simple as that. For example, in some parts of the world, there is a high suicide rate among rural farmers.

Genetic causes of mental illness

There is still scientific evidence for possible genetic causes of certain personality disorders, some forms of depression and some schizophrenic behaviour …

Where genetic causes are suspected, psychiatrists can use modern medicines to counteract the occurrences of chemical imbalances that are suspected. For example, boosting serotonin and noradrenaline levels in some depressives; prescribing Clozapine to reduce the symptoms of schizophrenia.

Other issues about seeking help

Sending a troubled person to see a psychiatrist may seem like a simple solution, but there are important questions to face.

How much should patients try to find out about psychiatry for themselves? The question applies to medicine in general. Is "a little knowledge a dangerous thing"? If a patient knows too much about psychiatric procedures, will that adversely affect what psychiatrists do? Some doctors think so. The approach in this book is to ask awkward questions and challenge the views held by some psychiatrists!

A psychiatrist is a medical doctor (M.D.) who has specialized in psychiatry. It takes about five years of study to become a medical doctor and another two of speciality in psychiatry.

Psychiatrists must belong to a recognized professional society. For example, in the UK a psychiatrist must be a Member of the Royal College of Psychiatrists, i.e. be a MRCPsych. In the USA, a psychiatrist is usually a member of the American Psychiatric Association. (Not to be confused with the American Psychological Association.)

Woody Allen

Only a small proportion of psychiatrists in the UK have had any training in psychoanalysis. It is used more widely in some other countries, such as the US and Japan. In fact, many psychiatrists are actively opposed to psychoanalysis.

So what methods do psychiatrists use?

Most psychiatrists, since they are doctors, take the medical **organic** view of mental disorders. This school emphasizes, as we have seen, the biological, chemical and neurological bases of mental illness. Examples where this is commonly recognized include: general paralysis of the insane, senile dementia, organic psychoses, mental deficiencies.

TREATMENTS ARE THEREFORE BASED ON MEDICINES THAT ALTER THE CHEMISTRY OF THE BODY, ESPECIALLY THE BRAIN AND THE REST OF THE NERVOUS SYSTEM.

THE NEXT PAGES LIST THE MOST COMMONLY PRESCRIBED DRUGS FOR MENTAL DISTURBANCES ...

Psychiatric drugs in four main groups

1.Sleeping
(also called hypnotics)

Benzodiazepines
(also used to treat short-term anxiety)

(longer acting – more hangover)
flunitrazepam (e.g. Rohypnol)
flurazepam (e.g. Dalmane)
nitrazepam

(shorter acting – less hangover)
loprazolam
lormetazepam
temazepam
Warning: can cause psychological and physical addiction. Only used for severe insomnia.

Non-benzodiazepine
chloral hydrate (e.g. Welldorm)
chlormethiazole (e.g. Heminevrin)
dichloralphenanazone
triclofos
zaleplon (e.g. Sonata)
zolpidem (e.g. Stilnoct)
zopiclone (e.g. Zimovane)

Antihistamines
(the drowsy effects can aid sleep)
diphenhydramine
promethazine

Antidepressants
(sometimes used to aid sleep)

Barbiturates
(now rarely used due to side-effects)

Alcohol
(a poor hypnotic due to sleep disruptions that include having to use the toilet)

2.Anti-anxiety
(also called anxiolytics or sedatives or misnamed "minor tranquillizers")

Benzodiazepines
(for short-term relief of severe acute anxiety)
alprazolam (e.g. Xanax)
clobazam
chlordiazepoxide
clonazepam
clorazepate (e.g. Tranxene)
diazepam
lorazepam
oxazepam
Warning: can cause psychological and physical addiction.

Beta-blockers
(for muscle tension or tremors, also used for migraine)
oxprenolol (e.g. Trasicor)
propranolol (e.g. Inderal)

Other
buspirone (e.g. Buspar)

Warning: both sleeping and anxiolytic tablets can cause drowsiness the next day and can be dangerous when operating machinery.

3.Antipsychotics
For treatment of psychosis, schizophrenia, paranoia, manic

depression, personality disorders, etc.(Also called neuroleptics or misnamed "major tranquillizers".) (Most are thought to work by blocking dopamine receptors.)

Phenothiazines
chlorpromazine (e.g. Largactil)
fluphenazine
perphenazine
prochlorperazine
promazine
thioridazine
trifluoperazine

Butyrophenones
benperidol
haloperidol

Thioxanthenes
flupentixol (e.g. Fluanxol)
(also used for depression)

Other ("atypical")
amisulpride
clozapine (e.g. Clozaril) – *Warning: needs blood monitoring.*
olanzapine
quetiapine
risperidone
sertindole
zotepine

Antimanics
(for manic depression)
carbamazepine
lithium – *Warning: needs blood monitoring.*
valproic acid
(Other antipsychotics and benzodiazepines are also used.)

4.Antidepressants
For major depression, panic disorders, obsessions, phobias.

SSRIs (boosts serotonin)
citalopram (e.g. Cipramil)
fluoxetine (e.g. Prozac)
fluvoxamine (e.g. Faverin)
paroxetine (e.g. Seroxat)
sertraline (e.g. Lustral)

SNRIs (boosts serotonin and noradrenaline)
venlafaxine (e.g. Efexor)

Tricyclics
amitryptiline (e.g. Triptafen)
amoxapine (e.g. Asendis)
clomipramine (e.g. Anafranil)
dothiepin (e.g. Prothiaden)
doxepin (e.g. Sinequan)
imipramine (e.g. Tofranil)
lofepramine (e.g. Gamanil)
nortriptyline (e.g. Allegron)
trimipramine (e.g. Surmontil)

Tricyclic related
maprotiline (e.g. Ludiomil)
mianserin (e.g. Bolvidon, Norval)
trazondone (e.g. Molipaxin)

MAOIs *(Warning: dietary problems.)*
isocarboxazid
phenelzine (e.g. Nardil)
tranylcypromine

For **manic depression** see antimanics under antipsychotics.

Warning: St John's Wort should not be taken with antidepressants.

Sources: *BMA Guide to Medicines and Drugs* (New Edition); BNF 45 (March 2003).
Important: this summary is for general information only. All medicines must only be used as prescribed by a medical doctor.

Therapies and professionals

The **dynamically oriented school** uses a mixture of psychoanalytic ideas (based on Freud, Jung, Klein, Reich and other analysts) to diagnose and treat patients.

There are also psychiatrists who concentrate on "behavioural" or "cognitive" techniques – some combining the two as the **cognitive-behavioural** approach – based on learning and problem-solving theories.

Another approach is used by the **systemic school** which is concerned with the communications between people, typically applied to family situations.

A psychiatrist should not be confused with any other professional, such as …

a psychoanalyst – any person who has received training in psychoanalysis at a recognized institute and who practises psychoanalytic treatment.

a clinical psychologist – a graduate in psychology who has post-graduate training and experience in treating the mentally ill, usually connected to a hospital.

any other psychotherapist – who may or may not have a degree but should hold some recognized qualifications.

a psychiatric nurse – a qualified nurse who has trained to work with the mentally ill.

a community psychiatric nurse – as above but, as the term suggests, visits day-centres and other places to meet patients away from the hospital.

... OR ANYONE WITH A PH.D. WHO CAN LEGALLY CALL THEMSELVES A "DOCTOR" ...

ASK POLITELY WHETHER THE PERSON CONCERNED IS A "DOCTOR" IN THE ACADEMIC SENSE OR THE MORE RECENT MEDICAL SENSE.

What does a psychiatrist do?

A psychiatrist works in a hospital, clinic or private practice. Psychiatric work, individually or as part of a team, may involve any of the professionals listed on the previous page.

Besides seeing patients, writing subsequent case notes and attending team meetings, a psychiatrist may be involved in writing reports for courts of law about defendants referred for psychiatric assessments.

PSYCHIATRISTS WHO SPECIALIZE IN LEGAL WORK ARE SOMETIMES CALLED FORENSIC PSYCHIATRISTS.

THE CHILD PSYCHIATRIST IS OFTEN A SPECIALIST WHO HAS PARTICULAR KNOWLEDGE OF CHILDHOOD DEVELOPMENT AND PROBLEMS.

FORENSIC PSYCHIATRY

THIS BOOK CONCENTRATES ON ADULT PSYCHIATRY ...

Who are the patients?

Patients can be roughly divided into **voluntary** and **involuntary**.

A **voluntary** patient will have been referred to the psychiatrist by their medical doctor (General Practitioner). As a general rule, patients should *always* first seek help from their MD, or another qualified doctor, who will then refer them to a psychiatrist if necessary.

What are the most common diagnoses and can they be treated?

Psychiatric patients have increasingly been treated at home. They do not have to stay in a hospital. In the UK, the population in psychiatric hospitals has dropped about 50% from its peak in the 1950s. Only about 1% of all those suffering from stress need hospital treatment.

Involuntary patients are those who get locked up, for their own safety and that of others …

Who gets "locked up"?

Patients are initially "locked up" in a psychiatric hospital only in cases of emergency. Those posing a danger to themselves – through Deliberate Self-Harm – or to others fall into this category.

What are the locking-up laws?

In the UK, for example, the law allowing a person to be locked up is the **Mental Health Act (MHA) 1983**. (Similar legislation exists in other countries.) Generally, with skill and patience, a sympathetic doctor can usually persuade a patient to accept hospital admission voluntarily. But if the patient remains uncooperative, then compulsory hospital admission and detention is possible.

Compulsory admission using MHA 1983, **Section 4: a 72 hour detention**, requires medical recommendation by any one doctor.

This section of the law is only used in emergencies, when there is not enough time to get an "approved doctor", and it is usually converted to a "Section 2" order after the patient has arrived at the hospital.

Section 2: a 28 day detention requires medical recommendations by two doctors, one being an "approved doctor" (e.g. senior registrar or psychiatrist) and the other preferably with previous knowledge of the patient (e.g. his or her MD). Also required is an application by the patient's nearest relative or an approved social worker.

Section 3: a 6 month detention is similar to Section 2 and must specify which of the four categories of mental disorder the patient is suffering from.

Section 5: a 72 hour detention is for someone already in hospital as a voluntary patient but who wishes to leave when the doctors advise against it.

ONE OF THE MOST IMPORTANT DECISIONS A PSYCHIATRIST HAS TO MAKE QUICKLY, IN THESE CIRCUMSTANCES, IS WHETHER OR NOT DSH HAS OCCURRED ...

What is DSH?

The psychiatrist looks at **motives** for DSH which may involve: the wish to die; a "cry for help" to change an intolerable situation; attempts at influencing others (e.g. make someone feel guilty); seeking unconsciousness to escape emotional distress; anger (against the self or someone else); or "testing fate".

Predictors of suicidal risk following DSH include:
– premeditation, i.e. planning in advance
– taking precautions to prevent discovery
– involving dangerous or violent actions
– carrying out the actions alone
– not trying to get help afterwards
– writing a suicide note or making a recent will.

Other significant facts to consider: any history of previous DSH; male sex; older age group, i.e. over 45 years; history of psychiatric illness (e.g. depression, personality disorders, alcoholism or drug dependency); social isolation; unemployment.

How is locking up decided?

In practice, there may not be the time or resources to assess the patient as thoroughly as would ideally be possible. Decisions about compulsory detention are often made rather hurriedly, for the sake of the patient's safety. (Hence the inclusion of Section 4 in the MHA 1983.) Also, full assessment may not be possible until detention has been obtained.

THE DECISION TO LOCK UP IS BASED ON MHA 1983 GUIDELINES ...

THE PATIENT MUST SUFFER FROM A MENTAL DISORDER OF A NATURE AND DEGREE WHICH WARRANTS HOSPITAL DETENTION FOR ASSESSMENT OR TREATMENT ...

(a) In the interests of the patient's own health or safety.

(b) With a view to protecting others.

The psychiatrist deciding about locking up must also consider the four categories of mental disorder:
(a) Mental illness
(b) Mental impairment
(c) Severe mental impairment
(d) Psychopathic disorder

The following are not regarded as mental disorders (under the MHA 1983):
(a) Alcohol or drug dependency
(b) Promiscuity or immoral conduct
(c) Sexual deviancy

The last two criteria may seem a little odd today. Yet, until as recently as 1973, the *Diagnostical and Statistical Manual for Medicine* (DSM), used in the USA and elsewhere, included homosexuality as a mental illness that could receive compulsory detention!

What should a patient know about psychiatry before seeing a psychiatrist?

Most psychiatrists would probably say that it is not necessary for a patient to know anything about psychiatry, and to treat an appointment in the same way as visiting any other doctor. But some knowledge of psychiatry might help patients to have insights into their own situations and remove initial fears about psychiatric procedures.

For example, this book is based on such massive works as *The Oxford Textbook of Psychiatry*, *The International Classification of Diseases (ICD)* and *The Diagnostic and Statistical Manual*, among many others. We could start with a few basic terms used in this book …

Common psychiatric jargon

aetiology (or etiology, pronounced "eaty-ology") = suspected original causes or explanations of an illness, e.g. genetic, physical, psychoanalytic, childhood experiences.

affect = (noun) emotion; **affective** = (adjective) emotional, as in the crude distinction between cognitive (thinking) and affective (emotional) aspects of mental life, e.g. a person may *believe* herself to be ill but not *feel* ill. **Blunted affect** is reduced emotional expression. **Apathy** is the loss of affect, i.e. a sense of detachment where little pleasure (or pain) is experienced.

anxiety = feeling of apprehension or tension when anticipating a perceived (external or internal) danger. When appropriate, a normal human reaction that aids physical and mental survival. When extreme and irrational, a debilitating condition requiring treatment.

clinical features = main signs (subjective, given by the patient) and symptoms (objective, observed by the doctor).

diagnosis = labelling or categorizing the disorder (including ruling out what it is not), e.g. "This is a personality disorder and not a form of schizophrenia."

dynamic = an adjective used in psychology and psychiatry to describe mental life using the analogy of forces in motion, e.g. the Freudian theories of tensions between the conscious and unconscious (controlled by defence mechanisms), or the "battles" between the id, ego and superego. Especially used to try to describe and explain mental conflicts and stress.

epidemiology = the groups of people usually affected, e.g. age group, sex, social class.

hypnosis = a condition of relaxation, accompanied by a diminished awareness of surrounding events, which allows the influence of suggestions from another person. (Or, rarely, the same person if it is "self-hypnosis".)

management = the treatment of the mental disorder, e.g. by drugs, psychotherapy, support.

phobia = an extreme, irrational fear, e.g. agoraphobia – the fear of being outside in exposed, open places.

prognosis = the predicted likely future course of a disorder (i.e. an educated guess), especially if treated successfully, e.g. "The personality disorder should improve as the patient gets older." Sometimes used more generally, e.g. the prediction of an educational, industrial or methodological programme.
(A prognostic test is any investigation used to make medical predictions.)

What actually happens when a patient visits a psychiatrist?

Patients attending an appointment with the psychiatrist will usually sit face-to-face in a private room. Rarely today is a psychiatrist's couch used at first – although it is possible. A second doctor may also be present.

The history of the patient includes personal details: age, marital status, occupation, source of referral, the presenting complaint (PC), the past psychiatric history (PPH), past medical history (PMH), family history (FH), family medical history (FMH), current relationships.

Personal history (PH) also considers birth (any difficulties), pre-school development, school, occupations and psychosexual history (e.g. age of puberty, sexual relationships, spouse, children).

Other relevant information might be: smoking, drinking, taking drugs, allergies, social circumstances (e.g. who else is in the household), forensic history (e.g. criminal convictions).

Mental state assessment

THE SECOND STAGE IS TO GAUGE THE PATIENT'S PRESENT MENTAL STATE ...

THERE ARE VARIOUS INDICATIONS OF WHAT MIGHT BE TROUBLING ME ...

Appearance and behaviour: dress, self-care, manner (helpful or hostile, amiable or aggressive), posture and movement (relaxed or tense, very slow or normal or overactive), appropriateness (aware of the situation, hearing voices).

Speech: spontaneous or hesitant, coherent or incoherent, pressured (trying to say a lot) or poverty of speech, neologisms (invented words).

Mood: subjective report (i.e. how the person says he or she feels), depression or elation, anxiety, irritability, fears, hostility, emotionality, suicidal ideas.

Thought: both in **content** (e.g. worries or preoccupations, obsessions, delusions, persecutions) and in **form** (e.g. pressure or poverty of thinking, thought blocking, loosening of associations, flight of ideas, interpretations).

Perception: hallucinations, illusions, depersonalization, derealization.

Cognition: orientation in time, place, person and age; attention and concentration (using standard tests, e.g. months of the year backwards – MOYB).

Memory: tested by the subject's own report on immediate memory (e.g. name and address); recent memory (e.g. menu of last meal); remote memory (e.g. events from several years ago).

I WILL ALSO TEST THE PATIENT'S **GRASP** ON KNOWLEDGE OF CURRENT AFFAIRS – FOR EXAMPLE, ASKING THE NAME OF THE COUNTRY'S LEADER.

MY SENSE OF **INSIGHT** IS QUESTIONED ... DO I BELIEVE I AM PSYCHOLOGICALLY ILL AND IN NEED OF TREATMENT?

Stage three: formulation or case assessment

Introduction: important features of the history, both positive and negative, are highlighted.

Current mental state: psychiatric labels are attached to the main apparent features.

Diagnosis: formulated according to a diagnostic hierarchy – personality disorders; neuroses; paranoid states; affective (emotional) disorders; schizophrenia; or organic disorders.

I WILL CHOOSE ONE OF THESE DIAGNOSTIC DISORDERS AS THE HIGH-PRIORITY CONDITION – WITH A MAXIMUM OF TWO CONDITIONS BEING CONSIDERED IN THE DIAGNOSIS.

THIS IS TO MAKE SURE THE PSYCHIATRIST HAS "SYNTHESIZED THE CASE".

EACH CONDITION MUST BE SUPPORTED WITH REASONS GATHERED FROM THE MENTAL STATE EXAMINATION AND HISTORY.

Aetiology: causes of the disorder, including the predisposing, precipitating and maintaining factors.

Investigations: requiring either more information (e.g. from relatives, spouse, friends, MD, school, employer, old case notes) or further assessments such as **physical** (e.g. blood and urine tests, X-rays, EEG, ECG); **social** (e.g. social worker's report, family interview); **psychological** (e.g. psychometric tests of intelligence, personality, etc.); **others** (e.g. observations of nursing staff, occupational therapy reports).

Management: considerations of possible treatments
– **short-term**: inpatient or outpatient?; compulsory detention?; immediate physical treatment?; involvement of other professionals?
– **long-term**: physical (e.g. drugs); psychological (e.g. therapy); social (e.g. involving other professionals, family).

Prognosis: stating reasons whether good or poor …

Clinical diagnosis and treatment

The symptoms and signs of mental disorders

The diagnosis of mental disorders, as in any branch of medicine, is based on the symptoms and signs.

66

Main categories of mental disorders

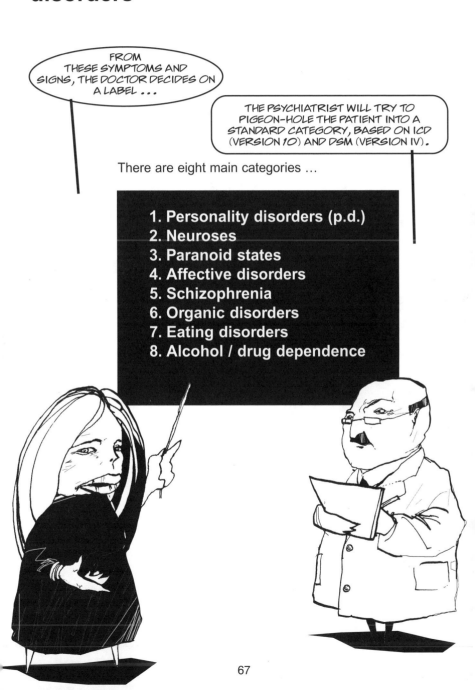

FROM THESE SYMPTOMS AND SIGNS, THE DOCTOR DECIDES ON A LABEL ...

THE PSYCHIATRIST WILL TRY TO PIGEON-HOLE THE PATIENT INTO A STANDARD CATEGORY, BASED ON ICD (VERSION 10) AND DSM (VERSION IV).

There are eight main categories ...

1. Personality disorders (p.d.)
2. Neuroses
3. Paranoid states
4. Affective disorders
5. Schizophrenia
6. Organic disorders
7. Eating disorders
8. Alcohol / drug dependence

What are the main treatments?

The management of psychiatric problems is usually divided into three main areas: physical, social and psychological.

Physical management mainly involves drugs, e.g. anxiolytics (to reduce symptoms of anxiety) and antidepressants.

Social management involves the support of others, including family and friends as well as professionals. For example, a "social phobic" will be encouraged to go out more.

Psychological management includes counselling and psychotherapies, e.g. relaxation training.

1. Personality disorders (p.d.)

Definition of p.d. concerns deeply ingrained, maladaptive patterns of behaviour, often from childhood or adolescence and continuing for most of adult life. The patient and others suffer, with adverse effects on both the individual and society.

Epidemiology: mainly aged 18–35, male, lower social class.

Clinical features:
I. *Affective* – in three groups: Depressive or Disthymic; Hyperthymic (cheerful); Cyclothymic (alternating)

II. *Anankastic* or *Obsessional* (repetitive; poor adaptability; humourless; sensitive to criticism; indecisive)

III. *Antisocial* (impulsive; lacking guilt; failure to form loving relationships; failure to learn from mistakes). Personality disorders can also be sociopathic or asocial.

Personality disorders continued ...

IV. *Asthenic* (weak-willed; compliant; avoiding responsibility; miserable)

V. *Avoidant* (low esteem; avoiding relationships; hypersensitive to rejection)

VI. *Borderline* (unstable; impulsive; bored; identity doubts; avoids being alone; self-injury; etc.)

VII. *Explosive* (outbursts of anger and violence but not otherwise antisocial)

VIII. *Histrionic* (theatrical play-acting; melodramatic; insincere)

IX. *Narcissistic* (self-importance; attention demanding; exploitative without returning favours; etc.)

X. *Paranoid* (suspicious; hypersensitive; etc.)

XI. *Passive-aggressive* (stubborn; difficult; etc.)

XII. *Schizoid* (very introspective; detached; shy; eccentric; etc.)

XIII. *Schizotypal* (superstitious; unrealistic; etc.)

SO, THERE ARE *13* RECOGNIZED CLINICAL FEATURES OF PERSONALITY DISORDER ...

HOW CAN YOU TREAT SO MANY DIFFERENT "SHADES" OF BEHAVIOUR?

Aetiology: there is little genetic evidence for personality disorders, although they correlate with some body types.

Management of p.d.
Short-term treatment by anxiolytic or neuroleptic drugs.
Long-term treatment involves:

- neuroleptics for paranoid and schizotypal p.d.
- social support from doctor, social worker or psychiatric nurse.
- group psychotherapy may be more useful than individual.

Category 2: Neuroses

There are five types:
(a) Anxiety
(b) Phobic Anxiety
(c) Obsessive-Compulsive
(d) Hysteria
(e) Hypochondriasis.

Anxiety neuroses
Definition: psychological and physical manifestations of anxiety; can occur as Panic Attacks or Generalized Anxiety Disorder (GAD).

Epidemiology: often begins in early adult life or middle age; more common in women; anxiety is the most common neurotic disorder (about 3% of the population).

Clinical features: symptoms and signs are fearful anticipation; irritability; restlessness; sensitivity to noise; worrying; difficulty concentrating; poor memory symptoms; weakness; numbness; dizziness; headaches; sleep disturbance, etc.

Aetiology: strong genetic evidence (in family and twin studies); increased secretion of adrenaline and noradrenaline; high lactate levels after exercise; psychoanalysis suggests an origin of primary anxiety during birth or subsequent maternal separation; possibly learned through imitation and reinforcement.

Management: possible drugs include benzodiazepine (short-term only), antidepressants (tricyclic or SSRI or MAOIs), beta-blockers.

Psychotherapy, counselling, relaxation techniques, Anxiety Management Training (AMT) by deliberately arousing anxiety, then reducing it.

Prognosis: with recent onset, most patients should recover quickly.

BUT IF THE ANXIETY NEUROSIS LASTS MORE THAN SIX MONTHS, THEN, IN ABOUT 80% OF CASES, IT WILL STILL BE PRESENT THREE YEARS LATER, DESPITE EFFORTS AT TREATMENT.

Phobic Anxiety Neuroses

Definition: neurotic states with abnormally intense dread of certain objects or situations that would not normally have such an effect.

Epidemiology depends on the type of phobic neurosis.

Simple phobic neuroses, e.g. fear of heights or spiders.

Social phobic neuroses, fear of meeting or being with other people, either generally or in specific situations, such as restaurants or theatres. Usually starts between the ages of 17 and 30. Equally common in men and women.

Clinical features of phobia

Simple phobic neuroses have a specific object or situation that causes intense anxiety, e.g. heights, spiders, dogs, darkness, thunderstorms – anything can be the focus of a phobia! Anxiety symptoms are identical to those of any other anxiety state and can be activated by anticipation of encountering that situation. The patient will habitually avoid such situations.

Agoraphobia, or fear of open spaces, can extend to shopping areas, bus and train stations, crowds, etc. Anxiety symptoms are identical to any other anxiety state, but sometimes the main fear is of fainting or losing control. In more extreme cases, patients may rarely or never leave the house. This used to be called "housebound housewife syndrome".

The aetiology of agoraphobia is explained by psychoanalysis as a displacement of unconscious conflicts that are not allowed conscious expression due to repression. Learning theory explains it as a series of conditioned "fear responses" with learned avoidance.

Social phobic neuroses are characterized by fear and avoidance of any situation in which the patient may be observed by others – eating out, shopping, using public transport, walking down the street. Anxiety symptoms are identical to other anxiety states, plus an associated fear of being humiliated or embarrassed, for instance, by shaking or blushing.

PATIENTS WITH SOCIAL PHOBIC NEUROSES OFTEN ALSO HAVE CERTAIN NON-PHOBIC SYMPTOMS SUCH AS DEPRESSION, OBSESSIONS AND DEPERSONALIZATION.

DIAGNOSIS NEEDS TO EXCLUDE SOCIAL INADEQUACY, PERSONALITY DISORDERS, OTHER NEUROSES, DEPRESSION AND SCHIZOPHRENIA.

The **aetiology** of social phobic neuroses is explained as a learned response based on the circumstances in which the first experience of acute anxiety occurred, plus a general lack of self-confidence in social encounters.

The management of phobic anxiety neuroses

Physical treatments include anxiolytic and antidepressant drugs, e.g. MAOIs (although there is a risk of relapse after the drugs are stopped) and tricyclics such as Imipramine (considered by some psychiatrists as the treatment of choice for agoraphobia).

Social management usually focuses on the accompanying avoidance behaviour …

Psychological treatments often use Cognitive-Behaviour Therapy and Modelling. These are techniques of controlled exposure to the situation or object being avoided, desensitization of imagined fears or comparatively rare phenomena (e.g. thunderstorms), and model examples of how to deal with them.

The prognosis of phobic anxiety neuroses depends on many factors, including the type of neurosis. Simple phobic neuroses in adults that have persisted since childhood can continue for a long time. Agoraphobia and social phobic neuroses that have lasted for one year can continue for five years. In all cases, the quicker treatment is obtained, the speedier the problems will be overcome.

Obsessive-Compulsive Neuroses (OCN)

Obsessions are recurrent, persistent thoughts, impulses or images that trouble the patient who struggles to ignore or resist them. Often the nature of obsessions is sexual or aggressive.

Epidemiologically, OCN usually starts in early adult life and is equally common in men and women.

Obsessions can appear in several forms.

Doubts about recent past behaviour …

Impulses that urge socially embarrassing, aggressive or even dangerous actions …

Phobias about illness …

Obsessional phobias can result from anxiety … the impulse to stab someone may lead to fear and avoidance of knives.

Ruminations on persistent themes … "the end of the world".

Thoughts of a repetitive sexual, violent or blasphemous nature.

Compulsions are sometimes called **compulsive rituals**, because the behaviour is repeated identically each time.

Aetiology of OCN

Learning Theory accounts for some OCN in terms of conditioned responses and imitation of others.

Psychoanalysis (Freudian theory) explains OCN in terms of repression of aggressive or sexual impulses, and possible regression to the anal stage of development.

Genetic evidence from the results of family studies shows that OCN appears in 5–7% of parents of patients with OCN (compared to about 0.05% prevalence in the general population). Twin studies show the concordance of OCN in identical (MZ) twins is 50–80%, while the concordance in non-identical (DZ) twins is about 25%.

PERSONALITY STUDIES REVEAL THAT ABOUT 70% OF PATIENTS WITH OCN HAVE THE PREMORBID ANANKASTIC PERSONALITY TRAITS OF CLEANLINESS, CHECKING, ORDERLINESS, RIGIDITY.

Diagnosis has to differentiate OCN from other disorders in which similar obsessional symptoms may occur – anxiety, phobic, depressive and organic disorders, and also schizophrenia.

Management of OCN

Physical treatments include anxiolytic drugs for short-term use or low-dose antidepressants for longer-term use, e.g. clomipramine (which is reported to have a specific action against obsessional symptoms). Other antidepressants may be used, such as SSRIs, e.g. fluvoxamine.

Social treatments involve the support of family members who are encouraged to adopt a firm but sympathetic attitude towards the patient.

Psychological treatments can involve psychotherapy. Cognitive-Behaviour Therapy can train the patient to relax and refrain from carrying out rituals.

Prognosis on OCN is generally good, with about two-thirds improving in one year. Poor prognosis is associated with certain personality traits (e.g. anakrastic), stress and severe symptoms. The sooner it is treated, the better.

Hysteria

The psychiatric term *hysteria* covers a wide range of symptoms beyond the patient's conscious control or awareness – amnesia, sleep-walking and multiple personality disorder, paralysis, blindness, deafness and other apparent physical disabilities.

Psychiatry refers to two uses of the term.

References to hysteria

Clinical features of hysteria

Hysterical dissociation involves major reactions such as **amnesia** (memory loss), **fugue** (wandering) and **somnambulism** (sleepwalking). The rarest is **multiple personality disorder** – which manifests as sudden alternations between two or more distinct patterns of behaviour in which the patient is unaware of becoming "others".

Hysterical conversion includes "classic" cases of **paralysis**, **fits**, **blindness**, **deafness**, **aphonia**, **anaesthesia**, **abdominal pain** and **abnormal gait**.

A famous example of hysterical blindness is the Biblical case of Saul's conversion on the road to Damascus, as a result of which he became St Paul …

Why does hysteria occur?

The diagnosis of hysteria must first rule out all demonstrable *organic* causes. Why would patients unconsciously inflict such extreme disabilities on themselves? The **primary gain** is considered to be the exclusion of anxiety, caused by a psychological conflict, from the conscious mind. (For example, Saul's unconscious guilt about murdering Christians.) A **secondary gain** for the patients can be some personal advantage, e.g. they don't need to go to work, they get the attention of others.

A psychiatrist has sometimes to be devious to rule out cases of **malingering** (i.e. pretending to be ill), for example, among prisoners and military personnel. Both malingering and genuine hysteria may be unwittingly reinforced by those in contact with such behaviours.

The aetiology of hysteria suggests genetic causes are unlikely. In family studies, incidence among close relatives is only about 5% above the general population and, anyway, this can be explained by family learning. Twin studies show no concordance for either identical (MZ) or non-identical (DZ) twins.

Personality research has found that 12–21% of patients with hysteria have premorbid histrionic personality traits.

Psychoanalytic theory offers perhaps the most convincing explanation.

Management of hysteria

Physical management has used small doses of sodium amytal injected to relax the patient sufficiently to relive the stressful events that are at the roots of the hysteria and to express accompanying emotions.

Social management generally focuses on trying to eliminate the factors that are reinforcing the symptoms – including the behaviour of family and friends – and on encouraging normal behaviour. For acute cases, lasting several weeks, treatment by reassurance and suggestion is usually appropriate.

Psychological management involves psychotherapy that explores past experiences …

Prognosis says cases of hysteria with recent onset usually recover quickly, while those that have already lasted over one year persist much longer.

Hypochondriasis

Hypochondriasis is a neurotic disorder of **the hypochondriac** excessively concerned with his or her health. Such worries are usually about some part of the body or, less commonly, the mind.

Epidemiology shows hypochondriasis to be more common among the elderly, men, lower social classes and those associated with disease.

CLINICAL FEATURES VARY WIDELY AND CAN BE GENERAL OR SPECIFIC . . .

pain, e.g. right iliac fossa, lower lumbar region, head.
worries about bladder.
concerns about appearance, e.g. shape of nose, ears or breasts.
concerns about sweating and body odour.
cardiovascular symptoms, e.g. chest pains, palpitations.
gastrointestinal symptoms, e.g. biliousness, nausea, abdominal pains, flatulence.

Diagnosis must differentiate hypochondriasis from personality disorders, anxiety neuroses, depression, schizophrenia and organic disorders, including dementia.

The **aetiology** of hypochondriasis is explained by psychoanalysis as a defence against psychosis or an expression of "anal fixation".

Management of hypochondriasis

Physical management may suggest a trial of antidepressants, e.g. a tricyclic.

Social management searches for the meanings of symptoms among family and other social situations, where possible. (Caution is needed, however, where symptoms serve powerful defence purposes.)

Psychological management may advise Cognitive-Behaviour Therapy to educate the patient about organic and psychological illnesses.

JUST BECAUSE I'M A HYPOCHONDRIAC DOESN'T MEAN I'M NOT REALLY ILL!

The prognosis is poor for chronic and established cases, but better for recent onsets and cases more associated with anxiety neuroses or depression.

Paranoid states

Paranoia is classified in five types.

Simple Paranoid State: delusions of being influenced, persecuted or treated in some special way. These delusions are usually of a fixed, elaborate and systematized kind.

Paranoia: permanent and unshakeable delusions, usually developing in middle or late life. There are no hallucinations and the personality is otherwise intact. The patient may continue working and maintaining a social life.

Paraphrenia: a late onset of systematized delusion, with prominent hallucinations. The personality and intellect are generally preserved.

Induced Psychosis (Folie à deux): a paranoid delusional system that develops in close relationship with another person with similar delusions, nearly always persecutory.

The fifth type of paranoia is subdivided into four special conditions.

Othello syndrome is a delusion, more common among men, that the marital partner is being unfaithful. It may be accompanied by other delusions, e.g. the spouse is trying to poison the patient or cause harm in other ways.

THE PATIENT OFTEN OBSESSIVELY SEEKS EVIDENCE OF THE PARTNER'S INFIDELITY BY EXAMINING CLOTHES OR BED-LINEN.

I WILL ALSO TRY TO EXTRACT A CONFESSION FROM THE SPOUSE - WHICH MAY LEAD TO AGGRESSION AND MURDER.

The patient is typically very moody: a mixture of apprehension, anger, irritability and misery. The prognosis is often poor, especially if the syndrome is well-established.

De Clerambault's syndrome is a delusion, more common among single women, that another person (the object), often of higher social status, loves the patient (the subject). The subject believes she did not initiate the situation but has been specially chosen by the object.

THE SUBJECT MAY OBSESSIVELY INTERRUPT THE OBJECT'S LIFE AND THEN, AFTER REJECTION, HER FEELINGS MAY TURN TO HATRED.

I AM CONVINCED HE CANNOT LIVE HAPPILY WITHOUT ME BUT, BECAUSE OF HIS STATUS AND OTHER REASONS, HE IS NOT ALLOWED TO REVEAL HIS TRUE LOVE.

Further paranoid delusions

Capgras' syndrome – a delusion that someone has been replaced by an impostor who is an exact replica of the original person. This is sometimes called an "illusion de Sosies".

FROM THE LATE 1960s, A NUMBER OF PEOPLE BELIEVED SINGER-SONGWRITER PAUL McCARTNEY, OF THE BEATLES, WAS REPLACED BY AN EXACT DOUBLE.

FREGOLI'S SYNDROME: THE PATIENT BELIEVES A SINGLE PERSECUTOR HAS SEVERAL DIFFERENT APPEARANCES.

FRUSTRATION OCCURS WHEN NO ONE ELSE REALIZES THAT THESE APPARENTLY DIFFERENT PEOPLE ARE REALLY THE SAME PERSON!

Aetiology of paranoia

Genuine cases of paranoia are extremely rare. Psychoanalysis theory explains paranoia as being a combination of two defence mechanisms: *projection* and *splitting*.

Paraphrenia is sometimes regarded as paranoid schizophrenia. Where the onset is late, there is good prognosis.

Induced psychosis or shared **folie à deux** delusion.

> PSYCHOANALYSIS EXPLAINS THIS AS PROJECTED IDENTIFICATION WITH A SUBMISSIVE PERSONALITY.

Othello syndrome is usually associated with personality disorders or neuroses; also with depressive disorders, schizophrenia, or organic disorders such as alcoholism and drug abuse.

> PSYCHOANALYSIS VIEWS IT AS A PROJECTION OF THE PATIENT'S OWN DESIRES FOR INFIDELITY, PROJECTION OF REPRESSED HOMOSEXUALITY, OR THE RESULT OF FEELINGS OF INADEQUACY.

De Clerambault's syndrome is linked with paranoid schizophrenia, or affective or organic disorders.

> PSYCHOANALYSIS CLAIMS THERE IS AN AMBIVALENT ATTITUDE TO THE PERSON IMPLICATED.

> FREGOLI'S SYNDROME IS ASSOCIATED WITH SCHIZOPHRENIA.

Management of simple paranoid states

Simple paranoia may be treated with antipsychotic drugs, e.g. chlorpromazine, haloperidol, trifluoperazine or thioridazine. The choice of drug and dosage depends on factors such as age, physical condition, degree of agitation and the response to previous medication.

Social management centres on the psychiatrist maintaining a good relationship with the patient. This requires skilful, compassionate interest without either colluding or condemning.

Psychological support is important, especially encouragement and reassurance.

Physical treatment

THE PSYCHOTIC PERSON IS IDENTIFIED AND GIVEN APPROPRIATE DRUGS.

Social management

THE AFFECTED COUPLE MAY BE SEPARATED.

THIS SOMETIMES LEADS TO THE DISAPPEARANCE OF THE DELUSION – OFTEN MORE IN THE RECIPIENT THAN THE INDUCER.

Psychological management involves supportive and family psychotherapy.

Management of Othello syndrome

Physical treatment begins with underlying disorders but, if they are not certain, phenothiazines (e.g. chlorpromazine) may help.
Social management advises temporary separation from the partner.
Psychological therapies may be used for patients with personality disorders or neuroses. Patient and spouse must be encouraged to express their feelings. Behaviour therapy may help by learning to avoid what might cause the partner's jealousy, refusing to argue and not responding aggressively.

Management of the other syndromes – De Clerambault's, Capgras', Fregoli's – centres on the treatment of underlying disorders.

Affective disorders

Affective disorders are characterized by mood disturbances, such as inappropriate depression or elation, often accompanied by abnormalities in thinking and perception.

Classification divides affective disorders into three types.

Unipolar (or monopolar) depression – recurring attacks of depression.
Bipolar depression – alternating between attacks of mania and depression.
Mixed affective states – where both manic and depressive symptoms occur.

All depressive disorders are twice as common in women, although bipolar depression is equally common among men and women. Depressive disorders are most common in the top and bottom social classes (I, II and V) and they are more common among the divorced or separated. Overall, about 3–4% of the general population is affected.

Clinical features of depression include a range of **physical** effects.

Sleep disturbance – especially onset insomnia (delay in falling asleep) and early morning waking, about 2–3 hours before normal. Some depressed people sleep excessively.

APPETITE AND WEIGHT CHANGES

USUALLY DEPRESSION CAUSES WEIGHT LOSS, SOMETIMES MORE APPETITE, WITH ASSOCIATED DECREASE OR INCREASE IN WEIGHT.

CHANGES IN MOOD AND ACTIVITY LEVELS

MOOD IS WORSE IN THE MORNING (SOMETIMES IN THE EVENING).

ACTIVITY SLOWS DOWN OR IS ACCOMPANIED BY AGITATION.

MOOD IS GENERALLY CHARACTERIZED BY MISERY THAT IS QUALITATIVELY DIFFERENT FROM NORMAL UNHAPPINESS, WITH THE ADDITIONS OF ANXIETY AND IRRITABILITY, LOSS OF ENERGY AND FATIGUE.

Loss of interests in work, leisure activities and sex.

Other bodily changes, e.g. constipation, amenorrhoea in women, aches and pains.

neglected grooming and clothing ✔

facial expressions – mouth turned down at the corners, frowning ✔

some patients maintain a smiling expression ?

reduced rate of blinking ✔

fewer gestures ✔

shoulders bent, head inclined, downward gaze ✔

poor speech ✔

hesitations – long delays before questions are answered

Depression also affects **thinking**.

past: feelings of guilt

present: generally seeing the unhappy side of life; thoughts of failure or considered to be a failure by others; loss of confidence; any success is due to luck rather than personal achievement

future: generally hopeless, expecting the worst; often thinking life is not worth living; death would be a welcome release; plans for suicide.

Depressive delusions

delusions about health – for instance, convinced of having cancer

persecutory delusions – others are trying to take revenge

auditory hallucinations, voices that repeat words or phrases

There are visual hallucinations, often of death and destruction.

Other possible psychiatric symptoms include: phobias, obsessions, hysterical symptoms, hypochondria and depersonalization.

Clinical features of mania (or hypomania)

Sleep disturbance

Appetite and weight changes

Changes in mood and activity levels

Mania affects **appearance** and **speech**.

Mania also affects **thinking**.
expansive ideas

Insight is usually impaired, so the patient will not realize that he or she is ill and in need of treatment.

Delusions may occur of a grandiose type.

Or may be persecutory.

Or self-referential.

Hallucinations, auditory or visual, may be experienced.

Schizophrenic symptoms occur in 10–20% of manic patients.

Aetiology of affective disorders

Genetic evidence is strong: family studies show bipolar depression is shared between 15–20% of close relatives, with unipolar depression between 10–15%, compared to the prevalence in the general population of 3–4%. Twin studies show a concordance rate in identical (MZ) twins of about 80%, compared to 20% in non-identical (DZ) twins.

Biochemical theories concentrate on three bio-neurological imbalances.

Monoamine neurotransmitter levels are *low in depressives* and *high in manics*. For example, reserpine depletes monoamine and depression follows. Whereas amphetamines cause the release of monoamines and euphoria follows.

Two of the main groups of antidepressants are the monoamine oxidase inhibitors (MAOIs) and the monoamine reuptake inhibitors (tricyclics) which both effectively increase levels of monoamines, creating elevated mood.

The neurotransmitter serotonin is found decreased in urinary and post-mortem studies of depressives. Hence, the use of selective serotonin reuptake inhibitors (SSRIs, e.g. Prozac) as antidepressants.

Endocrine abnormalities include raised levels of cortisol in some depressives. Decreased levels of thyroid stimulating hormone (TSH) and growth hormone (GH) occur in some depressives.

Electrolyte disturbances include increased intracellular ("residual") sodium in depression, with further increases in mania.

Psychological theories of depression cover a wide range of perspectives.

Parental relationships may be important, with maternal deprivation in particular being possibly one factor in later depression. Patients with mild depression sometimes remember their parents caring less or being over-protective. Animal studies also suggest that the loss of an emotional bond with another individual may cause depression.

Psychoanalysis draws on Freud's ideas to explain depression.

Psychodynamic theory generally sees mania as a *defence mechanism* against depression.

Cognitive theories of depression include **Aaron Beck**'s (b. 1921) idea that someone who habitually uses "faulty thinking" may be more likely to develop depression when faced with minor problems.

I IDENTIFY FOUR TYPES OF THESE.

1. *arbitrary inference*, i.e. drawing a false conclusion, despite the evidence.
2. *selective abstraction*, i.e. focusing on irrelevant details while ignoring more important features of a situation.
3. *over-generalization*, i.e. drawing a general conclusion based on a single incident.
4. *minimization and magnification*, i.e. the patient's own performance is underestimated while their errors are exaggerated.

Aaron Beck

Learned helplessness (based on the work of **Martin Seligman** (b. 1942)) explains depression as the result of good outcomes being believed unlikely, while bad outcomes are believed likely.

PATIENTS ARE CONVINCED THAT NOTHING THEY DO WILL CHANGE THE OUTCOME ANYWAY.

Martin Seligman

Personality can be an influence on affective disorders. Bipolar depression is associated with the cyclothymic personality trait of repeated mood swings. Unipolar disorders are associated with anankastic personality traits and predisposition to anxiety.

Sociological theories investigate family and life event factors. For instance, a 1975 study of working-class women in London found depression was more likely when …
1. Three or more children under 15 years were at home.
2. Not working outside home.
3. Husband was not supportive.
4. Mother had been lost, through death or separation, before age 11.
5. There was an excess of major difficulties before the depression.

Life event studies show that depressives tend to experience more life events (e.g. bereavement, separation) in the six months before depression starts, compared to controls.

Management of affective disorders

Physical treatment of depression channels mainly through antidepressants:

Tricyclics, e.g. amitriptyline (sedating) for agitated depression, or imipramine (less sedating) for retarded depression.

MAOIs (monoamine oxidase inhibitors), e.g. phenelzine for severe chronic depression with anxiety symptoms.

Tetracyclics, e.g. mianserin, which usually has no anticholinergic side-effects, has minimal cardiotoxicity (therefore safer in overdose) and rarely causes convulsions.

SSRIs (or 5-HT reuptake inhibitors), e.g. fluvoxamine which usually does not have daytime sedation or other unpleasant side-effects, although sexual disfunction can occur in males.

SNRIs, i.e. serotonin and noradrenaline reuptake inhibitors.

Lithium carbonate, usually as a last resort for drugs, reduces the rate of relapse in unipolar and bipolar depression.

ECT (ELECTROCONVULSIVE THERAPY) FOR SEVERE DEPRESSION HAS BEEN USED MUCH LESS IN RECENT YEARS ...

THERE ARE CONCERNS ABOUT ITS LONG-TERM EFFECTS ON MEMORY AND OTHER FUNCTIONS.

Physical treatment of mania is usually by antipsychotics, e.g. chlorpromazine (sedating) or haloperidol (less sedating), which can bring the symptoms under rapid control. Lithium carbonate is also sometimes used but is much slower in effect.

Psychological treatment of depression

Psychotherapy provides support. Psychodynamic therapies help the patient to confront inappropriate defences and find new approaches to problems. Interpersonal and family therapies may help with relationship difficulties.

Cognitive-Behaviour Therapy (CBT), using Beck's approach, may help with faulty thinking ("cognitive distortions").

Prognosis for unipolar depression

Prognosis for bipolar depression

NEARLY ALL YOUNG PATIENTS RECOVER, ALTHOUGH NOT ALL ELDERLY PATIENTS DO.

Outpatients' Waiting Room

NEARLY ALL MANIC PATIENTS RECOVER EVENTUALLY, DESPITE RECURRING EPISODES. PERSONALITY IS USUALLY WELL-PRESERVED BETWEEN EPISODES OF MANIA.

Schizophrenia

Classification of schizophrenia traditionally names four types: Hebephrenic, Paranoid, Simple, Catatonic.

Hebephrenic schizophrenia is characterized by "silly or childish" behaviour, affective symptoms and thought disorder, delusions and hallucinations. Onset is usually in late teens or early adulthood.

Paranoid schizophrenia typically displays prominent persecutory or grandiose delusions, hallucinations and delusional jealousy.

Simple schizophrenia is a syndrome of insidious development of social withdrawal, notably odd behaviour and declining performance at work.

> THERE IS USUALLY AN ABSENCE OF DELUSIONS, HALLUCINATIONS AND THOUGHT DISORDER.

Catatonic schizophrenia is characterized by catalepsy, i.e. staying still for long periods, or just rocking back and forth, and stupor with intermittent excitement.

> PATIENTS ARE OFTEN AUTOMATICALLY OBEDIENT AND REPEAT WHAT'S SAID TO THEM (ECHOLALIA).

Outpatients' Waiting Room

Clinical features of schizophrenia

Epidemiology shows schizophrenia is equally common among men and women, with an average (median) onset for males at 28 years, females at 32. It is more prevalent in lower social classes and among those born in winter months. Prevalence rate is about 1% of the general population.

Clinical features are different for acute and chronic syndromes.

Acute schizophrenia is typified by delusions, hallucinations, interference with thinking, inappropriate emotions.

Chronic schizophrenia has these main features: apathy, lack of drive and initiative, social withdrawal, poor social skills and antisocial behaviour (e.g. shouting obscenities in public), slow actions, poverty of thought and speech, being unemotional most of the time.

IT CAN BE BROUGHT ON BY SOCIAL OVER-STIMULATION.

IT CAN BE BROUGHT ON BY SOCIAL UNDER-STIMULATION.

A patient showing signs of schizophrenia will use "odd language", for example, making up words (neologisms) or using ordinary words in unusual ways. Ideas are often linked together like a "free association" exercise.

Thoughts are often blocked and there is difficulty in thinking about abstract ideas.

Mood tends to be unpredictable. Depression is followed by unexpected euphoria or anxiety or irritability.

Delusions can be grandiose or persecutory or self-referential.

There is generally lack of insight.

Aetiology of schizophrenia

Research shows that genetics and biochemistry can be important in schizophrenia, but so too can social factors.

Genetic studies
Family studies show that prevalence rates are influenced by other family members, varying from 14% in children of one schizophrenic parent, to 46% in children of two schizophrenic parents. (Compare 1% in population.)

Twin studies show concordance of 45% in identical (MZ) twins, and 10% in non-identical (DZ) twins.

Biochemical theories of schizophrenia

Dopamine levels are usually found higher in postmortem research. Drugs that increase dopamine can produce paranoid psychoses similar to schizophrenia, e.g. amphetamines, MAOIs. Antipsychotic drugs that block dopamine receptors can reduce symptoms of schizophrenia. There is some evidence against the theory that there is simply too much dopamine in schizophrenia. Increasing dopamine levels (by administering L-dopa, apomorphine, etc.) can also sometimes lead to reduced schizophrenic symptoms.

Monoamine methylation can be abnormal in brains of those suffering schizophrenia.

EVIDENCE COMES FROM RESEARCH WITH MESCALINE, A HALLUCINOGEN, WHICH IS AN ORTHO-METHYLATED DERIVATIVE OF DOPAMINE.

BUT THERE IS ALSO EVIDENCE AGAINST THAT TOO ...

NICOTINIC ACID (A SUPPOSED METHYL ACCEPTOR) DOES NOT HELP REDUCE SCHIZOPHRENIA.

Psychological theories of schizophrenia

Arousal levels are high in some schizophrenics, especially those more socially withdrawn chronic patients.

Attention, concentration and perception are poor with schizophrenia. Some abnormalities of perception, including hallucinations, may be caused by an overwhelming input of visual stimuli.

Thought disorders are common in schizophrenia – inability to think in abstract terms, inability to separate irrelevant ideas. Personality tests show abnormal constructs, i.e. lack of coherence and inconsistencies in assessing personality.

PSYCHOANALYSIS EXPLAINS SCHIZOPHRENIA AS A "WITHDRAWAL OF LIBIDO" WHICH MAKES THE WORLD SEEM MEANINGLESS, RESULTING IN THE DEVELOPMENT OF ABNORMAL BELIEFS.

MY THEORIES EXPLAIN SCHIZOPHRENIA AS A FAILURE TO PASS THROUGH THE "PARANOID-SCHIZOID" STAGE.

Klein

IN NORMAL DEVELOPMENT, THIS IS WHEN A CHILD DEALS WITH INNATE AGGRESSION BY SPLITTING THE EGO (AND THE MOTHER'S REPRESENTATION) INTO WHOLLY "BAD" AND WHOLLY "GOOD" COMPONENTS – LATER REALIZING THAT GOOD AND BAD CAN EXIST IN THE SAME PERSON.

Social influences in schizophrenia

Lower social class situations, such as inner-city poverty and deprivation, can produce higher incidences of schizophrenia. Since schizophrenia can be found in all social classes, there might also be a tendency for "social drifting", i.e. sliding down the social scale.

Immigration has been linked to schizophrenia. For example, there was an increase in hospital admissions among Norwegians emigrating to the USA.

Abnormal families and schizophrenia

Communication problems in families may be a cause in schizophrenia. A "double-bind" situation occurs when instruction to a child is contradicted by the same or other parent. Consequently, the child is reduced to ambiguous or meaningless responses.

DISRUPTED AND NON-SEQUENTIAL COMMUNICATIONS FROM AND BETWEEN PARENTS MAY BE A CAUSE OF SCHIZOPHRENIA.

THE "SCHIZOPHRENIC MOTHER", A CONCEPT SUGGESTED BY ERICH FROMM (1900-80), COULD BE ANOTHER SOURCE OF SCHIZOPHRENIA.

I FOUND THAT MOTHERS OF SCHIZOPHRENICS HAD AN EXCESS OF PSYCHOLOGICAL PROBLEMS.

Erich Fromm

Other abnormal family set-ups include "marital skew" where an eccentric parent dominates the family; or "marital schism" where parents have contrary views that force the child to have divided loyalties.

Neurological abnormalities in schizophrenia

General neurological signs include clumsiness and unusual gait. Brain examination demonstrates thickening of the corpus callosum – the tissue that connects the brain's two hemispheres. Other brain abnormalities include enlargement of some ventricules and unusual EEG measurements, e.g. increased theta waves.

SOME RESEARCHERS BELIEVE A VIRUS INFECTION CAN CAUSE SCHIZOPHRENIA!

Differential diagnosis must exclude drug-induced psychoses (e.g. amphetamines, alcohol) or epilepsy, especially in younger patients. Among older patients, tests need to exclude acute organic syndromes (e.g. encephalitis), dementia and other brain diseases (e.g. GPI – General Paralysis of the Insane).

Management of schizophrenia

Physical treatment prescribes antipsychotic drugs, e.g. chlorpromazine, haloperidol, clozapine.

ECT – OR "SHOCK TREATMENT" – LESS SEEN TODAY, HAS BEEN USED ON CATATONIC PATIENTS AND WHEN SEVERE DEPRESSION ACCOMPANIES SCHIZOPHRENIA.

SOCIAL MANAGEMENT INVOLVES WORKING WITH RELATIVES, EITHER WITH OR SEPARATELY FROM THE PATIENT.

REHABILITATION PROGRAMMES FOR THE PATIENT INCLUDE DAY CENTRES, HALF-WAY HOUSES AND SHELTERED WORKSHOPS WHERE UNDERSTIMULATION OR OVERSTIMULATION CAN BE CONTROLLED AND AVOIDED.

Psychological support may come from psychotherapy or Cognitive-Behaviour Therapy for social skills training. Patients can benefit from direct instruction (using operant techniques) combined with modelling (demonstrating examples of social interaction). "Token economy" has been used to encourage and reward institutionalized patients for specific behaviours.

Prognosis of schizophrenia

SINCE STATISTICS ARE RATHER VAGUE, TWO "RULES OF THUMB" HAVE BEEN USED FOR PROGNOSIS (TAKE YOUR PICK) ...

The Rule of Thirds
1/3 eventually show complete recovery.
1/3 recover but repeatedly relapse.
1/3 never seem to recover.

The Rule of Quarters
1/4 show complete recovery after one attack with no further symptoms.
1/4 recover but still have some persistent symptoms.
1/4 show partial recovery with persistent symptoms.
1/4 never recover and steadily deteriorate.

GOOD PROGNOSIS DEPENDS ON CERTAIN CONDITIONS ...

The conditions are: no past psychiatric history; the onset is acute; episodes are short; there is a clear precipitating factor; a good employment history; signs of strong personality traits, sexual adjustments and social relationships. It can also help if the person is married (but not guaranteed!).

Relapse occurs most commonly when the psychiatrist tries to reduce the medication or the patient stops taking the medicine against advice.

Organic disorders

Classification gives two types: *acute* (delirium) and *chronic* (dementia).

Clinical features of acute organic disorders
Impaired consciousness, e.g. slowness, not sure what time it is, poor concentration.
Behavioural changes, either overactivity (noisy, repetitive, purposeless movements) or underactivity (slow, repetitive, purposeless movements).
Speech reduction.
Mood changes, e.g. anxiousness, irritability, depression, lability, fright, agitation.
Thought problems, e.g. slow, muddled, persistence, delusions (reference or persecution).
Perceptual disturbances, e.g. misinterpretations, visual and auditory hallucinations, depersonalization.
Cognitive problems, e.g. being disoriented in time and space, memory difficulties, learning difficulties.

Aetiology of acute disorders

Acute disorders can be caused by alcohol or other drug intoxication (e.g. opiates, overdose of medication).
Metabolic causes include: cardiac, respiratory or hepatic failure; electrolyte imbalance; porphyria.
Endocrine causes: hyperthyroidism; hypothyroidism; hypopituitarism.
Infective causes: intercranial infection (e.g. encephalitis, meningitis) or systemic infections (e.g. pneumonia, septicaemia).
Vitamin deficiencies: B1 (thiamine), B12 and Nicotinic acid.

Clinical features of chronic organic disorders

Consciousness is clear but there may be a general impairment of personality, intellect and memory.

Behaviour is characterized by a reduction of interests, orderliness with rigid routines, sudden explosions of anger or other emotions ("catastrophic reaction").

Speech contains errors, e.g. words in the wrong order (syntax); sometimes the patient only mumbles, makes meaningless noises or becomes mute.

Mood varies, e.g. anxiety, irritability, depression, lability.

Thought is typically slow and poor in content, with delusions of persecution and little abstract thinking.

Perception may be dominated by hallucinations.

Cognition, e.g. many learning difficulties, disorientation in time and place, poor attention and concentration, forgetfulness (especially of recent events), confabulation (i.e. inventing experiences to hide memory deficits); poor insight into own problems.

Aetiology of chronic disorders

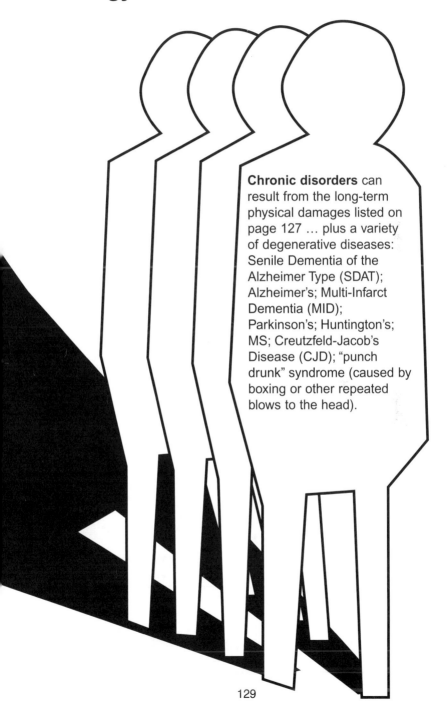

Chronic disorders can result from the long-term physical damages listed on page 127 … plus a variety of degenerative diseases: Senile Dementia of the Alzheimer Type (SDAT); Alzheimer's; Multi-Infarct Dementia (MID); Parkinson's; Huntington's; MS; Creutzfeld-Jacob's Disease (CJD); "punch drunk" syndrome (caused by boxing or other repeated blows to the head).

Diagnosis of organic disorders

Detailed diagnoses of all possible disorders cannot be given here. But the example of **senile dementia of the Alzheimer type** is a useful one for demonstrating the complexities involved.

A POPULAR MISCONCEPTION IS THAT ALZHEIMER TYPE DISEASES ONLY AFFECT MEMORY ...

Signs and symptoms include: memory failure; lability; apathy; depression or paranoia; Parkinsonism; parietal lobe syndrome (e.g. inability to copy drawings – "constructional apraxia"; inability to get dressed – "dressing apraxia"; getting lost in familiar places; inability to recognize, name or point to parts of the body; inattention); general deterioration of personality and intellect.

ALZHEIMER'S DISEASE SHOWS THE SAME SIGNS AND SYMPTOMS, EXCEPT THAT IT IS PRE-SENILE – ONSET MAY BE AT A MUCH YOUNGER AGE.

Management of organic disorders

Acute organic disorders are treated by general measures. The patient is nursed in a well-lit room, preferably a side ward, with frequent reassurance from medical and nursing staff ...

Chronic organic disorders are also generally treated, including help with self-care and prevention of accidental self-harm. Mostly this can be managed at home with the suitable support of "home helps" or district nurses. Specific measures depend on the causes, e.g. vitamin B tablets for deficiencies. Drug treatments depend on the main symptoms at the time, e.g. benzodiazepines or phenothiazines for anxiety; antidepressants for depression. There is no specific drug treatment for dementia.

Eating disorders

Eating disorders concern both overeating and undereating, various expedients to lose weight, such as laxatives and bulimia – vomiting to empty the stomach. One eating disorder especially has received media attention and appears on the increase in recent years …

Epidemiology shows anorexia is more common in females than males, with the ratio being about 10:1. In females, the onset is between 16 and 17 years, seldom after the age of 30. In males, the onset is about the age of 12 years. Anorexia is more frequent in upper and middle social classes, with a prevalence rate among middle-class teenage girls of about 1%. There is a particularly high prevalence in certain occupational groups, e.g. ballet students.

Clinical features of anorexia

The main characteristics are a body weight approximately 25% below the norm for the person's age and height; an intense desire to be thin; amenorrhoea, i.e. cessation of monthly periods. A fear of being fat is accompanied by relentless efforts at reducing weight.

Attempts at weight loss will involve eating little and particularly avoiding carbohydrates (e.g. sugar products, bread, potatoes, rice); induced vomiting by using emetics or sticking the fingers down the throat; excessive exercise and use of laxatives. Some patients indulge in "binge eating", followed by feelings of guilt and vomiting, with increased intentions of losing more weight in the future.

Sensitivity to cold increases, with risks of hypothermia; constipation; low blood pressure; bradycardia; amenorrhoea; leucopenia and abnormalities of water regulation.

Some hormone levels are raised (e.g. growth hormone, GH; prolactin; cortisol); while others are reduced (e.g. thyroxine, T4; Tri-iodothyronine, T3; oestradiol; testosterone; follicle-stimulating hormone, FSH; luteinizing hormone, LH). Erratic food intake can cause serious dysfunction of the hypothalamus.

Aetiology of anorexia

Family studies show 6–10% of female siblings of patients with anorexia suffer the condition. Other family influences extend to over-protectiveness, rigidity, enmeshment, lack of conflict resolution.

Psychological causes can stem from dietary problems in later life; parents preoccupied with food; family relationships that leave the child with a poor sense of identity.

Diagnosis needs to exclude neuroses (e.g. phobic anxiety and obsessive compulsion), depressive disorders and schizophrenia. Organic disorders also have to be excluded (e.g. hypopituitarism, malabsorption, diabetes mellitus).

Management of anorexia nervosa

Physical treatments can resort to antidepressants (e.g. tricyclics) and antipsychotics (e.g. chlorpromazine). But these would be temporary measures to promote weight gain.

Social management depends on building a good relationship with the patient, so that a firm approach is possible. The first priority is to establish and maintain a healthy weight.

Psychological treatments can also prove effective.

> PSYCHOTHERAPY PROVIDES SUPPORT, INCREASES SELF-ESTEEM AND IMPROVES PERSONAL RELATIONSHIPS.

> FAMILY THERAPY MAY BE IMPORTANT WHERE SUCH RELATIONSHIPS ARE A MAJOR FACTOR.

Cognitive-Behaviour Therapy may be used to control eating habits, e.g. setting weight targets and providing positive reinforcement through praise and privileges. Cognitive approaches concentrate on changing the patient's attitude towards eating and improving self-image.

Prognosis of anorexia

Where cases are left untreated, the prognosis is very poor and anorexia can be fatal.

IN TREATED CASES, THERE IS AGAIN A "RULE OF THIRDS" ...

1/3 fully recover
1/3 partially recover
1/3 little improvement, with possible chronic disablement or death.

CERTAIN FACTORS ARE ASSOCIATED WITH POOR PROGNOSIS ...

– long illness
– late age of onset
– bulimia (vomiting or purging)
– anxiety when eating with others
– great weight loss
– poor childhood adjustment
– poor parental relationships
– male sex

The mortality rate is 5–10%.

Alcohol dependence

Alcohol dependence is defined by using seven criteria.
– Subjective awareness of the compulsion to drink alcohol.
– Stereotyped pattern of drinking.
– Increased tolerance to alcohol.
– Preferring drink to other activities.
– Repeated withdrawal symptoms.
– Drinking to relieve stress.
– Returning to alcohol dependency after a period of abstinence.

Epidemiology shows alcohol dependency is more common in males, although with increasing incidence among females. Heaviest drinkers are men in late teens or early twenties, and increasingly among young women. The lowest occurrence is in the middle social classes.

DEPENDENCY IS MORE COMMON IN THOSE DIVORCED OR SEPARATED ...

AND IN HIGH-RISK OCCUPATIONS – COMPANY DIRECTORS, DOCTORS, WRITERS ...

Ethnic factors are interesting. For example, dependency is more common among Irish than Jewish people.

Clinical features of alcohol dependence

There are four alcohol-related psychiatric disorders.

Intoxication phenomena include **pathological drunkenness** in which acute episodes (e.g. outbursts of aggression) are caused by relatively small amounts of alcohol; and **memory blackouts** which last from a few minutes to several hours.

Withdrawal phenomena characterized by **general withdrawal symptoms** (e.g. trembling or "the shakes", affecting hands, legs and trunk; agitation; nausea; sweating; visual distortions; hallucinations; convulsions); and **delirium tremens** which includes the above plus clouding of consciousness, disorientation in time and place, recent memory impairment, delusions, fearfulness and prolonged insomnia.

IS THAT IT FOR DRUNK AND DISORDERLY?

NO, THERE ARE TWO MORE DISORDERS YOU CAN SUFFER ...

Further alcohol-related disorders

Nutritional or toxic disorders leading to **thiamine deficiency** can cause either **Wernicke's disease** (i.e. ophthalmoplegia, nystagmus, memory disturbance, ataxia) or **Korsakoff's psychosis** (i.e. recent memory impairment, confabulation, disorientation, euphoria, apathy, lack of insight, ataxia). Another possible outcome is **alcoholic dementia**.

Associated psychiatric disorders:
Alcoholic hallucinosis, often auditory, e.g. voices uttering insults.
Affective disorders.
Personality deterioration.
Suicidal behaviour.
Sexual problems.
Pathological jealousy – "my partner is being unfaithful".

Aetiology of alcohol dependence

There are a number of possible factors.

Genetics may be one influence, as shown by the results of twin studies which reveal a higher concordance in identical (MZ) twins than non-identical (DZ) twins. Adoption studies have also shown significantly higher levels of alcoholism in adopted individuals whose biological parents were known alcoholics, compared with a matched control group.

Biochemical factors include abnormalities in alcohol dehydrogenase and neurotransmitters (although what is cause and what is effect is not clear).

Learning may influence children to adopt their parents' drinking habits by a combination of imitation and conditioning.

PERSONALITY STUDIES SHOW ASSOCIATIONS WITH CHRONIC ANXIETY, SELF-INDULGENT TENDENCIES AND LOW SELF-ESTEEM.

SOCIAL INFLUENCES WILL DEPEND ON APPROVAL OF ALCOHOL USE IN CERTAIN SOCIETIES, ITS GLAMORIZATION IN ADVERTISEMENTS, TV PROGRAMMES AND FILMS.

Management of alcohol dependence

Physical treatment starts by ceasing intake and detoxification. The following is a typical programme.

Sedation by drugs, e.g. chlormethiazole (Heminevrin) or chlordiazepoxide (Librium), with special care taken to avoid the potentially fatal effects of combining alcohol with these medications.
Vitamin supplements particularly to provide thiamine.
Rehydration to correct electrolyte imbalances.
Glucose to correct hypoglycaemia.
Antibiotics to treat any infections.
Anticonvulsants to treat convulsions.

Social management usually includes a **goal-oriented treatment plan.**

THE AIM IS TO DEAL WITH THE **MAIN DRINKING PROBLEM** BY TOTAL ABSTINENCE OR CONTROLLED DRINKING.

AND TO SOLVE **ACCOMPANYING PROBLEMS** OF HEALTH, MARRIAGE, JOB AND SOCIAL ADJUSTMENTS.

Other agencies may provide support, such as Alcoholics Anonymous (AA) or Hostels (for rehabilitation and counselling, especially in cases of homeless drinkers).

Psychological treatments

Psychotherapy ranges from simple counselling and advice (education about alcohol dependency) for the individual to group therapy in which patients can experience their own problems mirrored in others and work out their own solutions.

Cognitive-Behaviour Therapy tackles the drinking behaviour itself by tactics of self-monitoring.

Prognosis

GOOD PROGNOSIS IS PREDICTED ON THE FOLLOWING CONDITIONS ...

- early treatment.
- patient's motivation.
- social stability, e.g. fixed abode, family support, regular employment.
- absence of antisocial personality traits, e.g. ability to control impulsiveness, to defer gratification and to form meaningful relationships.
- age (with older patients generally being more successful).
- adequate intelligence.
- good insight into the situation.

Drug dependence

Like alcoholism, drug dependency is defined as a state, mental and physical, resulting from the use of a drug. It is characterized by behavioural and other responses that always include a compulsion to take the drug on a continuous or periodic basis in order to experience its psychological effects and avoid the discomfort of its absence.

Epidemiology suggests drug dependence is more common in males, with the highest rates in the 20–30 year age group and a slight peak in middle age. Social class associations vary among different countries, e.g. in the UK it occurs in all social groups, but in the USA it is associated mainly with underprivileged, minority ethnic groups.

Clinical features of drug dependence

As you would expect, these vary according to the drugs used.

Opiates (such as heroin) cause both psychological and physical dependence, with typical features of constipation, constricted pupils, chronic malaise, weakness, impotence, tremors.

WITHDRAWAL EFFECTS ARE MANIFESTED BY SHIVERING, ABDOMINAL CRAMPS, DIARRHOEA, DILATED PUPILS, YAWNING, AGITATION, RESTLESSNESS AND INTENSE CRAVINGS FOR THE DRUG.

Barbiturates (such as pentobarbitone) also cause both psychological and physical dependence. Its features are slurred speech, incoherence, dullness, drowsiness, depression. Withdrawal effects include clouding of consciousness, disorientation, hallucinations, twitching, major seizures, anxiety, restlessness, insomnia, hypotension, nausea, vomiting, anorexia.

Other drugs

Hallucinogens (such as LSD or lysergic acid diethylamide) cause psychological but not physical dependence. The mental effects of LSD develop during the two hours after consumption and last from about 8 to 14 hours.

Mood changes are often dramatic, ranging from exhilaration to acute anxiety and distress. Sensory perceptions can be very distorted, including synaesthesia (confusion between the senses, e.g. tasting colours or hearing sounds of colours) and distorted body image (e.g. hands may appear to be very large). These experiences can lead to panic and fears of insanity.

Amphetamines (such as dexamphetamine) cause psychological but not physical dependence, although physical toleration can occur.

Low doses cause physical increases, e.g. raised heart and breathing rates. The main problem with higher doses and chronic use is the risk of **amphetamine psychosis**, indistinguishable from acute paranoid schizophrenia. (This can occur regardless of whether the amphetamines are taken intravenously or by mouth.)

Features of amphetamine psychosis

Hostile and dangerously aggressive behaviour.

Persecutory delusions.

Auditory, visual and tactile hallucinations.

THE CONDITION USUALLY SUBSIDES AFTER ABOUT A WEEK OF DISCONTINUED USE, BUT MIGHT PERSIST FOR MONTHS.

Cannabis (active ingredient tetrahydro-cannabinol) causes psychological but not physical dependence.

Effects of cannabis

Exaggerations of existing moods, e.g. euphoria, depression, anxiety, aggression.

Distortions of space and time.

Heightened awareness of aesthetic experiences.

Intensification of visual perception with possible visual hallucinations.

Reddening of the eyes.

Dry mouth and throat.

Irritation of respiratory tract, often with coughing.

Decreased body temperature.

Increased appetite ("getting the munchies").

Cocaine causes psychological but not physical dependence.

A MAJOR PSYCHIATRIC FEATURE OF COCAINE IS THE PHENOMENON OF "COCAINE BUGS" ...

... THE BIZARRE TACTILE HALLUCINATION, AS THOUGH INSECTS ARE CRAWLING UNDER YOUR SKIN.

Benzodiazepines (e.g. diazepam, lorazepam) can cause both psychological and physical dependency.

clinical features	withdrawal effects
Drowsiness	Anxiety
Dysarthria	Appetite disturbance
Nystagmus	Confusion
Unsteady gait	Delirium tremens like symptoms
	Insomnia
	Restlessness
	Tremors

Aetiology of drug dependence

The first factor is the availability of drugs, followed by social pressures to take them. A young person might start drug-using to achieve status or just keep "in" with the peer group.

SOME PEOPLE ARE MORE VULNERABLE TO DRUG ABUSE THROUGH PERSONALITY DISORDERS AND A HISTORY OF CHILDHOOD UNHAPPINESS.

Tolerance to drugs and physical withdrawal effects can be explained, for example, by hypertrophy of the brain's neural pathways and dysfunction of endorphin metabolism.

Management of drug dependence

Physical treatment depends on the drug abused.

Opiate withdrawal may involve the use of methadone (although that can cause dependency too!) in decreasing amounts or using medication for the relief of symptoms, e.g. chlorpromazine and analgesics.

Barbiturate withdrawal usually starts with decreasing dosages.

THE SYMPTOMS ARE ALLEVIATED BY A BENZODIAZEPINE (TAKING CARE NOT TO REPLACE ONE DEPENDENCY WITH ANOTHER!).

ANTICONVULSANTS MAY BE NECESSARY. HENCE, WHY THIS PROCESS SHOULD BE UNDERGONE IN HOSPITAL.

Benzodiazepine withdrawal may include changing from a short-acting benzodiazepine (e.g. lorazepam) to a long-acting one (e.g. diazepam), plus an overall reduction in dosages. Symptoms may be relieved to some extent by using an antidepressant (e.g. dopiethin).

Rehabilitation of drug abusers

Social rehabilitation generally aims to remove the addict from the drug-taking social group and develop new social contacts. This may involve moving home and changing employment. The interest and care of a supportive person is usually important.

Psychological treatment may include individual psychotherapy.

This concludes the summary of what adult psychiatry actually is today. We shall now consider the criticisms of psychiatry, its historical interpretations in postmodern times and its possible future.

Social criticisms of psychiatry

The economic straitjacket of psychiatry
There not only remains a great deal of social stigma attached to mental illness but we must also consider the economic consequences. For example, a history of mental illness may be used as a reason for not giving applicants certain jobs, denying insurance, or refusing tenancies or mortgages for homes.

Lloyds TSB Essential Healthcover Insurance	
Benefits	**Cover available**
Hospital charges	Yes
Consultants' fees	Yes
Diagnostic tests	Yes
Radiotherapy	Yes
Psychiatric treatment	No

Economic considerations can also directly harm patients. Doctors may prescribe cheaper drugs rather than more efficacious but expensive options.

Such short-term "economizing" may help the immediate problem of low medical budgets, but in the long term it may cost society much more through additional financial support for the patient.

Anti-psychiatry

By the 1960s, a wave of criticism swept through psychiatry, often from within the profession itself. **Ronald David Laing** (1927–89) studied medicine in Glasgow, Scotland, and practised psychiatry from 1951 to 1956. He then moved to the Tavistock Clinic, London, in 1957, and specialized in the study of schizophrenia. His psychiatric training was orthodox but he was strongly influenced by the dissident existential analyst Ludwig Binswanger (see page 36) and the existentialist philosophers Heidegger, Jaspers, Sartre and Tillich.

In *The Divided Self* (1959, 1965), Laing claimed such utterances contained comprehensible responses and – when analysed more closely – had meaning from the perspective of the schizophrenic.

The self and others

R.D. Laing emphasized that a schizophrenic's behaviour can be better understood by studying his or her family background – a theme he developed in *The Self and Others* (1961, revised 1969). Often, he claimed, people diagnosed as schizophrenics were brought up in families that subjected them to intolerable contradictions.

A PERSON CAN BE CAUGHT IN A "DOUBLE BIND" OF CONFLICTING INJUNCTIONS.

I'M IN A "CATCH-22" SITUATION ... WHATEVER I DO, I SHALL UPSET SOMEONE!

THE SCHIZOPHRENIC MAY SIMPLY BE SOMEONE WHO HAS BEEN UNABLE TO SUPPRESS HIS NORMAL INSTINCTS AND CONFORM TO AN ABNORMAL SOCIETY.

Laing developed these ideas further in *The Politics of Experience* (1967) and *Sanity, Madness and the Family* (1970). Laing's existential colleagues also wrote influential books, including: David Cooper, *Psychiatry and Anti-Psychiatry* (1967) and Aaron Esterson, *The Leaves of Spring* (1971).

Anti-psychiatry communities

David Cooper first coined the term "anti-psychiatry" to describe his "experiment" on a ward in a large mental hospital in 1962. He tried to "allow a greater degree of freedom of movement out of the highly artificial staff and patient roles imposed on people by conventional psychiatry". Patients decided on their own leave periods, attendance at meetings and getting out of bed. These "anti-rules" were the practical manifestations of "anti-psychiatry". Laing himself did not like the label "anti-psychiatrist".

Cooper, Esterson and Laing became founder-members of the Philadelphia Association Ltd (1965) named after a biblical quotation:

"Behold, I have set before thee an open door, and no man can shut it." (To the church at Philadelphia, *Revelations* III, 8.)

The Association challenged traditional approaches to mental health by setting up therapeutic communities in London households. The first was in Kingsley Hall (opened 1964) where a group of people, previously diagnosed as "mentally ill", lived outside the mental-hospital system. In keeping with the spirit of the times, these households were more like hippie communes.

Other anti-psychiatrists

Other critics of psychiatry also appeared during the 1960s. In Italy, the best-known was Franco Basaglia who edited *The Institution Denied – report from a psychiatric hospital* (1968). This described the hospital of Gorzia with its open doors, removal of gratings and nets, abandonment of physical restraints and administration by the patients' community.

I DENOUNCED THE USELESS SADISM OF THE MENTAL HOSPITAL ...

IN ITALY, AS ELSEWHERE, MENTAL HOSPITALS WILL CLOSE AND WE WILL BUILD NEW STRUCTURES OF ASSISTANCE AND CARE FOR MENTAL DISEASE.

Franco Basaglia

Even more militant was the Socialist Patients' Collective, the SPK, of former patients from the Heidelberg Clinic in West Germany. Dr Wolfgang Huber was convinced mental illness was created by capitalist society and, therefore, could only be cured by its destruction. Fighting capitalism was itself considered therapeutic. Consequently, patients were taught to make bombs instead of baskets! In 1975, six SPK members were responsible for murdering two diplomats and blowing up the West German embassy in Stockholm, after demanding the release of colleagues in the terrorist Baader-Meinhof gang.

The "myth of mental illness"

Although anti-psychiatrists were generally against traditional diagnoses and treatments, most did not deny the existence of mental illness. However, **Tom Szasz** (b. 1920) even rejected this concept in his book, *The Myth of Mental Illness* (1961). He argued there is a small group of genuine "diseases of the brain", such as Alzheimer's, but the vast majority of so-called "mental illnesses" are really "problems in living", e.g. relationships with partners, families, friends, work colleagues. Consequently these should be seen as social not medical problems, as described in his *The Manufacture of Madness* (1972) …

"MADNESS" IS MANUFACTURED SOLELY IN ORDER TO LABEL THOSE PEOPLE IN SOCIETY WHO DO NOT CONFORM TO THE RULES OR CONVENTIONAL STANDARDS OF MORALITY.

THIS LABELLING SERVES TO CONTROL PEOPLE BY REMOVING THEM FROM SOCIETY AND LOCKING THEM UP IN PSYCHIATRIC HOSPITALS.

Tom Szasz

Szasz was the first to question madness itself on a more deeply philosophical level.

The anti-Oedipus criticism

Other critics of both psychiatry and capitalism included Gilles Deleuze and Felix Guattari who together wrote *Anti-Oedipus: Capitalism and Schizophrenia* (1972). In this complex, jargon-filled work, they propose a new materialist form of psychoanalysis based on the concept of the "autoproductive unconscious" which is "a desiring machine in a universe of desiring machines". Although, according to them, capitalism does not invent "Oedipus", it exploits it cynically and mercilessly, supported by modern, capitalist, neurotic, Oedipalizing psychoanalysis.

Felix Guattari

Schizoanalysis

Schizoanalysis is far more than just a critique of the Freudian Oedipus complex. It portrays a political and philosophical position invoking Karl Marx and Friedrich Nietzsche, as well as Freud, and acknowledging the importance of human sexuality.

THE TRUTH IS, SEXUALITY IS EVERYWHERE: THE WAY A BUREAUCRAT FONDLES HIS RECORDS, A JUDGE ADMINISTERS JUSTICE, A BUSINESSMAN CAUSES MONEY TO CIRCULATE ...

Gilles Deleuze

HITLER GOT THE FASCISTS SEXUALLY AROUSED. FLAGS, NATIONS, ARMIES, BANKS GET A LOT OF PEOPLE AROUSED!

Schizoanalysis had a profound effect on our postmodern understanding of psychiatry, environmentalism, feminism and cultural studies. The question raised is how to *interpret* the history of psychiatry in terms of the social, economic and political forces that shaped its theories and practices.

Foucault and postmodern history

Michel Foucault (1926–84) is the controversial postmodern historian of psychiatry in such works as: *Madness and Civilization* (1961); *Birth of the Clinic* (1963); *Discipline and Punish* (1975); and *The History of Sexuality, Vol. 1* (1976) and *Vols 2 and 3* (1984).

Foucault "archaeologized" the concept of madness itself as constructed through changes in institutions, such as "the birth of asylums". The sociologist Erving Goffman also argued that asylums, prisons and armed forces are self-reinforcing and dehumanize the individuals within them – in his *Asylums*, 1961. Foucault's idea is that the politically repressive nature of psychiatry and medicine advances with power shifts in knowledge.

THE FIRST TASK OF THE DOCTOR IS POLITICAL ...

MAN WILL BE TOTALLY AND DEFINITIVELY CURED ONLY IF HE IS FIRST LIBERATED ... BUT "LIBERATION" DISGUISES A BENIGN SELF-REPRESSION.

Michel Foucault

Towards a new psychiatry

Objectors, like Foucault, condemn the whole system of medical practitioners who impose their own particular (and often peculiar) views on society and pursue pecuniary interests in the exercise of their profession. The justice system conspires to work as an accomplice and legalizing body for these medical manipulators.

Psychiatry should not be a penal institution, but it is nevertheless liable to the arbitrariness of doctors with uncivilized powers at their disposal, such as physical punishment (e.g. being strapped to a bed) and the use of personality-changing drugs. All this contradicts the normal freedom-creating functions of a modern democracy.

A new concept for "madness" should be found to oppose this situation – contributing towards a New Psychiatry.

Changes in psychiatry today

Psychiatry has been influenced by reformist critics such as R.D. Laing and Szasz. For example, in the UK, since the Mental Health Act of 1983, many psychiatrists try to avoid labelling a person "a schizophrenic", preferring to describe specific behaviours that may be signs of schizophrenia.

Community care has become a major feature of psychiatry (e.g. through the UK Community Care Act, 1990), helping people to take more control of their lives. Community Mental Health Centres support a wide range of clients with aims that include the reduction of stigma. Other staff, such as Community Psychiatric Nurses, are involved with providing care and support.

The need for psychiatry

There is still a growing need for treating mental illness. This was highlighted by a datamonitor survey, published in 2003, of psychiatrists in the UK, USA, France, Italy, Spain and Japan that found 47% of patients had suicidal thoughts and more than 20% of patients with depression had attempted suicide before being diagnosed. The report said this also reflected the stigma attached to mental illness and suggests depression is still chronically undiagnosed, with doctors needing to understand it better.

There is perhaps more tolerance of mental illness in society generally, but the problem of stigma clearly remains, as does fear of consulting a psychiatrist.

Internet problems

New psychiatric problems are likely to emerge from abuses of advanced technologies. The rapid growth of the internet has provided information and communication previously unavailable in the history of the human race. But it has many negative aspects and is already causing concern because of the **addictive** aspects of the medium.

Effects of internet abuse

Many children and adults spend hours each day at computers, playing games (on and off line), entering "chat rooms" or just "surfing". The long-term effects on children are still not known.

Long-term psychiatric problems may come from the lack of physical exercise and possible radiation effects from being close to electro-magnetic sources for extended periods. Some people already believe that some cases of Chronic Fatigue Syndrome may be associated with intense computer use.

Internet pornography

One of the most potentially harmful aspects of the internet is the pornography, previously very difficult or impossible for most people to obtain, which is now freely available at the click of a mouse.

OBNOXIOUS WEBSITES PROMOTE ALL KINDS OF PORN, INCLUDING PAEDOPHILIA, INCEST, SADISM AND BESTIALITY.

PSYCHIATRISTS IN THE FUTURE MAY WELL BE TRYING TO DEAL WITH A HUGE INCREASE OF PROBLEMS CREATED BY THESE INTERNET SEXUAL PERVERSIONS.

THE ADDICTIVE NATURE OF PORNOGRAPHY HAS BEEN UNDERSTOOD FOR A LONG TIME BY PSYCHOLOGISTS AND PSYCHIATRISTS ...

Ivan Pavlov

The conditioning effect

Classical Conditioning theory (as developed originally by **Ivan Pavlov** (1849–1936)) can explain the powerful reinforcements provided by sexual arousal and release when viewing pornography.

Salacious internet images, whether deliberately sought or received unsolicited (in emails), have the potential for both initiating addictions which would have never otherwise begun, and reinforcing addictions to the point of psychiatric need.

The availability and nature of the internet is such, therefore, that sexual addictions and perversions could escalate dramatically in the future and cause unprecedented psychiatric and social problems.

Future pharmacy

New drugs are being developed all the time. There may be future medications to help psychiatric problems in ways beyond our current knowledge. However, the history of psychiatric drug development has not always been unproblematic, as instanced by the addictions and serious side-effects of barbiturates and other widely used drugs.

The heavy reliance on "taking pills" to solve psychiatric problems needs to be continuously questioned. Both the medical profession and the general public must realize that drugs alone are not answers and that changes in life-styles – combined with personal responsibilities – are the keys to mental health.

Psychiatry in crisis?

If the current trend continues, there will steadily be fewer psychiatrists in the future. Unless the professional image of psychiatry changes dramatically, from both the inside and outside, it is in real danger of disappearing in its current form altogether. Some people might even say that is a good thing.

More psychiatrists should be trained now for the future. Training should include changing the ways psychiatrists work to improve their effectiveness in helping people. The impersonal authoritarian behaviour deliberately employed by many psychiatrists (indeed, medical doctors in general) is not appropriate or acceptable to many patients. We all respond better to personal interaction.

"Proactive psychiatry"

Perhaps psychiatry as a profession could become much more proactive and do more preventative work, rather than just being there *after* personal crises have occurred.

Educational programmes could be developed to help the general public become more aware of psychological dangers, for instance, by recognizing symptoms of excessive stress in themselves and others. Employers could be far more involved in work-place stress-reduction and stress-management – which would actually be of benefit to their organization as well as to individual employees.

"Open psychiatry"?

Psychiatry as a profession needs to do something about its poor image. Past and present tendencies to keep psychiatry a closed "secret society", in which only select initiates are allowed to participate, need to change in favour of access and involvement by others. A more "open psychiatry" (to coin a phrase) would help remove the mystique and stigma attached to the profession.

At present, psychiatrists are able to write reports that are not necessarily seen by the patients themselves, despite various "freedom of information" laws in many countries (e.g. the Data Protection Act in the UK). Even if a patient does see a personal psychiatric report, there is usually no equivalent of an "appeals procedure" to get the report changed or re-written.

PARTICULARLY INSIDIOUS IS THE WAY IN WHICH PSYCHIATRISTS CAN SAY ANYTHING THEY LIKE ABOUT PATIENTS – TOTALLY UNCHALLENGED – WHICH THEN BECOMES A PERMANENT PART OF EACH PATIENT'S MEDICAL FILE FOR THE REST OF HIS OR HER LIFE!

Meanwhile, at least books like this are becoming available for the general public – enabling more people to learn about and benefit from the positive aspects of psychiatry. We hope it has been informative, interesting and useful!

Help and further reading

Help

Anyone seeking help for any suspected mental disorder should start by consulting a medical doctor, who can make a referral to an appropriate specialist such as a psychologist or other health professional.

For information, different countries have their own legally approved bodies, e.g. the UK has the Royal College of Psychiatrists, which can provide help and publications (e.g. *The British Journal of Psychiatry*).

Other organizations can provide information and support, e.g. in the UK: MIND (National Association for Mental Health); BABCT (British Association for Behavioural and Cognitive Therapy); BACP (British Association for Counselling and Psychotherapy).

General information on all types of illness and therapies can be found on the International Society of Therapists website: www.isot.org.uk.

General reading on psychiatry

Gelder, M., Gath, D. and Mayou, R. (1989) *Oxford Textbook of Psychiatry*. Oxford Medical Publications. (A standard textbook for doctors, easy to read.)

Harrison, P., Geddes, J. and Sharpe, M. (1998) *Lecture Notes on Psychiatry*. Blackwell. (A concise clinical approach including community practice, integrating psychiatry's three elements: biology, psychology and sociology.)

Levi, Michael I. (1992) *Basic Notes in Psychiatry*. Kluwer Academic Publishers. (An excellent, succinct summary of adult psychiatry; a major source of reference for this book.)

Puri, Basant K. (2000) *Saunders Pocket Essentials of Psychiatry*. W.B. Saunders. (A handy summary, including DSM-IV and ICD-10 classifications.)

History of psychiatry

Ellenberger, Henri F. (1970) *The Discovery of the Unconscious*.

BasicBooks. (A classic work, a large 932pp tome but easy to read; a major source of reference for this book.)

Criticisms of psychiatry

See any writings by: Mary Barnes, Gregory Bateson, Joseph Berke, Robert Coles, David Cooper, Aaron Esterson, Leslie H. Farber, Michel Foucault, Edgar Z. Friedenberg, Erving Goffman, Jan B. Gordon, R.D. Laing, Theodore Lidz, Kenneth Lux, Bob Mullan, Benjamin Nelson, Thomas J. Scheff, Peter Sedgwick, Miriam Siegler, Thomas Szasz.

About the Author and Artist

Nigel C. Benson is a psychologist and author of the international best-selling *Introducing Psychology* (1999) and *Introducing Psychotherapy* (2003) by Icon Books. He contributed to the Reader's Digest series *Brain Power* (2002), including *The Healing Brain, A Good Memory* and *The Conscious and Unconscious Brain*. He is a member of the Writers' Guild of Great Britain.

Piero is an illustrator and graphic designer. He has been working as an illustrator, animator and graphic designer in London since 1997. His work has twice been included in the Royal College of Art's *The Best of British Illustration* (1998, 1999). He illustrated *Introducing Shakespeare* (2001) and *Introducing Anthropology* (2002).

Acknowledgements

The author would like to thank Richard Appignanesi (for asking me to write this book and for extensively editing it, when he probably could have done it all much better on his own!). Thanks also to everyone who provided help and support, especially Gill Cliff and William Greig (for lending me books); Andy Crooks; Duncan Heath and Ruth Nelson (for proof-reading and sub-editing at Icon, Duxford); Lavinia Hunter (at the Philadelphia Association); Lorna Marriott and Peter Randall; Dr Nash Popovic; Eppie Saunders; and of course my parents Ralph and Heather Benson.

The artist would like to thank Richard Appignanesi and dedicate this book to his parents, Rosana, Carolina, Mora, Rocio and my soulmate Silvina.

Index

(important pages in **bold**)